Finding

Anna Harvey

Copyright © Anna Harvey 2020

The right of Anna Harvey to be identified as the author of this work is asserted in accordance with the Copyright, Designs and Patents Act 1988.

All rights reserved. No part of this publication may be reproduced, stored in a retrieval system, or transmitted in any form or by any other means (electronic, mechanical, photocopying, recording or otherwise), without the prior written permission of the author, nor be otherwise circulated in any other form of binding or cover other than that in which it is published and without a similar condition being imposed on the subsequent publisher.

All characters in this publication are fictitious and any resemblance to real persons, living or dead, is purely coincidental.

Cover Design © More Visual Ltd UK

ISBN 9798636844655

Dedicated to the memories of Rob Godfrey who encouraged me to set out on my writing journey

and Nick Petrartos for showing how to live life with humour, resilience and resourcefulness.

"We are all creatures of each other"

Adapted from Tom Main (1975)

Contents

Author's note	1
Playlist	3
Maps and Genealogy	5
Prologue	8
Chapter 1	12
Chapter 2	21
Chapter 3	38
Chapter 4	57
Chapter 5	81
Chapter 6	99
Chapter 7	118
Chapter 8	146
Chapter 9	173
Chapter 10	200
Chapter 11	224
Chapter 12	246

Chapter 13	264
Chapter 14	293
Chapter 15	321
Chapter 16	339
Chapter 17	372
Chapter 18	393
Chapter 19	408
Chapter 20	422
Chapter 21	445
Chapter 22	463
Chapter 23	493
Telegony	513
Ithaki by Konstantine Kavafy	515
Ithaka (English Translation)	517
Glossary	519
Selected Bibliography	522
Acknowledgements	524
About the Author	526

Author's note

Greek names:

Where possible, the original Greek spellings have been retained throughout the story. Consequently well-known characters or place names may be less familiar to the reader than the common English forms derived from Latin. In particular the Greek letter *k* is commonly replaced by the Latin *c* (there is no c in the Greek alphabet). An example of this is the spelling of *Klytaimnestra* instead of the traditional English version of *Clytemnestra*. In addition, Greek words typically ending in *-os* often became Latinised by adding the suffix *-us* in Latin i.e. *Menelaus* for *Menelaos* with some exceptions, most notably the name *Odysseus* which is written in Ancient Greek in this form.

In Modern Greek, there is a huge controversy and numerous ways of spelling the name of the Ionian island Kefalonia. Here the latter form is adopted as the modern contemporary spelling, but the ancient part of the story retains the original spellings from Homer of *Kephallenia* and *Kephallenians* for the people who lived across the island kingdom, the descendants of the hero founder *Kephalos*.

Natural Phenomena:

In Ancient Greece, natural phenomena such as the winds, rivers and dawn were traditionally perceived as divine entities in their own right. Similarly geological features like caverns or grottoes were often believed to be inhabited by semi-divine creatures or local deities such as water nymphs or sea spirits. This also extends to ancient explanations and understanding of civil states such as *Strife, Peace* and *War*. Internal psychological or mental states, such as having an idea or experiencing a particular emotion, also would be perceived more readily as stemming from the direct action or influence of a higher deity. In keeping with this tradition, the novel adopts a similar practice and denotes such phenomena by the use of the proper name in italics, for example *Hope, Dawn* and *Sleep*.

The Playlist

As music played a key role in the creation and envisioning of the story, a playlist is included to accompany the reader through their journey. Each chapter has a soundtrack, but the lyrics should not be taken literally (especially concerning Bronze Age Greece), but rather used to evoke a particular feeling or sentiment linked to that juncture in the story. It is hoped that the playlist enhances and enriches your experience and enjoyment of the story, but this is for you the reader to decide and a matter of personal choice.

Finally, although this book is a work of fiction, the details concerning the conceivable location of Odysseus' palace are based on authentic historical and archaeological research. Any names, characters and incidents are however the product of my, the author's, imagination and are used fictitiously. Any resemblance to actual events or persons, living or dead, is purely coincidental.

Anna Harvey

Leeds

2020

Playlist

Prologue : The Shadow of the Plane Tree – *Oh Very Young* (Cat Stevens)

1. Beginnings – *The In Between Days* (The Cure)

2. The Return – *Adventure of a Lifetime* (Sarah Menescal)

3. Troy – *Your Move* (Yes)

4. Goatherds and Panegyri – *Beautiful Day* (U2)

5. Quarrel – *Running Up That Hill* (Kate Bush)

6. Books – *Oxford Comma* (Vampire Weekend)

7. The Fall of Troy -*The Dog Days Are Over* (Florence and the Machine)

8. Vrechei – *Rain* (Mika)

9. Xenia – *Heart of the Sunrise* (Yes)

10. Hospitality – *Will You Love Me Tomorrow?* (Carole King)

11. The Witch – *I Hear You Now* (Jon and Vangelis)

12. Courtship – *There's Too Much Love* (Belle and Sebastian)

13. Departures – *The Rhythm Changes* (Kamasi Washington featuring Patrice Quinn)

14. Reunion – *Sweet Disposition* (Temper Trap)

15. Feasting –*Wonderous Stories* (Yes)

16. Pascha – *Heart's on Fire* (Bronwynne Brent)

17. Home-coming – *Land of Confusion* (Genesis)

18. Revelations – *When You Said Goodbye* (Bronwynne Brent)

19. Restitution - *Can't Turn Back The Years* (Phil Collins)

20. Rejection –*Feelin' Good* (Kaz Hawkins)

21. Apollo's Feast – *So Long Ago, So Clear* (Jon and Vangelis)

22. Discovery – *Can We Still Be Friends* (Robert Palmer)

23. Endings and Beginnings – *I'll Find My Way Home* (Jon and Vangelis)

24. Telegony – *A Sky Full of Stars* (The Cooltrane Quartet)

Maps and Genealogy

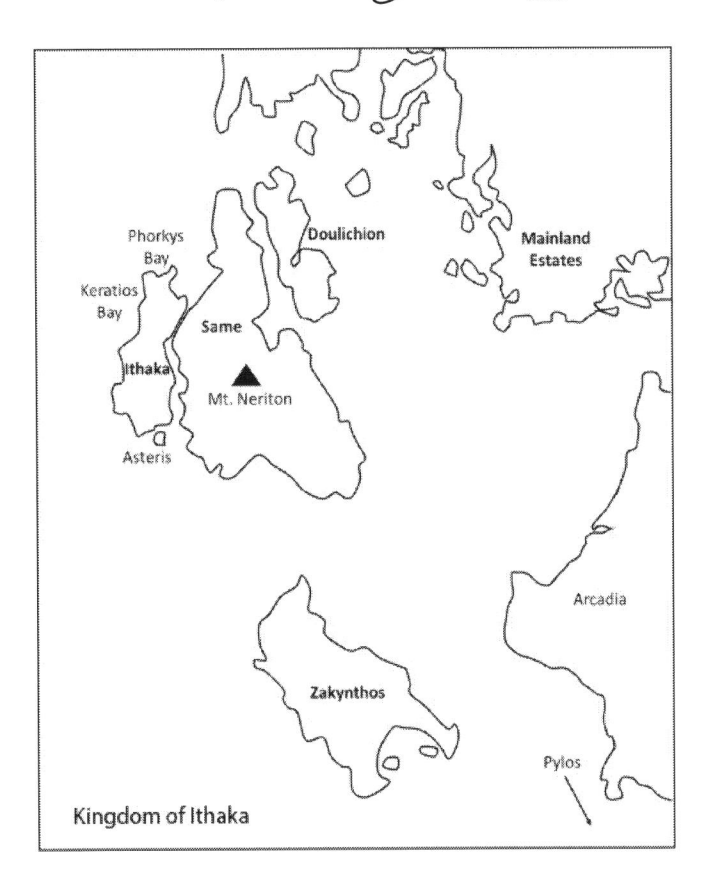

Kingdom of Ithaka

The Mykenaian World

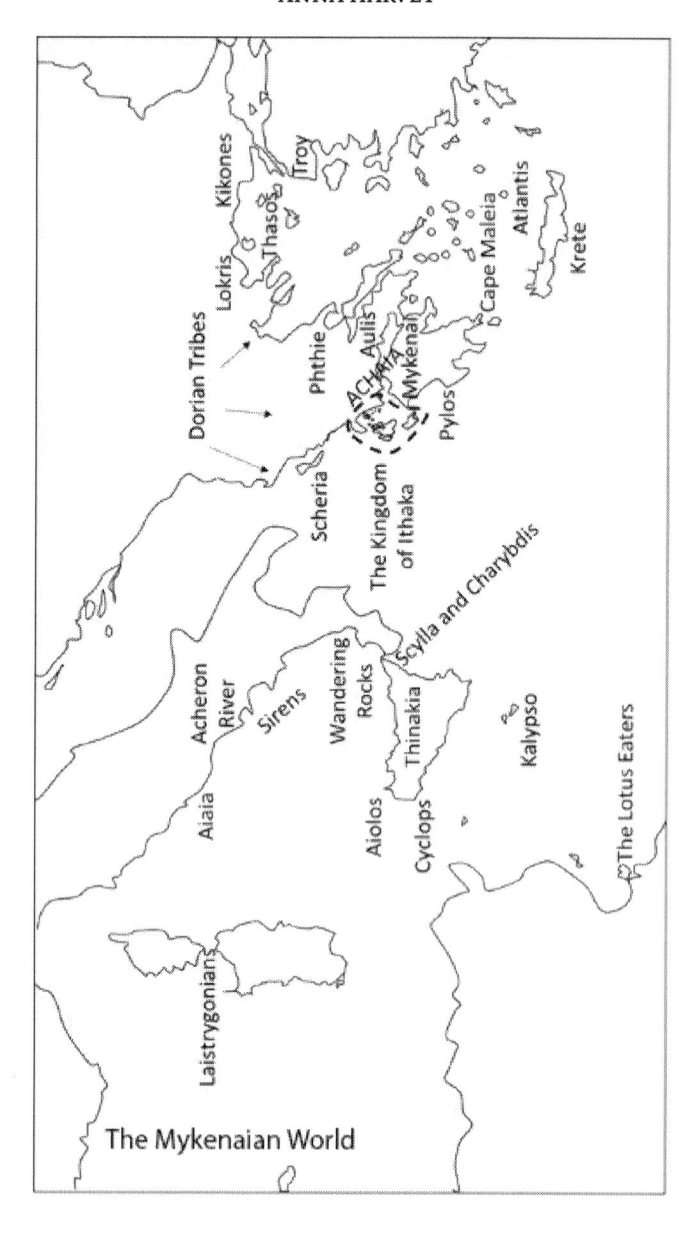

FINDING ITHAKA

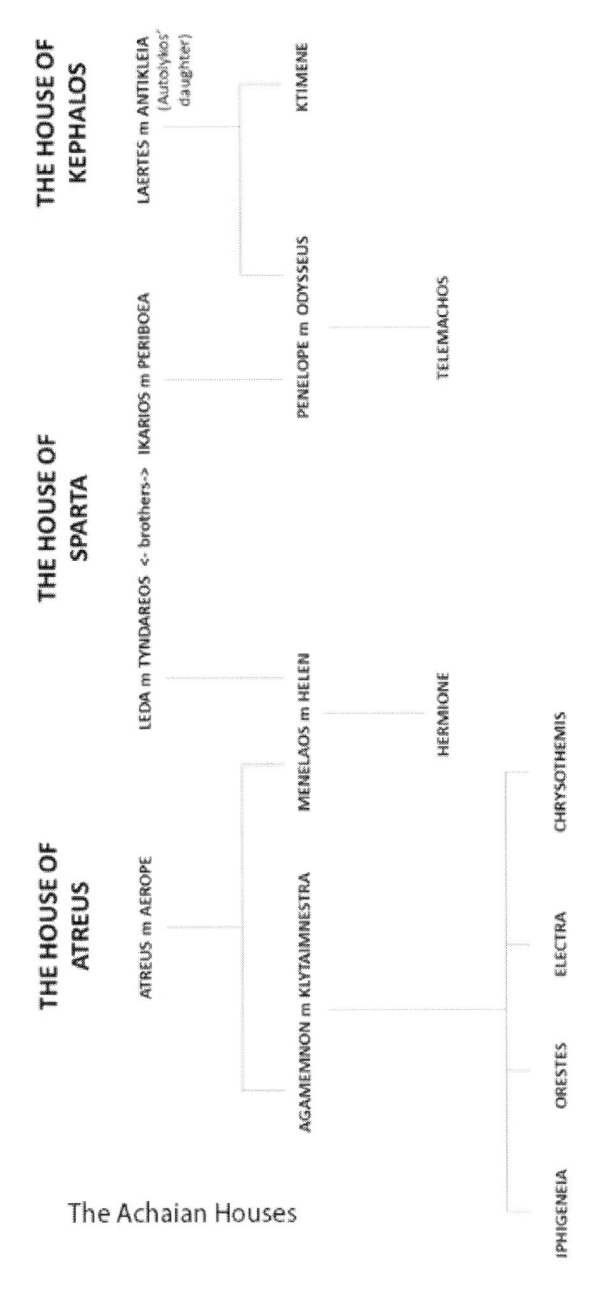

THE HOUSE OF KEPHALOS

LAERTES m ANTIKLEIA (Autolykos' daughter)

KTIMENE

THE HOUSE OF SPARTA

LEDA m TYNDAREOS <- brothers-> IKARIOS m PERIBOEA

PENELOPE m ODYSSEUS

TELEMACHOS

THE HOUSE OF ATREUS

ATREUS m AEROPE

MENELAOS m HELEN

HERMIONE

AGAMEMNON m KLYTAIMNESTRA

IPHIGENEIA — ORESTES — ELECTRA — CHRYSOTHEMIS

The Achaian Houses

Prologue

The Shadow of the Plane Tree

A sweat broke out across his forehead and dripped into his eyes as he wielded the sword high above his head. The battle was only half begun but already he had slaughtered an army of enemies who threatened the island kingdom. Now he wearied as Helios beat down on his body with full heat. If only he could slake his thirst, but he could not quit the field while the fight was still raging.

"Die you dog!" he cried as he swung the blade into the air with all the strength his limbs could muster. He pulled his weapon up sharp so his enemy would not get the better of him.

"Odysseus!"

At the call of his name, he glanced across taking his eye off the prize. But his father beckoned him with a commanding wave he dared not disobey. Odysseus put aside his child's game and re-sheathed the play weapon, running across the dusty palace yard. His father was seated beneath the broad leafy plane tree in the coolness of the shade.

"Come sit with me," said his father, patting the stool beside him, a smile playing on his lips at the boyish spectacle. As he climbed onto the wooden perch, his father handed him a cupful of water, which he greedily swallowed down. He waited expectantly, his eyes mesmerised by the gold foil of his father's robes. He looked up and noticed the heavy expression his father wore and how the burden of kingship weighed heavily on him. At last his father, King Laertes spoke.

"I think the time draws near to find you a teacher who can instruct you in becoming a warrior, now you are nine summers old and not far from manhood. Perhaps your grandfather Autolykos, who knows all wiles as well as fighting skills, can teach you his crafts." His father threw his head back, breaking into a laugh. "Yes, he is an astute fellow, full of invention and resourcefulness. He would teach you well."

His father's eyes now misted up with tears, as he studied his son. "One day this kingdom will be yours," he said, his hand pointing to the distant horizons. "These islands of the Kephallenians: Same, Zakynthos, Doulichion, the mainland estates and Ithaka itself. You will be a great warrior following your forebears, bringing *kleos* to myself and your family." And Odysseus' youthful eyes gazed out beyond the stone ramparts where the land dropped away and the town dwellings huddled to the slopes, across the gulf to the island of Same with towering Mount Neriton and south to purple-misted Zakynthos.

"And I will be proud to call you my son," his father continued, "the only offspring of King Laertes. It is for the reason of *kleos* for his service in war, that your paternal grandfather was granted these wheat-yielding lands, the fine acres of orchards, and all the fruit-bearing vine and olive groves you see before us. For it is through individual heroic deeds on the battlefield, that a warrior gains much in wealth and possessions and is honoured above the rest."

Odysseus craned his neck around until his eyes rested upon the palace itself, with its straight undeviating walls, looming over them and dominating the skyline. Its four-sided block was perfectly shaped with rows of high-set windows cut square into the walls, their frames brightly painted with blood-red ochre. At its entrance, a row of columns stood upright like bow-legged sentries, guarding admission to the great audience chamber and the inner reaches beyond. In the distance, he noticed gathering clouds that cast a looming shadow over the mountainous island kingdom.

"Honour," continued his father gravely, "is the highest virtue of the warrior. And if you follow this code dutifully, your fame will live beyond your mortal years, should the gods see fit to countenance this. But all is in vain, if the warrior cannot prove himself worthy and is not prepared on the battlefield to spend blood or life to meet his obligations. "

Despite his tender years he listened, grasping the role he was assigned to play from birth: the future leader of the Kephallenians. As he surveyed all he saw before him, he committed his father's words into his heart.

"Have no fear, father. I will do my duty."

Chapter 1

Beginnings

He gazed out across the bay, as the east *Euros* wind buffeted his body. The waves deafened against the shore, whipped up into a white foaming frenzy, without any sign of stilling. In the distance grey storm clouds had gathered. He paced restlessly as he surveyed the scene, feeling a tightness grip his chest. The thought struck him that he could be enjoying the comforts of family life on Ithaka instead of shivering on this beach forsaken by the gods. This place was Aulis, where Agamemnon, their overlord, had chosen to muster the Greek forces for war.

For thirty days, they had been trapped in this accursed spot. The winds blew this unfavourable easterly gale, hemming in the fleet and refusing to grant them passage across the sea to the Troy. He pulled his *himation* closer to him. Across from the headland loomed the deep back-bone of the island of Euboea, which sheltered them from the worst of the tempest. Before him was assembled the fleet of Greek ships, their dark-pitched hulks hauled upon the strand as protection against the crashing waves. From his position, he could see the blue smoking campfires below and the billowing tents pounded by the *Wind*. With the delay, day by day the men had grown restless and edgy, as if sensing this mission was ill-conceived.

He looked around him again and at the distant headland. It was a strange setting for a wedding, he thought to himself grimly. At least the arrival of the bridal party two nights before had brought cheer to the camp. The excited chatter and laughter of female voices had lightened the throng of male warriors and relieved the endless wait. Perhaps a marriage ceremony was indeed what was needed to lift the gloomy spirits in the Greek encampment.

"Odysseus!" At the call of his name, he turned to discover one of Agamemnon's men had been sent to fetch him. "It is time," the man panted. He nodded his head in acknowledgement, perplexed why their overlord, the great *Anax*, had gone to the trouble of having him summoned.

Without questioning, Odysseus followed the man back down the steep cliff path to where the gathering had assembled. At his approach, the troops parted in waves for him to join the

Greek leaders waiting at the altar. Odysseus took his place towards the end of the line, as befitted his status as the leader of a small island kingdom.

"Surely you would not have missed this spectacle," quipped Ajax, son of Oileus, through hooded eyelids, a mocking smile playing on his lips. Holding his head high, Odysseus chose not to answer. *Rumours* abounded amongst the troops about how he had tried to escape Agamemnon's call to arms and been a reluctant combatant in this venture.

Odysseus' eyes fell on his own men, able-bodied warriors he had recruited from across the island kingdom standing proud within the gathered throng. He knew their faces and could call each by name. There were some older veteran faces within the troop, but most were like himself, men newlywed or young fathers to infant children. It struck him again how their numbers were small amongst the assembled forces. Odysseus smiled inwardly to himself, remembering how he had not pushed any man who held back, suspecting a bloody long drawn out conflict. Rather he had allowed any who willed it to carry on with their trades of *Peace*, tending their fields and animal herds. He had not outwardly defied Agamemnon, but when he had presented to Aulis with his twelve ships, he Odysseus suspected the *Anax* deep down had known his resistance.

And now Agamemnon, overlord of all the Greeks, took his place. As customary, Menelaos stood at his side, the younger of the two brothers from the house of Atreus. It was for his sake, Agamemnon had rallied a Greek force to right the wrong and humiliation inflicted by a Trojan guest for stealing his brother's wife Helen.

From close quarters, Odysseus took time to study Agamemnon himself. He was tall-boned and fine featured in appearance that often was pleasing to women, unlike his own diminished stature and ruddy complexion. As the father of the bride, the *Anax* had taken extra care in his dress, wearing his kingly robes festooned in famed Mykenaian gold. But he noticed Agamemnon's grim face and tightly clenched jaw, more fitting for a funeral pyre than a marriage celebration. The wedding procession interrupted his thoughts as just then the wedding chorus struck up and the sweet sounds of feminine singing filled the air.

The procession began as the female attendants advanced through the male throng scattering, at their feet, herbs gathered from the hill slopes. And then finally the bride, Iphigeneia herself, radiant and finely dressed, her hair braided, with a row of neat curls framing her face. Though tightly pinched at the midriff to reveal her slender waist, her fine tunic scarcely showed the mounds of her breasts. At her approach, the *Euros* wind buffeted her progress, clutching and tugging at her robes as if trying to pull her back. Odysseus could see Iphigeneia shiver as the caress of the breeze chilled her body. But despite the squalls and the long dusty journey from her home city of Mykenai, the bride appeared in full bloom unfolding like a flower. From the pink flush on her cheeks, he imagined the excited wedding preparations for the day. Her mother Klytaimnestra would have eagerly gathered together the finest clothes and jewellery for her daughter's dowry and offered her instruction as a new bride. At last the maiden procession reached the altar and the young bride took her place at her father's side.

The priest started to mumble the words of an incantation, pouring a libation into a cup and raising it high towards the heavens. He was a strange fellow, wild-eyed and zealous, who Agamemnon himself had summoned from the city of Megara less than one moon ago. Even the men avoided the priest's gaze and shrank back at his approach.

Now Odysseus' eyes darted around the amassed crowd, suddenly wondering which warrior was to be honoured as the son-in-law to the great *Anax*: for the choice had been kept secret. Without warning, a tightness weighed his chest and in his throat he could taste sour bile. He searched around wildly, trying to discover the reason for the dread that gripped him. Only then did he glimpse the flash of burnished metal. The look of joy on Iphigeneia's face had frozen with horror, as the priest plunged the knife into her chest. There were screams and the sickly sound of metal cracking bone. In her betrayal, the maid took faltering steps, her eyes reaching desperately for her father who looked on like hardened stone.

Instinctively Odysseus stepped forward, his sword arm flecked and moving towards his sheath to draw his weapon. Hastily his eyes fell on his men amongst the ranks, reckoning up their numbers. But the pressure of a restraining hand stopped him.

"Know your place or you might be next." The words were softly spoken, but the grip on his hand was flint-like. Nestor, the old king, bowed his head in warning. Odysseus swallowed his outrage and stepped back in line, glowering at Agamemnon and the priest.

He forced himself to stay motionless, remembering his father's words and not wishing to bring dishonour to his family's house. He lifted his eyes to witness Iphigeneia's body now collapsed and limp held upright in her father's arms, the fine wedding garments fouled with blood as her spirit descended to the underworld. But a heaviness weighed down upon his breast and Odysseus could barely lift his head to meet the eyes of his men in the throng.

The fire raged for the full afternoon, stoked by the firewood piled beneath the corpse and the fury of the *Euros* wind. Holed up in his tent, trying to shake the image from his mind, Odysseus had seen plumes of grey smoke billowing upwards. Even then, the smell of death and burning flesh lingered over the camp, the bitter taste sticking in his throat.

The shadows were lengthening, when Odysseus finally brought himself to draw near to the funeral pyre. The timbers were glowing red and white hot, as his eyes searched for Iphigeneia's body in the blackened heap. But all that remained of the once youthful maiden were piles of ash and charred bone. He approached the unlikely pair, stationed beside the dying embers. The priest was kneeling at the head, still muttering prayers of supplication to the gods, while Agamemnon stood at a distance, his head bowed staring out across the sea. No longer was he dressed in all his finery and shining gold but a simple plain tunic. As Odysseus approached, a swell of anger burst out of his chest towards the priest.

"How could you let him do that, Kalchas?" he hissed under his breath. "To plant the seed inside Agamemnon's mind to kill his own daughter?"

"Hush, still your tongue," Kalchas snapped through thin cracked lips. "For you cannot undo what the gods have ordained. Agamemnon offended the gods and atoned for his transgression through sacrifice. Without it the Greek fleet could not sail for Troy."

"But to sacrifice his own child." He cast his glance askance at the *Anax,* who, lost in thought, had not stirred.

Slowly the priest raised himself until he reached his full height, sizing Odysseus up as if dealing with an irritating insect. "Put an end to your raging. I have heard of your reputation for wiliness but even your cleverness cannot outrun what the *Fates* intend. Beware you do not upset the gods or those better than you as this will only bring down trouble on your head."

"Let him be, priest." Both men looked up, caught by surprise, to see that Agamemnon had finally rallied himself. His face was pallid like the ashes on the funeral pyre but tears glimmered in the corners of his eyes. "Do not rage, Odysseus," he said laying his hand on Odysseus' shoulder to console him. "This is a sad day for us all. The time will come to right wrongs once we set foot on Trojan soil. So spare your strength for that fight."

Odysseus bowed his head, pushing down the

feelings that raged in his chest. The words almost stuck in his throat. "Of course, oh *Anax.*"

He awoke with a start, gasping for air and a cold sweat pouring from his body. As he blinked back *sleep,* for a moment he could not fathom where he was. He stretched out and felt the soft pillow beneath his head and the padded mattress of a bed. Through the half-light, he could make out the swell of a slumbering shape at his side and the gentle murmurs of a sleeping woman. Finally his mind grasped he was home on Ithaka. He inhaled a few breaths to steady himself, slowly untangling himself from the dream. The images the gods sent him had come thick and fast, throwing his mind off balance.

Odysseus cast his attention around the darkened room, listening for sounds of the household servants moving around the building. Rose-coloured *Dawn* could not have yet made her appearance, as the house was still wrapped in silence. He rose and threw on a robe. He would wait for the appearance of Helios' light in the great hall, to dispel the horror of the *Dream* that the gods had sent. For that day was forever branded on him and on any who witnessed the slaying of that innocent maiden, Iphigeneia.

Yes, he thought grimly, *it had been an ill-omened wind that blew no good.*

Chapter 2

The Return

Thea stepped off the plane and breathed in the cool spring air. As always the mountain ridge loomed above, punctuated by red-tiled roofs, low rise buildings and cypress trees. Now in the foreground stood the airport terminal, raised by migrant workers during the winter season. Already it was ageing, the concrete pillars shedding their painted skin in long strips. As Thea joined the procession of passengers filing across the open expanse, an elderly airport worker walked towards her. For a brief moment their eyes met and between them passed a flicker of recognition. Thea averted her gaze, staring blankly ahead, and continued her anonymous walk across the concourse.

In the arrival zone, a small scrum of people jostled to meet the daily Athens flight. Thea made her way through the crowd to a man holding up a sign bearing her name in bold letters, "Dr Sefton".

"Hello, can I help you" enquired the man in perfect English, mistaking Thea for a foreign holiday maker. His appearance was unremarkable, slightly shabby-looking, and he would have blended into any crowd. Dressed in a casual dark suit and open neck shirt, he had the appearance of a taxi driver, academic or general fixer, only the expensive branded wristwatch and polished leather shoes suggested affluence.

"I think you must be waiting for me," Thea said to the man, reaching out her arm to shake his hand. "I'm Dr Sefton."

"But we were expecting a man," he replied, a frown momentarily crossing his face, before he recovered himself. "Please excuse me, I didn't...," he corrected himself, "we didn't realise you were a woman." He was now vigorously shaking her outstretched hand. "My apologies. Allow me to introduce myself. I am Stelios Ioannou from The Foundation and have come to meet you."

"*Yeia sas, o afenti mou*. It's a pleasure to meet you. Please call me Thea. "From his quizzical look, instantly she realised her mistake. Her use of a local dialect word betrayed her and had not escaped his notice.

"That is an expression I hear only on this island. So you've been to Kefalonia before. Unfortunately I myself am not from these parts."

"I'm a language specialist," Thea lightly replied, recovering her error. "So I have a special interest in collecting dialect words."

He didn't reply but directed her across the carpark to a high-end German SUV, expensive by Greek standards. It was clear that this man's presence was not coincidental or his position within The Foundation insignificant. The freshly valeted and immaculate interior of the vehicle only deepened her impression.

They had left the airport perimeter behind and were travelling towards the main town, past olive groves, pieces of cultivated land and boarded-up tourist pensions. Thea was deliberating whether to break the awkward silence that had descended when Stelios spoke up.

"So you are going to help us find this palace?" The tone was casual but there was a hint of mockery.

"I hope so. That's the reason I'm here."

"You don't have much luggage. Your colleagues brought boxes of equipment with them."

"I travel light. Just a couple of books and a laptop. I'm an academic, rather than a field archaeologist."

"So you are a bit of a Schliemann then?"

"I suppose you could say that," Thea answered assuming that Stelios, like most Greeks, had been reared as a child on the Iliad and the Odyssey, the stories that told of the Trojan War and of the hero Odysseus' return. It had been the German archaeologist Heinrich Schliemann, armed with only a copy of the Iliad, who had located the lost city of Troy. Then the discovery had caused an overnight sensation across the salons of nineteenth century Europe, propelling Schliemann into celebrity status.

"So you are hoping to do the same?" Stelios continued, raising his eyebrows. "To become our own Schliemann?" He briefly turned towards her throwing a long sideways glance. "Certainly you don't look like the archaeologists we see around these parts."

Without flinching, she returned his gaze as they drifted back once more into an uncomfortable silence. She steered her attention to the view outside, where an ugly gaping wound of the abandoned quarry scarred the hillside.

It was just then, as they came over the brow of the hill with the sunbeams breaking through the clouds, that she saw it. First the stretched out island in the foreground but then behind the peninsula itself, the low lying land gently swelling out of the sea: Paliki. Like a magnet, the spur of land held Thea's gaze captive, beckoning her towards it with a strange emotional pull.

So this is Ancient Ithaka, she thought, taking a deep inward breath. *If the palace is there, I'm going to find you!*

****

"Welcome to our hotel! You have been expected!" the hotel receptionist greeted them exuberantly, her smile revealing a large gold tooth. "I'm Electra," she said, her accent thick and aspirated. Her bright translucent blouse was modestly cut but barely concealed the contours of her body beneath. Her face was otherwise evenly balanced and handsome, except for the disruption of a large mole.

"Let me check you into your room," Electra continued, handing Thea the registration form with her manicured hands, the fingernails painted in a deep crimson colour. "Don't worry about payment, the Foundation has already taken care of your bill."

Thea quickly read through the form, written in a mix of Greek and English, conscious of Stelios watching over her shoulder, as if scrutinising her personal circumstances. So close was he standing, Thea could feel his breath stroking her neck and taste aftershave. With the pen poised over the line "next of kin", she could feel the pain welling up remembering her separation from David and her new single status. With a stroke of the pen, she suppressed the feelings and wrote the name of her closest friend. As she handed the completed form back, Stelios' intrusion into her personal space was starting to get on her nerves. Trying not to betray her sentiments, she turned towards him.

"Thanks for meeting me at the airport, Stelios. If you will please excuse me, I'd like to go up to my room."

"Of course, *kyria*. I'll leave you to the hospitality of *kyria* Electra and look forward to renewing our acquaintance at the reception tonight." As he turned, he paused, holding her gaze with his eyes. "Please let me know if there is anything that I or The Foundation can do to make your stay more comfortable." He thrust into her hand a business card on which a personal telephone number had been inscribed.

"So you have met our Stelios Ioannou, Dr Sefton," Electra said, following Stelios' back with her glance, as if reading Thea's aversion to her new acquaintance. "You know he's a big man on the island. Very close to those people in The Foundation." She dropped her voice, rubbing her fingers together, "You know big money!" She nodded conspiratorially before returning to her official voice once more. "I'll arrange to have your bags brought up to your room."

****

The library was uphill from the main square, tucked away between the residential apartment blocks and civic buildings. With its portico of white columns, the outside echoed an old classical temple, except that the walls were painted a bright cherry-red. In the entrance porch, Thea was greeted by a line of the island's eminent citizens, their features hardened in alabaster, wearing elegant morning coats from a bygone era.

Excited chatter emanated deep from within the building and Thea followed the sound. She pressed against the heavy double doors which opened into a large *megaron,* where walls of books stretched up to the ceiling. This evening, the room had been transformed into a public meeting space and rows of stiff-backed chairs had been stationed in regimented lines.

Thea cast her glance around, searching for a familiar face. There was a pack of young male students engaged in animated conversation, all wearing eager and self-assured expressions. A peal of female laughter rang out from the centre of the group, but her attention was instantly captured by the young woman poised on the periphery, her gentle oriental face wearing a thoughtful look. Feelings of protectiveness stirred as Thea started to make her way over, when a familiar voice interrupted her.

"So you made it!" Thea looked round to discover her dear friend and university colleague, Mark Hatton, standing beside her. His appearance was always surprising, as the slender body, pale skin and dark brown curls gave Mark the appearance of a Bohemian artist rather than a field archaeologist. "Thanks for covering for me in the departmental meeting," Mark said, flashing a smile. For the first time since setting foot on the island, Thea felt the tension in her shoulders ease.

"No problem. Lucky you missed all the talk about the budget and increasing class sizes." There was a playful irreverence in her voice that was characteristic of their relationship.

"Laurence sends his love. He was sorry to hear about you and David splitting up. We always thought you two would stick together."

"Thank Laurence for me," she said feeling the edges of her nerves fraying and vulnerability creeping in again. It had only been autumn, as the seasonal London drizzle had spluttered against the windows, when they had all dined together on Laurence's home cooking. After the long drawn-out winter that seemed a lifetime ago.

"Ah Thea, you're here at last! So glad that you could join us!" The voice boomed out like that of a Shakespearean actor performing in a public theatre.

Heads turned round as Richard Mortimer, the project director, came forward to greet her. He was at least a generation older than Thea, with greying hair, and an air of old school charm, cultivated in public school and followed by a spell at Oxford. Possessing a rare talent for censuring people in a way that left them flattered Richard, now a professor of archaeology, would have excelled in the diplomatic corps had he not entered academia.

Thea shook his large proffered hand, smoothing down her feelings. "Hello Richard. Sorry for my late appearance. I'm so looking forward to working on the project."

"You come highly recommended," Richard beamed, his features lighting up. "And allow me to introduce Alistair and Elizabeth Woodward," Richard gestured towards a middle-aged couple, his voice stuffed with self-importance and grandiosity. "You will no doubt be familiar with their exceptional work in Aegean Pre-history."

Elizabeth held out her hand towards Thea. "Pleased to meet you at last. I've heard a lot about your work tracing the migration of peoples through the language. A brilliant piece of work using indigenous animals and vegetation!" Her handshake was cold, mirroring the taut lines on Elizabeth's face. The hair had been scraped back into a coiled bun and her paisley blouse high-buttoned to the neck. From Elizabeth's outwards appearance, one could not guess at her formidable academic abilities and yet she exuded no warmth.

"I'm hoping Thea can assist us in a similar way in locating our missing palace", said Richard.

"I didn't realise my work was so well known," Thea modestly replied, noticing the warmer touch of Alistair's fingers. "My apologies I couldn't get here sooner."

"Don't worry, you are not the last to arrive," replied Alistair reassuringly. There was a trace of a soft Edinburgh accent in his voice, toned down presumably through exile from his Scottish roots.

"Yes," said Elizabeth coldly, "we are still waiting for our renowned geology expert, if he ever escapes his icecap."

Richard shot her a sharp look, pumping out his chest. "I was surprised indeed by Dr Hughes agreeing to join our project. His services are in high demand these days."

"Let me get you a drink," said Mark, steering Thea towards the corner of the room where an obligatory table of alcoholic beverages had been set up. "What would you like?"

"Just a Nescafe with milk," Thea said, keen to keep a clear head. She lowered her voice not wishing their conversation to be overheard.

"I was surprised when I heard we were meeting here, rather than at the hotel."

"Richard wanted a dry run for tomorrow's press conference," came Mark's light reply, spooning into a cup a generous helping of coffee granules.

"And he didn't want to involve the whole team?"

"Probably saving the crowning glory for himself. I hear Richard is quite chummy with the chair of The Foundation" They exchanged a glance of mutual understanding.

"Okay everyone, if you can please take your seats." Richard's voice echoed around the large hall, as he took charge of the proceedings. Carefully balancing her cup of coffee, the lukewarm contents in danger of spilling out, Thea seated herself at the front.

As the lights dimmed, Richard slid effortlessly into addressing his captive audience. "I would like to take the occasion to welcome everyone formally to the Odysseus Project. As you will all know, our goal is to discover the whereabouts of the palace of Odysseus, one of the great archaeological mysteries of our age." Richard paused for deliberate effect to emphasise the significance of the task at hand. It was easy to see how his style of delivery might grate sometimes on students and colleagues alike, giving Richard a mixed reputation of brilliance and pomposity.

Trying to quell her rising impatience, Thea noticed a clock was ticking somewhere, disturbing her attention. As in the time frame of the story of the Iliad there were fifty days exactly to complete their modern day task. Richard was settling into a long-winded discourse.

Thea knew the story well: fascinated by the mythical hero Odysseus, the countless expeditions to the nearby island of Ithaka to find the palace. Faded images flashed up on the screen of men in old-fashioned work clothes with picks and shovels standing proudly in symmetrical rock-dug trenches. The small island had been turned over with a fine toothcomb, but the palace had eluded them all, stubbornly refusing to be found.

Only recently some amateur scholars had proposed this new heresy: that the Paliki peninsula of Kefalonia had once been separate, before a huge landslide had snatched away its island identity.

Thea shifted awkwardly in her chair, checking her watch. After a long convoluted journey, Richard finally seemed to be reaching the climax of his talk. "So assuming Paliki is in fact Ancient Ithaka" he announced pointing to the map, "and the palace is located in this upland area, we plan to survey from this village here radiating the search outwards."

It was at that moment, Thea started to feel a strange light-headedness creeping over her body. As her eyes flicked over the familiar contours of the island, the black outline danced in front of her, refusing to focus. She shrugged it off as she tried to catch Richard's next words.

"We are most grateful to the Archontakis Shipping Foundation for their financial support. If we are successful this season, they have agreed to fund a fuller excavation next year." Richard, basking in the limelight, beamed as he glanced round at the reaction on the faces. "May I also thank Mr Stelios Ioannou, for his excellent handling of the practical arrangements of our arrival on the island."

Twisting her head to follow Richard's gaze, Thea noticed Stelios was standing at the back of the room. He must have slipped in unnoticed and now seized her glance with a broad grin. She immediately flinched at the unwelcome familiarity and a wave of blackness gripped her again.

"Please now permit me to introduce someone whom I have had the pleasure to be acquainted with since his undergraduate days." Richard's voice drifted far far away. Thea grasped her stiff chair to steady herself. "My valued and distinguished associate, Dr ...." The words hardly registered on her mind as the darkness enveloped her and the floor came up to meet her.

****

"Stand back everyone. Give her air." Thea blinked back at the harsh glare of the overhead lights. Her mind had splintered into fragments of confusion, refusing to coalesce to make sense. She recognised at once Mark leaning over her, wearing a concerned expression but the other face was unfamiliar.

"Thea," the stranger appeared to have taken charge of the situation. "I'm just checking your pulse to make sure you're alright." She felt a light pressure squeezing her wrist and a strange tingling sensation sweeping her body.

"You'll live" the newcomer grinned reassuringly. "Looks like a sudden drop in blood pressure. When did you last eat?" At last some of the fog engulfing her mind was starting to disperse as she thought back. In her haste to catch the connecting flight in Athens she had skipped lunch.

"Breakfast time."

"Let's help you back onto your chair and I'll grab some biscuits for you to nibble." She felt herself being lifted gently onto feet that refused to obey and eased into a chair. The stranger dug into his bag and unwrapped a foil pack, which he placed in her hand. After a couple of chews, the sugar appeared to be taking effect and her body was becoming trustworthy again.

"Thank you" she said gratefully.

"I don't think you've met Dr Rob Hughes," said Mark "our geophysics specialist for the project. Rob and his assistant are going to be staying behind with you when the team relocates to Paliki."

"Pleased to meet you Thea." The accent was educated, but neutral, suggesting Hampshire or the Home Counties. With his weathered skin, blanched hair and uneven trimmed beard, it was not the most handsome face Thea had ever encountered but there was a humour behind the eyes.

"Please don't let me hold you up," Thea said noticing the hall had drained of people.

"Don't worry," Mark said reassuringly. "Richard has gone on with everyone for pizza. Are you up to joining us for tomorrow's early start? You have a full day ahead with an excursion around the island, while Richard and I hold the press conference, followed by dinner hosted by The Foundation."

Thea shook her head feeling a mounting frustration at how her body was behaving. Her limbs felt weak, still tingling and bristling, as if shot through with a bolt of electricity. For weeks she had been speculating on possible locations for the palace, but this threatened to jeopardise her work. "I think some fresh air and an early night will do me good," she replied.

"In that case you had better take these," said Rob reaching into his bag and stuffing an unopened food pack into her hand. "It's from the flight but it will save you searching for something to eat. You know troops can't go into battle on empty stomachs!" It was an odd turn of phrase, but Thea accepted the package gratefully.

A voice from over Thea's shoulder interrupted them. "I would be most happy to escort Dr Sefton back to the hotel, to ensure her safe return." She twisted her head to discover Stelios, who must have observed the whole incident, hovering in the background.

"No that won't be necessary," Thea replied, firmly declining and feeling uneasy at the way this man singled her out. "Please don't trouble yourself as I will be perfectly fine."

They accompanied her out of the library, Mark holding tightly onto her arm as they descended the white marbled steps onto the darkened street.

"Now go," she said, releasing Mark's hand from her arm as they reached the street corner. "Enjoy your evening."

"If you are sure?" She nodded her head and then watched their retreating shapes, conscious that Stelios was hanging back in the half-light.

"Allow me to call you a taxi at least," he said reluctant to desert his post.

"Thanks but I can find my way. The walk will do me good."

"Of course, Dr Sefton, I forget that you have been on the island before." The comment punctured her feelings and Thea felt grateful for the darkness to conceal her reddening cheeks. "My boss is flying in tomorrow for the press conference," Stelios continued. "I have no doubt he will be most keen to make your acquaintance." He rolled his eyes over her body, as if admiring a prized acquisition, a satisfied expression playing on his lips. "In the meantime, if there is anything I can do, please do not hesitate to call me."

"I appreciate your concern but I'm sure you must have other pressing matters. If you will excuse me, I'll say goodnight." And without waiting for his reply, Thea turned and ventured out into the blackened town.

Chapter 3

Troy

The household was starting to stir. Odysseus could hear the movement of the servants in the kitchen areas, as the first bread was being rolled out, kneaded and prepared for baking. Already the smell of smoke hung in the air as the palace ovens were being lit and stoked for the day. Yet still the main hall was quiet as he nursed his thoughts from far away on a distant plain. The other members of the household appeared to be sleeping. "Untroubled by the dreams the gods sent them," he thought wistfully.

"Oh *Basileos*, may I put more kindling on the fire for you? Surely you must be cold sitting here, now the flame has died?" the maid servant asked anxiously. He knew that the question came partly out of care but was also tainted by fear. Although unspoken within the household except perhaps in hushed whispers, the events from the past and the fate of her predecessors were not forgotten. And the festival of Apollo was nearly upon them, which marked the twentieth year since his return.

"Yes, that would be agreeable." Odysseus responded with forced cheerfulness, trying to assuage her fears and pulling his cloak closer to him. "And can you fetch me something to drink. Perhaps a cup of mixed wine if there is some left over from last night."

"Certainly, master."

"And bring me some meat and bread too from the larder." Odysseus added, thinking with satisfaction of the palace well-stocked, the result of years of good management and order within the *oikos*. The gods had certainly been good in providing all. Again he thought of the approaching feast to celebrate Apollo's day, where the marks of his well governed *oikos* and kingdom would be on display for all to see.

"Of course, at once." The young woman quickly refreshed the firewood, the flames greedily licking the fresh fuel and billowing out plumes of thick grey smoke. Then she retreated to do her master's bidding. Odysseus recognised her as one of the slaves captured in a raid on the northern mainland some years ago. Then she had been just a slip of a girl of perhaps twelve years. Now she must be at least twenty years old. It occurred to him that she must be of a similar age to him, when as a younger warrior he had first set foot on the plain of Troy all those years ago. He and this young woman, now a lowly serving maid, had shared a similar fate of youthful exile from their home *polis,* far away from their family and those who were dearest to them.

Odysseus recalled that very first time he stepped off the ship, beached along the sandy shore with the other blackened hollowed-out boats. His men were in buoyant mood, chattering excitedly and bristling with hope that the war would be brought swiftly to an end. With his farming eye, he noticed the wide swathe of flattened land as the chilly *Boreas* wind blew down from the straits and buffeted his *himation* around him. These were not the craggy and rugged contours of Ithaka, where vines and olives flourished in the loamy soil, but open grassland and pastures ideal for horse-breeding and cattle raising. And watching over the plain, flanked by the low hills, he glimpsed for the first time Troy, with its high commanding towers and impenetrable walls, and shuddered. *To take the city was not going to be easy,* he thought.

They were setting camp close to the mouth of the wide meandering river *Skamandros*, when the messenger arrived.

"You are urgently summoned to the war council," the man panted, "by the great *Anax* himself."

"Are you sure it is I who am required?" Odysseus asked, taken by surprise, as he lashed the canvas to a wooden stay. With his small contingent of men, he had doubted his place amongst this inner council.

"Apparently your reputation for smooth words and persuasion goes before you," the other answered.

"So you will be elevated far above us," his captain, Eurylochos, quipped. Odysseus looked across and noticed how the other man's jaw had hardened and the body broadened out under the labour of rowing from the sea voyage. Certainly they had come a long way from those boyhood days when they had wrestled and swum together from the harbour beach.

"Let's see if we can bring a swift end to this business and return to Ithaka," Odysseus said, buckling his sword around his waist and reaching for his horsehair plumed helmet.

He found the leaders of the Greeks already assembled in the billowing tent of Agamemnon, who was seated on a bench cushioned by animal pelts. He raised his head and acknowledged Odysseus through long eye lashes as he entered.

"Ah Odysseus, please join us in our deliberations." He turned his head to the side and snapped, "Fetch food and wine, wench!"

Though they were newly arrived, clearly Agamemnon had already procured a woman to warm his bed.

Odysseus glanced around at the other gathered men recognising the faces. As customary Menelaos, with his softer features and golden hair, flanked his brother. Standing several heads taller than the next man and solid as oak, stood Ajax, son of Telemon. The men had nicknamed Ajax "The Big One" as he towered over them strong, broad and unbendable. Odysseus recognised at once Nestor but there was also a stranger amongst them, whom he assumed must be Idomeneus, famed for throwing the spear, newly arrived from the hundred-citied Krete. A shudder ran down Odysseus' backbone as he spied Ajax son of Oileus in the corner a mocking smile playing on his lips. *Who knew what vile deeds this man might commit if he was left unchecked?*

"We were considering how best to take the city," the *Anax* continued. "I say we prepare for battle at first light and take them by storm. With the finest Greek warriors it will not take long to bring those Trojan dogs to their knees."

"If I may be so bold, *Anax*." The voice belonged to Nestor, the king of Pylos, a kingdom on the mainland only three days sail from Ithaka. The words resonated loud and weighty. "I once encountered a not dissimilar occasion as a young man, many moons ago. Though we were many and brave warriors, that heavy-armed and well-defended citadel inflicted much death and injury upon us. For this reason, I say better to lay siege to the city and wait patiently. If I may recall..."

"Perhaps there is a third way," Odysseus interjected, aware of Nestor's fondness for reminiscence of stories from the past and battles from long ago. "For those walls are impenetrable and we may have to wait until we are all old men to Troy see fall. Might we send a delegation to the Trojans to seek for terms of *Peace* and appeal to their king to return Helen and make amends to Menelaos, her wronged husband? For our arrival will not have gone unnoticed by the Trojans and they also will be eager to see us gone and avoid a long drawn out war."

Agamemnon glanced at his brother and there was a slight discernible bow of Menelaos' head. "Very well Odysseus, you have persuaded me. Menelaos shall lead the delegation and, as you have a way with words, you shall accompany him."

They set out at first light, crossing the open plain by chariot, uncertain what fate awaited them. The thundering of the horses filled Odysseus' ears, as their hooves pounded the earth, and then he realised that the noise also came from his own heart beating wildly. The image of his infant son flitted across his mind and tearful pleading eyes of his mother as he tore himself away from her embrace. *The mission had to be successful to put a stop to this madness.* He glanced across at Menelaos, noticing in his haste to reclaim his errant wife, he had not groomed himself that morning. With a flush rising on his cheeks and eyes shining, he realised the man whipping the horses was driven by passion rather than reason.

Close-up those city walls seemed even more impregnable with the towered gateways and thickened ramparts. They could easily repel a swarm of warriors like a bull flicking off an irritating fly with its tail. *They were right to sue for peace* he thought again.

They were met at the city gate by a small delegation and allowed to pass through, escorted to the citadel on high. The city was in the throes of preparing for *War*. Banks of suspicious eyes and stolen glances greeted them as they passed through the narrow streets, mothers shielding their children with their bodies and craftsmen halting their hammering to watch. Silence followed their steps as if their presence heralded the arrival of death and destruction. Only the wails of babies punctuated the air. Though these were strange peoples of whom he knew so little, Odysseus could see the fear rubbed on their faces.

When they entered the throne room, the hall was crowded with a throng of people, all richly attired and flashes of gold hanging from their bodies. With shock, he noticed that the women, even those of marriageable age, did not veil their faces to receive strangers. On Ithaka, never had he seen his own mother expose her face outside the chamber, let alone his young wife.

"Welcome strangers." An older man, distinguished by his long white beard and purple robes, addressed them. "I am Priam, king of the Trojans and ruler of this city." He was sat on a high stone-carved chair, purple robes and a profusion of gold distinguishing his status as a high-born. Besides him sat his queen, Hekabe, a woman past her childbearing years but her face bore a dignified and regal beauty. Despite his wife's ample skills with the loom, suddenly Odysseus felt under-dressed and ill-prepared in his simple warrior's tunic in the face of this dazzling display of wealth.

The king gestured for them to sit on two wooden benches, hastily set out for them and waited for them to settle before continuing.

"And this is my trusted and wise counsellor Antenor," he said gesturing to an upright man standing beside the throne, "and my eldest son, Hector." They exchanged courteous nods of acknowledgment. It was obvious from the flecked muscles of the sword arm and tough strong body that Hector was a prime warrior like himself. Yet the son had a forbearance that was much to his liking and, under other circumstances, they might have formed a strong guest friendship.

"And these are some of my many sons and daughters," the old king continued, motioning to the throng of young people gathered around him, "through birth or marriage." It was rumoured that Priam had sired over fifty sons by his multiple wives and concubines, but his brazenness caught Odysseus by surprise. Then the thought came to him that despite the strange custom, this was an intended display of the power and the might of the Trojan kingdom. For those tied through blood would fight harder to defend their home city.

"So please, tell us your names and the nature of your visit," Priam asked, his pale eyes still intent upon them.

"I am Menelaos, son of Atreus and king of Sparta." began his companion, courtesy only thinly veiling his words from the seething rage beneath. "My brother Agamemnon leads the Greek contingent. This man is Odysseus, king of Ithaka and the proud hearted Kephallenians. Surely you know why we have come, sir."

"Your arrival has been expected, but please go

on."

"Your son Alexandros stayed in our kingdom as a stranger and was accorded the full rites of guest hospitality. However, he abused these blessed ties of *xenia,* that the gods gave us to bind one stranger to another to maintain peace and harmony. He charmed my wife with smooth winged words of deceit and then abducted her. I believe she is being held against her will within these city walls. I ask that she is allowed to return to her rightful husband and suitable reparation is made to our satisfaction for the harm and trouble that has been caused."

"That is a lie!" The source of the outburst came from a strikingly handsome young man, his features blended like those of a woman such was the perfection and flawlessness of his appearance. He had hair golden like sunlight and deep blue pools for eyes, which would have enchanted even the female gods. Concealed by his siblings, it had been hard to notice him. It was clear this was the wayward son who had brought trouble to the city gates, Alexandros of Troy. "She came of her own volition. I did not force her!" Odysseus could feel Menelaos' body tense beside him and he put out his hand to stop his companion from acting at the provocation.

"Silence Alexandros!" Priam spoke out firm and commanding. "Let us hear what these men have to say." He knew that Menelaos was struggling to keep his passions in check, so this time Odysseus stood up and spoke, keeping his eye firmly fixed on the royal couple.

"Sire, King Priam, I know that you are a wise and just ruler." His mind worked fast, as if impelled by one of the gods themselves. He chose his words carefully, mindful that the speech he uttered was the only chance of averting a long and bloody conflict. "We are not concerned with how this unfortunate juncture came about. Previously the peoples of Troy and the Greeks have lived in peace and harmony. Let us not allow this matter of a woman to come between us. Both our peoples stand to lose much if we enter into war and many on both sides will die and there will be much sorrow. Let us find a way to bring this unfortunate incident to a swift end. So that we each can return to our normal lives and the rightful order of the world can be restored according to the gods' wishes. All we ask is the return of Helen, the rightful wife of this man here, Menelaos, and for some recompense to make up for the harm that has been done. Then we Greeks will be happy to leave your shores and return to our homes once more to raise our families, tend our crops and govern our lands. Hateful *War* will only bring calamity to both our peoples."

In the uncomfortable silence, his words were

starting to carry weight as Priam watched him intensely with those pale grey eyes. Alexandros also must have sensed it too, for he burst out shouting "No, father, don't listen." He would have sprung on Menelaos had not brotherly hands held him back. "You cannot let Helen go," the voice bawled, the display of passion uncomfortable to witness. "Remember your vow to us, when I first brought her to Troy. You said that she would always be welcomed as my wife and protected within these walls. Father, I urge you, stay true to your words. Don't let her be sent away from this city. Our city is strong and well protected. We can withstand and hold out against any Greek attack."

"Silence, my son. Silence I say. I have heard enough from all sides." A sternness entered Priam's voice this time, warning those present to take heed. Alexandros had ceased struggling and a hush descended on the assembled group as Priam pondered the matter, his fingers drawn up to his lips. In that moment, the fate of his city and his people rested in his hands, that of the living and of those yet to be born. At last, he broke the silence, fixing his gaze unfalteringly upon Menelaos.

"I do not approve of what my son has done. To break the rules of *xenia* and take another man's wife is wrong. For this defies the laws of the gods. Yet Alexandros speaks the truth that when Helen entered this city, I vowed to honour, treat and protect her like my own daughter." Priam paused and Odysseus felt his body brace at the judgement about to be passed.

"Helen herself came here of her own free will and her place is here in Troy as is that of any child that may be produced from her union with Alexandros, should the gods wish this." Priam raised his head, his shoulders squared to them. "I cannot grant your request but I am prepared to provide ample reward that would satisfy you and recompense my son's transgression many times over. We are a wealthy city and can offer you plenty in terms of precious metals and gold."

Odysseus felt dismay fill his heart at Priam's words. He knew that Menelaos, who sat beside him with hunched shoulders and burning cheeks, could be won over. For the man keenly reproached himself for the troubles his failed marriage had heaped upon his fellow Greek warriors. But instinctively Odysseus knew this proposal would never be acceptable to their great *Anax*, King Agamemnon, as appeasement for the wounded honour of the house of Atreus. The sacrifice of Iphigeneia had put paid to any prospect of compromise.

Odysseus' thoughts were interrupted by Hekabe, perhaps observing the shadow that weighed down on him and Menelaos' deafening silence. There was an astuteness in her countenance and perhaps like him, the Trojan queen grasped the heavy price. Her words rang out in pure Greek across the hall, each one enunciated in a northern Thracian accent.

"Gentlemen, I am a Greek by birth from the city of Lokris. It was as a girl I first came here to Troy to serve as a priestess in the temple of Athene before my marriage to my lord Priam. Our peoples, those of the Greeks and those of the Trojans, have always been close and our fates intertwined. I know my husband's words may not entirely please you or win you over completely, but I urge you to consider these matters. I am sorry for your loss Menelaos and my husband can more than recompense you with wealth and goods so that through your *kleos* you may find a fitting bride. One who you will be satisfied with and perhaps in the fullness of time will bear you children. With my husband's wealth, you will not lack noble families offering their daughters in wedlock to you. I beg you to consider this offer and take it to your brother the *Anax*, great Agamemnon. Our peoples need to be at peace once more and avert a terrible war."

"I thank you for those words, Queen Hekabe," Odysseus replied, nodding in acknowledgement. The words were kindly meant but brought no relief to Menelaos who slumped further into silent humiliation. The man was brittle and fragile, like a clay pot that might smash into a hundred shards. "We will lay the terms of your peace before Agamemnon and the other Greek leaders to weigh up."

"May I see my wife before we go?" Menelaos suddenly asked, raising his head, the sound of his voice catching them by surprise. "I wish to hear from Helen's own lips that this is her true wish to remain with this man in Troy."

"I'm sorry Menelaos," Priam's voice was conciliatory and kind, "but she refuses to speak with you."

"Perhaps I can go if that is acceptable?" Odysseus said, the thought appealing to him. He wished to ensure this was not some trick meant to deceive. "I am her kinsman through marriage to Penelope, her cousin."

Priam turned to his counsellor and the two men spoke in hushed urgent whispers. "That will be possible due to your claims of kinship," the king finally replied, returning once more to his mild disposition. "Antenor will take you Odysseus to his apartment, where you can see Helen but Menelaos must remain here. My eldest son Hector will entertain him." The two Greek warriors exchanged glances and Odysseus bowed assent to answer for them both.

He was taken to a well-proportioned apartment, where the walls were richly furnished with elaborate tapestries to insulate the room and keep the winter chill out. *If there was a war*, he thought ruefully, *the Trojans would not be shivering in their tents*. Antenor was a pleasing host of uncommon refinement and in normal circumstances he Odysseus would have appreciated his company. The sound of light footsteps on the passage steps alerted the two men to the approach of another and then the door creaked open. Helen entered, her breathtaking beauty illuminating the room. Her face was uncovered, and she wore her hair down in ringlets, a fitted girdle emphasising her slim waist and full breasts. It was clear why this woman was so coveted by the warrior men and why her fame surpassed the kingdoms of Achaia.

"Odysseus, my kinsman, you are here." She reached out to clasp his hand and he accepted her embrace his body stiffening. "How is Penelope your wife, my dearest cousin?"

"Very well, madam, when I left her with our new-born son."

"She must miss you very much and long for your return."

He tried to summon his patience and respond mildly rather than with recrimination. "Indeed so and we both wish heartily that I may return back home as soon as the gods allow it."

"Come let us sit." Odysseus led her to a bench,

where beakers had been poured by his convivial host. He waited for her to take a sip of the wine and then began. "Dearest Helen, I regret we meet under these strained circumstances and this is not easy for both of us." She was looking at him directly and her exposed ravishing beauty unsettled him. "I come as a deputation to Troy on behalf of Agamemnon and the Greeks. Menelaos is in the city anxious for your return, but King Priam says you are here of your own volition. Does he speak the truth?"

"I'm sorry Odysseus..." She broke off, her voice faltering as she averted her gaze and her face blushed from shame.

"Helen, I did not come to condemn you but tell me is this truly what you choose? To stay here with this man in Troy rather than return to Sparta. I must ascertain with my own ears that this is indeed your true wishes?"

Helen looked down at her long slender fingers, letting out a deep regretful sigh. "That is my deepest desire, Odysseus. I want and need to be with Alexandros." Tears sprung into her eyes, beneath the long silky eye lashes, even then it enhanced her beauty. "I know that this is madness and perhaps the goddess of love herself, Aphrodite, has put this feeling in my heart and taken away my senses. But I love Alexandros and have given myself to him. No longer can I bear to be parted from him."

Odysseus studied her demeanour and thought of some infatuated love-struck youth, naive in the ways of the world. He tried again still patiently but from a different tack. "You know that Agamemnon has mustered a Greek army to take you back by force if necessary. He is a man not to be trifled with and can be most determined. It may not end well for the people here in the city and those who would love and protect you. Are you sure you want to risk taking this path and stay with this man and these alien people?"

The tears were falling freely from her eyes, as she raised her head towards him. "I love Alexandros," she cried, sobs racking her body. "Forgive me my dearest Odysseus." He beheld that luminous face demanding his sympathy, trying to fathom the promptings of her heart, but realising further talk was pointless. Helen was consumed by this passion and beyond reason.

As Odysseus and Menelaos crossed the wide open plain back towards the battle lines of the Greek troops, a grim silence hung over the two men and Odysseus found himself lost in his thoughts. The mission had been a failure and the Trojans were unwilling to surrender Helen without a violent struggle. It was worthy of Priam that he chose to stay loyal to his son and his ill-advised choice of bedfellow. Always he had respected Helen, his kinswoman, though her beauty marked her out for competition between the male warriors. But love or no love, the lovers' recklessness to allow this potential blood-letting was hard to stomach. He could almost taste the bitter bile in his mouth. For it seemed a madness that the gods had instilled into these two people conducting their lusty affair. Could this love-making be worth the slaughter of others, leaving their lives early to descend down into Hades? Perhaps it was these thoughts that had influenced Odysseus' own decisions in the future yet to come. That was still far away. But with a heart heavy and foreboding, he returned to the Greek camp to break the news to Agamemnon, knowing that the course towards war had been set.

Chapter 4

Goatherds and Panegyri

Thea leaned over the boat rail, as she took in the scene around her. The landmarks were familiar: the old sea mill, now desolate and deserted, silhouetted against the pine-wooded hillside; then the lighthouse with its white rounded portico jutting out into the straits and finally the stretch of open water. As the ferry's path cut swathes through the water, the crossing was relatively smooth for the time of year and already the sun's rays had dispelled the morning chill. Looking back across the lagoon, Thea saw the island's mountainous spine stretching up to Mount Oenos and felt the knot coiled inside her unwind. It caught her by surprise how much she had missed the island with its natural beauty.

"Have you recovered from last night?" Her body jolted startled by the sound of the voice. It was the same enquiry that Mark had asked as Thea had pulled up her chair at the breakfast table. No doubt Mark was concerned about Thea putting herself under too much pressure so soon after the marriage break-up. Masking the truth, she had reassured Mark fixing a smile to her face. He had not pressed the matter as Richard's booming voice announced his entrance into the breakfast room.

"Much better," she said, glancing across at Rob, brushing off the concern. "You were right, it probably was low blood sugar from skipping lunch." She saw a quizzical look cross Rob's face, aware that the dark shadows under her eyes betrayed her disturbed night's sleep. Perhaps the return to the island had unsettled her: for the old dream had struck, where she was chasing a man's shadow through dense woodland, always one step ahead and always just out of reach. Only with the arrival of early dawn, had she finally drifted into sleep.

"The biscuits usually do the trick."

"Your help was very timely," Thea conceded, noticing Rob leaning against the rail, apparently taking in the view and in no hurry to leave her side. He was taking deep breaths of the pure air as if absorbing the very fabric of the island.

He glanced at her quickly. "Forgive me, I hope I'm not intruding. You did seem lost in your thoughts."

"No, not at all," Thea replied lightly, rallying

herself and forcing herself to make the effort. "I was just enjoying the view." Not for the first time, she wondered whether her decision to return to the island was a mistake. In those long winter months she had wrapped herself in solitude, avoiding the sympathetic looks and enquiries, comforting herself alone in the deafening silence of the London flat as the empty days stretched out in front. Feeling now the soothing spring sunlight, she banished the anxious and fearful memories.

"We've worked out an itinerary for today," Rob continued. Instantly her attention was grabbed and she felt again the mounting excitement. The beach had been suggested and though ambitious for the time of year, Thea had come prepared. "We've managed to incorporate your Potso Kaliki as well as visiting some interesting geology around the lighthouse area. That should give us plenty of time to be back for the big event tonight," he said, a hint of irony in his voice.

"You mean Porto Katsiki?" Thea corrected him, noting though he was a renowned specialist, languages were clearly not Rob's strength.

"Alistair and Elizabeth were keen to drive close to the field survey site to gain a sense of the local geography." This was welcome news as at least the day would not be entirely wasted and divert them away from the main thrust of their work.

Rob had turned his face towards Thea as if studying her intensely, the daylight emphasising his pitted skin and playing on the lively intelligent eyes. The beard had been neatly trimmed and the blonde-copper hair swept back. He wore a casual grey sweatshirt, which only thinly disguised his muscular arms and strong upper torso. "Do you want to ride with us? There's a spare seat in the front. Sophie and Belinda are riding in the back with Matthew, my assistant."

Thea glanced behind Rob where the group had spread out across the bright orange plastic chairs of the open air deck. Belinda was holding court, her long blonde tresses falling over her face whipped by the wind. Thea's eyes flicked over the male students, all fresh-faced, whose names of Jamie, Daniel and Toby oozed confidence or prowess on the sports field. As usual Elizabeth sat clamped to her husband's side like a conjoined twin. Finally Thea's eyes alighted upon the young woman who had caught her attention only the previous night and to whom she could now attach the name Sophie.

"Thanks for the offer. That would be great," she replied, noticing that the cream apartment blocks and houses of the provincial town were quickly coming into view, signalling the end of the ferry crossing.

"I think we'd better get down to the car," said Rob catching her glance.

Shortly afterwards, Thea found herself seated in the car front seat, watching as the ramp of the ferry was lowered with a clanking and juddering of heavy metal. As engines revved and people pressed forward, there was a surge of activity as the vessel expelled its human and metal cargo. Undaunted and without hesitation, Rob steered the vehicle through the chaotic commotion, closely tailing the car in front as if roped by an invisible umbilical cord, until they emerged into the quietness of the sleepy provincial town.

It was early afternoon, when they finally arrived at Porto Katsiki. Their journey had taken them to the western extremity, where a remote lighthouse overhung the precipitous cliffs. A young pup had bounded out to greet them, its panting tongue lolling side-wards, revelling in the arrival of potential playmates. Belinda and Jamie took turns to throw brushwood for the hound to retrieve as Rob explained in an animated voice the deceptiveness of the place, where the cliffs plummeted into the depths of the Mediterranean Sea.

The road had then taken them north through a labyrinth of country lanes, skirting an old monastery, the iron gates padlocked, and a clutch of small villages. All day they had passed very little traffic and even fewer people, despite the signs of well-tended fields. So it was unsurprising when they pulled up onto the strand at Porto Katsiki to find the place deserted.

The fragrance-laden air filled Thea's nostrils, as she stepped out of the car. She glanced around noting the epithet *Porto* seemed rather misplaced as the port consisted of a few fishing boats bobbing in the harbour and a cluster of shuttered houses. Despite the air of neglect and the overgrown gardens, there was a profusion of flowering plants and trees weighed down with fruit blossom. A mounting excitement gripped her when Sophie interrupted her thoughts.

"This place is lovely! Do you mind me asking why you were so keen to come here?" Thea glanced at the younger woman noting the eagerness in her voice. Her openness tempered with inexperience reminded Thea of her own younger self.

"I wanted to see this place for myself," Thea replied, suddenly feeling overdressed and clammy in her long sleeved tunic in the full sun. She reached for her wide-brimmed hat to cool herself as beads of sweat pricked her skin. "The Odyssey describes a place where Odysseus first sets foot on Ithaka, when he finally arrives home from the Trojan wars. The place is called *Phorkys* or *old man of the sea* and was thought to refer to the monk seals, which breed off this northern coast."

"I've never heard of seals in Greece."

"I'm not surprised. They're shy creatures so raise their young in underwater sea-caves beyond human reach."

"That's such a shame!" the younger woman exclaimed "they've been driven to the edges of their natural habitat. So do you think this place matches that description?" The group had gathered and were observing the conversation with attentive eyes and listening ears.

"See there," said Thea, pointing out to sea where the two headlands jutted out to create the long shallow bay. "Homer describes exactly such a sheltered bay, where it was possible to leave boats untethered even in a winter storm."

"The bay is very different from the main body of the island we drove through this morning," Sophie picked up, her head gazing round.

"That's right," said Thea, impressed by the young woman's swift perception. "So much so that Odysseus doesn't at first realise he's arrived home."

"Certainly the wide stretch of sand fits well with an ancient bronze-age harbour for beaching a boat," Alistair interceded, standing stiffly and raising an eyebrow. "Is there something specific we are looking for as perhaps we need to go on?"

"Actually a cave, where Odysseus hides the friendship gifts presented to him," said Thea, feeling as if she was being gently reprimanded for delaying the group.

"We've still got plenty of time," said Rob, glancing down at his watch. "Perhaps we can try the path over there and explore a bit?" he said, motioning towards an earth-beaten path that followed the steep shoreline towards a small harbour.

After a fruitless search, they retraced their steps to the sandy strand of beach, crossing to the other side of the beach. It was as the path started to climb upwards towards the village, that Thea glanced back over her shoulder and saw it. A cave hidden from view, just as Homer had described all those millennia before, covered by an olive tree and some distance from the shore.

"There it is," she cried, her startled shout stopping everyone in their tracks, "Odysseus' cave!" Her heart sank as she realised without a boat nor any villager in sight, swimming was the only way to reach it.

"We could quite comfortably wade over or swim, if you want to take a look," Rob offered reassuringly, perhaps noticing the frown crossing her face. "The water doesn't look too deep or cold for this time of year."

"I'm afraid we must decline your suggestion," said Elizabeth, suddenly alert to the conversation. "I'm surprised you could even contemplate such a thing at this time of year," she said, twisting her lips.

"I assure you I have encountered much worse," replied Rob good-naturedly, his enthusiasm undaunted. "So who's up for it?" he asked, his question meeting several nodding heads.

Thea gasped as she plunged into the ice-cold water. Her body protested, as it took a moment for her limbs and torso to acclimatise to the biting chill. Behind her, she could hear the shrieks and splashes of the others braving the water, but without hesitation Rob had set off at a pace, his powerful arms cutting through the water surface. Bracing herself, she submerged her body and followed his lead.

Rob was already stretched out on the white shingle floor of the cave, when they emerged from the salt water.

"You obviously keep yourself fit," quipped Matthew as he collapsed beside him, panting for air.

"You're just not used to the cold," said Rob laughing, stretching out his legs and rolling onto his back. He lifted up his eyes and shot an admiring glance towards Thea, as she threw herself gasping on the pebbled ground.

"So this is the cave where Odysseus himself may have been," Sophie remarked, finally catching her breath.

Thea nodded, reaching over and seizing a handful of smooth pebbles, struck by being almost in touching distance of her legendary hero. Perhaps he too had sat in this very spot and looked up at the same jagged rock protrusions that formed the cavern ceiling. She cast the stones aside and sat upright to take a better look around her. Over time the cave entrance had been shaped by the elements into a portico, like arches in a cloister.

"You know the ancients used to believe that behind every natural phenomenon like a river, the sea, the wind, there was a local god," said Thea.

"So this cave would have been a sacred place?" remarked Sophie.

"Exactly," Thea nodded, struck again by Sophie's quick turn of mind. "And that entrance over there," she continued, gesturing to a smaller side opening blocked off by a rock fall, "would have led down to the nymphs' home."

"We must be crazy to be swimming out here in March," Belinda protested, rubbing herself vigorously and trying to wrap herself up in her arms and legs. Her fashionable brief neon bikini was perfect for the beach in the scorching heat but inadequate in blocking the spring chill.

"You look freezing!" Thea said, noticing the raised goose bumps on Belinda's skin and her chattering teeth. "If everyone has seen enough, perhaps we should get going before someone catches a chill."

****

It had been Thea's idea to explore the dirt track leading up the steep hillside from the shore to the village above. It was as if her body, shocked by the chilling sea, had become energised and the weight burdening her mind had lifted. She had given the tangible reason of wanting to check out the distance to the nearby settlement as the possible location for the hut of Eumaios: the lowly herdsman who first received Odysseus on his return. But there was a deeper reason which Thea had felt unable to articulate: that walking in his footsteps and seeing what he might have seen might bring her closer to this mythological Greek hero. Certainly the olive groves cultivated on the slopes, their trunks wizened and split apart with age, looked as if they might have witnessed Odysseus' hike up the mountain.

They were over halfway up the steep path,

when the frenetic jangling of bells announced an approaching herd. Around the bend, a flock of goats feeding on the slope obstructed the gravel path. The drove now stood alert, twitching, their heads jerking round to weigh up the newcomers. Slowly the herd parted like a wave, allowing the strangers to walk steadily through their midst.

A scream rang out ahead, disturbing the calm as the panicked herd bolted. Thea rushed forwards towards the noise to witness a goat charging at Sophie. On contact, the young woman's body crumpled and collapsed to the ground. Only then did Thea realise Rob was by her side.

He grabbed a heavy stick and put out a restraining hand towards Thea. "Stand back. I'll deal with this."

Ignoring his words, Thea pushed past the outstretched arm. "Let me handle this," she replied firmly. "Nobody move!" she commanded shooting a warning glance around the group. Sophie was writhing on the ground, her face contorted with pain, clutching the wound where the blood was oozing between her fingers. The agitated animal was pawing the ground preparing to charge again. Making a cooing noise between her teeth, Thea approached steadily, reaching out her outstretched hand to stroke the beast. As the goat permitted her touch, Thea could see the blood of afterbirth clinging to its shaggy haunches. "Ssh," she cooed soothingly, gently caressing it until she could feel the stiffness of the animal's body relax. ""It meant no harm. It's only wanting to protect its young." She glanced up, searching for the kid and spied it bleating, camouflaged against a rock. Clasping the bony horns, Thea steered the doe from the path, reuniting the mother with her new-born, speckled with the blood of its birth.

By the time Thea turned her attention to the injured Sophie, someone had thought to pull her off the path and Rob was kneeling beside her. The others appeared transfixed by the spectacle, like game caught in the beam of a headlight. Rob anxiously threw her a glance.

"Sophie," she said calmly. The young woman was cupping the wound with her fingers, as the blood pooled, staining her clothes like ink on blotting paper. "I need you to take your hand away so I can examine the injury. Is that okay with you?" The younger woman nodded slightly, through gritted teeth wincing with pain.

Carefully Thea unfolded Sophie's fingers, as the blood oozed out of the wound, where the animal's horn had ripped the flesh. The slash had cut into muscle but had missed the bone. Fear and pain were written on the face of the injured woman. "Don't worry, it looks worse than it is," Thea reassured her soothingly. "I will give you something for the pain and will dress the wound until we can get you back." Sophie nodded faintly, biting her lip to hold back her cries of agony. Thea rummaged in her bag and pulled out a small quilted bag, unfolding it carefully. She picked out a small dark bottle and emptied some drops into a small cup of water, which she raised to Sophie's lips. "This will work quickly to ease the pain."

"What is that?" Elizabeth had suddenly sprung into motion. "I've some pain-killers in my bag."

"This will work better and has no ill effects. I prepared the tincture myself from natural herbs." Sophie nodded and tipping back her head, drained the cup. Next Thea pulled out some gauze and like a trained field medic deftly started to clean and dress the wound. "The ointment I've applied, should help the skin bind together and prevent scarring," Thea explained. "It will be sore for a couple of days but should heal well. Just to be sure, I'll arrange for a doctor to visit you tonight when we get back."

She lifted her eyes to see Rob watching her movements, as if spellbound. Perplexity must have been written on her face for he lowered his glance. "I'm sorry," he said, "I didn't realise you were medically trained?"

"Not at all," said Thea shaking her head, tearing the strip in two to fasten and secure the bandage. "Okay, all done!" She raised her head towards Sophie and gave a reassuring smile. "But I don't think you can walk very far," Thea said, helping the injured woman slowly to her feet.

Rob began checking the satnav on his mobile phone. "About half a kilometre up, the track meets the road. Do you think you can walk there? I'll fetch the car and meet you further up the track."

"I think I can make that," replied Sophie weakly. "I don't want to spoil everyone's afternoon."

"Don't worry about that Sophie," Thea assured her. "Perhaps with Matthew's help, you can lean on the two of us so you don't put too much weight on that leg." Matthew nodded in agreement.

"We need to be getting back anyway," said Elizabeth. "There's the big important event planned for tonight. Richard will be expecting us."

"Yes, all the great and the good will be there, Sophie, so it is important you look your best!" Rob added teasing her to raise a thin smile. "Don't worry, we'll get you there. I'll fetch the car and be as quick as I can." After he disappeared, the three of them started to make their way slowly up the pathway, leaving the others to follow Rob.

"Thank goodness you were there, Thea," said Sophie, putting her weight on their shoulders, "and knew what to do. I can feel the pain-killer working already."

"Good. It should help."

"Yes, you and Rob work really well together," added Matthew. And for the second time that day, Thea felt disconcerted.

****

At 8 o'clock prompt, they were all seated at the restaurant as instructed. It was situated on the outskirts of the town near the *katavrothes*, a rather select venue frequented by locals rather than tourists. They made up a large party in the *taverna* but were not the only arrivals.

"I'm afraid my boss isn't here yet." Stelios had immediately come over to greet them, attentive as always. He had changed out of his drab suit and was wearing a clean pressed shirt. "We're expecting him very soon and he is extremely keen to meet you all. I've told him a lot about you," he said, a slow smile building on his lips as he glanced at Thea.

There were vigorous handshakes and exchanges of introductions. The place was bursting: a crescendo of noise, jabbering and rising excitement. Two long trestle tables had been allocated for the party. Thea found a place towards the end of one of the tables. Sophie and Matthew had already seated themselves there and were absorbed in conversation. Here Thea would be able to observe events from a position of half concealment. It caught her by surprise when Rob pulled up the chair beside her.

It was hard to talk above the deafening noise. Despite being assembled specialists with a common purpose, the conversation struggled and came in fits and starts. Thea had heard similar discussions many times before: the trading of lists of personal connections, research and published articles to determine social ranking within the academic hierarchy. From her vantage point, she felt an inexplicable anxiety mounting, as if warned by her night's dream, but as she scanned the room, she recognised no one. Just unknown faces of peoples whose lives had been lived separately except for this brief moment of time.

And then the music struck up and the dancing began. Thea identified the familiar strum of the bouzouki music and a well-known song, bellowed out whenever Greeks came together in groups. It was a song of the Aegean Sea, conjuring up images of the surf, seabirds and turquoise waters. Some of the Greeks sang along mouthing the familiar words, while others listened, all animated. Then a single male dancer took to the floor. He was middle aged, greying but still sinewy in his movements. Thea recognised the etiquette: that when a single dancer performed, only he could command that dance and take centre stage. Around him, others kneeled, observed or clapped. Thea watched his movements, the twists, the turns, the drop to the ground and then the sudden spring: like a deer stag in its prime, rutting to establish its dominance. The watching children joined in the spectacle, tearing up and throwing pieces of serviettes like confetti. Once upon a time, it was broken glass on which the males danced, demonstrating their bravery, prowess and the determination of mind to control the heady shots of wine and ouzo. Now it was harmless paper.

Thea watched the movements and started to catch the rhythm of the music, like the beating of her pulse. Taking a sip of her wine, Thea felt its warmth pulsating through her body, as if the life force was returning to her and coursing through her arteries, mellowing her jangled nerves. She relaxed, reassuring herself that her fears were groundless. But it was at that precise moment, she saw him. A stir in the *taverna* announced his arrival, but she spotted him as soon as he stepped over the threshold. He moved effortlessly like a big cat, warmly accepting the gestures of welcome. A handshake here and an embrace there, his presence drawing all eyes to him. He was dressed immaculately in crisply pressed chinos and a white cotton shirt, which accentuated his dark complexion. With his thick curls of jet-black hair, she would have recognised him anywhere, only the fresh boyish looks had given way to a masculine maturity. Dimitri Kampitsis.

But he was not alone. There was a stunningly striking woman at his side, presumably his wife. Immaculately coiffured and attired, she was dressed in chiffon trousers the colour of sand and a long flowing emerald silk tunic. Gold jewellery jangled on her neck, arms and ears, indicating wealth and privilege. Her slim stomach and pinched waist belied the obvious fact that she was the mother to the two children at her side. The children themselves, no older than ten years old, were a completely different proposition. A solemn boy and girl, both slightly overweight with dark hair and circles around their eyes, dressed in mourning black. It was as if all the beauty and radiance had been bestowed on the parents so that nothing had been spared for the children.

The picture punched her body, as her limbs stiffened and the pit of her stomach sank, like a lift hurtling down a shaft.

Keep calm, she inwardly commanded herself,

as she cast around weighing up her predicament. From her half-concealed position, she could see the glamorous couple were still exchanging greetings and noticed Stelios eagerly approaching the newcomer and clasping his hand. Then her mind suddenly clicked inside. *This was the absent boss Stelios had mentioned. This was the head of the Archontakis Foundation who was funding the project.* A wave of nausea and total horror gripped Thea at the realisation. Richard had now joined the small party, vigorously shaking Dimitri's hand, which only strengthened Thea's suspicions. Panic now took hold, spreading through her body, as she realised the glamorous couple might turn their attention to her table and they would be brought face to face.

Thea cast her glance around, her heart beating wildly, feeling as if the ground was collapsing beneath her feet. *How could she have been so stupid? How could she not have realised! She had to get out of here. Find an excuse.* Her mind had gone blank as she desperately racked her brain, when she felt the pressure of a hand on her arm. The grip was solid, strong and reassuring. Thea looked up to see that Rob had turned his head towards her, his slate-grey eyes questioning. There was a slight jolt of fire in the pit of her stomach, but it was enough to bring her back to her senses.

"Are you alright, Thea? You look quite shot." There was an anxious tone to the enquiry as Rob studied her face.

She could feel her body trembling and tried to rally herself. "I think I might have a migraine coming on," Thea stammered. The excuse sounded only half convincing, but it was the best she could muster.

The family group had now been seated at the table opposite. The immediate moment of danger had passed, but she needed to get out of there. For the moment Thea sat unobserved, surveying the shape of Dimitri's familiar head which had caused her so much anguish. *Was she watching her own fate that had never quite come to pass?* she wondered as she caught snatches of the conversation: a female name *Clemmie*, the shipping company *Archontakis* and finally his name *Dimitri*, the sound once so treasured. There was a toast of *Yeia mas* as the details started to stitch themselves together.

"Do you need to leave?" asked Rob solicitously, punctuating her thoughts. "I can accompany you." *Yes, she did need to get out of here. She needed some time to think about how on earth she was going to handle this situation.*

"Perhaps better I leave before the headache gets any worse," Thea replied, seizing the opportunity. "Can you make my apologies?" She hesitated, looking towards Sophie, giving her the briefest of nods. "Can I entrust Sophie to your care to ensure she gets back alright to the hotel? Her leg will still be very sore." Rob nodded, a puzzled look on his face.

Thea grabbed her things and steered her way out of the tavern, careful not to draw unwanted attention. It was not hard as everyone was engrossed by the new arrivals, the feast and the dancing music. Once outside, the raucous sound and bright lights of the tavern gradually gave way to the chirruping of cicadas and the tree-lined avenue blanketed in darkness. As she walked back, Thea tried to calm herself and get a grip on the emotions churning around in her mind. *She was a grown woman of thirty eight years of age, no longer the naïve nineteen year old young adult*, she reasoned with herself. And yet the wound still physically hurt and throbbed even after this passage of time. She was walking faster and faster, almost running, back to the refuge of the hotel.

"You're back early," commented Electra as Thea retrieved her room key. "Did you not enjoy the gathering?"

"I'm afraid I'm not feeling well," replied Thea, repeating her lame excuse.

"What a shame!" exclaimed Electra. "You're not having much luck! I understood the big man himself, Dimitri Kampitsis was going to be there. He's quite the looker and all the women round here swoon over him!" His name grated on her ears and Thea took her key with a brief nod.

Alone in her room, it took Thea some time to regain her composure. The possessions scattered around gave some sense of security. She needed time to think. To process this development. To work out a plan as to how she was going to handle the situation. She knew Dimitri was on the island, but he didn't necessarily know that she was. He wouldn't recognise her married name of Sefton. So she had time. All she needed to do was to keep a low profile. It wouldn't be too surprising if she was buried in the local library archives for days on end. That was after all ostensibly why she was here. That would provide a perfect excuse and she could "politely" decline any invitations to meet him. She suddenly realised that Stelios might be a complication. She needed to take extra care to ensure nothing got back to Dimitri. He could not be alerted to her presence or know that she was here.

Her thoughts were disturbed by a soft knock on the door. Now feeling irritated, Thea flung it open to find Rob filling the doorway.

"I just wanted to make sure you were alright," he said, concern written on his face, "and especially after you fainted yesterday. I wasn't completely comfortable with you walking back on your own."

"That was very thoughtful of you," Thea said, fastening a convincing smile on her face. "I'll be fine with rest. Probably just overdone things over the last few weeks in the push to get here."

He moved towards her and but then hesitated, as if wrestling inside with something. "I just wanted to say Thea," Rob finally said, swallowing hard, "I really enjoyed your company today. Sleep well." And with that he was gone.

Thea hurriedly closed the door. For a moment she had glimpsed something in Rob's expression but dismissed the thought. There were enough complications already. After changing into her night clothes, she reached for her well-thumbed edition of the Odyssey beside her bed, drawing comfort from the familiarity of the words.

Chapter 5

The Quarrel

It had been as he Odysseus had feared. The offer of peace and recompense had been dismissed out of hand. Nothing less than the return of Helen to her husband would satisfy the honour and restore the reputation of the house of Atreus. And so the army had laid siege to Troy, expecting the city to fall quickly in the face of the overwhelming might and pride of the Greek forces.

In those first lunar months, the young fresh troops had been optimistic that soon they would return to their homes, once more to pull their ploughshares and take up the trappings of *Peace*. There had been raids into the hinterland and the lands beyond the city, below the wooded slopes of Mount Ida, taking from the land the well fed flocks of animals and other natural plunder for the army to feed upon. Then there had been raiding parties to some of the smaller cities, allies of Troy, but vulnerable to attack without the same impenetrable walls to protect them. From those devastated burning cities, they had carried off grain, oil, wine, treasure, precious metals and of course women. The air had been filled with the cries of screaming women, clutching wailing children to their breasts, begging for their homes to be spared and mercy for the men folk about to be put to the sword. It was not a pleasant sight to behold. But by this process of strangulation, tightening the grip on the land around that Trojan fortress, it was hoped that slowly but surely life would be squeezed out of that great city with its mild mannered king and stubbornly resistant people.

Only gradually did the horror of *Strife* unleashed make its presence known amongst the troops. In those first grim encounters, the young men of the troop started to learn the truth of warfare. Men didn't die swiftly and cleanly as the bards sang, giving up their spirit easily to the shades of Hades. There was no single blow and a quick dropping to the ground, headlong, spent. Instead there was gore and mess, the bloody stench of which seemed to cling to the body and blood spattered garments despite repeated washing and cleansing. There were groans of men, calling out in their agony for their mothers or to their comrades for a quick dispatch. There were those who endured slow agonising death throes, sometimes lingering days as wounds grew infested and blackened, despite the ministrations of the best skilled Greek healers.

But more than that it had been a chaotic business. In the heat of the battle, warriors had fought over the spoils of the bodies, each trying to strip and carry off the precious metal armour of the dead or dying. It was in the recklessness to win these coveted prizes, that men would be vulnerable and take risks exposing themselves to death from a well-judged spear. There had been no discipline amongst the troops, each fighting for personal glory or his own contingent. Brother had fought alongside brother, often dying together in a single attack spelling disaster and an uncertain future to their families and kinsfolk far away. Young sons, husbands and lovers in the fullness of youth had been cut down, their lives ended when they had just begun. Then the reality of war and *Strife's* full measure had hit them.

In the winter a cold wind swept over the plain blowing from the straits of the Hellespont sometimes with whirling flurries of snow. Then they had shivered, miserably huddled in their coarse tents or around the campfires trying to warm frozen fingers, hands or toes. In the heat of the hot season, that same open plain turned into scorched land, where the dust infiltrated everything: the men's tents, their clothes and their dry mouths. Then the stench of the cesspits, the filth of countless men, fouled and polluted the air itself. They had idly passed this time of stand-off as best they could. In the tedium of their waking time, someone had invented a new game etching markings on a stone, which they had called "*dice*". At first, it had been not too uncomfortable for Odysseus and the proud hearted Kephallenian warriors to spend the time idly chatting, practising their combat skills or singing songs from their island home. There were always duties to be done: the washing, the endless cooking, securing the provisions for the day's meal, gathering brushwood for the campfire and sharpening spears and weapons. But mostly it had been boredom.

Each morning Odysseus had looked out from his tent across that flat plain to that great city Troy, with those impenetrable walls. Each morning he hoped that the day would break the stalemate. Each morning he hoped that the gods would grant them *Victory* and finally they could return home. But the years had dragged on with no end in sight, an interminable waiting game. Only he had watched himself and those troops around him slowly grow older together, past the prime of youth. He was still a fit and vital man, now approaching his thirtieth summer, but it was the time spent away from home that troubled him most. As the years passed by, his thoughts had turned increasingly to Ithaka, anxious for news of his family, his wife Penelope but most of all Telemachos, his young son. Would his parents, his dear mother, still be alive to welcome him by the time he returned, which was long in the coming, or was his fate to die here in this strange land?

When had those doubts about their leader and overlord, the *Anax*, first appeared? Odysseus could not be sure. Perhaps it had been at that first war council when he had glimpsed the signs of Agamemnon's weakness and indecision. Sitting on his lofty wooden chair, padded with deer and fox skin, the look of arrogance and self-belief had slipped from that dark fine-looking face as the leader of the Greeks had surveyed those thick city walls. Perhaps it had been during the madness of battle, when Agamemnon had accused him of cowardice for not plunging his brave-hearted Kephallenians headlong into the chaos. Or perhaps it had been in the ninth year of siege warfare, when recklessly Agamemnon had tested the resolve of the troops, suggesting they give up the fight and depart for their homelands. The man Agamemnon was a headstrong imperious fool! For he had sent the Greek warriors bolting for the hollow ships in disarray. And there would have been a mass exodus on the spot had he, Odysseus, and the other Greek leaders not cajoled, commanded and exhorted the fleeing men, stamping order on the troop once more. And he confessed there had been times when gladly he Odysseus could have done the same, had he not been determined to stay and see this bloody business out to the end. But it had been during the famous quarrel, with Achilles who was destined to die young, that things had come to a head, in that tenth year of the war.

It had started simply enough after Agamemnon had sent away a priest, Chryses, his name. The pitiful man, his face pinched with grief, had come in supplication to beg for the return of his beloved daughter, a war spoil now warming the *Anax*' bed. In his haughty manner, Agamemnon had disrespected the old priest with harsh words, threatening to beat him to death with cudgels if he ever clapped eyes on him again. That was when the real trouble had begun. It must have been Apollo, outraged by the contempt displayed towards his priest, who sent a pestilence as punishment amongst the troops. At first it had started with one man here or there taking sick to his bed, unable to be aroused in the morning, refusing all food and sustenance. Then more and more fit healthy troops had succumbed to the sickness, labouring to catch their breath and complaining of an intense internal fire, the tell-tale signs of plague. It was only on the tenth day of the sickness, when the sickly smell of death hung over the Greek camp and they had started to bury bodies heaped in pits, that Achilles, the leader of the Myrmidons, had summoned an assembly and stood up amongst them all.

"Son of Atreus," he had begun giving due honour to Agamemnon, "I think that we will be driven back to the ships and forced to flee these shores unless we can ascertain the reason for this sickness that the gods have unleashed. Is it possible that we have neglected the temples or not offered adequate sacrifices of oxen, lambs or goats? We need to find some priest or diviner who can explain what has angered the gods to send this pestilence amongst us." Achilles had voiced the fears of each man present, that of an ignoble death without *kleos,* drawing their last breath covered in the filth of their own vomit and excrement.

It was then that Kalchas, that accursed priest, had stood up. He wore the simple light robes of his position, but his eyes set within the narrow bony face were hard. This was the very same man who had advised that terrible sacrifice of the lovely and innocent Iphigeneia at the outset of the expedition, all those years ago. Since the death of his daughter, Agamemnon had little time for the man, perhaps seeing his own guilt reflected in the man's face. However the priest now had the courage to stand up and speak out.

"Most god-like and shining Achilles," the man began a slight quiver in his voice. "I think I can give you the answer, but first you must promise to protect me from harm, if my words unwittingly anger someone, even the great *Anax* himself." His face was pale and beads of sweat had broken across his brow.

"With my mother, an immortal goddess, as my witness, you have my promise," replied Achilles without hesitation. "Come, speak your mind priest!"

"Noble Achilles," proclaimed Kalchas taking confidence from Achilles' protection, "it is not because of any missed offering or promise that this affliction has been sent. Rather it is because of the priest Chryses, whom Agamemnon dishonoured and sent away empty-handed. To make reparation, the daughter Chryseis, without delay or ransom, must be returned to her father and the appropriate offerings made. Only this action will appease the anger of the god Apollo."

"That is impossible." Agamemnon had jumped up, his cheeks reddened with anger at the priest's words. "Chryseis shares my bed. I am quite taken by her and even prefer her to my own wife Klytaimnestra. Indeed she is her equal in all ways, being clever, of pleasing looks and accomplished in the skills of the home." Odysseus remembered shuddering at the sound of these words, praying silently to the gods they never reached the ears of the wife now dishonoured before all.

"Priest!" Nestor had intervened sharply. "You should remember to choose your words more carefully when you speak of these matters concerning our overlord, *Anax*. He is a great man and you must in future accord him due deference and respect as befits our leader." The priest was visibly trembling with fear, expecting to be run through with a sword by the old man. But Nestor instead had turned his attention to Agamemnon, speaking now with smooth flattering words. "My lord, if you will allow me to speak so boldly. If it is as the insolent priest says, then you must be the great leader that you are and think of the troops. Surely it is more important to consider the men dying and the success of this mission, than hold out over a woman. For a woman, even though she may excel in the beauty and loveliness of Aphrodite herself, is not the equal and match of a single warrior."

Agamemnon sat silently for several minutes, his fingers lightly stroking his chin, his olive eyes dark and gleaming. Finally he replied.

"Very well, Nestor. I am persuaded to give the daughter Chryseis back if that is for the best. However I expect appropriate recompense to be made to me, as is befitting my position as the overlord and leader of the Greeks. It is not right that I should be deprived my share of the prizes, when others keep their own rewards."

"But that is impossible." Achilles, always hot-headed and impetuous, had responded without tact or diplomacy. "Lord Agamemnon, you know that all the spoils have been shared out already and there is nothing that can be offered now to recompense you." His eyes had widened and his cheeks flushed. "Each warrior was assigned a reward according to how he performed in battle. We cannot now reapportion those prizes. Surely you must know that. To do this would only be seen as personal greed which is unbecoming in a leader. You will be recompensed three or fourfold once we take the city and sack Troy."

"So what would you have me do?" snapped Agamemnon. "Carry off your prize, or that of the Ajaxes, or perhaps my good fellow Odysseus here. Is that what you are proposing?" A menacing tone had crept into the exchange and anyone else might have heeded the warning in front of the assembled troops.

But Achilles always headstrong and so sure of himself could not let the matter go. "So you would take away a trophy from us who fight here day after day," he retorted. "You cannot do this! Rewards won by our sweat and blood in battle! It wasn't on our account we came here to do battle. I have no quarrel with the Trojans. I did not come to be insulted. I am taking my Myrmidons out of the battle. We set sail tomorrow!"

"Go, if you feel like that." Agamemnon had stood up. "Run away like a coward or dog. We don't need you. We can win this war without you. And since I am losing Chryseis, then I claim your prize, the woman Briseis. So that you will know how much stronger I am than you."

It was at that point, Achilles looked as if he might kill Agamemnon on the spot. The blue veins of his temple throbbed as his fingers hovered over the sheath of his sword. Somehow the younger man managed to control his impulse, turning and walking away. But this quarrel set off a disastrous chain of events for the Greek contingent.

It had been he, Odysseus, who had been entrusted to return the girl Chryseis to her father. She had been freshly attired with a finely woven tunic and her hair well-groomed to reflect the magnificence of her captor, Agamemnon. The old priest, stumbling to greet them, had received his precious daughter with eyes swollen by tears. It was a brief touching moment in the whole sad affair as father and daughter fell into each other's arms weeping. *At least here was something good in this bloody conflict,* Odysseus had thought to himself. To appease the anger of the god, they had then made sacrifice on the temple altar. An offering to Apollo himself: a herd of beasts brought with them, lowing oxen and whining goats. This seemed to placate the god for soon after the plague lifted and the men had stopped dying.

At first, things had not gone too badly for the Greeks, despite the loss of their most able warrior Achilles and the fierce-hearted Myrmidons. Achilles had not sailed home to Pthie as he had threatened, but had stayed in the camp, licking his wounds but refusing to fight. Then suddenly their fortune in battle had turned. The Trojans had grown in confidence, perhaps spurred on by rumours of dissent and division within the Greek camp. Some had even claimed Achilles beseeched his mother Thetis, the sea nymph, to ask Zeus himself to grant the Trojans success on the battlefield so that her son's honour might be restored.

It had been a hard day of fighting when the Greek army under heavy pressure had been pushed back to the very beachhead itself. In the privacy of Agamemnon's tent, they had all gathered round to take council, all those heroes whose names the bards now recounted. Agamemnon had sat on his customary wooden chair, his arms folded across his body and his face drained of colour. The mood had been solemn and downcast. But Odysseus had insisted they first all ate. "We troops can't go into battle on empty stomachs," he said summoning the servants. After their plates had been piled with meat and the diluted Thracian wine poured, it was Nestor, the diplomat, who began. He had looked nervous, his aged face flushed with wine, and he fiddled with the gold griffin ring he always wore on his right hand.

"Oh Agamemnon, son of Atreus, you are a great king and to you the gods have given wisdom to rule over the peoples you command," Nestor began. "We all look up to you and acknowledge your rule and authority. But in this matter, I cannot condone your treatment of Achilles, who is a fine warrior, taking his woman and dishonouring him in front of the troops. We must find a way to end this quarrel and bring reconciliation between you both. You must make amends to Achilles for publicly shaming him."

Agamemnon, perhaps fully aware of the seriousness of the Greek position, was quick to agree. "You are right Nestor and you have given sound advice. I admit I was deluded, overcome by a passion that the gods must have sent me. I am willing to make amends and amply compensate with material things for the injury I have caused. Tell Achilles I am prepared to offer bronze tripods, gold bars, metal cauldrons and horses from my own possessions to make up for the injury that has been caused. But more than this, if I should return safely to my kingdom Mykenai, I will treat Achilles like my own son and marry him to one of my two daughters. He can choose which ever he pleases and is the fairest to him. Let him know that I will settle on him rich lands as the wedding dowry. However, he must bow to my position and acknowledge me as leader."

"That is a very generous offer, lord Agamemnon," Nestor replied, choosing his words carefully. "But I'm afraid that gifts alone will not be enough to compensate Achilles' honour. Things have gone too far and it will require words as well to soothe the injury to his *kleos*. Let Odysseus lead a delegation, as he is most skilled with words. He can appeal to Achilles better than anyone and explain our current predicament. Let Ajax the Greater also go with him and Phoenix the healer, who tutored Achilles as a boy and who he holds in high esteem."

Agamemnon's open contrition and the proposed plan to put things right had briefly alleviated Odysseus' misgivings about the man, their leader. But the mission had been a failure. The young Achilles, of whom Odysseus had always been fond, had warmly welcomed and entertained them with food, listening respectfully to them all. Suspecting that the gifts alone were not enough for a man like Achilles, Odysseus had tried to reason with him.

"I know you have no love of the man, Achilles, and that you cannot change these feelings. But at least think of the plight of the Greek army and take pity on them. Each day, more and more of them are dying, in your absence from the battlefield, cut down by Trojan weapons. If you return to the fight, who knows you may even kill the Trojan warrior Hector, which would add to your *kleos*. But if these words have no effect and you are still consumed by anger, a passion that can blind men from reason, then at least remember your father's advice who urged you to control and master your feelings."

He had consciously omitted to mention Agamemnon's demand to be acknowledged as Achilles' superior. But despite the best attempts of Ajax, Phoenix and himself, still the answer had been the same. An outright "*No*". And although Achilles, too swayed by his passions, held onto his grievance, he Odysseus couldn't help ascribing the bigger portion of blame to Agamemnon, son of Atreus. He was their *Anax* after all, their appointed overlord and leader. Knowing Achilles' hot temperament, Agamemnon should have been man enough to not let this quarrel get out of hand.

But it was in the very darkest hour of the conflict, when the Trojans had pushed them back all the way to the beach camp itself and were threatening to burn the ships. It was then that he had finally lost patience with the man and those doubts turned into something else. Something deeper and darker that fills a man with disgust and loathing to the bottom of his spirit.

The fighting that day had been particularly heavy. He and Agamemnon, had been forced to retire early from the battlefield nursing new wounds. Many of their best warriors were now injured and had to leave the field. Leaning on their spears, the two injured men had been ordering the able bodied men to hastily shore up the defences and haul up the boats into a defensive circle. Agamemnon was shrieking at the men to work harder, a sweat breaking out across his brow. The situation had become critical and the Greek defences were in danger of being overpowered by the Trojan swarm. It was at this point that Nestor had approached them for orders.

"What are you doing here?" snapped Agamemnon, sternly rebuking the older man. "Why are you not with the troops, fighting on? Do your eyes not see the gravity of the situation?"

"They do indeed, my lord." The older man was

panting and struggling to catch his breath. "I came to ascertain your command, as we are close to being overrun by the Trojans. What is your plan?"

It was then that Agamemnon had proposed the unthinkable. "Prepare some of the ships and let's make a run for it," he barked, gazing wildly around him. "Escape from this place is better than death. We can gather together the rest of the fleet at nightfall, when the fighting has died down."

Odysseus looked at the man beside him in fury: Agamemnon, their supposed leader! "What kind of king are you?" he demanded furiously. "That you propose to quit the field. After all we have suffered and endured, you would run away like some snivelling child. For your advice will destroy us all and in the disarray of retreat we will be slaughtered to the very last man. None of us will make it back to our homelands alive. No Agamemnon. Give the men the proper leadership they deserve and the army will follow."

"So what do you propose?" asked Agamemnon, wild-eyed with fear.

Odysseus plunged his spear upright into the ground before him. "We stand and fight," he announced. "Enough of this talk. Nestor, go haste and rally the troops." The older man nodded and hurried away towards the thickest of the fighting. "You there," Odysseus pointed at one of the foot soldiers, "help me on with my armour. And Agamemnon too. We must get into battle right away. There will be time to nurse our wounds later."

"You are right Odysseus," replied Agamemnon, his head bowed but his cheeks blazing. "Well man," he shouted at the common soldier, "do as your better says. Bring me a spear and sword. Quickly now."

So they had fought on, the danger averted. But in that moment of crisis, something changed. He Odysseus could never respect the man as leader. Even after he had healed that rift between Agamemnon and Achilles, reconciling the two men in public before the army, he could not shut off the feelings roused in him. He would do his duty and serve the Greek cause, but he could no longer stomach the man.

Chapter 6

Books

A clanking of metal rattled in her ears, as Thea took the last few bites of her *tyropita,* cheese pie. In the labyrinth of narrow streets, the March sunlight was catching the trees and shrubs, just coming into bud. In high spring, there would be a full display of lemons, hibiscus and brightly coloured osteospermums. From somewhere, the sounds of drilling and clanking of metal came again disturbing the peace. It was workmen already hard at work, repairing the buildings damaged in last year's earthquake. As the hum, bangs and clatter subsided, an almost beguiling sense of tranquillity returned.

Going through the library gateway, Thea admired again the neo-classical white-washed mansion from a by-gone age. The lush greenery of the garden with its olive and orange trees gave off the sense of an oasis of peace and calm tranquillity in the midst of the noise and industry of the busy town. Thea walked up the marble steps and entered the hallway, where a staff member welcomed her with the customary greeting of *Kalimera*.

It had been four days since that fateful evening at the *taverna* when Dimitri had re-emerged in her life. For four days, Thea had waged an internal battle with herself, refusing to dwell on the feelings that came crowding in or the tears that pricked her eyes. And yet she had conducted herself like a seasoned commander, carefully crafting a campaign strategy. After the departure of the team for Kalodia, each day she had set out early on her mission, before any of the other hotel guests were a foot. Holing herself up in the protective confines of the library, she had then hunkered down to her work. As the light faded, she took refuge in a small tavern, under the cover of a book and the extensive menu, while keeping watch for the final ferry departure of the day.

Against her denials, protestations and the evidence of her own eyes, she had hoped that this disciplined routine would provide some security and time to think. And yet, no matter how hard she tried, she could not dispel the knowledge that finally he had shown up: like woodworm emerging from rotten timber. After days of Mark coaxing, persuading and pressing her, it was the fear she had dreaded most when she had uttered her agreement to return to the island.

She slammed the door shut on those thoughts as she entered the reading room, a part still vigilant as she surveyed the space. The room was light and airy, with its chequerboard tiled floor and high panelled ceiling, decorated with rosettes and intricate geometric patterns. She had requisitioned one of the desks as a temporary workspace and books from the previous day were still piled there.

"Good Morning, Dr Sefton. Is there anything I can help you with today?" The question came from the only other apparent occupant in the building, the librarian, a middle-aged woman of unremarkable appearance except for her full head of jet black hair. At first Thea had judged her austere and officious but gradually through their conversations, had discovered her to be warm and generous with her assistance. Vassiliki had positively beamed on discovering the interest being taken in her region, the home of her family's village.

"I was hoping to look again at the old ledgers," Thea replied, her eyes flicking over the empty tables. "I'm interested in any references to the northern villages."

"*Sto anogeton*?" Vassiliki queried.

"Yes," she confirmed, trying to relax the strained muscles of her smile, "the villages in the upland region." Vassiliki nodded and disappeared into the back of the library, emerging shortly afterwards with a neatly labelled box file.

"These are all the original hand-written documents," Vassiliki said. "Not well organised I'm afraid, nor easy to decipher."

"That's fine," said Thea, feeling lulled by Vassiliki's voice and the familiar antiquated smell of decaying paper. "I was expecting that."

The librarian still hovered over her, a questioning look on her face. "I think you must be a very educated woman for the ledgers are not easy for even Greeks to read. Let me get you a pair of gloves so you can handle the pages."

"Thanks," Thea replied, glad to wrap herself in the ordinary trappings of her research routine. She flicked open her laptop and switched on the screen.

Her initial plan had been to work through the old Venetian tax records to uncover the original village names on the Paliki peninsula. For place names were notoriously conservative, passed down and preserved from one generation to the next. But names like Damoulianata, Monopalata, Mantzavinata, with an -*ata* ending, betrayed their Venetian masters. So after many hours of searching, Thea had reluctantly concluded that any such evidence was either lost or resided somewhere in the vast archives of the Catholic Church in Rome. It could take months rather than weeks to gain access to the Vatican records.

Instead this realisation had forced Thea to improvise and adjust her strategy. Over the past few days, she had listed the current villages known from historical times, plotting them on a map. By cross referencing these to the archive ledgers, she could work out the points where the land was most fertile and might support a prehistoric palace settlement.

Thea began to read the first entry on the ledger, where the public notary had recorded in crammed writing a series of property transactions between the good island citizens: the inheritance of a farm here, the transfer of a field there or listed olive presses liable for taxation. As the hours of the day stretched out, occasionally the solitary footsteps of a fellow visitor punctuated the silence or the excited chattering of a party of school children.

The afternoon was well advanced, when finally Thea's attention and eyesight began to fade. Despite her efforts, the tangled letters of the cursive script refused to unravel as Thea strained to read the entries. She could do with a break. She glanced at the map beside her, now heavily scored with bright yellow marker pen, her finger tracing Porto Katsiki on the creased page, where they had visited only a few days ago. *At least it gave a fixed reference point,* she thought as an idea suddenly struck her.

Thea approached the librarian working quietly at her desk, who looked up and smiled.

"I don't suppose the library keeps any archaeological journals that I could take a look at?" Thea asked, already suspecting that any records would not be digitalised and she would manually have to search the paper records.

"Unfortunately we don't have anything like that," Vassiliki explained with a frown, shrugging her shoulders helplessly. "You could try the other library in the main town but it's probably closed already due to austerity measures."

"Never mind." Thea reassured her, trying mentally to readjust her schedule. "I can visit first thing on Monday."

"Is there any particular area you are interested in?"

"Kalodia."

"Isn't that where they're conducting a field survey? It's been in all the local press here and caused a lot of excitement. There was a very good photograph of one of your colleagues on the front page," Vassiliki continued, obviously referring to Richard. "But I was surprised when I heard the survey was in Kalodia as I've never heard of anything archaeological from there.

But please tell me something," Vassiliki hesitated and looked up at Thea, wearing a puzzled expression on her face, "why aren't you searching on the island of Ithaka itself?"

Thea ventured a smile at the familiar question. She had lost count of how many times the question had been posed to her. "We discovered evidence that the main town on Ithaka was known in historical times as *Dolicha*, very similar to the *Doulichion*, the island mentioned in Homer. It seems likely that they mistook the island in ancient times and renamed it as Ithaka."

"You know so much about our history." Vassiliki beamed at her, the puzzlement vanishing from her face. "But why Kalodia? I always thought that it was vine growing and wine making country." Vassiliki glanced quickly around to check that no one else occupied the room, before continuing her chatter. "Did you know that the chairman of the Archontakis Foundation has connections with Kalodia? His maternal grandparents come from the village and the family still own a house there?"

Thea's body stiffened, as she tried to digest this new information. "Who exactly do you mean, Vassiliki?"

"Why Mr Kampitsis of course. You know the one who married the shipping heiress and is now the head of the Archontakis Foundation.

As a boy he used to spend his summers at his grandparents' house."

The sound of his name on Vassiliki's lips jarred Thea's ears. She looked askance at the other woman, willing her to take back the words as the truth gripped her. In that instance, the awful realisation of the extent of the man's involvement hit her. For a moment, she felt barely able to hold back the torrent of emotion that had been threatening to burst through, overwhelming and engulfing her.

"You know they found Mycenean tombs in Mousatoi," Vassiliki volunteered helpfully, not registering the effect of her previous words. At the sound of the village name, Thea raised her head, her scholarly curiosity piqued.

"Mousatoi? When?" Thea demanded, now fully alert to the conversation.

"I can't say, as it was a long time ago, well before I was born. But you've heard of Karellis, the famous Greek archaeologist?"

"The one who excavated on Crete and demonstrated the destruction of a pre-historic palace by a tsunami? Of course, everyone has heard of him."

"Well he came from the same village and as a young man excavated around the island, including his own village."

For a moment, Thea could have swept Vassiliki off her feet and hugged her, any previous fears banished. "Thank you, thank you Vassiliki." She grabbed the surprised woman's hand, vigorously shaking it. "That's a really useful lead."

Thea checked her watch, impatient to follow up this new revelation. If she went back to the hotel now, she could check the online data bases this evening. For one night, she could risk an early finish she thought, as she felt a rush of adrenaline.

"Could you store the documents away until Monday?"

"*Malista*. Of course," replied Vassiliki, still basking in the glow of Thea's demonstrative appreciation. "The library will be closing shortly anyway."

Thea began gathering her things together, carefully placing the ledger and the old documents back into the folder as if handling a new-born infant. When everything had been meticulously gathered up, Thea presented the neat pile to Vassiliki.

"Thanks for your help, again," Thea smiled.

"*Parakalo*," the other replied. "You're most welcome and have a good weekend."

It wasn't until Thea reached the ferry dock, that her burst of excitement at the new discovery started to waver, clouded by the gnawing fear creeping back to jangle her nerves. She paused to watch the small boat coming into view, as it plied its trade across the island straits. The breeze was strengthening and was starting to whip up the waves. Already grey rainclouds were gathering, shrouding the sky and insinuating a wet day for tomorrow. *It was going to be a rough passage but having come this far, she wasn't going to turn back now.* She smoothed down her feelings, refusing to give into the unspoken sentiments that threatened to capsize her, and setting her jaw boarded the boat.

At the hotel, Electra as always was posted at the reception desk, ever present to the guest's comings and goings.

Electra set down her Greek fashion magazine *Gynaika*, Woman, she had been reading to hand Thea her key. Her thick layer of deep cherry red lipstick offset her close-fitting gold metallic shirt.

"Good evening, Doctor Sefton. How are you today? We've hardly seen you these last few days. I was afraid you might feel a little bit lonely, now your colleagues have left?" The enquiry invited confidence, which Thea ignored but couldn't help feeling her movements were being closely watched. Certainly little seemed to escape Electra's notice.

"I'm fine thank you. Just a bit caught up with

my research," she reassured Electra, as she turned away with her key.

"Doctor Sefton?" The note in Electra's voice made her stop.

"Yes, what is it?"

"I have to tell you something," said Electra, firing out the words in a torrent of Greek, her voice shrill and excited. "Stelios Ioannou telephoned to speak to you less than half an hour ago. It's the fourth time today he has called." A conspiratorial grin lined her face. "He said you had your mobile phone switched off!"

Instinctively Thea touched the smooth plastic screen of her mobile, which had been switched to silence. "Yes, I've been working in the library and must have forgotten to switch it back on," Thea replied, knowing that this was not strictly true but ignored Electra's insinuation. It had been part of her battle plan since that night at the *taverna*. She had scrutinised carefully all incoming calls, partly expecting Stelios' call to come one day.

"Of course I told him you were out," Electra continued undaunted, holding out a folded slip of pink paper. "So he asked me to give you this message."

"Thank you, Electra," said Thea, involuntarily flinching as she took the folded note. Climbing the stairs, she hastily scanned the note written in Electra's spidery handwriting, partly anticipating its contents. It was not the first time Stelios had called in the last few days, seeking a meeting with his boss, the chairman of the Archontakis Foundation. She had been left in no doubt that Mr Dimitri Kampitsis was eager to make her acquaintance and discuss her role on the project.

A shudder ran through her body as she crumpled the note in her hand and tossed it into the bin, as soon as she closed her door. *If only one thing was certain, she had absolutely no intention of clapping eyes on Dimitri Kampitsis ever again.*

The room was as it had been left from earlier that morning: the bed hastily made; her clothes neatly folded in a pile; her books and papers stacked on the small dresser now a make-shift desk. She filled the small kettle with water to boil, before settling down in front of her laptop.

****

The insistent tone of her mobile phone, startled her as it rang out in the room, demanding attention. Thea checked her watch. Nearly eight o'clock and it was dark outside, the blackened mountain side dotted with the lights of the small villages. The name of the caller flashed on the mobile screen, as she reached for her phone.

"Hello Richard. How are you?" she said, answering on the sixth ring.

"Thea, my dear. I hope I'm not disturbing you." The voice on the end of the line was smooth and silky.

"Not at all," she quickly reassured him. "I'm just about finished doing an on-line search of some archaeological journals."

"My apologies we haven't managed to speak over the past few days," Richard began, clearing his throat. "I wanted to check that everything was alright." The enquiry caught her by surprise as each night she had dutifully sent an update of her progress. Clearly there wasn't a good Wifi connection up in the village.

"It's been disappointing really, Richard," Thea admitted experiencing a shrinking feeling inside. "I've been going through the island archives all week, but there is very little left of the old tax records." Her words were upbeat, but she paused, wondering how she could soften the disappointing news for Richard. "I think we might be on a wild goose chase there, but the property sales records look more promising." The suppressed silence on the end of the line suggested this was not the primary purpose for Richard's call.

"How are things holding up your end?" Thea enquired.

"It's been a bit of an anti-climax. Quite frankly

awful to survey as the terrain is rugged and heavily cultivated." Even on the crackling line, the voice sounded tired and weary.

"Let me guess, with grape vines?" Thea asked lightly.

"Yes and olive groves. How did you know?"

"I have my sources," Thea admitted laughingly, thinking of her earlier conversation with Vassiliki. On the island, everything was open to village gossip and public knowledge.

Richard paused as if gathering his thoughts. "I also received a call from Stelios Ioannou. I understand our benefactor, Mr Kampitsis is quite anxious to meet you, as he didn't get an opportunity to do so the other night. I know you are very busy, but I can't stress how important Mr Kampitsis' personal support is to the project." At the sound of his name, Thea could feel her fingers grip the phone, so tightly the muscles were almost in spasm. "We wouldn't have got off the ground without him" Richard continued confident in his argument. "You'd be doing me a huge personal favour if you could give Stelios a call and set something up."

"I'll see what I can do," Thea finally agreed keeping her voice measured but the tone was noncommittal. "It'll be the other side of the weekend."

"If you can get back to him as soon as you get

a chance. By the way, Dr Hughes is paying us a visit tomorrow with Matthew and bringing some things over. Do you want to join them?"

"Certainly I'm limited over the weekend as the libraries are shut. I've a possible lead for some Mycenean graves so I wanted to take a look at Mousatoi."

"That's practically on the doorstep! Just eight kilometres away on the other side of the valley. I'll text Dr Hughes to let him know," Richard said without giving Thea chance to respond. "Would nine o'clock suit you?"

"Okay, nine o'clock."

Thea ended the call, watching the bling of the grey screen, her heart still racing. Since that awful evening, she had hardly seen anything of Rob or Matthew, whom she assumed like herself had both been engrossed in work. So she would spend the day in their company. *It would not be the worst thing in the world,* she told herself. At least being the other side of the island put her as far away as possible from the danger of encountering Dimitri or rebuffing Stelios' phone calls.

****

The book lay open on Thea's lap, where she had reread the same sentence for the third time, but the words failed to lodge in her brain. Glancing across at the small travel clock on the bedside table, she saw the evening was getting late. The remains of a drink can and half eaten takeaway souvlaki littered the desk. Suddenly there was a sickening click as the room plunged into pitch darkness. It took seconds for Thea's vision to acclimatise to the gloom, as the shuttered windows blocked out the streetlights. Thea reached over the bed and fumbled for her shoes. With her fingers, she could make out the smooth texture of the leather and stuffed her feet inside them. Deprived of her sense of sight, Thea groped for the edge of the bed, bruising her knee on the sharp wooden corner.

To her relief, the lights at the end of the hallway illuminated the stairwell, acting like a beacon to guide her through the dimness. The corridor was quiet, with no other signs of guests. As she approached the reception desk, she heard the phone slam down and discovered Electra with her head in her hands. She looked up startled at Thea's approach.

"Oh Kyria Sefton, I am so sorry," Electra gasped as tears pricked her eyes. "The electricity has gone off. I have called and called the electrician but he's not answering his phone at this hour. He's probably in a bar or in bed." A scowl momentarily passed across her face. "What am I to do?" she complained, throwing up her hands up in despair.

"Is all the hotel affected?" Thea asked, looking up at the lighted stairwell.

"No, just your corridor." The words flew out between the gasps for breath. "Two other rooms are occupied but the guests are out. What am I to do? *O popoi!* " Electra threw up her hands again and looked pleadingly at Thea willing her to summon a miracle from the heavens.

Just then the lobby door swished open as Rob and Matthew strode in together chatting. Rob stopped abruptly in his tracks. "Is everything alright?" he asked, grasping the scene, a concerned look crossing his face.

"Oh, Kyrie Hughes. It's a catastrophe!" Electra's body heaved with sobs. "The electric power has blown and there is no electricity for my guests." Rob turned his eyes towards Thea with a questioning look.

Thea stepped in. "All the lights on the first floor suddenly went off. The rest of the hotel seems okay."

"What shall I tell the other guests?" Electra wailed. "Perhaps I can move them to another corridor," and she started to flip through the room register, almost ripping the pages with her fingers.

"I don't think that will be necessary," Rob said

genially, putting out his hand to reassure her. "Sounds like one of your fuses has blown. Do you want me to take a look at the circuit box?"

"Oh please, please, would you," Electra gushed, clasping Rob's arm and squeezing it. "I would be so grateful." She grabbed a tissue and blew her nose loudly.

Rob gestured to Matthew. "Can you run back to the lab and grab a screwdriver and some pieces of equipment?" He turned his attention once more to Electra. "So let's take a look at this fuse box. Don't worry, we'll have it sorted in no time." He winked at her playfully.

"You show Dr Hughes where the box is and I shall make you a drink," Thea said, fondly stroking Electra on the shoulder.

"Okay," she nodded, smiling thinly at Rob, the heaves of her chest diminishing.

It was not long before full power was restored and light flooded the upstairs stairwell. "Oh Dr Hughes, how can I thank you," gushed Electra, her face beaming and her arms spread open. "You are my hero. And you too young man" she said, turning to Matthew to include him in her praise, who smiled bashfully. "You are all so kind. Please sit! *Kathiste!*" Matthew was hovering awkwardly but obediently sat next to Rob at Electra's command, as she commandeered a large bottle of ouzo and several shot glasses.

Rob sunk back into the chair and lifted his head

towards Thea, a good-humoured smile playing on his lips. "Will you join us for a quick drink?" he asked expectantly, gesturing towards the unoccupied chair beside him. "Richard phoned earlier to let us know you're joining us tomorrow."

"No, but thank you" Thea said shaking her head, involuntarily blowing out a stream of air. Still preoccupied from the earlier conversation with Richard, her instinct was to retreat and regroup in the solitude of her room. "It's been a long day. If you don't mind, I'm going to turn in."

"Of course," Rob agreed, the smile not diminishing on his face but his shoulders deflating. "No worries. Electra and Matthew will keep me good company. See you tomorrow then." Thea turned to leave. As she ascended the stairs she heard the chink of glasses and good natured laughter.

Chapter 7

The Fall of Troy

It was dark and musty. The space was small and cramped, hardly room to draw breath. Odysseus could feel the pressure of Diomedes, his dear friend, squeezed up against him. It would be daylight now but in the gloom it was hard to discern anything. He could only sense the other warriors by the odour of male sweat and the moistened air as they exhaled. They were so tightly packed, like fish in a barrel, hardly room to move and impossible to shift position. They had sat like this since nightfall, man against man, body pressed against body, limb against limb, fully armoured. The only compromise to comfort being the horse plumed helmets bulky on their laps. Still, but ready primed warriors, waiting.

The air inside had already grown hot and stale with the rising heat of the day. Helios must have progressed well into the sky by then, when they heard the sound of human voices.

Initially it was low murmurings, indistinct but then came chatter in the clear Asiatic accent as the talking grew louder. Beside him, the body of his companion had tensed. The fear inside was palpable and he could almost taste it inside his mouth. Any moment their hiding place might be discovered and condemn them all to a grim death.

The plan had been he Odysseus' idea. Things had never been the same after that famous quarrel, which had set in motion the sequence of events culminating in the death of Patroklos. Achilles, mad with grief at the loss of his gentle beloved companion, had gone on a frenzied killing spree. He had murdered the noble warrior Hector, the son of Priam, hideously defiling the body and dragging it round the city ramparts. It was said that he only stopped this despoliation of the body when Priam himself had secretly come to his tent to make supplication. The old man had begged for the return of his son's carcass, so they could make proper funeral arrangements. Even the elaborate funeral games thrown by Achilles, to honour his precious Patroklos, had been overshadowed by yet more tragedy. Ajax "The Big One" had done the unimaginable, killing himself by thrusting his sword into his own chest. He had been in the war from the outset and it was hard to imagine fighting without that wall of a man. And even the circumstances of his death were hard to comprehend: his body discovered lifeless after Odysseus had bettered him in a wrestling match. They had competed fiercely for the honour and *kleos* of the win. The man had been a worthy opponent, but losing was no disgrace and hadn't merited the taking of one's own life. Perhaps the long drawn-out war had undone the man's spirits but it troubled Odysseus that he had missed the signs of despair. It would have been easy to relax his grip and allow the other man to win. No *kleos* was worth such a sacrifice.

And then quickly following, there had been the early death of Achilles himself. Fighting in the midst of the battle, he had been shot in the heel of the foot by a poisoned arrow. The bright dazzling Achilles, their most brilliant warrior, cut down by the barb of an arrow fired by some cowardly marksman cosseted away from the violence of battle. After those deaths, despondency and despair had fallen over the Greek camp, creeping into the spirits of the troops and turning everything dark, like the ink of an octopus in the clear blue sea. Odysseus had not been immune from the general gloom. Despite all those long years of fighting and self-sacrifice, the capture of the city seemed as far away as ever.

He had continued his unspoken ritual each morning of looking out at the well defended city walls, hoping that day would bring victory. An end to the stalemate. Perhaps some god had put this in his mind. But it was then it had come to him. This plan.

It had not been a straightforward business. The other leaders, including Agamemnon, had agreed readily to the idea. Perhaps they had been keen to shake off the despair and despondency that had enveloped the Greek camp. But it had been the seer Kalchas, that disruptive influence, who had come up with an unexpected obstacle. A new prophecy.

"Troy will only fall when the goddess Athene has left her temple," the diviner had announced examining the signs of sacrifice. His brow was furrowed and stern.

"What do you mean?" Odysseus asked, sensing he would dislike the reply.

"The holy Palladion, bearing the image of the goddess Pallas Athene, must be first removed from her temple, before Troy can be taken," had come the answer.

That night, Odysseus had sat mulling the matter over in his mind as he and the battle-weary Kephallenians gathered around the campfires. The flames were greedily licking up the tinder wood, changing the men's features and weary limbs to partial shadows in the fire's glow. Eurylochos, his commander, was sat beside him. He had known these men from Ithaka most of his life, but recently it had become harder to share memories of their native soil or talk about their home-coming. It was in this frame of mind that his dear friend Diomedes had joined him, sitting down in the small circle.

"What ails you, brother? I haven't seen you looking so low-spirited." Diomedes offered a bemused smirk, slaking his thirst with a swig of wine from one of the skins. He wiped his lips on his sleeve. "You look as if you have been to Hades and back. This mood seems to be catching, like some pestilence sent by the gods."

"Perhaps, we are indeed being punished," Odysseus replied. "This whole business wearies me. At last I thought we had found some way of ending this cursed deadlock of the war. I didn't want to end my days here on this ill-starred land, my bones being picked clean by scavengers. But now Kalchas, that accursed priest, puts barriers in our path." He scowled, clenching his jaw. "He tells me that first we must remove the sacred image of Pallas Athene from Troy before the city can be taken. Another fool idea like that of sacrificing the innocent Iphigeneia. Will this war never end?" He had spat out those last words with anger and frustration.

"But Odysseus, is that all that stands between you and your plan!" the other man replied enthusiastically, clapping him on the back. "Then let me dispel your gloom. I think I know a way!" Odysseus looked across at his companion sceptically, but listening with his full attention. Diomedes had come late to war and was the younger man. But they were like kindred spirits, well-matched in cunning, wits and boldness. And they had been through so much together. Once on a nocturnal mission, they had even laid in the blood-sodden battle-field together, hiding themselves amongst the dead and dying, hearing the wounded struggling for breath and the release of death. That had been a daring raid, when the Greeks were hard pressed against the ships, and the two men had returned victorious, slaughtering the newly arrived Thracian king Rhesos, carrying off his prized horses. That was a rare breakthrough in the long protracted war.

"So tell me what is this way?" he asked, grimly, not convinced that a path lay ahead.

"Well, you will recall one full moon ago, I was scouting the city walls with my men." An easy smile now played on the younger man's lips. "There was a small hollow, behind the city, where a clear spring comes out of the hillside. There appeared to be an entrance as the stone was all carefully hewn by the hands of men in a triangular shape. Myself and another man could easily walk through the entrance passage at head height, only stooping a little, although the water came up to our waists. We did not fully explore what we found, as we had brought no flame with us and it disappeared into pitch darkness. But -."

"You believe it is an entrance passage to the city?" Odysseus interrupted him following the line of reasoning.

"Yes, indeed. A secret entrance to the underground cistern, which supplies Troy's water."

The new revelation excited Odysseus. He had always puzzled how the city had kept itself supplied with water throughout the stranglehold siege. "So in the cold season," his mind was quickly reasoning, "the passage is completely flooded with the waters from Mount Ida. But in the spring and summer heat, the water level falls. And the tunnel becomes traversable."

"Exactly!" exclaimed his friend with satisfaction. "Sufficient at least for two bold and brazen men to crawl through the passage and gain access to the city."

"Have you thought who that might be?" he had asked, knowing already the answer. The two men exchanged a broad grin slapping each other on the back.

"Well, I couldn't allow you to have all the excitement," Diomedes replied.

"Come, let us drink to that idea and may the gods sanction it," he had said, summoning the herald to fill up the mixing bowl with sweet diluted wine, which they shared between them. As the wine was drained from the vessel, a merriment in mood swept over the Kephallenian camp and for the first time Odysseus had felt *Hope* return. Some of the men, filled with the warm liquor, had broken into song, singing of sailing ships and of their women back on their island home. He and Diomedes had sparred with one another to come up with the most audacious plan to break into Troy. In the end they had settled on the plan to disguise themselves as destitutes with ragged and unkempt clothing. In the haze of the crackling fire and warming wine loosening his limbs, a surge of affection had come over him for these comrades and this man.

"You know, Diomedes," he said his words slightly slurred, clasping his friend around the shoulder. "From this mess some good has come. I will miss these brave hearted warriors, who have been with me from the beginning, but also you." He rubbed his hand over his face to brush away any sign of tears. "You have made this ill-fated war more bearable. When I am back in Ithaka, I will think of you."

"Some god must have taken your mind, Odysseus!" laughed Diomedes. "You will be too busy warming your bed with that wife of yours." They both laughed but looking back how hollow those words felt.

The next day, the two men found themselves peering into a dark hollow, not far from the city walls. Diomedes had described it well. A spring of clear water bubbling from the hillside, flowing into a channel covered by overgrowing bushes. The passage had been there all along, through those long weary ten years: the secret key to the city.

"We should go as soon as possible while the water level is still low." he said, inspecting the passage. The stream was only a trickle of a stream, as the gods had not thought to send rain for some days to offset the heat of early summer. "If there is heavy rain, the passage will be flooded and the opportunity will be lost."

"I agree," replied Diomedes.

"And I think it should be as we discussed, just the two of us disguised as beggars in rags. To avoid detection by the Trojans."

"If it is to be under cover of darkness, then perhaps tomorrow night. The moon will not be so high."

And so it was that Odysseus found himself wading through the water in the darkened tunnel, the tallow torches they carried the only illumination. To give truth to their story if caught, they had dressed in plain, dirty and torn tunics, taken from two slaves captured in war. The passage proved as even and proportioned as its entrance, continuing on its straight purposeful course beneath the city walls. Whoever had been responsible for the construction had taken the task seriously. Even the ice chillness of the water was not unpleasant after the heat of the day. At the end of the passage, it narrowed to a small gap, with just enough room for a grown man to squeeze through.

"Let us leave a lighted torch here on a higher ledge. We can collect it on the way back," Odysseus whispered to his companion. Through the narrow gap ahead, they could make out a symmetrical pool in the gloom. Beyond was the beginnings of a flight of steps. His mind was working quickly now. "I will extinguish my torch, Diomedes, so we have enough tallow to find our way back. Leave your own burning. Take time to look around so that if the torches are lost, we can retrace our steps in the dark."

"There looks no way of getting round the cistern," said Diomedes.

"So we will have to swim for it. I hope they teach you how to swim in Argos."

"Like a babe to his mother's breast," grinned Diomedes, plunging into the ice chilled dark water.

In the dark, they had felt their way, stone by stone up the twisting stairway until they emerged out into the night air. The quickness of Odysseus' heart lessened as with relief he realised no one had thought to guard the cistern, confident that the water or the protection offered by the local god of the spring barred the way. The lower city streets appeared to be deserted with the townspeople safely in their beds or guarding the lower perimeter walls and gates. Above, the palace and the higher citadel loomed over them, casting a deep shadow over the city.

"Come, I think we should go this way," said Diomedes.

"Let us first wring out these wretched clothes, so it will be easier for us to move quickly and unnoticed," Odysseus suggested. They stepped back into the shadows of the cistern staircase, each man hastily removing his rags and standing naked as they squeezed out the water. Less encumbered and re-clothed, they stealthily walked through the empty town, trying to keep to the shadows. The lower gate to the citadel was unguarded, perhaps due to complacency, after ten gruelling years of the siege. Odysseus' sight had now grown accustomed to the darkness.

"I recognise this way from when I was here

many years ago."

"You've been here before?" asked Diomedes, curious.

"Now is not the time to explain. I think we need to go this way." Odysseus led the way, silently crossing over the open space of the citadel beckoning Diomedes to follow him. On one side, he recognised the reception rooms and sleeping quarters of King Priam and his family entourage. Close by was the smaller apartment of Antenor, where he had once met with Helen, hoping to persuade her to return to Menelaos. At the far corner of the ground, Odysseus recognised the outline of the temple, dedicated to his own personal goddess and protector, Pallas Athene. The shrine was in the open air, flanked by a wooden colonnade but he could make out the altar at the centre. The Palladion could not be far away. The image of the goddess carved onto a sacred piece of wood. The two men found it easily, standing upright just behind the altar.

Quickly they stashed the wooden plank, bearing the sacred image of the god, inside the rough sewn sack Diomedes had brought for the task. They needed to escape before they were discovered and the alarm raised.

"Quickly, let's go," hissed Odysseus in the dark, his unease increasing with every moment that passed within the temple.

It was as they crossed the open land once more, *Trouble* struck. In the dark, he lost his footing, stumbling and falling headlong with a heavy thud. Diomedes stopped and started to turn back.

"No," he rasped in the dark, "you go ahead. I will follow shortly." He waved the younger man away. It was then he heard the sounds of footsteps. His fall had been heard.

"Who are you and what are you doing here?" The pitch was youthful, almost like a maiden's. Odysseus looked up to find long spears pointed at him, clasped by two warriors. In the darkness, he sized the guards up as only recently come of age. They lacked experience and appeared nervous at challenging him. Slowly he got to his feet, hoping that Diomedes had opportunity to make good his escape. As he did so, he couldn't help reflecting ruefully that he Odysseus was no longer quite as swift of foot as he used to be.

"Forgive me. I am a poor beggar," he began, trying to emulate the local Asiatic dialect. "I only seek a safe place to sleep for the night. The sentry took pity on me and allowed me inside the city wall, as I feared to be murdered by those villainous Greek warriors." He quickly assumed the part, spitting on the dusty floor as he pronounced the last words. He had picked up some of the Trojan dialect from the servants captured in battle, listening to their exchanges over many years. He could see the two sentries were hesitant, eyeing him suspiciously. At that moment another shape emerged from the darkness.

"My lady," acknowledged one of the guards, lowering his head.

"What is the meaning of this?" The voice was clear and rang out in the gloominess of the night. Odysseus couldn't quite see who spoke. Their face was obscured by their cloak and veil, but the accent was familiar.

He continued to play the part. "Forgive me, lady, whoever you are that I disturb your presence." He bent his head low in deference. "I am but a poor beggar seeking a comfortable place to rest my weary bones. I came seeking shelter close to the sanctuary of the sacred temple, that I may find comfort in the goddess' precinct."

He could hear the sweet sound of her breathing, as the woman drew near to inspect him more closely. Instinctively his stronger hand reached for his sword, but the finger tightened over empty air. His heart skipped a beat, as it had done many times just before battle, but he held fast. "Cast down your weapons!" the woman declared. "Can you not see this man is just a poor wretch and poses no threat? He is only an unfortunate seeking comfort and a place to sleep. Leave us and I will see to him myself."

"Are you sure, my lady?" asked one of the warriors, his voice hesitant.

"Of course," she answered tersely. "Now go, lest my husband hear of your disobedience."

"Certainly madam," the bolder one mumbled more humbly and they both withdrew. As the two men walked away out of earshot, the woman spoke again, this time more sharply.

"Odysseus, my kinsman, what in the gods' name are you doing here? That I find you in the citadel of Troy itself. Are you mad or have the gods' deprived you of your wits?" the voice hissed in the dark, now speaking in a clear Greek enunciation.

"Helen?" he exclaimed, peering into the dark. Suddenly the disassembled voice and shape fell into place. "Can it really be you? What are you doing out at night?"

"You should thank me that I decided to come to make prayers to the goddess. Your accent deceives no one except those young inexperienced fools. You are indeed fortunate that I came across you as you would be surely tortured and murdered if they discovered you." Helen looked around anxiously as she spoke in a harsh whisper. "The goddess herself must have put it in my mind, for I could not sleep. Quickly, you must get out of here before you are discovered! Which way did you come?"

"I entered from the lower city."

"Then follow me. I will walk with you part of the way, in case you are challenged again. Leave me to do the talking if we are stopped. You may be full of clever strategies, but you are no man of languages. Come!"

Helen set off walking without glancing behind. He lumbered after her still playing the part of a beggar. As they walked close to the royal apartment, another figure stepped out of the shadows. The frame was diminutive and belonged to a woman.

"Helen!" The songful sound of a woman's voice rang out, stopping Helen in her tracks. "Why are you out so late and who is this man?" Instinctively Odysseus reached for his sword but grasped only a handful of wretched rags. This was a dangerous turn of events and he waited holding his breath.

"Forgive me mother. I could not sleep. I found this unfortunate trying to seek comfort in the temple of Athena." He realised at once who this must be, the mother of Alexandros and wife of Priam herself. Queen Hekabe.

"Come here man, let me have a look at you!" the voice commanded him. He could not see Hekabe's face direct in the shadows, but he felt the heat of the flickering torchlight on his face as she closely scrutinised his features. He would be undone if this woman recognised him. He thought he heard a slight intake of breath escape her lips as she looked closely at his face. Then a pause …a momentary shudder ran through his body.

"You act properly, daughter, in giving this man care," spoke the older woman. "Show him a place where he can bed down for the night, but then hurry back. For you do not know who may be lurking around the city at this hour."

"Yes, mother, at once." Helen bowed her head to the older woman in deference and quickly continued her path. He could feel the stare of the queen boring into his back as they walked away. Hekabe knew. She had recognised him.

They were now approaching the passage that led back to the lower city, when Helen halted and stepped into the shadows.

"I must leave you here Odysseus," she whispered breathlessly. "I dare take you no further. Can you find your way?" Even in the gloom, the moonlight pooled in her eyes that could undo many a man and loosen his reason.

"Without doubt," he whispered, his voice low, careful that they would not be discovered a second time by the guards in the lower city. "I will take my leave of you here and thank you for your help, kinswoman."

He was about to descend the stone-carved stairs, when Helen turned to him, almost as an after-thought and asked the question.

"Tell me Odysseus. Do you think this cursed war will last much longer?" He could not see her expression, but he heard the anguish in her trembling voice. Helen wrapped her arms around herself as if it would soothe her pain. "For sometimes I cannot bear it. You must know Alexandros died in battle and they married me to his brother." She used her cloak to wipe away the tears, as she burst into heaving sobs. "If only I had listened to you. So much suffering and bloodshed might have been averted!"

"Hush Helen." He looked round anxiously, his ears keen for any approaching guard, before seizing her hands. "You must calm yourself and keep strong. For I think this may be over soon and then Menelaos will accept you back."

"Thank you, Odysseus, for your kind words." She brushed his hands with a wet kiss before releasing him "May the gods go with you" and she turned to leave him standing alone.

When he reached the passage entrance, Diomedes was waiting for him. "So my brother, we've done it," he laughed, clapping Odysseus on the back.

"Yes, we did," Odysseus replied, as he changed back into his warrior clothes, discarding the borrowed wet rags. But he felt no sense of comfort or elation. Only a gnawing feeling of apprehension for those left inside the city.

What fate awaited these people? he wondered.

Once back at the Greek camp, the plan was set in motion. Epeios, renowned for his craftsmanship with wood and carpentry, was summoned and tasked with the job of building. For nearly a whole lunar cycle, the craftsman had laboured with the soldiers to assemble the wooden structure. Work parties had been sent out to the lowlands of Mount Ida to fell timber and then drag the wooden stumps back across the plain into the camp. It was a gigantic task. An effort worthy of the Titans themselves. Men, with sweating bodies and sinews tort, banging, shaping and forcing the timbers into place until at last it finally emerged. The Wooden Horse.

The day before they had met in Council. Under the wide billowing awnings of the tent, a welcome relief from the scorching heat, they had discussed the strategy.

Agamemnon took command, perhaps hoping to take some of the credit for the audacious plan. "So Odysseus, it is finished, I hear,"

"Epeios the carpenter assures me so and I have inspected it myself. A trap door has been made to conceal the warriors inside." Odysseus had taken no chances and each day without fail he had journeyed to the workshop to satisfy himself that his wishes were carried out, as slowly the edifice took shape sculptured out of planks of wood and hammered nails.

"Nothing must go wrong." Agamemnon's handsome face was composed, but beads of sweat pricked his brow. "Odysseus, I want you to lead the men concealed in the Horse. This needs to be our elite warriors so handpick who you will."

"I have already given that some thought." Indeed Odysseus had deliberated on it in his mind, sat by the shore gazing out across the wine dark sea. He knew his proposal broke the rules of *kleos*. He looked round at the expectant eyes waiting for his words. "I would like Diomedes as my deputy and Kephallenian warriors handpicked from my contingency. These are men I know and trust will fight bravely." There was an audible sharp intake of breath and murmuring from those assembled in the Council.

"But surely we need our noblest warriors inside this horse!" It was Neoptolemos who spoke, his cheeks flushed with pique. He had inherited the god-like looks and temperament of his father Achilles, only the features were harder set and there was a curl to his lip. After Achilles' death, Odysseus had fetched the young lad from his childhood home of Leros. The son had quickly established himself as a pitiless killing weapon against the Trojans. "I for one wish to be included and I am sure the other leaders here also," Neoptolemos continued. "For how will we win *kleos*, if the future bards sing of lesser men taking the city?"

"Don't fear Neoptolemos. There will be plenty of glory for all of us." Odysseu grinned at the young man, clapping him on the back. "And if the bards do sing of this, there is no reason why your name and the other nobles here should not be mentioned. For who is to know that you were not inside the horse."

Agamemnon had been listening closely and nodded. "Very well, have your wish Odysseus. We will not stand in your way."

"And you all know the plan." Odysseus continued. "The camp must be destroyed. Nothing must be left on the ground so it will look as if the troops have given up and returned home."

"My scouts have already found a place to conceal the fleet." It was Menelaos who now spoke. "There is a small island, Tenedos, twenty stadia distance, where we will beach the ships on the far side of the island."

Odysseus nodded in assent. "Good. It must be made to look as if the horse has been left as an offering to one of the Trojans' gods. Once it is taken inside the city, we will come out under the cover of darkness and open the city gates. My kinsman, Sinon, has agreed to stay behind after the army has departed and will light a beacon to signal the troop to return."

"Is there any way the plan might fail," asked Agamemnon, anxiously. Odysseus' glance fell on the *Anax*. Even now the man could not keep his nerve.

"If they discover that it is a trap," Odysseus slowly replied. "I believe they will not deal with us kindly. Or the Trojans might decide against taking our generous gift inside their city walls." Laughter broke out and he held up his hand to silence them. "That is why our elite warriors must be inside it, as any sound or loss of spirits will give us all away. He looked around scanning the faces of the Greek leaders as each gave their nod of assent.

He paused. "One more thing Agamemnon. The men are weary after so many years fighting. There are women and children inside the city as well as their menfolk, who have fought bravely to protect them. We must ensure that we still act as men and not beasts of the forest. That the passions of our warriors do not get carried away. For our actions will be watched by the gods and judged accordingly."

Agamemnon, a mocking smile attached to his fine face, met Odysseus' eyes. "If indeed this plan of yours is successful and Troy is taken, it will be hard to keep the army in check. But Odysseus, if it pleases you, I promise that I and the leaders present here will do our best to curb the bloodlust and restrain the men." Odysseus shifted his gaze at each of the leaders, a depleted group since they had first arrived on these shores. Their leader Agamemnon, bedecked in his fine clothing; Menelaos the gentler and soft-hearted of the two brothers; the snowy haired Nestor of good counsel; Idomeneus, the seasoned warrior; the newly arrived Neoptolemos, still young and impetuous; Ajax son of Oileus and of course Diomedes, his brother in arms. As Odysseus regarded each man in turn, a shiver ran through his body. He felt a sense of foreboding and growing apprehension.

So here they sat, man pressed against man in the cramped space and rising heat. No one dare move lest they unwittingly give away their hiding place. Outside, Odysseus could hear human voices murmuring and a talking taking place. The sounds of the speech were too muffled to hear clearly, but he recognised some of the harsh single syllables of the local Trojan dialect of *che tsuk cha* and *tak*. There seemed to be some sort of disagreement as the quiet murmurings had changed into raised voices. It was at that point, a maiden shrieked out and no doubt his companions heard it too. Even through the thickness of the wood and his limited understanding of the language, Odysseus could make out the words "Fools. Don't trust the Greeks bringing gifts." He could sense the tension inside the dark space, each man knowing that the next few moments would decide the success of their plan. Sitting here in the dark, they were vulnerable. The *Fates* holding their future by a thread, ready to cut it at any moment.

After what appeared to be an endless time, the voices subsided and quiet descended outside. Odysseus could feel one of the men was about to speak and hastily put his hand to his mouth. Guards might be sat outside so any sound could be their undoing. Then came the sound of metal striking stone again and again in a cacophony of sound. It was now clear the Trojans had decided to take the Horse into their city. The unbearable heat of the day was now declining when they felt the structure move. The Horse with its deadly load was being taken into the city accompanied by festive songs and celebration. Even then they were almost undone. It must have been as the Horse was pulled over the city wall that suddenly it came to an abrupt jolting halt. The sound of metal weapons striking weapons rang out. After what seemed an age, they were on their way again, slowly being pulled into the heart of the great famed city of Troy.

The noise and festivities seemed to go on for ever. Clearly the townspeople thought that the war was over after these long years of *Strife*.

At last they were free of their enemy. When all had grown quiet, Odysseus gave the signal to Epeios to release the trap door. The men, slowly unfurling themselves, emerged from their hiding place and climbed down the rope ladder into the heart of the city.

"What now Odysseus?" asked Diomedes. The city was bathed in full darkness and silence. Nothing stirred. The townspeople were slumbering, spent after their drinking and festivities.

His mind worked quickly, grasping the situation. "The beacon should have been lit by now. The fleet must be well on its way back. You men go to the city gates and make sure they are secured and open for when our comrades join us. The rest of you, follow me to the citadel." He uttered those final fateful commands. "Spare those who are disarmed and who offer no resistance. There are men here who have fought bravely to protect their city as well as blameless women and children."

It was hard to try to recall the rest of that accursed night. He had spent years trying to loosen the memories. To forget the details of what he had witnessed. There had been the anxious wait for the army to return but then it had been like Hades itself had been unleashed. The carnage and massacre began as the army ran amok. There had been screams of women, crying children standing dazed not knowing where to turn, watching their homes burn. So much slaughter and blood as the city was sacked.

In the midst of this, he had come across Agamemnon. In his fury, he had thrown him against the wall, grabbing him by the throat.

"Why in the gods name are you allowing this to happen?" he raged. "You are king, our *Anax*. Can you not keep the men under control? This is not *kleos* when the men are acting like swine, killing and committing all manner of atrocities. You must restrain them."

The man had shrugged and rolled back his eyes. "Do not rage Odysseus. This is out of both our hands. The men have waited too long for this day. They will have their revenge for all the suffering they have endured."

"I hope the gods will not punish us for *hubris* with these excesses," he had replied, releasing his grip. Nevertheless, he had ordered his own band of Kephallenian warriors to maintain discipline. With his men he had protected the house of Antenor, the counsellor who so long ago had unsuccessfully advocated the return of Helen. When he came across his former adversary Glaukos and his wounded brother pursued by a blood-thirsty mob, he had intervened. He had spared both men from death at the hands of his fellow comrades. Where he could, he had tried to moderate the killing.

It had been a terrible night when unspeakable and wicked acts had been committed. The slaughter of the citizens had been indiscriminate. The old king Priam had met his end by the sword of Neoptolemos, seeking shelter at the altar of Zeus. No mercy had been shown. His body had been despoiled and thrown to the dogs to feed on. Astyanax, Hector's young son, had been hurled from the battlements to his death. His fate had been sealed on the day he was stripped of his father. Even the temples of the gods had not been exempt from violence and desecration. What horror had he witnessed! The sight of Ajax raping the young priestess in the sacred shrine of Athene, still clutching the image of the goddess. He could still hear her screams and cries resonating in his ears.

He awoke from his reverie with a start. It was now the full light of day and a woman was shrieking nearby. He roused himself to investigate the noise, stepping through the porch into the yard.

One of the older servants, her face etched with lines, was stood rigid. At her side, a bucket had been overturned, spilling water over the dirt. "Whatever is the reason for your screams?" He sharply rebuked her. "Don't you realise that you are disturbing the peace of the household?"

"Look master," the woman said pointing, her voice high pitched. "Do you not see it?"

Glancing across he saw a white bird perching on the wooden rafters of the palace. "It's only an owl," he replied.

"But master, don't you realise. It's an omen. A sign of death within the household."

Chapter 8

Vrechei (It Rains)

Heavy splutters of rain were beating on the glass pane of the window when the clock sounded the alarm. The high-pitched ring echoed around the room. The night had been stormy and a loose shutter had been knocking rhythmically against a wall somewhere. The wind was still rattling the balcony window, an inauspicious sign for the day. Thea checked the time. It was still early. Despite the temptation to lie in beneath the warm bed covers, Thea forced herself to climb out of bed. At nine o'clock promptly, she descended into the marble-tiled hotel lobby.

"Good morning!" The loud female voice called out. It was Electra, already stationed behind the reception desk. All signs of the previous evening's drama had vanished and instead Electra wore a wide smile on her lips.

"Good morning, Electra." Thea returned the greeting, her glance caught by the heavy coat of lipstick, a vibrant cerise today. The shade clashed with the crimson patterned viscose blouse and not for the first time it puzzled Thea how Electra found time to attend to her wardrobe, when she spent all her waking hours at her desk.

"Your colleagues are already outside in the car park. Oh Dr Hughes and his assistant were so wonderful last night. He is so polite," Electra gushed. "And always says good morning. A real English gentleman."

"Yes, I suppose he is," Thea agreed.

"But I'm afraid our weather is not so good today," Electra continued, tightening her face into a grimace. "They say the rain is going to last most of the day. At least you have a good coat!" Kitted out in her waterproof jacket and sturdy walking boots, Thea had anticipated the temperamental spring weather.

"Wait!" Electra dived under the counter and pulled out a white plastic bag. "I have something for you all." The contents inside had been wrapped with great care. "I made them myself for Dr Hughes. *Spanakopita*, spinach pies, in case you all get hungry."

"Thank you," said Thea, wondering how Electra had found the time to conjure up the pastries. The shadows etched around her eyes suggested it had been an early rise. "I'm sure Dr Hughes will appreciate them."

"Have a good day," Electra called out as Thea turned and walked through the wide double doors. Outside the rain threatened a miserable day.

Across the car park, Thea spotted the familiar figures of Rob and Matthew, their faces obscured by their stiff waterproof jackets. They were both preoccupied with packing an assortment of bags, boxes and metal rods into the boot of a red hatch-back. There was an urgency to their movements. In the heavy downpour, it was hard to keep anything dry and ordered. At Thea's approach, Rob immediately glanced up and a broad smile broke out on his lips.

"Good morning, Thea." Despite the late evening drinking, he appeared remarkably fresh-faced. "Don't hang around. Get in the car out of the rain. Take the front seat as it's cramped in the back."

"Electra sent you some pastries."

Through the downpour, Rob looked over at the plastic bag. "That's very generous of her."

As Thea climbed in, Matthew mumbled a greeting and she noticed the dark circles under his eyes. Splashes of rain swept inside the cabin, as the car doors opened in quick succession, allowing Rob to climb into the driver seat with Matthew following closely behind.

"So we've not seen so much of you," Rob remarked casually, as he started the ignition. He glanced over his shoulder to reverse the car, catching her eye.

"I've been working over in the other town," Thea replied lightly.

"Richard tells me you want to visit a village near the survey?"

"That's right, Mousatoi."

"We'll probably get to the base at Kalodia later in the afternoon. First Matthew and I need to make a short stop around the landslide area to take some samples." She noticed he was making an effort to explain things to her.

"That sounds fine and thanks for the lift."

"Matthew was feeling isolated being left behind in the lab with just my company. Isn't that right?" He paused for a moment, as Matthew ventured a response. "So he's spending the weekend at Kalodia with some fresh faces."

They were now driving along the promenade, passing the ferry terminal on the sea front and avoiding the main town square. The old Debosset Bridge, now used only by pedestrians, had come into view. Its low elegant arches spanned the width of the Koutavos lagoon. The journey took them inward, encircling the lagoon, passing through small industrial yards punctuated by eucalyptus and cypress trees. After passing the old town cemetery at the far side of the old bridge, the road began to climb hugging closely the contours of the mountain. As they left the main town behind, Thea could feel the tautness lift from her body, as if she could breathe freely again. Despite the steep drops into the sea, Rob's self-assured driving seemed to infiltrate Thea's mood bringing increasing equanimity with every passing mile.

The wet streets were deserted, as most local people had sensibly chosen to stay indoors. Nevertheless, there were signs of local industry: the fish farm out in the gulf, the circular hoops arranged in neat regimented rows; and signs advertising local mountain honey for sale. It was hard to see where the bees might feed on such a precipitous slope. They drove in silence except for the frantic rhythmic sound of the car wipers, sweeping away the torrent of raindrops spattering the windscreen. Rob tried to tune the radio but had given up, having been rewarded by a loud soulful *tragoudia* broken up by the poor signal. At times the vehicle slowed almost to a standstill to negotiate unexpected hazards: piles of stones and boulders swept down by the winter storms; a herd of goats clambering over rocks, their bells jangling in agitation; and road maintenance, where flimsy orange netting displaced metal crash barriers and impacted earth replaced the tarmac.

"Can we stop for a moment?" Thea asked, suddenly spotting a small parking area. "I'd like to take some photographs."

"In this rain?" Rob replied in disbelief. "Sure." He glanced in the mirror and brought the car to a careful halt.

Thea undid her rucksack, pulling out a small compact camera and a canary yellow waterproof. She stepped out, quickly pulling her jacket over her sweater. Despite the rain, there was a reasonable view across the water to Paliki, although the contours of the distant hill line were partially obscured by mist. Thea glanced across the gulf. From this vantage point, she could make out some hillside villages in the distant background, silhouetted against the green and wooded higher land. A rounded hill drew her attention. It had a distinctive conical shape. She started to take some photos.

"You seem very interested in this part of the peninsula." Rob had stepped out of the comfort of the car to join her. He glanced around at the view in front of him. "I thought the landslide would interest you more. What's captured your attention?"

Thea twisted her head towards him, their eyes meeting momentarily, and again felt a strange sense of connection. With his broad shoulders and solid frame, Rob instilled a feeling of trust and dependence.

"I've been reading again some passages from Homer. I was thinking that it would make sense for the palace to be somewhere over there." She pointed towards the peninsula where the land swelled up just below the small conical hill. "It's maybe tucked away but it is on the edge of some really fertile land. It would be within a day's walk of Porto Katsiki, if that is the place where Odysseus first came ashore."

"You're taking this search for the palace very seriously." Rob grinned, a playfulness in his voice. "Is that the reason you want to look at the other village, Mautauki?"

"Mousatoi," she lightly corrected him. "Yes, the librarian on Paliki told me that some old tombs were excavated there. If there are graves then there must be a settlement. But I haven't been able to get hold of the archaeological journals to check it out."

They got back into the car, the dampness on their faces, skin and waterproofs following them inside. The car set off once more. At a crossroads, where the arm of Paliki came up to meet the main part of the island, they took a sharp turn, descending into a plain. The road was newly surfaced but already the black tarmac was streaked with stress cracks, a tell-tale mark of seismic activity. About a third of the way down, they pulled off onto a small dirt track, jolting and shuddering on the rough uneven surface. With the rocking of the vehicle and the rain obscuring the windscreen, it was hard to make out where they were going.

"Is this where you think the landslide took place?" asked Thea.

"That's right," Rob answered. "At least that's what we're hoping to prove."

"We've been taking samples from across the isthmus to see if we can find evidence of sea vegetation", explained Matthew enthusiastically. "Rob is an absolute expert in soil and rock analysis."

"Thanks Matthew for the compliment," laughed Rob, throwing back his head. "This looks a promising spot for today." He pulled the car over where the track broadened out, allowing two vehicles to pass. "Matthew, can you get the equipment and we can take a couple of soundings." Matthew obligingly got out, quickly pulling on his waterproof and started to unload the equipment from the boot.

Rob now turned his attention towards Thea. "We're going to be about forty-five minutes. Do you want to stay in the car? At least you'll stay dry."

"Don't worry about me," she replied reassuringly. "I can occupy myself. I've brought a couple of things to read."

"Don't tell me." Rob grinned, the laughter lines on his face now crinkling into Crow's feet. "A copy of The Odyssey!"

"How did you guess?"

"We'll see you in a bit."

Alone, Thea checked her watch and then opened her bag to pull out her book. She could use the time usefully to study again Homer's descriptions of Ithaka. The pages were scored with brightly coloured markers to highlight passages containing potential clues. The book fell open at the place where the spine was most creased. She re-read again Odysseus' description of his homeland:-

"I live in clear set Ithaka. A Mountain stands there, Mount Neriton with its quivering leaves. Around it lies several islands very close to each other- Doulichion, Same and wooded Zakynthos. Ithaka itself is low lying and the furthest out in the sea to the west, while the other islands are away from it towards the rising sun. It is rough land, but a good place for bringing up children: I tell you, I can think of no sweeter sight than one's own country." Odyssey 9.21-30 (translation Martin Hammond)

She was thinking quickly. The topography made sense: the gentle swell of Paliki conspicuous during the drive. Certainly it was the furthest west of the islands. There were no steep cliffs as in the main part of the island or most of the Greek islands she had visited. But Mount Neriton baffled her. There was higher land in the background but it was hardly a mountain. But Mount Oenos on the main part of the island, that seemed to make sense. It loomed large above the whole island and would have been a welcome landmark for ancient mariners at sea. Now a national park, it was covered in natural woodland. Thea turned to an earlier excerpt, where she had picked out the phrase *upo neriou*. *Upo*, the unaspirated word usually meant *under* or *below*, so would translate as *under Mount Neriton*. But what if Homer meant *across from*, so opposite the mountain, which seemed to fit better. By the time the two men returned, Thea was fully immersed in her new theory, her fingers flicking between the different passages.

"Okay, we're done," said Rob, opening the car door, the sudden sound startling her. She hadn't noticed their return. "I hope you've managed to occupy yourself. At least the rain has eased off."

A glance at Thea's watch told her that a whole hour had past. "Yes, I've been fine," she reassured him, looking up. It felt hard to pull herself away from this new line of thought. Somehow being close to the actual physical places felt so real and a different experience from reading about it in the comfort of her London flat. She glanced at Matthew, who looked slightly pitiful in his sodden clothes, whereas Rob just seemed to throw off the rainwater like water running off the back of a water fowl.

"We'll probably be in Kalodia within the next half hour," Rob said, starting the ignition. The vehicle set off, bouncing down the dirt track until it reached the low coastal plain. Through the rain and misted windows, it was hard to make out any signs of an ancient landslide. Eventually, they turned off the main road climbing up a steep hillside for several kilometres. The narrow lane snaked its way around sharp hairpin bends and narrow village passages, until at last a sign for Kalodia appeared. On the outskirts of the village, Rob pulled the car into a covered parking bay, overshadowed by a tall modern residence standing on its own. The sound of the car must have announced their arrival as instantly Sophie and Daniel came to greet them.

"We weren't sure what time you would get here."

"Hi Sophe", said Matthew, tossing his bag out of the back of the car. "How's it going?" A shy glance passed between the two younger people and Thea realised that a definite attachment was blossoming.

"Fine," Sophie replied." It's been a bit of a quiet

day as the rain has confined us to barracks. The field work got cancelled. Daniel was planning to do a blog about the survey until he realised we don't have an internet connection." Daniel looked up briefly at the sound of his name, forcing a smile that faded quickly. From his grim mood, it was clear that the imposed disconnection from the world did not sit comfortably with him.

"And how is the injured leg?" Thea enquired turning her attention back to Sophie.

"It's healing really well. I can walk on it now without any pain. Whatever you put on it was miracle stuff!"

"It can work wonders sometimes."

They followed Sophie into the house, where the entrance opened into a huge hallway with wooden stairs leading to the floor above. "This is massive, Sophe. Does anyone else stay here?" exclaimed Matthew, sizing up the dimensions of the building.

"No, just us. It's huge. We even have our own housekeeper who does the cooking." They had now entered a living room where some of the others had congregated to pass the time, dressed in several warm layers of clothing. Richard was there too. Even he had had to make a concession to the weather, discarding his usual pale light-weight suit in favour of a casual sweater. His extrovert unflappable manner was unchanged.

"Here you all are! You found us in our village hide-out!" he greeted them affably. Already Richard had a full glass of red wine in his hand, although it was only mid-morning. It reminded Thea of the gentlemen's club of archaeologists from the last century. Richard wouldn't have looked out of place in his usual white linen suit and Panama hat excavating the palace of Knossos with Arthur Evans.

Mark appeared round the door. "Hello everyone." He glanced at Thea. "Are you joining us for lunch? I can ask our housekeeper Mrs Florakis to set some extra places."

"I'm easy with that, if you are happy Thea," said Rob, deferring the decision to her.

"That would be good," Thea replied. There was still plenty of time left in the day and she welcomed the opportunity for company after her enforced solitude. "Provided we won't be an inconvenience?"

"Don't worry about that," Sophie quickly reassured her. "Mrs Florakis has developed a soft spot for Mark."

"Then we'd love to," Thea replied. She could imagine the Greek housekeeper fussing around Mark, wondering why such an eligible man didn't have a wife and children.

****

"Do you have time to take a look around, Thea?" enquired Mark. The lunch pots had been cleared away. Most of the team had melted away, Elizabeth and Alistair quickly returning to their work after limited conversation. Thea glanced across at Rob, who was in deep discussion with Richard.

"Sure, I'd be interested to see how you all live here."

"I'd be most happy to show you around, if you wish," offered Mark smiling.

The house proved to be enormous and well furnished, but it was the garden that impressed Thea the most, with its overhanging foliage, pots of geraniums and intimate secret corners. "It's lovely out here," Thea remarked. "You must be out here all the time."

"Not at the moment," Mark shrugged. "The weather hasn't been up to it and we've been full on with the project."

"At least the warmer weather will be arriving soon," Thea offered encouragingly.

"And here is the "Find Shed"," said Mark pointing to an open air covered work area, where a large table had been set up and open shelving stacked neatly with numerous boxes. Each had been meticulously labelled in a neat uniform handwriting with a date and a sequence of numbers. Elizabeth was bent over the table, focusing on several small earth-covered objects scattered in front of her. Each find was being recorded in a large moleskin bound book. Alistair had set up a makeshift studio on the side bench and was photographing a small find. At their entrance, Alistair gave a cursory nod, but Elizabeth didn't glance up. Although unspoken, their presence felt an unwanted incursion so they chose not to linger.

"So how's the survey going?" Thea asked, seizing the opportunity to speak with Mark privately. "I understand that it hasn't turned up anything of significance yet?"

"Yes, that's right. To be honest Thea, it's an absolute nightmare to survey. There are a lot of closed properties around here, as you may have noticed. So we haven't been able to work out who are the landowners to approach to get permission. So what we have tends to be small holdings, heavily cultivated with vines or that have been left to go wild. A lot are really badly overgrown with brambles and undergrowth. And then we also have to look out for the wildlife."

"You mean snakes?" Thea shuddered thinking of the small silver vipers, difficult to spot but highly poisonous.

"They're attracted to the vines. So not the best

of starts. I think Richard is already feeling the pressure. I have wondered why this spot was chosen and whether we ought to be looking elsewhere."

"It's strange, isn't it." Remembering her conversation with Vassiliki, Thea chose not to be drawn. "So very quiet around here," she said suddenly, shifting the conversation and refusing to allow her thoughts to dwell on Dimitri Kampitsis. "I haven't heard a single car since we arrived."

"So you've noticed. We don't see many people, just a couple of the locals. There is a sense of the pied piper about the place. All the young people and anyone under fifty years old has been lured away by the attractions of city living."

"Isn't there a *taverna* or a *kafeneion* in the village where there is a bit of village life?"

Mark sighed. "There used to be but that closed down a few years ago. The nearest eating place is now two villages away and only open at weekends. After the earthquake, even the church has been closed and is still in a state of disrepair."

"So lots of time to read and contemplate." It was hard imagining Mark, a man who enjoyed his urban living and city amenities being available twenty-four seven, settling for the rural country life.

Mark looked across at Thea, concern written across his face. "You know I worry about you. You've not seemed yourself since you arrived what with the fainting fit and then leaving dinner early. Is something else going on I should know about?"

"Don't worry about me," Thea replied, trying to enthuse her voice with conviction. Though she trusted Mark absolutely, it was too long and complicated a story to explain at that moment. "I'm perhaps just over tired. You know what it is like in the run up to the end of term," she said brushing off the concern.

Apparently convinced, Mark glanced towards the director and scientist, who were standing on the porch deep in conversation.

"You know I googled him?" said Mark, speaking in a conspiratorial undertone his eyes lingering on the shorter thick-set man.

"Who do you mean?"

"Rob of course. The man's the real deal. He's a string of publications as long as your arm and sits as a climate expert on several governmental and international panels. I can't believe he's helping us with our small little project."

"I think the two of them go back a long way," replied Thea. Inadvertently, her eyes rested on Rob, trying measure him up and hang this new piece of information on the unassuming appearance. From the corner of his eye, Rob caught Thea's gaze and hurriedly broke off his conversation, clapping Richard on the back.

"I've been delaying you," Rob said attentively, an apologetic expression on his face. "Do we need to be leaving?" They said their farewells quickly and had started towards the car, when Richard caught Thea's arm, taking her by surprise.

"Would it be possible to have a quick word Thea? " The words were lightly spoken but the hand grip was insistent.

"Of course," Thea replied.

Thea followed Richard into a quiet corner of the garden where they could talk without being overheard. The sun had started to shine giving the foliage around them a feel of freshness. But at once, she sensed something was coming and that she wouldn't like it.

"Stelios rang me this morning, about setting up a meeting with Mr Kampitsis, next week. He's heard a lot about you and is really keen to meet with you in person. I can't stress to you how important this is as we're seeking further funding and our negotiations are at a delicate stage." He paused and took a deep cough to clear his throat. "I know that you are working hard on the research, but I want you to be at that meeting." There was a steely look on Richard's face giving his words more weight.

Thea felt her body lurch, as if hit by an invisible hand. Despite her best avoidance tactics, she had underestimated Stelios' persistence. She searched quickly in the corners of her mind for an escape but could only draw a blank. "Okay," Thea agreed reluctantly, "I'll be there."

****

Thea sat in silence on the drive over to Mousatoi, all the joy sucked out of the day. The village straddled a hill and Rob parked the car in a quiet square opposite an old church. Despite the cluster of houses, the village seemed deserted. It was clear that some of the homes were still closed up for the winter by absent owners or simply abandoned, left standing shabby and neglected.

"Are you okay?" asked Rob, looking at her quizzically sensing her subdued mood.

She was aware Rob was doing her a favour and she needed to snap out of this dread. "I'm fine," Thea replied, tight-lipped. "Can we walk around the village and see what we find."

"Alright." They were both equipped with walking boots and rain coats, though the sun was starting to shine brightly through a gap in the clouds.

From their elevated spot, they could see a panoramic view of the bay across to the main part of the island, with the faint outline of Zakynthos visible in the grey distance. In the foreground, the view opened up to reveal a fertile green valley, with vines, olive groves and fields for growing wheat.

"Whoever lived here, really did control the land," commented Rob.

"And it's perfect for Mycenean agriculture," Thea said, noting to her satisfaction the view of Mount Oenos opposite. It seemed to confirm her earlier theory. They walked on past gardens where the bougainvillea and pink floribunda roses were just coming into bloom. Before their neglect, the garden plots had been well cultivated by the owners. Grapevines had been carefully trained to provide a canopy of shade from the summer heat.

"Let's explore down this way," Rob suggested, his face now animated. He was pointing at an old farm track, which descended sharply away from the village and led out onto open land. He was striding ahead, humming to himself. Thea followed, trying to focus her mind away from the conversation with Richard. After a couple of minutes walking, it became clear that the old track was twisting its way across to meet the distant shoreline. And then Porto Katsiki beyond.

All of a sudden Rob halted and stood motionless like a sentry, wearing a strange expression on his face. He didn't raise his head when Thea approached him.

"Do you hear that?" he asked.

There was something about his voice that made Thea look round straining to catch the sound. "Hear what?" Except for the breeze rustling the leaves of the olive trees, she could hear nothing.

He looked up at her, his eyebrows raised. "I thought I heard lots of shouting and laughter. I could have sworn there was a big party taking place in that olive grove over there."

Thea slowly shook her head, her ears pricked up for any sound. "I can't hear anything." They were on the village outskirts but no one was around.

Rob shrugged his shoulders, dismissing the thought, but the perplexed look remained on his face. "I must be imagining things. Do you want to go on?"

The old farm track was definitely leading them out towards the northern coast but it would require time to explore. It could be a marker that the palace was not far away. "Let's leave it for now and see if we can locate the tombs," Thea suggested.

They retraced their footsteps up the hillside to the main street of the village. It was then a small truck pulled up, the only vehicle they had encountered since their arrival. The driver, his face thick set and rough shaven, wound down the window.

"What are you doing and where are you from?" the man demanded in Greek, his voice deep and gravelly, suggestive of years of tobacco smoking and ouzo drinking. His age was hard to tell: it could be any number between fifty and seventy years. Rob attempted to take charge of the conversation, struggling with the unfamiliar tongue. A torrent of Greek followed: long sophisticated words delivered in a strong local accent.

"I'm sorry, I don't understand", replied Rob, shrugging his shoulders. "Can you speak more clearly?" He had slowed down the pace of his speech, heavily annunciating his words, as if the man was hard of hearing. "We are archaeologists looking for some archaeological tombs near here. Tombs. Do you know if there is anything in the village?"

The man's eyes narrowed and another torrent of Greek emerged, except this time fiercer and more hostile. As he puffed up his chest to square up to Rob, Thea stepped in.

"He thinks that we're thieves and have come to steal treasure," Thea said before switching into Greek, "*ochi, den eimaste*", explaining the Odysseus Project. "We heard some Mycenean tombs were discovered by the village. We wondered if you know anything about them?"

"Archaeologists, you say?" The man questioned still suspicious." You're sure you're not here to steal. You know the word "*klepsia*"? How do you say this in English?"

"Theft," Thea responded, unperturbed, "but we're not here to steal."

The man appeared partly reassured, a slow smile building on his lips. Already, Thea could see the stranger was mellowing, reassured by hearing his own language. "You know I heard it rumoured there was an excavation here many years ago." the man said, "About one and a half kilometres from here. Would you like me to take you?"

"That's really not necessary," Thea said, politely declining the offer, anxious not to inconvenience their new acquaintance.

"Then let me point it out to you," the man said, jumping out of his truck and from the roadside indicating somewhere in the distance. They grouped round him, following the line of the stretched finger but nothing stood out, only the undulating contours of the fields.

"*Efcharisto gia ti voithea sas*." Thea courteously replied, looking the man squarely in the face, covering her initial disappointment. "Thank you for your help."

The man was in no hurry to end the conversation, now confident in the identity of his two new acquaintances. "Can I invite you to my home for coffee?" he asked, his instincts for *philoxenia*, warm hospitality, kicking in. "My wife and I would be happy to entertain you."

"You're very generous," Thea replied, tipping her head back, "but we have to decline as we need to leave soon."

They exchanged their farewells and the man was about to turn away, when he stopped suddenly. "Your friend?"

"Yes?" Thea nodded in encouragement. The man was staring at Rob, his mouth falling open.

"He's familiar to me but I cannot think where I have met him. He's not from around these parts?" Thea nodded in agreement. "Please apologise to him if I have treated him discourteously." The man bowed in slight deference to Rob, who watched on blank and puzzled. Then the older man got in his car and drove away.

Rob was studying Thea, his eyebrows raised. "He responded to you like a local. I hadn't realise you'd been on Kefalonia before."

"Naturally I speak Greek as languages are my trade," Thea replied modestly, side-stepping the question but feeling an ugly mottling rising on her neck. Was it so obvious that she had spent time on the island?

"Let's check the Mycenean tombs," Rob suggested agreeably, not pushing the question further. "I rather like this place."

****

The car was where they had left it in the empty childless square, under the watchful bell tower. The lane meandered through the village, where pastel-painted and cream-coloured dwellings clung to the steep sided slope, before emerging into open fields. They loosely followed the instructions of their local guide, but there were no traces of stone structures, either ancient or modern, just cultivated lands.

"I think we should go this way," said Rob, swinging the car abruptly into a narrow side road. It led to a disused quarry, where huge boulders and piles of rubble barred their way. Rob's brow knitted with perplexity, as he suddenly halted the car with a screech of the brakes.

"I felt sure we'd find something here," he said disconcerted, scanning the pockmarked landscape. He glanced across at Thea, shrugging his shoulders, as he turned to reverse the car. "I must have been mistaken. Do you want to keep searching for these tombs?"

"It's getting late. Perhaps we should head back," Thea suggested, puzzled. For the past few minutes, she had started to experience the strange tingling sensation again, as if her body was trying to tell herself something. *The palace is close*, she thought.

The sky was darkening as they left the village and a gloom had descended over the landscape with the thickening clouds. The distant outline of the isthmus had just come into view, when the car suddenly jolted to an abrupt halt.

"What's happened?" asked Thea, turning to look at Rob.

"That's strange. Electra would have a field day. I think that the car electrics have just failed," Rob replied slowly. Casually he got out of the car and started to look under the bonnet. After a couple of minutes, he returned, a frown on his face.

"It looks like a fault with the electrics. I've never known that to happen in a modern vehicle. We're going to need a garage to fix it." Rob started to reach for his mobile phone. "I'm phoning the hire company to get someone out here." His fingers quickly dialled the number on the key pad. He waited for a response and then abruptly snapped the device shut.

"What is it?" asked Thea.

"There's no signal," he said, stuffing the mobile back into his pocket. "The phone isn't calling out."

"We must be in a blind spot. There isn't a hundred percent coverage for the island." Her mind was working quickly. "We'll have to walk to the next village to find a *taverna* or shop with a landline."

"That sounds a good plan. Okay, walk it is!" Despite the absence of traffic, Rob grabbed a piece of tarpaulin from the boot and hastily covered up the samples and boxed equipment.

"Just a precaution," he grinned as he handed Thea her rucksack.

Just then, Thea felt a gust of wind against her cheek: the weather was turning." I think we'd better get moving."

Chapter 9

Xenia (Strangers)

"Telemachos!" He warmly clasped the younger man to his chest. He could feel the taut muscular arms and the powerful body taking the strength into his own limbs. Odysseus stepped back to inspect his son more closely. He stood a full head taller with the same close set eyes and tight cropped beard. Only the softer lighter hair was now greying at the edges. No longer was Telemachos the youth of Odysseus' return, but a man full grown with two fine sons of his own.

"You look well, my son. When did you arrive back on Ithaka?"

The younger man greeted him with a wide smile. "Late last night, father. When all the palace was abed. The servants said I would find you here in the yard. You are about early this morning."

"I wanted to inspect the preparations for tomorrow's feast day. Will you walk with me?"

"Of course."

There was a sudden hiss of air, like an arrow shot from the bow. A pebble skimmed past, narrowly missing them. Feathers fluttered in mid-air, but the stone had not struck its target. The presence of the white owl had disturbed the peace of the household. Since first light, the servants had been throwing stones at the creature to scare it away.

"Careful, woman!" Odysseus put on that familiar scowl, as he turned to the offending female servant. From a body stooped with age, her throw had been surprisingly agile. "There would be more trouble if you hit your master, than from this bird."

"Forgive me *Basileos*," the old woman anxiously replied, lowering her head. "I was scaring the owl away. For the bird will bring death upon this house." She bowed before hastily hurrying back into the kitchens, leaving father and son alone.

"Do you believe the servant speaks the truth, father?"

He shrugged off the notion. "Of course not, they are just the ramblings of her over anxious mind. A servant believes every rustle of the wind is a portent from the gods. I have endured too much to fear a harmless bird perched on our roof." He casually put his arm around Telemachos. "Come son, let us walk on and look at these preparations."

The two men fell into step as they descended the steep track leading out towards the open fields. The day's labours were already well progressed. In the fruit groves, the women had been picking ripened fruit hanging down from the heavy laden trees, while the men toiled to bring in the first harvest of wheat and barley. It looked as if the gods had bestowed a fine crop. The granary would be restocked with grain for bread making and barley-broth. In the rough hedgerows, some young children were gleefully scrounging for red berries. Their squeals of delight rang out in the chill morning air. All around were signs of industry: men, women and children working together.

In a flat piece of land, facing the palace hill, a canopy had been strung between the trees for shade to protect from the heat of Helios. A throng of servants were setting out long wooden tables and benches in preparation for the feast.

One of the stewards had seen them and came up to join them. Odysseus recognised him immediately and greeted him.

"Ah, Eurymachos, I see the work is well progressed. Will everything be ready in time?"

"Indeed my lord," the steward replied. Odysseus knew him well. He had been the eldest son of his esteemed captain, Eurylochos. His father had acquitted himself well with much glory and valour. If only the man had not challenged and disobeyed his orders. He Odysseus had set the boy to work on the estate to honour the father who never returned from that accursed war.

"We are expecting many guests from the kingdom to whom we wish to offer full hospitality."

"You need not worry my lord. The gods have seen fit to provide for five hundred if that is required," Eurymachos replied.

"Well done, you have served well." And he clasped the faithful steward on the back. "I am proud of you as your father would have been if he had lived to see you."

"Is there anything you wish me to show you, *Basileos*?" he asked, his eyes welling up with tears.

"No, Eurymachos. Do not linger on our account. We will make our way round," he said. "Come Telemachos." And father and son continued on their way. Surveying the land, Odysseus felt satisfied. The well governed land was providing a bountiful harvest, through the will of the gods and the hard work of the people. Even if each day brought more and more people to the kingdom, fleeing violence on the mainland. There would be enough for all.

"So why is this festival of Apollo so important father?"

"My dearest son, I was once a stranger, dependent on the kindness of strangers. There were those who took me in. Who fed me, bathed me, and even clothed me when I was destitute. They will stay in my heart through their generous *xenia* to strangers." He could feel his emotions stirring. "But also there were those who abused the rules of *xenia* and who behaved like beasts, destroying my men and my ships." He shuddered at the memories from the past. "If the gods should grant me *kleos*, then I do not wish to be remembered for my guests going hungry or cold."

By now, the sun god Helios had driven his chariot well up in the sky. The burning rays had grown intense and the shadows short. Suddenly Odysseus felt overcome with a weariness deep in his bones. His strength seemed to be deserting him more each day. As if the gods pressed on him the weight of his years.

"Perhaps we could rest a while, Telemachos. Until the heat of the day is past."

The younger man glanced at him concerned. "Of course father. I will ask the servants to lay some coverlets down under the shaded tree. They can fetch us some food and wine from the palace, so we can take our fill outdoors." He gestured over one of the servants and sent him on with his instructions.

After they had eaten their fill, Odysseus found himself lying down on the blanket. There was a gentle breeze in the shade, which he felt against his well-trimmed beard. As his eyelids closed, the thoughts of bad *philoxenia* filled his mind: all the pain and suffering that had beset them on that ill-fated journey back from Troy. Slowly he succumbed to the fatigue and allowed *Sleep* to cover his limbs, as his mind drifted back to distant shores.

When had that journey home turned bad? Odysseus wondered. *Had the Fates always decreed so right from the moment of my birth? Or sitting aloft on Mount Ida, had the gods witnessed the terrible outrages of the Greeks as the city was sacked?* He did not know. It had been Agamemnon's orders to put Troy to the torch. For five whole days huge fires had ravaged Troy, reducing the famed city to piles of ash and rubble. On the beach head, it was a pitiful sight. The Trojan women and children huddled together, weeping and clinging to one another. Some blank eyed, numb with shock. As the city lay smouldering, they waited lamenting their fate. There felt no *kleos* in the warriors' task of dividing the spoils and apportioning out the captives to be taken into slavery.

It had been a terrible spectacle. Even the most hardened men had watched in horror as the beautiful Trojan princess, Polyxena, had plunged a stolen knife into her breast: she had preferred death in the land of Hades than life as a concubine. And what of the lot of the noble Andromache, the wife of Hector? The *Fates* had been cruel in apportioning her lot to her child's killer Neoptolemos, the son of the man who had slain her husband. Now this monstrous pairing was destined to share a conjugal bed. Odysseus had involuntarily shuddered remembering his own son and family on Ithaka. This was what happened when a kingdom was ruined and the male warriors no longer there to protect their kin. It was a relief he was only ten days sail away under oars from his island kingdom.

And what of the booty allotted to him. Through the smoke and ash of the windswept beach he had glanced at her sat hunched by the shore, unveiled and in ragged clothing. It was as if over the night, the gods had drawn her life's breath out of her body. Her hair was falling lankly at her sides, covered with ash and dust thrown in lament. Her cheeks were hollowed with grief mourning the loss of her husband and sons. He approached her. This former queen of Troy, Hekabe.

"Lord Odysseus, I would keep away from that woman." Eurylochos put out his hand to restrain him. "Some god has taken her wits away.

She spits and scratches anyone who goes near."

"We should kill her," muttered one of the other men joining in the conversation. "That would put her out of her misery and stop her wailing tormenting our ears."

"Silence, hold your tongue!" At his rebuke, the men ceased their chatter and cast their heads downwards. "Don't worry. I can take care of myself," he continued more mildly. Already a plan was forming in his mind. He went up to her, approaching her slowly as he might a wild animal. An animal cornered, trembling and fearful, which might strike out in terror.

Ensuring the men were out of earshot, he knelt beside her. "Queen Hekabe," he whispered, "it is I, Odysseus, the kinsman of Helen." The woman barely seemed to register his presence but sat still with her head bowed. "I am sorry for your loss. Through fate your husband was our enemy but he was a good man. If times had been different and the *Fates* had allotted us another path, we might have been linked by ties of *xenia*. You showed me kindness when you did not expose me to the guards. For that I owe you my life. I swear you an oath now by the gods that I will protect you. No bad fate will befall you."

The woman slowly looked up. Her whole countenance had been transformed by grief. "And how will you do that, pray tell me Odysseus. You have seen the fate that befell my husband. They killed him at the altar and despoiled his body. So even now in death the dogs and scavengers feed on his unburied corpse. How can I believe anything you say, when you Greeks behave like animals. I spit on you all." He quickly put his arms out to calm her.

"Hush. Do not rouse yourself more than you need. The gods will take their revenge on me if what I say is untrue. You are a Thracian Greek princess. We speak the same language and worship the same gods. Before you were taken as a bride by Priam, you came here as a Phrygian maiden to serve at the temple of Aphrodite as is the tradition of your people. I plan to return you to the town of your birth. But for the moment, keep this to yourself. So that none can raise opposition before our departure."

Hekabe looked at him attentively through her tears and grief. "You need not do that, Odysseus. Perhaps you are moved by a generous spirit but you prolong my suffering. For my life is over, like that of my husband, my beloved sons and this once noble city."

He left the woman still consumed in her grief and returned to his men. Already the preparation for the long sea crossing ahead were well advanced. Those skilled in carpentry had been hard at work repairing the planking and decking, ensuring that the boat timbers were seaworthy. Even now their rhythmic beats and clattering of tools reached his ears. All twelve ships had been newly coated with black pitch to prevent the seawater seeping through the planks. For otherwise the sea would overwhelm them, dragging them down to the kingdom of Poseidon as food for fishes. High on each ship's bow, the blue indigo eye, the eye of *Protection*, had been freshly painted. On the shore besides had been piled the war spoils apportioned for him and his Kephallenian warriors. As soon as the ships were seaworthy, the precious cargo would be loaded.

"Are the boats nearly ready?" Odysseus asked his captain, Eurylochos. The man had been with him from the start. On Ithaka they had played as boys, together learning to swim in that glistening turquoise sea. Under Trojan skies, the soft-skinned boyish face had become deep creased and leathered through the years of fighting. He tipped his head skywards and the mouth broke into a beaming smile.

"They are indeed. I thought this day would never come," Eurylochos replied, his voice full of joy. "We have only three more boats to finish. Everything should be ready by sunset tonight."

"Good! Then load everything on board and take on supplies of fresh food and water. We set sail tomorrow at first light." Some god propelled him to start the journey home with haste. He had stayed away too long. "Hopefully we will be back home before the next full moon." The cheerful words masked his gnawing unease and growing apprehension.

Eurylochos nodded in assent. "Of course, my lord Odysseus. And will you not stay with us?"

"Later," he answered, tight lipped. "There is first a matter I must settle."

He found Agamemnon in his tent with his brother, Menelaos. As he approached, he could hear their raised voices arguing over Helen's fate.

"The slut deserves to die brother!" Agamemnon's voice rose to a roar. "She has heaped disgrace on our house of Atreus."

"And I say we are reconciled." The pitch was milder and more malleable.

"Are you a mule head! That your mind is turned by a pair of women's bare breasts!" The argument was now attracting attention from within the camp, as heads raised to glance at the quarrelling brothers.

As he entered, they fell silent and Menelaos withdrew to the corner of the tent, turning his back and pacing from side to side.

"Welcome, Odysseus" Agamemnon greeted him with a ready smile, recovering his temper. "Our hero of Troy! You catch us quarrelling."

Menelaos turned, bolted upright like a spear, his face flushed and his fists clenched. "Over a woman. Your kinswoman Helen."

Agamemnon was sat on his bench, cushioned with animal pelts. Beneath his leather corselet, he now wore a fine murex purple tunic and bright gold-leaf crown both plundered from the city. In victory, the man had become even more arrogant and insufferable. Odysseus quickly assessed the situation.

"If I might be so bold to speak, my lords."

Agamemnon nodded in encouragement. "Speak your mind."

"Enough blood has been shed on this Trojan soil. We came to war so that Menelaos might reclaim Helen, his rightful wife. Let her live if that is his pleasing. For he has been the more wronged."

"Is that your counsel, Odysseus?" A shadow crossed Agamemnon's face, darkening the fine looking features. Since the sack of Troy, his hair had been cropped close to his brow and the beard carefully trimmed.

"It is, *O Anax*." His tone was deferential, but Odysseus stood full shoulder to him, staring him squarely in the eye.

"Very well, Odysseus." A beam now broke out on Agamemnon's face. "As the city fell into our hands by your brilliant strategy, I agree."

He turned to his brother. "You may do as you please with Helen. For the gods have blessed us with this day. Our treasuries will be filled with gold, silver and precious copper. Our names will be famous and known to men for generations to come. So much wealth and *kleos* we have gained. Let us set this quarrel aside." He held out his arms generously for the two brothers to embrace.

"But you came to speak to me about something," Agamemnon said, turning his head now towards Odysseus, scrutinising his expression.

"Indeed. There is a matter that must be raised with you. That concerning Ajax, son of Oileus." Odysseus paused waiting for a response. The cheerfulness still hung on Agamemnon, but the eyes had narrowed. When no answer came, Odysseus went on. "He defiled the temple of the god Apollo by raping the priestess holding the sacred image. I believe that he must be punished, or by his reckless actions we are all endangered."

"Yes, I know of it." Agamemnon said steadily, shrugging half-heartedly. "That is why I have taken the priestess, Kassandra, into my care. The Trojan girl will accompany me back to Mykenai and live out her days in my household."

He could read at once what Agamemnon was implying. Despite her despoilment, the beauty and graceful looks of the priestess had caught his eye.

"And what of your wife, Klytaimnestra?" He had only a distant memory of the queen of Mykenai, proud and regal. Installing a slave mistress could only bring shame and dishonour to her. "Will she not be displeased?"

Agamemnon looked at him directly. His body was rigid, like unflinching granite. "Klytaimnestra's thoughts are of no concern", he said, his expression now stone-like. "She will do as commanded by her husband and her king." Odysseus held his counsel. There was nothing to be gained from pressing a man so consumed by his own *hubris*.

Menelaos now stepped forward, breaking the tension. "They say, Ajax has already escaped from the camp, Odysseus." His words were softer and conciliatory. "When he heard you were demanding his death, Ajax claimed sanctuary in a neighbouring temple. He is beyond the reach of us all. Only the gods can decide justice."

The feeling of foreboding rose up in Odysseus again, like the bitter taste of bile from the spleen. This was not the news he had wanted. "Then I hope the gods do not punish us all for his actions," he replied grimly.

"Come, why so gloomy, Odysseus." Agamemnon's face had softened and the easy smile had returned. "You are our great conquering hero! Come drink with us!"

"I'm afraid I must take my leave of you, if there is nothing more to be done here. There is still much to do before our departure. I bid you both farewell. May we meet in more peaceful times." His words were courteous, but he could barely disguise his contempt for Agamemnon.

He retraced his steps along the well-trodden path to his own camp of the Kephallenians. His heart still heavy, he hardly noticed his dear companion, Diomedes, until he was almost upon him. They embraced warmly.

"Why so glum Odysseus," began Diomedes, "when I hear you leave at sunrise."

"You hear right, my dear friend." He pulled the younger man closer, playfully tussling his hair. "May the gods grant us favourable winds and safe passage. And you my friend?"

"We will not be off so speedily. The eighty ships will take time to make ready and watertight. We plan to put to sea on the eleventh dawn to make the journey back to Argos. So you will be back on Ithaka before we have even set foot on the Greek mainland."

"Indeed so!"

"You know Diomedes," Odysseus said more quietly, staring down at his feet. "We have battled side by side like brothers for so long. I don't regret that this war is over, but I will miss you. I will drink from the *kylix* and think of you, when I am back on my estates."

"Perhaps we can extend the ties of guest friendship on our return. You will be my guest at Argos and be richly entertained."

"And I you." He paused and then continued. "I only pray that the gods are not enraged by what we have done here and wreak revenge on us. Agamemnon would not restrain the troops." He felt the anger once more rising up. "Now he refuses to exact justice from Ajax, son of Oileus, for desecrating the sacred image."

"Do not fear on your own account, Odysseus. You have done everything with honour and *kleos*, as befits a noble man. You have no reason to fear vengeance from the gods. Come, let us shake off this gloomy mood. I expect you at my camp at dusk. Let us share food and drink wine one last time together."

****

The next morning Odysseus felt fresh and revitalised as the ships were pushed out into the shallow bay, ready to board. A band of the warriors had gathered on the beach to bid them farewell. Diomedes had been amongst them, as too the old man Nestor and the sons of Atreus.

He had embraced each in turn, his daily companions of these last ten years.

When it was Nestor's turn, the older man had clasped him eagerly to his breast. Odysseus had grown fond of the old warrior, this survivor of countless battles, despite his bewildering quickness to side with Agamemnon.

"You travel straight to Ithaka?" Nestor asked.

"We do and I hope to be there before the next full moon," he replied, keeping his inner counsel to himself.

"Then take a care to cross to Lemnos and break your journey there," Nestor said, offering advice. "That will be a good place for you to pull in and rest your men. You should then head towards the island of Skyros and follow the shoreline down to the Cape of Maleia."

Odysseus smiled indulgently and clasped the older man to him. "I thank you for your advice Nestor, which you offer with a good heart. I trust we may meet again, for our two kingdoms are not so far apart."

"Perhaps our houses may one day be joined through marriage," offered Nestor graciously. "For I hear that you have a strong healthy son who one day may be in need of a bride."

"That would be a joyous day indeed!" he agreed laughing aloud.

"Here Odysseus, take this clay piece, which is

stamped with my griffin insignia. If you should come to Pylos, show this and you will be recognised at once as my guest-friend." And the older man had placed a disc of hardened earth into his rough callused hand.

The troublesome priest Kalchas had also shown up to make offerings on the shore for their safe passage. The man had not been well-liked amongst the warriors and even shunned whenever possible. As Odysseus turned to board his boat, the priest now barred his way. He looked askance at the man, dressed in his dirt-stained priestly robes and long ash-grey locks.

"What is the meaning of this, Kalchas?" he demanded.

"I have had a vision, as I made offerings just now," the man rasped through chaffed lips. The years had not treated the priest kindly and Odysseus doubted he would survive the long sea journey ahead. Perhaps a fitting punishment for his part in the sacrifice of the innocent maiden, Iphigeneia. "The gods themselves put this in my mind to tell you," Kalchas continued, the words rasping from his throat. "Your death will come from the sea."

"I thank you for your words, Kalchas. But nothing will stop my journey home."

With that he passed the priest and waded through the shallow waters to his ship. But his sense of foreboding swelled, like the ripples on the sea before the storm.

The boats had been launched as one flotilla in the bay. The masts had been positioned upright on each boat, newly painted with the indigo eye on the bow. It was a sight to behold: the Kephallenian fleet. Twelve ships manned by the two hundred and forty proud-hearted Kephallenian warriors, the survivors of Troy. The rowers had stripped down to their tunics, ready and primed for the arduous journey. Loud cheers of men rose up, as he boarded his ship. Their exhilaration at the long awaited departure cut through the air. He glimpsed Hekabe, seated below the deck, her head hung low and clutching her cloak close to her chest.

"Do we make sail westward?" asked Eurylochos, his face full of joy.

"No, we head north on the prevailing wind," he answered cheerfully. "I have one more raid in mind before we are done. A chance for more plunder!" Eurylochos had shot him a look but the order had been obeyed. Even if his true motive had been suspected, no one had said anything.

At first the voyage had gone smoothly enough. At Lokris, the land of the Chersonese, they had weighed anchor and unloaded their cargo: Hekabe, the Trojan queen. The woman seemed confused, no sign of joy or recognition crossing her face at the sight of her native city. Wrapped in her filthy rags, her body resembled a bag of dried up bones.

"Why have you brought me here, Odysseus?" Hekabe had asked him, raising her pitiful face.

"So that you may live out the days that the gods grant you amongst your own people."

"My family is dead," she angrily retorted. "You do me no favours but only prolong my agony. Would that I have died too!"

He looked at the woman. The face still showed traces of noble beauty, only crushed by grief. He spoke kindly looking into her blank eyes. "At least here, you can mourn as you see fit and find comfort from your people. I offer this for the kindness you showed on that night in Troy." Hecuba simply turned her back and said no more.

As he boarded his own ship, a bank of suspicious faces greeted him. Eurylochos spoke on their behalf.

"So this is why we sailed north, my lord. To return our Trojan goods! We could have headed straight for Ithaka." The words carried an angry rebuke.

"Indeed not!" Odysseus replied, not wishing to betray any kind-hearted sentiment. "We still have unfinished work. I hear the Kikones, allies of the Trojans, escaped the worst of the fighting. So they will have no complaint if they offer us some hospitality." His grabbed the tiller, his eyes wide and shining. "I have a thirst for the famed Kikonian wine. Let us row on and test the land. Afterwards we can wait for a favourable wind to take us down to the Cape."

A big grin broke out over Eurylochos' face. "Certainly my lord." Turning to the rowers, he barked out the command "Rowers to the oars! Raid!" As they dipped the oars into the wine-dark sea, a big roar of hollering rose up.

The attack on the land had been initially successful. The battle-seasoned Kephallenians had caught the townspeople by surprise and quickly overwhelmed the citadel of Ismaros. But with victory, the great conquering heroes had grown careless, over-confident and unruly. Instead of a speedy departure, they had idled for several days, seduced by the heady Kikonian wine and the pleasures of the women. Perhaps that was when the *Fates*, the hideous sisters *Atropos*, *Clotho* and *Lachesis*, had changed the men's luck. The delay cost them dearly. Mustering their neighbours, the Kikones had come upon them at *Dawn*, lulled by *Sleep*, their bodies sprawled out, mouths agape, heaving with loud snores. Hard-pressed they had fought back bravely but the Kikones punished them severely for their bold raid. Seventy two warriors in all descended to Hades, their lives cut short in the full-pitched battle.

In disarray, they had boarded the ships, rowing as hard as they could to escape death. The men had sweated and heaved, their bodies straining at the oars. This time the course was set for the Cape of Maleia and beyond Ithaka. As they crossed the open water, birds had skimmed overhead and then familiar landmarks came into view: the island of leafy Thasos, the rugged contours of Lemnos and small countless islands until at last the long coastland of Achaia itself. Each night they pulled into a shallow harbour to setup camp and take rest. But their progress was tempered by adverse weather sent by Zeus and the sorrow of losing so many, when the war was over and done. And then disaster truly struck.

It happened as the ships were rounding the Cape. The god Zeus had whipped up a storm, for the sky turned into night and the winds blew cruelly against them. The ship's timbers had groaned, as the waves battered the wooden hull, soaking their bodies with the briny water. As hard as the men battled against the wind and tide, they could not overcome the force of the waves which pushed them further and further away from home. For days they had rowed. And each day brought neither any sighting of other ships nor land to beach the ships and take shelter for the night.

Only the vast boundless sea and endless waves in front of them. Wearied by their efforts and nights sleeping at their oarlocks, the men's eyes had grown dull and their limbs stiff. He could see the fear in their faces. In despair, he had prayed to his goddess Athena to show some sign of favour. But there was nothing. No bird in flight, no dolphin leaping from the sea, no promising lightening flash. The gods had abandoned them, horrified by their deeds at Troy. A shudder passed down his spine as he recalled Kalchas' words of prophecy, "Death will come from the sea." He gritted his teeth. He refused to accept that ignoble fate for him and these conquering heroes of Troy: to be food for fishes.

On the tenth day, land appeared. The people had been friendly and welcoming but it was a strange seductive place, where the air tasted sultry and heavily laden. Even the vegetation was unfamiliar: there was a honey-sweet brown fruit, its skin leather-brown and wrinkled; a rounded fruit, red-skinned and bulbous like an onion, which when split revealed a hundred jewelled seeds; but the most seductive was the Lotus flower. There was a mesmerising beauty in its delicate star-shaped petals, the colour of murex purple. But any who tasted it were robbed of their senses and memories of all that was most precious. Alarmed, Odysseus had ordered them to put to sea immediately.

They had dragged those unfortunates, still under the Lotus' spell, writhing and screaming onto the ships.

Once at sea again, he had tried to navigate them back on course, following the Little Bear in the sky which pointed towards Ithaka. But for days there was only the grey-green sea and swell of the endless waves, an emptiness all around devoid of land, ships or other living creatures. It was then, he had to admit to himself, they were lost. This was no longer the civilised domain of the Greeks he recognised, with its rules of *philoxenia* and hospitality. A strange world, with new lands and strangers who might not obey the rules of the gods. But he had been curious too and keen to discover all he could.

On one mountainous land, a small party of them had gone ashore seeking food and supplies from the local people. The land was fertile but uncultivated and had never been put to the plough. Whoever lived here, led a troglodyte existence. They had found a hollowed cave packed with young lambs, kids and curdled cheese.

"We should take our fill and go," one of his companions had urged him, looking around anxiously. But he had closed his ears, curious to see what kind of fellow lived there. It was almost dark, when the herdsman arrived back from tending his flocks of goat and sheep. He was a strange unkempt fellow, a giant of a man towering above them. On his forehead was a blue spiral body-painting like an extra eye. It was not *philoxenia* he had offered them but death. The Spiralled One had flown into a rage, killing two men with his bare hands on the spot, pitiless like a mountain lion. With his monstrous strength, the brute had rolled a boulder in front of the entrance, entombing them so he could kill them off one by one. But in the darkness of that cave, Odysseus' wits had not forsaken him. He had devised a plan to save them. First, he had offered the wild man a skin-sack of heady Kikonian wine. Never tasting liquor before, the brute had taken the bait, quickly guzzling down the wine and falling into a drunken stupor. Then using a stake of green olive wood, heated in fire, they had blinded him. Finally clinging to the underbellies of the well-fattened rams, they had escaped that tomb. But six companions had been killed by the *Cyclops* beast, violating the rules of *philoxenia*.

Then there had been Aiolos. A strange island which from a distance floated above the sea, ravaged by winds from all four corners. There ruled a brother and sister, who shared a marriage bed siring two children. At first the two rulers had received them well, entertaining them with fine food and shelter. They had departed on a north-west wind, which carried them towards the Little Bear and Ithaka. For ten full days they had made good progress across the wide boundless sea. They had come almost within sight of Ithaka itself. But then a sudden storm, whipped up by Zeus, had descended upon them, driving them back the way they came. That time, the king of Aiolos turned his back and refused to help them, claiming it must be the will of the gods. They had been driven off the island, truly hated by the immortals.

Then there had been the Laistrygonians on whose island they had sheltered within a natural harbour to beach the ships and taken rest. Instead of comfort and hospitality, they had been pelted with boulders and rocks from the cliffs above. There had been the hideous sounds of men screaming and ship timbers tearing apart. The gentle sheltering cove had turned into a deadly trap. Odysseus' was the only ship to survive, cutting the cable ropes and rowing out to open sea. Their losses were heavy. Yes, he knew well the effects of bad *xenia*. With each encounter, the survivors from that ill-fated war had dwindled.

They had sailed on with heavy hearts, once more across that endless sea. The men had grown silent, their faces frozen, as they strained at the oars. Now looking back, it was hard to believe that fateful meeting was so close at hand.

They were steering once more towards the Little Bear. It had been four full cycles of the moon since they had left Troy. He could smell the chill in the air. The seas grew turbulent and squally. Winter was fast approaching. The need to reach Ithaka or find suitable wintering quarters had become pressing. He had driven the men hard, barking out orders, taking his turn at the oars, anything to quicken their passage. So when Aiaia had come into sight, with its distinct mountain and fertile green land, they had felt only despair. Some of the men had wept openly, no longer able to hide their feelings. He Odysseus had understood this unexpected land mass as a barrier, blocking their sea passage home. The thought of her so close, even now had the power to move him deeply. But then as they beached the boat, all they could do was collapse on the sandy beach, spent from endless rowing.

Chapter 10

Hospitality

"Which way do you think?" Rob asked. They were at a T-junction, in front of a worn signpost, the painted letters rusted and faded. The left arm pointed towards a village two kilometres away and the right arm towards a tourist beach over twice the distance. The clouds had now thickened and the blackening sky intimated the approach of a storm somewhere out at sea. Just then there was a flicker of light, for a split second illuminating the landscape. In that moment everything was caught in a ghostly light, like a sepia photograph. It was soundless but there was no mistaking the lightning flash.

"The village looks closer," Rob broke the silence. He furtively glanced at the gathering storm clouds.

Breaking out of her thoughts, Thea finally answered. "I think we need to head towards the beach. It's a longer walk but we're more likely to find holiday apartments or a restaurant. Somewhere that has a phone we can use. Judging from today's experience, I'm not confident that we'd find anything in the village except locked doors." The rain had now begun to fall again in heavy droplets.

"We'd better get moving then as this storm is closing in quickly." Rob's voice had taken on an urgency as another flash of lightning out at sea lit up the sky. This time there was a deep growling of thunder and the juddering vibration of the earth.

They set off down the asphalt road which skirted a steep hill, the edge falling away into a tree-clad valley. The lightning flashes were intensifying but also the growls of thunder. They quickened their steps. Thea glanced across at Rob. Beneath the layer of waterproofs, his solid frame seemed to possess an almost superhuman vigour. It wasn't long before Rob's agile strides outpaced Thea. He must have realised as he slowed his pace to allow Thea to catch her breath.

"You know that in ancient times," Thea said, gasping, struggling to make herself heard through the pelting rain, "people believed thunder was a sign of the gods' anger.".

"Well they seem pretty upset right now," Rob retorted, a gust of wind carrying away his words. The rain was now sheeting down, the wetness penetrating their waterproof clothing and soaking any flesh or clothing left exposed. "This storm is getting worse," Rob shouted above the tempest, his words almost drowned by the heavy downpour. "We need to find shelter." Thea nodded in agreement. But there was no immediate sign of any building or rocky outcrop to take refuge, only the smooth stretch of road disappearing behind a distant bend.

They had been walking at a fast pace for some time, when at last some sign of shelter came into view. It was where a lush green valley gave way to scrubland; where the road met the edge of the coastal cliffs and where the grey frothing sea waves could be glimpsed. There perched above, overlooking the bay, was a small pension.

"Let's check if it's open" Rob said.

Thoroughly soaked, Thea nodded her agreement. They climbed up the marble steps and walked past the patio and swimming pool, where the rain was ricocheting off the paved tiles. The marl stone flags were now awash with rainwater rather than sunbeds, tubes of sun-cream and holiday-makers. The glass fronted doors slammed shut behind them, as they entered the vestibule, announcing their arrival. In the stillness of the guesthouse, their presence felt like an intrusion. Somewhere from within the building, a shrill female voice called out, followed by footsteps and then a middle-aged woman emerged. With her hair swept back behind her face, her appearance was plain, verging on world-weary, but the woman's welcoming expression transformed her features.

The glass doors banged again from the storm ranging outside, rattling and echoing around the hard floor and bare walls. "I assume you would like me to do the talking and enquire about the telephone," Thea said to Rob, speaking in a low voice. "I suspect my Greek is slightly better than yours."

Rob shot Thea a look, but amusement danced in his eyes. "You're teasing me!" He had just removed his waterproof, to reveal his hair dripping with raindrops. In the circumstances, he looked remarkably relaxed and composed. "On this occasion, I'm happy to let you do the talking."

Rob stepped back, as Thea introduced them in her politest Greek, explaining their circumstances. The woman gestured Rob over, placing an old phone in his hand.

"She is saying it's no problem," said Thea, translating the jumble of words. "You're welcome to use the phone." As Rob dialled the number, the woman tugged away his sodden coat from beneath his arm, hanging it on a nearby stand.

"*Kafe?*" the woman whispered to Thea under her breath. When Thea nodded, she disappeared into the back of the building. It was a relief to find shelter, where they could at least have a hot drink. Thea shivered. Not only did she feel soaked from the lashing of rain, but also surprisingly cold. She walked across the lounge area to watch the storm raging outside, wrapping her arms around herself for warmth. Through the wide panoramic windows, the mountain side fell away to the crescent shaped bay. Below was a shingle beach and white circling cliffs, now obscured by mist and rain. On a summer day, with the sun setting over the bay, it would be breathtakingly beautiful but with the storm raging, it felt primordial and menacing, as if there were more powerful elemental forces at work. The sky was suddenly illuminated by a short lightning streak and a quieter roll of thunder. The storm was losing its ferocity.

"I've spoken to the car rental office in the main town." The sound of Rob's voice startled her as she had not heard him walk up behind her. "They can't get anyone out here tonight. Not in this weather." He spoke rapidly to cover any awkwardness, as if sensing this news might displease her. "They promised to come out first thing tomorrow. Unfortunately for tonight we are stranded."

Thea felt her body stiffen, but she checked her reaction. At that moment, the woman returned with a tray loaded with steaming cups of coffee and honeyed pastries. "*Ela*," she beckoned them over, carefully setting down the contents on a small wooden table. "Weather, no good," she tutted to Rob in sympathy, raising her forehead in disbelief. "Eat please," she gestured to them both.

Thea smiled and thanked her, taking a mouthful of the coffee. She grasped the hot cup with gratitude, allowing the warmth to spread slowly through her hands and into her body. Rob was watching her attentively, as her body started to shiver in her damp clothes. Except for small traces of pastry and honeyed nuts, the plate in front of him was empty.

"What do you want to do," Rob asked concerned. "You look cold and wet." He refilled her cup with hot coffee and handed it to her. "I have another sweater in my bag, if you want it."

Thea shook her head, hunched over her coffee cup. "I'll be fine," she reassured him, deliberately throwing off his concern, although she shivered in her wet clothes. "I didn't expect we'd get caught in such a storm." She rubbed her arms for warmth as she quickly considered the options before them. "Let's see if we can rent a couple of rooms for the night," she said, taking charge of the situation. "How many euros do you have? They probably accept only cash here."

Rob reached for his wallet. It was made of soft brown leather, well-worn and scuffed. He tipped out the contents in front of her, placing a handful of notes on the table. Thea silently counted them. Adding her own limited cash, it didn't appear enough.

"Let me speak with the proprietor and see what I can negotiate," Thea offered. The woman looked up from the reception desk as Thea approached her. The conversation now flowed easily in Greek, as Thea explained their predicament. But as they discussed the room rental for the night, Thea could feel her anxiety mounting as she gripped the wad of notes tightly in her hand. The response was not what Thea had hoped. Finally beaten, Thea returned to Rob, who had been sat watching the exchange.

"What did she say?" asked Rob. "You don't look happy."

"She can offer us room and board for the night, but," she hesitated slightly, trying to steady her voice, "we'll have to share."

"*Echei dyo krevatia, to domatio* ?" asked Thea turning once more to their propietress, wanting to reassure herself that at least the beds would be separate.

"*Echei dyo krevati e diplo, opos theleis,*" nodded the woman, trying to put her mind at ease.

"She can offer us a twin bedded room," explained Thea, omitting to translate the whole sentence. The beds, either as singles or doubles, could be arranged as they wished. Although she didn't know why, being deprived of her solitary refuge unnerved her as did being in close proximity to this man.

"Don't worry. I'm used to bunking up with colleagues down in the Pole." Rob was sat comfortably on his chair, his arms stretched out behind him. "I'm sure we'll manage for one night."

Keen to secure their business, the proprietor now motioned Thea over to accept the offer. "*Einai poly oraio to domatio,*" she said encouragingly.

"She is saying it is a lovely room", Thea translated.

"Well at least let's take a look," Rob suggested casually and he nodded his approval. They followed their Greek host up an external white staircase. The wind was still gusting and rain spattered the white marble steps. The light in the upstairs corridor was muted but everything appeared clean and well kept. Part way along, the woman unlocked a dark wood-stained panelled door.

"Very nice," the woman said beaming in broken English, turning to Rob. She obviously recognised him as an ally for the deal that was being brokered.

A single light shade illuminated the room, casting a yellow pallid light. The room was simply furnished with pine furniture, a polished tiled floor and white-painted walls, giving the illusion of airiness. But it was the two beds pushed together in the centre of the room which instantly caught Thea's attention. The only splash of colour was the pair of curtains, bright scarlet like a warning beacon, which the woman now pulled back to reveal the balcony beyond. The dim light of the dying storm entered the room, revealing the sudden drop to the bay below.

"The view looks stunning," Thea commented biting her lip, still feeling uneasy at the proposed arrangement and begrudging having to share her personal space.

"This will do fine," said Rob without hesitation, "let's take it," overruling any doubts. He nodded at their host, who broke into a broad grin. The woman busied herself in the wardrobe, pulling out a stack of woollen blankets.

"*Kryo*," she said, rubbing her arms and mimicking shivering for Rob's benefit. "You sleep well tonight," and she handed the pile to Thea. The transaction completed, the woman withdrew, leaving them alone in the room together.

"Which bed do you want? Left or right?" asked Rob, flinging his wet rucksack on the floor with a heavy thud. At once Thea realised any opportunity to change the lay-out of the room had passed. It would only draw attention to her intense discomfort. The furniture would have to stay in place.

"I'll take the side nearest the window," Thea responded, now resigned to her situation.

"You seemed to be talking to our hostess for a while. What were you discussing?" Rob asked.

"I enquired whether we could have help bringing the equipment and samples here. I'm assuming you would prefer not to leave anything valuable in the car overnight. Her husband will be back soon and can give you a lift so you can pick up what you need. You can store the equipment overnight in the storeroom next to the hotel."

"That sounds good." Rob grinned at her, fixing his eyes on her face. "Thanks for organising that. If you can translate for the husband, I can manage the rest."

"Angeliki will have dinner ready when you get back. Do you want to shower first, assuming there is hot water?" Thea paused, looking uncertain before the level-headed part of her took over again. "I noticed there's a hair dryer.

I could have a go at drying some of the wet clothes."

"Thanks," Rob said with a broad grin. "I could get used to this."

****

Darkness had fallen by the time Thea and Rob took their seats at the small table, set in a corner of the vestibule. The storm had eased to a rhythmic spattering of raindrops on the wide windows panes and squally gusts. The panoramic view was now obscured by black-ink darkness except for the light from a single fishing boat bravely venturing out into the vast expanse of sea. There was the smell of vanilla and wax from a burning tea-light candle, set in the middle of the table and creating a soft warm glow. A jumble of fresh flowers had been displayed on the table along with an assortment of appetisers: a plate of olives, glistening in an oily sheen, freshly cut bread and honey-coloured wine. It was obvious that their hostess Angeliki had gone to considerable trouble. As Thea cast her eye over the laid table registering the markers of intimacy, she felt a lurch in the pit of her stomach. Her skin was now bristling from static energy, the fine hairs stood on end. Was this a left-over from the storm or something about the presence of this man which disturbed her? Whatever it was, she quickly dismissed her anxiety.

It was for only one night, she told herself, *and at least she couldn't be ambushed by any unwanted phone calls*.

"So, how did you get involved in finding Odysseus' palace?" asked Rob, settling into his chair. "You seem pretty obsessive?" He was dressed in the fern-green fleece, half-zipped, he had worn earlier. The flickering candlelight danced on his face, accentuating the copper-blonde streaks of hair and the rugged creases of his skin. In the half-light, his eyes had become glassy and Thea noticed how the blue irises were flecked with hazel and the whiskers on his jaw grew not quite symmetrical.

"You're not the first person to say that to me," Thea replied, a memory shooting through her mind. A Sunday afternoon in London, when families or loving couples would be out strolling arm in arm on Hampstead Heath, enjoying the first touch of spring. A dappled light had filtered through the flat window onto her desk and the open books piled in front of her. And then a glance around the door and the stern expression on David's face speaking of disapproval, before the door had slammed shut. Thea's preoccupation, the search for a lost palace, had eroded their marriage and pulled them apart as surely as conducting an extra-marital affair. And yet in the early years together, that same academic drive and intellectual work had bound them together.

"It's a long story," Thea said, shrugging her shoulders to banish the memory. "I was always drawn to the story of Odysseus. I must have been a child of about nine years old, when my father first read it to me as a bedtime story." Her face lit up at the memory and she took a sip of wine. "Perhaps it was my father's story telling but the tales always fascinated me. The account of Odysseus' travels with the semi-magical places and mythical creatures he encountered like the Cyclops, the snake-headed Scylla and the whirlpool Charybdis. He always struck me as the true leader of the Greeks rather than Agamemnon." As she spoke more animatedly, she noticed how her skin had reddened under the influence of the wine. No doubt blotches had appeared on her throat and chest and without thinking, she lightly caressed the inflamed skin with her fingers. Rob reached towards her and carefully replenished her wine glass.

"So when Richard asked me to join the project," Thea continued, omitting Mark's role in convincing her, "naturally I said "yes". It was the opportunity of a lifetime." She looked up at him, smiling lamely and noticed he had been listening to her attentively.

"And is there anything you particularly admire about Odysseus?"

Thea hesitated, looking down for the moment, gathering her thoughts. "His shrewdness," she replied finally, feeling herself unravelling like flower petals in the sunlight. "His capacity to apply his human intelligence, no matter what the circumstances. For that he is my archetypal perfect man," she said, speaking unreservedly. The wine was loosening her tongue. "You could say I'm a little bit infatuated." The blush spread from her neck to her face, as the heat of the alcohol rose up in her body.

Thea glanced across at Rob. His eyes, bright and intelligent, were fastened on her face. The connection with this man sitting opposite struck her again. Thea popped an olive in her mouth, tasting the bitter flesh, as she tried to fathom where they had met before.

Had Richard introduced them at some point in the past? Thea wondered, but nothing readily came to mind.

"So what about you?" Thea asked, shifting the conversation from herself, still puzzled by the sense of familiarity. "How did you get involved with the Odysseus Project?"

There was a sharp intake of breath. "To be honest," said Rob, his fork poised over his plate, "I don't quite understand it myself." He turned his face upwards towards Thea wearing the same puzzled expression from earlier that day. "I've known Richard from my undergraduate days, so when he approached me and explained the work, I felt drawn to come." He paused to take a mouthful of food, before continuing. "Our work is at quite a critical stage, so it makes no logical sense for me to be here."

"You work in the Antarctic?" Thea asked, her curiosity aroused, recalling Richard mentioning this fact. "What do you do down there?"

"I'm one of the geo-physicists at the Halley Research Centre," Rob answered modestly without any conceit. "Myself and the team study climate change and its impact on the polar ice-caps and weather systems." His words did not betray his eminence Mark had enlightened her of.

"That must be interesting. And worthy too," she added.

A broad grin broke across Rob's face. "The pole is certainly a very magical place, the last wilderness on earth. In the winter the sun never sets and in summer it never rises." There was a faraway look on his face, as if recalling an absent lover. "And we suffer severe weather," Rob continued. "Blizzards that can keep us trapped inside for days until a window in the weather opens. Then we work day and night to collect samples from the field." A gust of wind suddenly rattled the pane and a door slammed shut deep inside the building. "It's very methodical work," he said, his face lighting up with enthusiasm, "not glamorous," but his expression spoke otherwise.

"So I guess today's storm was a stroll in the park."

"You could say that."

Thea glanced at Rob with renewed respect. For a man living at the extremes of nature and prominent in his field, he rather understated his feats and accomplishments.

"Have you always worked there?"

Rob poured out more wine for them both, a droplet of wine dampening the table-cloth. "Since I got my doctorate, I've spent six months each year down there. It can get pretty cramped at times, but we stay connected to the outside world through satellite. And of course it gives me lot of time to computer model things and write academic papers." He looked up, measuring her response as if expecting her to censure him.

"I can imagine that must have been hard on your personal life." It was difficult to imagine this vibrant man cloistered away from civilisation for months on end, with only a few other human beings for company.

"Yes, it took its toll on my marriage." A look of pain stole behind Rob's eyes, almost imperceptibly. He took a mouthful of wine, quickly swallowing it. "Jane and I met at University," he continued, "and married when we were young. I was away a lot through work, so Jane more or less was left to raise our son single-handedly." He paused, toying with the collar of his sweatshirt, struggling for words. "Unfortunately through my absence we drifted apart and eventually she did meet someone else. Someone who could give her the companionship she craved." Rob smiled wistfully and Thea noticed the roots of his hair had flushed crimson. "To be fair, my work was very hard on Jane."

He turned his chin upwards towards Thea. "And you? I understand from Richard, you're not in a relationship?" Her ears immediately pricked up that her marital status had been a subject of gossip and speculation.

"Yes, it's true," she replied brushing aside any offence. "David, my husband... I mean former husband", Thea said quickly correcting herself, "and I split up about six months ago. In very different circumstances," she said her voice cracking. Somehow speaking the words out aloud made her situation more real.

"I'm sorry." Rob said sympathetically. "Had you been together long?"

"About ten years." She looked down at her glass, refusing to betray her pain, as her fingers played with the glass stem. "It was sad, but it had just run its course." The words came out measured but she knew, now in her late thirties and with the biological clock ticking, her decision to leave the marriage childless and abandon the prospect of parenthood had fractured her. She paused for a moment to compose herself, repressing the tangled web of grief. "I think it had become a marriage of habit, like a comfortable pair of old shoes. David was always a very safe and reliable person," Thea continued, surprised by how easily she was unburdening herself to her dining companion. "But perhaps in the end, that was the problem." She sat back in her chair and now regarded Rob directly, noticing his attentive and sympathetic eyes. "We took each other for granted. We got ourselves into a rut, which we found impossible to get out of. And he came to resent my work and obsession with Odysseus."

The metal clank of serving dishes heralded the entrance of Angeliki with a tray laden with food. They fell into an awkward silence, the intimacy suspended, as their hostess carefully set down the bowls of food in front of them. A waft of sweet cinnamon and fried potatoes permeated the air.

"Let's eat," said Thea, changing the mood, scooping the home made Moussaka and *choriatiki* "peasant" salad onto their plates. They devoured the food with pleasure, discovering they shared a voracious appetite.

"*Einai endaksi?*" Angeliki their hostess hovered nearby, anxious to check that her cooking met with her guests' approval.

"*Poly kala,*" Thea replied with a warm smile.

"What did she say?" asked Rob, feeling left out of the exchange.

"I was assuring Angeliki that her food is really good," Thea explained. Rob nodded and grinned his appreciation to Angeliki. Pleased with her guests' response, a beaming Angeliki picked up the empty wine carafe to refill it.

"You know that hospitality and generosity is extremely important to the Greeks," Thea explained always taken by surprise by the heart-warming experience. "It's in their DNA. They even have a special word for it," she added, "*filoxenia*, a love of strangers."

Angeliki had returned with a refilled carafe in her hand. As she set it down on the table, she gave Thea a knowing glance and wink, like a village match-maker. Thea ignored the signals hoping they had gone undetected by her dining companion. Covering her awkwardness, she chose to move the conversation onto safer ground.

"So is there much evidence for climate change?" she began.

At once the mood shifted and Rob's face became more sombre. This clearly meant something to him. "Unfortunately yes," he replied after a sharp intake of breath. There was a hint of anger, but the expression on his face was steady and calm. "We are seeing the ice-sheets shrink back and the edge of the sea-line moving, year by year. But the danger isn't only from temperature change." He paused, holding his wine glass in front of him, turning it in the flickering candlelight, which danced on the crystal. "Dumped plastic waste and micro-particles are emerging in the seas, the wildlife and even virgin snow." His brows knotted together and it was the first time Thea had observed him scowling. "The Antarctic is the last wilderness on the planet, but it has become an expendable commodity, a casualty to overconsumption and modern human lifestyles. To meet modern demand, we would require three or four planet earths. But forgive me, I'm preaching at you."

He fell silent, a sense of despair lingering in the air. To dwell on this uncomfortable truth was too hard and he carried a heavy burden on his shoulders.

"It reminds me of the myth of Prometheos," Thea hesitantly offered.

Rob looked up puzzled. "How so?"

"You know the story of how Prometheos

helps mankind?" Taking Rob's silence for a *no*, Thea continued. "At the dawn of creation Epimetheos, his brother, is tasked by the gods to share out all resources amongst living creatures. Unfortunately Epimetheos, whose name means *No Forethought*, is not very smart." She noticed she had captured Rob's full attention. "So he happily distributes different characteristics to all species but forgets about humans who are left naked and cold."

"Go on," Rob said encouragingly, she assumed out of politeness as the connection with climate change was not obvious.

"So taking pity on them, Prometheos, his brother, steals fire and the technologies belonging to the gods, like science, the arts and writing. All the outward symbols of a civilised society. But the gods severely punish him for upsetting the order and balance of the cosmos."

"Is that the hero where an eagle feeds on his liver each day, which then regenerates overnight?"

Thea nodded. "The Greek gods made the punishment fit the crime, for Prometheos taking what did not belong to him and disturbing the natural ordering. Because," she paused, lifting her chin for the punchline, "Prometheos elevated the human race to semi-divine status. Consequently in Greek wisdom, humans were perceived as being in constant danger of overstepping themselves, what the Greeks called *hubris*, making them the most dangerous creature on the planet."

"I guess there's a strong ring of truth in that story," Rob replied thoughtfully. "Especially as the liver rids the human body of toxins and waste. Certainly we act as if we own planet earth, rather than respecting it and living in a sustainable way. But please forgive me, as I'm lecturing you again."

"It's clearly something you care passionately about and is massively important." And a moment of understanding passed between them.

"But tell me," Rob said steering the conversation back to her. "I think this is not your first visit to the island. You seem to know your way around here so well and speak Greek like a local."

"Yes, when I was younger. It was a long time ago and probably even Richard doesn't know." Thea tried to respond lightly and brush off the question, but she could feel her body tense and her face burning. "It was a time in my life that was very difficult so I'd prefer not to talk about it." The memory of the earlier conversation with Richard flooded back and panic gripped her again.

How on earth could she avoid this meeting with Mr Dimitri Kampitsis? Thea wondered. Rob must have picked up her sudden change in mood as he did not press her with further questions.

"It's getting quite late. Shall we turn in?" Rob suggested. "We have an early start tomorrow."

"Yes, of course."

They both rose together making their way out of the empty dining area. Thea expressed thanks to their hostess, who had been watching out for their departure. After further compliments for the hospitality and "*Kali nikta*", they stepped out into the chill night air, climbing the external staircase to the room.

Thea busied herself in the bathroom still distracted in her thoughts. With the familiar routine of cleaning her face and teeth, using the basic toiletries she had procured, she hoped to calm her jangled nerves. The ice-cold water splashed on her face brought her back to her senses.

She would have to give this meeting further thought, she told herself, as she brushed her teeth. *It could wait until tomorrow.*

Turning off the tap, she glimpsed her appearance in the tarnished mirror. The flush on her face had vanished, replaced by a pale luminescent reflection with almond shaped eyes framed by copper-spun hair. As she stepped into the room, Rob was sat awkwardly on the bed fiddling with his phone.

"Bathroom is free," she said, holding the door open.

"Thanks," Rob nodded. He brushed passed her and immediately she felt it: the sensation like an electrical charge striking her body. Turning her head upwards, Rob was staring down at her with the same quizzical expression he had worn earlier, scrutinising her face. For a second they stood transfixed, each regarding the other. Only when Rob leaned in towards her, his mouth reaching for her lips, was the spell broken.

Chapter 11

The Witch

He could feel a slight breeze on his face, stroking the whiskers of his beard. The air was sweet-laden with the smells of the first harvest, of ripening golden barley and yellow bitter-sweet fruits. He could feel the rays of Helios on his face, but softer and mellower than before, bathing his face in a warm glow. From the far distance, came noises of chatter. The shrill cries of the women and the deeper calls of the men as they worked the land.

A familiar voice was whispering into his ear. It came again, so close he could feel the moist breath. "Father?" In his half-sleep, Odysseus recognised it as Telemachos. But he was not ready to wake-up, not yet, not now. He knew his bones were growing old, as never before would he have slept while others toiled. With old-age now upon him, surely the gods could allow him this grace. A soft woollen coverlet had been placed over him, against the *Zephyr* who took mischief in the afternoon, whipping up the sea and foaming the waves. He wrapped the blanket tighter around himself, as *Sleep* overpowered him this time with sweet dreams.

For two whole days, the men had slept on the edge of that beach, where they had first made landfall. Their bodies aching from the endless rowing, barely had they stirred except to slake their raging thirst. Only on the third day, he felt at last the strength returning to his weary limbs. While the men slept, Odysseus had roused himself early, his heart restless to take measure of this new land. They appeared to be on an island: on which a steep mountain rose up, its slopes covered in dense woodland.

At least, he calculated, *they would have fuel for the fire and timber to repair to the ship.* The pain of losing the other ships and men suddenly struck him like an arrow. *Had Agamemnon's recklessness brought this upon all their heads?* He could afford no time for sentiment if they were to survive the winter. He glanced around again. The land appeared to be fertile with plenty of game and wild boar to fill their bellies. But also, where they had beached the boat, there was a secure harbour with a fresh-water spring. The gods had favoured them with an ideal wintering place until the seas calmed.

Arming himself with his spear and sharp-blade

sword, he resolved to climb up higher to take in a better view of this strange island and any signs of people. The dappled light broke through the tall trees, as he clambered over the steep rocky hillslope, until he reached a point where the woodland gave way to a clearing. All was still and quiet, except for the murmuring of the breeze in the leaves and the beating of his heart. He gazed around from his vantage point. This was not an island as he had first thought but a promontory, stretching out into the water still connected to the wide-way land like a babe corded to its mother. But more significantly, he could see wisps of grey smoke from a hearth curling up through the trees. They were not alone.

Odysseus' first urge was to set off by himself to find the dwelling, but then he restrained himself. *If there were people nearby*, he reasoned, *could he be sure of a friendly reception? Better return to the men so they could explore in numbers.* He turned back towards the shore camp.

It was as he made his way down the mountain, *Chance* put into his path a stag deer. The creature stood poised, its high antlers upright, its nostrils sniffing the breeze. It had come to drink the cool water of the mountain spring. Making sure he was downwind, as his grandfather Autolykos had taught him, soundlessly Odysseus raised and aimed his spear. The animal issued a scream, falling to the ground in front of him, writhing in its death throes until its spirit departed.

At least the men could enjoy a full meal and satisfy their hunger, he thought.

The beast was too big to carry over his shoulder. So he cut off supple young branches to twine into rope by which he could drag the carcass back. As he entered the camp, for the first time in many waxes of the moon, *Hope* returned to him. At last the gods had provided something good for the first time since they had left Troy, to raise up the spirits of the men exhausted by hard sweat and misfortune.

It wasn't until the next day that he called the men together, after they had finished feasting on the stag roasted over an open fire. He glanced around at the expectant faces, some still gnawing bones stripping every last morsel of meat. It was the first good meal they had eaten in days. After the disastrous encounters with the barbaric Cyclops and the Laistrygonians, he knew in his heart they would not like his plan. They had lost so many dear friends and fellow warriors, the survivors of Troy, on that ill-starred journey home. But they were lost and to survive they needed help from these local people, whoever they might be.

Odysseus broke the news to his men of what he had seen, using his most persuasive arguments:

the smoking fire, signs of human habitation. The reluctance and fear of the men were palpable and he could see on their faces that the hardships of that return voyage had taken their toll. With their ragged clothes, their matted beards and soiled faces, weakened by misfortune, hunger and toil, he scarcely recognised them as the proud conquering heroes of Troy, full of confidence and bravado. But to survive, they had to leave the safety of the camp to explore this new land and learn who these strangers were, whether friendly or hostile.

As he divided the men into two parties, no one raised an objection. Perhaps they were too weak to protest.

"You Eurylochos," he said, addressing his captain, "shall lead one company and I the other." He glanced across at him. Since they had left Troy, the soft mouth had become harder set with a curled lip. They drew lots pulled from a bronze helmet with high set horse-hair plume, to decide who would venture out from the safety of the camp. The task fell to Eurylochos.

"Have a heed my dear friend," he said, clasping Eurylochos to his chest as they said their farewells. "And if there is danger, take no chances." Eurylochos nodded, confident in the long spears and burnished swords, with which he and the men had armed themselves. "And may the gods protect you," Odysseus added, his words full of emotion.

They had passed the time as best they could, gathering firewood, refilling the goatskins with fresh water and erecting a makeshift shelter. The Sun god Helios had reached his highest zenith in the sky, when Eurylochos burst into the camp, breathless and sobbing, scared out of his wits. He was alone. "There's a witch!" he yelled, panting, his voice cracked with fear. "She's bewitched the men and turned them into swine!"

He hardly recognised Eurylochos from the bold warrior who had strode out that very morning with the well-equipped party of armed soldiers. His face had turned ashen and tears were rolling down his cheeks. His encounter with the so-called witch had transformed him into a jabbering husk. The men were now crowding round and straight away he could smell the fear at Eurylochos' distraught appearance. If he Odysseus didn't contain this, *Chaos* would quickly stalk amongst them like the plague, draining their spirits and loosening their minds.

"Calm yourself Eurylochos," he spoke more sharply than he intended. "Tell us what you saw. What did you witness with your own eyes? So we may learn what you know and prepare ourselves for this danger."

He gestured to one of the men to bring his sword. "You cannot go," Eurylochos responded anxiously, openly sobbing. "For surely you will perish too!" He clutched Odysseus by the shoulders to restrain him.

"Of course I must go," Odysseus replied firmly. "The men out there are our comrades. How will we look their fathers or sons in the eye, if we do not try to save them? As they would do us. Surely you realise that."

At his words, Eurylochos grew more frantic. "I cannot go back Odysseus." His grip tightened. "Do not force me," he beseeched. "We must escape the witch while we can. I beg you Odysseus. Let us put the ships to sea and leave this accursed place."

Odysseus loosened Eurylochos' grip, covering his fingers with his calloused hands. "Come my dear friend, tell me what you know so I may discern whether this is an immortal living amongst us or a mortal woman." He spoke to him soothingly like a mother comforting a small child. So Eurylochos told what he knew, starting from the beginning to the very end.

At the end of the story, Odysseus was quiet for a while, weighing things up in his mind. Finally he steadily replied. "I have heard of such stories, long ago, but never believed they were true. Of men being changed into forest beasts. Myself and three others will go and witness for ourselves this Sorceress. We will return with the men." He glanced around him to see nods of approval. "But before we go, a god has put in my mind a thought. There is a plant, Moly, said to grow as the moon wanes and to protect against the magic arts. These hill slopes would favour it. Let us search for it before we set out."

In a shady hollow not far from the camp, they found the pungent herb growing. They dug it up out of the earth and four of them quickly chewed the creamy bulbs. Buckling his sword sheath and slinging his bow over his shoulder, he set out.

They made their way through the woods, following in the direction where he had first glimpsed the dwelling with the smoking fire. There was no discernible path, so their progress was slow as they made their way along the rough ground, their feet obscured by undergrowth and shade loving plants. The shadows were growing longer when at last they came across a clearing. Human hands had stripped back the forest. They stood completely still, silent, listening for sounds on the breeze. Apprehension was in the pallid faces of the men and their bodies stiff, as they gripped their weapons. Odysseus nodded and cautiously they ventured into the clearing, no longer under the forest's protection.

A small bird landed on a branch, so close that

the turtle-shell markings could be seen on the wing feathers. It chirruped a sweet warble undisturbed by their presence. Strips of torn cloth had been hung on the tree branches, giving the place a strange enchanted atmosphere. It was then they had noticed the animal enclosures, made from woven willow twigs and supple branches. Odysseus' brow furrowed. Dangerous wild animals, mountain lions and wolves that ranged in the mountains, were caged inside quite contentedly.

"The witch must have beguiled them," whispered Neritides, beads of sweat running from his forehead. "How else would these creatures stomach being kept like pet dogs?"

"This has the appearance of a sacred precinct," said Odysseus quietly as he turned his head to observe the neat and ordered pens in the clearing. Someone tended the beasts well. "Perhaps a local cult practised by the people here. Come, let us discover more." They stealthily advanced, passing the animal enclosures and tame wild deer and boar grazing unperturbed by their presence. They could see a well-built lodging, stone clad not unlike the great *megara* he had seen at Mykenai. It was then they spied the lost men. It was as Eurylochos had described, they were grovelling through the dirt ground on all fours acting like swine. Softly they called out their names, but the bewitched men took no notice and continued with their scavenging.

He could feel the anger rising in his chest at the scene he had witnessed. *Whoever had done this to his men, would pay a dear price*, he thought, as he reached the steps leading up to the dwelling. His companions now faltered, frightened perhaps by Eurylochos' tale or the shock of seeing their warrior comrades transformed. The pride of the Greek army crawling in the mud like pigs. Witch or no witch, he was determined to discover the cause, whether this be the work of a god or a mortal.

As he climbed the polished stone steps, he could taste the bitter outrage in his mouth. The heavy-studded wooden doors were barred shut. There was no sign of life. He was in no mood for the rules of *xenia*.

"Come out, whoever you are and show yourself," he shouted, banging his fist on the door. "I would speak with you!" He strode across the columned porch, his metal sword scrapping on the stone floor.

For a moment nothing stirred. Then the double doors slowly opened, as if taunting him, and she had stepped forth: the witch.

She stood silhouetted in the dark doorway holding a wooden baton. Her hair was unbraided, snaking down her sides in long curled tresses, deeper in colour than spun copper. She wore a simple mantle dyed fern-green, which modestly covered the length of her body. The witch was stood upright, contemplating him with her clear green orbs.

"Welcome, strangers to our house." Her soft voice rang out clearly, addressing him in his own language. "You have come to the sacred precinct and shrine of the goddess Feronia. My name is Kirke, named so after the wild falcon that nests in these hills. Please enter," she said gesturing them inside, "so that we may entertain you with wine and food as befits a traveller." Her words belied the tales he had heard of her.

It was not as he had expected. On the surface she seemed well born, even educated and spoke his language. Odysseus' first instinct had been to run her through with his sword, like a skewered piece of meat. He had marked the spot to plunge his weapon into her heart, just where the rounded bosom swelled beneath the tunic. He steadied his hand. *Whatever spell they were under, he needed to find out.* He suppressed his rage and with gritted teeth followed the witch.

She showed him into the ante-chamber of the house, where well-appointed tables and chairs had already been placed. Their arrival was not unexpected. There was murmurs in the background: light youthful voices. In the shadows, he caught a glimpse of maiden figures, eyeing him with a mix of curiosity and suspicion.

"Will your companions not also join us?" the witch asked calmly. "For I will ensure you are all looked after well. Please call them inside, while I prepare a drink for you."

Her back was turned. He had no doubt that she was tampering the wine-bowl with some drug of bad intent. He gestured to the men to cross the threshold. They stood guarded, shifting from side to side. None was inclined to sit and rest.

"Here," she said unperturbed, handing out the wine cups one by one. "Please drink, as is right for guests to this house." Courteously she pressed a cup into his hand but was watching him keenly. *It was a trick*. Finally his wrath got the better of him as he hurled the cup away, smashing it into pieces on the floor.

The witch flinched taken by surprise, the sweet smile fading from her lips. He reached for his sword and jabbed it against her throat, pinning her against the wall. As the blade pinched against her skin, even then she held her nerve and did not recoil.

"Please, put away your weapon." Her voice was calm, as she looked him straight in the eye without fear. "There is no need for violence," she urged.

"You would trick me witch! Use your sorcery

on us as you did with my men." He almost spat out the words at her, such was his fury. He could hear the pounding in his head as he readied to dispatch her. "With my own ears and eyes, I've witnessed your work. Do you think we are fools?"

"You are right," the witch replied. "I did give the men who came before a drugged potion. It is harmless and will wear off within two sunrises, when the men will be their selves again. They will be thick-headed for a while but otherwise will suffer no other harm. Please, put away your sword. I mean you and your men no harm. My intention was only to protect this sacred precinct."

He loosened his grip and slowly lowered his weapon, gesturing the men to hold back from further attack. He backed away, his eyes still firmly bolted on her as if watching a venomous snake.

"You speak my language," he asked, curiosity beginning to take over. "I have not heard Greek spoken in these strange lands. Tell me how did you learn it? And why should I trust you not to put an enchantment on us, if I let you go?"

Smoothing her tunic, where his hand-hold had gripped her, Kirke stood square to him. "I am mortal woman not a witch," she replied evenly, holding her chin high. "Many years ago my grandfather took in a man who was shipwrecked near these parts. He was the only survivor of a ship and claimed to come from the lands of the Achaian Greeks. It was he who tutored me as a child in your language. He prophesied that one day other men from Achaia would come to this sacred place. So your arrival was expected." Kirke lowered her glance, lighting on where he still clasped the sword-hilt. "Please sheathe your weapon and to demonstrate no harm is meant, allow me to entertain you unaccompanied in my private chamber."

Before he could answer, Kirke clapped her hands summoning a group of young women, who had been listening close by. Most were not long out of childhood, so smooth was their skin and lithe their bodies. They approached cautiously with bowed heads, their bodies trembling. Kirke addressed them in a language Odysseus' ears did not recognise to which the maidens nodded in response.

Turning to Odysseus once more, she spoke again. "These young women have been placed under my care in the service of the goddess. I have explained to them that it is safe," she paused, looking him directly in the eye. "That you and your men will not harm them." He nodded his head to re-assure her. "They will show you a spring where you can wash yourselves and will provide oil for your skin, as I believe is your custom." She regarded his stained and thread-bare warrior clothing, where the long sea crossing had frayed and torn the cloth, and a look of understanding crossed her brow. "We can offer fresh garments to you and your companions."

Suspecting a trap, he had answered sharply. "No, we are fine dressed as we are."

Understanding his distrust, Kirke smiled. "As you wish. Then when you are ready," she continued, "and have cleansed yourself of the warrior's stain, one of the maidens will show you to my quarters." With that, she had turned and left him open-mouthed.

****

"Surely you will not go to her chamber, *Basileos*?" Neritides had stopped him, grabbing onto his arm. "It is a trap to poison you with magic herbs or entrap you by some other mischief."

"What fear can I have," Odysseus answered with certainty. "For she is only a woman." He felt restored from bathing, ridding from his body the brine which clung to his skin and hair. "Besides I will keep my sword close by," he grinned.

As he stepped in the chamber, it took time for his eyes to adjust to the darkened room. A lighted torch hung against the wall flickered, giving off a soft golden glow. It smelt of candle fat, smoke but more pleasantly of mountain herbs. The room was simply furnished with a small window high set in the stone built walls, letting in the fading glow of Helios.

He had not seen Kirke at first, but the sound of her voice alerted him to her presence.

"Come, join me." She was sat on a well-carved chair, a table beside her. She gestured to the empty chair, similarly fashioned, beside her. "Please let me entertain you with food and wine." At her summons, several maidens entered the chamber, bearing baskets laden with fruits, meat and wine, which they set out before them and then, with a slight bow of their heads, left.

Alone, Kirke beckoned him to eat, pouring a beaker of undiluted wine and proffering it into his hand. She saw him hesitate.

"I mean you no harm," she began, noticing his suspiciousness. "If you are still afraid of trickery, I will taste the food and wine first to show it is safe." Kirke took his goblet out of his hand and swallowed. Next, she broke off a hunk of meat and slowly chewed it. Reassured, he took a sip of the wine and did likewise. The wine was palatable to drink and he could feel a warmth entering his bones and spreading through his body.

"You keep your own chamber?" he asked, studying her appearance more fully. He had never been alone in the company of an unveiled high born woman. He noticed her deep copper tresses had been braided and twisted, but some wisps of hair still escaped. She wore a long sleeved mantle, the colour of deep woodland, tied in a girdle at the waist. The cloth was well made although simpler than the exquisite loom-work of Penelope, his wife. But it was Kirke's eyes that unnerved him. The way she returned his gaze, without lowering her face or turning away.

"I do," she replied steadily. "This room is for my own convenience. The others sleep elsewhere in the house."

"Do you not have a husband whom you serve? To share your bed and protect you and the young maidens here?"

"I need no man," she replied casually, looking him in the eye with that same direct stare. Again he felt unsettled by this woman who acted like an equal to a man and spoke his language. "There are many men who have asked me as their bride," Kirke continued, "and were prepared to pay a bride price to my family. But my fate was decided long ago to be the priestess at this shrine. Here I hold sway over the sacred precinct and all those who serve the goddess Feronia. Why would I need to take a man as my husband?"

"How did you become a priestess?" he had asked, his curiosity fired.

She smiled at his question, so that he felt almost foolish like a smooth cheeked boy. "I have the gift of healing and the knowledge of plants and wild animals," she explained patiently. "These skills were taught to me by my mother, who acquired them from her mother before having been passed down through the generations. My mother was the priestess here at the shrine, before her marriage when she left the precinct to live as a wife with my father. Through her I learnt the old wisdom, how to tame the forest beasts, how to recognise plants with healing properties and how to prepare special potions for those who are afflicted."

He inhaled sharply. "So you are a sorceress?" he demanded.

"No," she replied, speaking firmly, "though it is sometimes suits us for men to believe that it is so. That they may stay away from harming us through fear. I am a healer."

"But you turned my men into swine!" His anger swelled again at the thought of his men grovelling in the mud like swine. "How can you not be a witch or a sorceress?"

"It was done only that we might protect ourselves," Kirke calmly replied. "Your men came dressed as warriors, entering the precinct armed with weapons of *War* and fighting. How could we know that you intended to do us no harm?" She looked up, squarely meeting his eyes, a smile playing on her lips. "You use weaponry to have your way, we use more peaceful methods."

"So tell me," Kirke asked, pouring more wine into his cup, "what is your name and why have you come to these shores?"

A shadow flitted across his mind, but he did not betray this sentiment. "You are correct in your assertion that we are warriors. My name is Odysseus, the king and leader of the bravehearted Kephallenians. We are returning from war, which we fought for ten long years on the distant shores of Troy, before capturing the city." He swallowed deeply, the words now sticking in his throat. "On our return journey, our boats were blown off course by storms and many grievous misfortunes have befallen us. Many men, dear companions, were lost along the way so what you see is now a depleted group." He felt again the urgency of their predicament bearing down on him. "Our islands are in the direction of the Little Bear and I fear are many days by sea. We are looking for a place to shelter over the stormy winter."

"I am sorry for your plight," Kirke replied kindly, not lifting her gaze from his face. "You and your men are welcome to stay here until the calmer seasons return when once more you may go on your way. Send word to your men, if it comforts you, to haul the ships onto the land and store your goods in the caves. Invite them to come and eat here, as we have food aplenty for all."

"You are very courteous," he replied, his spirit suddenly lifted by her words, like a huge boulder that had been pressing down on him had been raised from his back. A god stirred a feeling in his chest. He could not name it outright. Towards a fellow man, it might have been called "gratitude", but this was a woman. He lapsed into silence, remembering all the hardships and trials he had endured since they had left Troy.

After a pause Kirke spoke again. "I can see you have suffered much. You are a warrior, more used to fighting on land than to a life wandering the seas, at the mercy of the sea god. To see the lives of your men cut short, although the gods must have willed it, must cause you deep anguish. You are a man more comfortable with determining your own destiny." She reached out and touched his arm soothingly. "Though you may doubt it, I believe the gods will help you find your way home."

They had then spoken of sorrows he had never before dared utter aloud, not even to Eurylochos, his boyhood friend. The sea journey had been deeply disturbing, throwing him off balance and taking him away from all that was familiar. It was as if a god had given this woman the power to see into his mind and understand him. It was deeply unsettling how she addressed him as an equal but there was something about Kirke to which he felt strangely drawn.

He looked again at her anew, this time not as a foe to be skewered but as a woman. Her face was darkened by the sun, not pale from living indoors as a noble-born woman. The lines around her face intimated she was a woman in her prime, past the first bloom of youth. He noticed beneath her woollen mantel, the outline of her rounded body and full breasts, emphasised by the girdle. She was very different from his wife Penelope, who had been only just out of childhood when she had come as a trembling bride to his house. Sitting beside this perplexing woman, he found himself overcome by a passion. Perhaps one of the arrows of Eros had struck him: as one had struck his kinswoman Helen, when she eloped with her Trojan lover.

He felt his member rising and recognised it as *Desire*. It felt like a madness he'd never experienced before. Never at Troy had he taken pleasure in womanising, unlike Agamemnon, seeing it as an obstruction to their mission and his return to his life on Ithaka. He tried to summon up the memory of his youthful love for his wife. Her raven hair, the silky skin and the small mounds of breasts. It was so long since he had beholden her face, the image was clouded and far away. But the more he struggled to fight *Desire*, the more the hunger raged. Finally he could stem the promptings of Eros no longer.

"I would lie with you, Kirke," he said. "Let us to bed."

Chapter 12

Courtship

She felt his weight on her body, his mouth urgently seeking her own. His fingers were exploring her, feeling her face, her arms, her shoulders and breasts. His embrace on her skin felt strange but also familiar, warm and encompassing. He fluctuated between respectful hesitancy and raging passion. Initially her body had resisted his pressure, but then yielded allowing him to enter her deeply. So intoxicating was the sensation, that even if she had wanted, her body now refused to pull back. She gave into it, responding to his rhythm until a crescendo was reached. She clung tightly to him as she felt him spend himself and heard her own voice crying out in the night.

Afterwards they slept together peacefully, their bodies closely entwined. As daylight filtered through the shutters, he leaned into her again, his touch light as he caressed her smooth skin with his coarse weathered hands. This time he made love to her slowly and tenderly, no longer with frantic urgency, until they both succumbed to exhaustion.

When Thea awoke, beams of silver light were flooding into the room. She reached across and felt the empty space next to her. The indent on the ruffled sheet was cold to the touch and instinctively Thea realised that side of the bed was empty. He had gone. Blinking back sleep, Thea raised herself onto her elbows and glanced around. It was then she saw a note, a torn piece of paper, neatly folded on the bedside table beside her. Reaching over for it, she read the words hastily written. *Gone to the car. Back shortly. Rob x.* Only the cross hinted at any sign of affection.

Thea grimaced, pulling herself out of the cold sheets. *What had she done?* She felt a moistness on her body. *She needed a shower.* The water from the solar heating system was tepid, as Thea hastily bathed and scrubbed herself. Her crumpled clothes were still scattered across the bare stone floor, which she picked up, quickly dressing herself. Angeliki was waiting for her, as she descended into the foyer.

"*Kalimera.*" Her hostess' welcome was somehow comforting and stemmed the deepening anxiety rising up inside.

"*Kalimera-sas.*" Thea said, returning the greeting and allowing herself to be directed to same table, which they had occupied only the previous evening. Angeliki disappeared, re-emerging with a tray of hot coffee, fresh rolls, juice, pots of honey and apricot conserve. Her hostess stayed briefly to chat and keep Thea company. It did not take long to discover Rob's whereabouts. He had left with Angeliki's husband an hour ago, as Thea slept, but there was uncertainty when he would return.

"*Einai o andros sou?*" enquired Angeliki with a knowing smile.

The directness of the question startled Thea. "*Ochi,*" she replied firmly, raising her eyebrows, as she explained Rob was not her husband but a colleague.

"*Omorfo zevgari!*" With that Angeliki departed for the kitchen, leaving a perplexed Thea to stare after her.

Despite her natural aversion, Thea for once appreciated the warm instant coffee. Eagerly she took sips of the piping liquid in the hope of it clearing her head clouded from the wine. She felt slightly nauseous from the bitter taste of last night's meal and the skin of her ankle was inflamed from a mosquito bite during the night. Thea pulled her woollen sweater closer round her, glad for its comfort and warmth. With the taste of bile in her mouth, she didn't feel like eating but made an attempt for the sake of her hostess Angeliki.

The promise of the early morning with its sunlight had vanished and thick clouds shrouded the full view of the bay. The sea was grey and tempestuous against the chalk-white cliffs. Thea hardly noticed the view, listlessly toying with her food. Since awakening, a gnawing sense of foreboding had been growing inside her. Angeliki's comments about making a good couple only unnerved her further. *What had happened must be written all over her face.* She quickly dismissed the thought but the feeling of being caught out like a wayward youth remained. *How could she have allowed it to happen? When there was already the complicating matter of Dimitri Kampitsis. And though she liked Rob there was an uncertainty, which puzzled her.*

The urgent sound of a car horn tore Thea away from her thoughts. A vehicle had pulled up outside, its wheels scrunching on the loose gravel. Rob's familiar form sat in the passenger side, waving towards her. Within seconds, he was greeting her enthusiastically, still dressed in the clothes from the previous day. A shudder ran down her body at the memory of their night.

"I hope I didn't wake you?" Rob began, as he strode towards her. "I thought it better to leave you sleeping, while I met the mechanic. We've arranged to have the car towed to a garage. Dionysios," he gestured towards the driver, "is here to drive us with the equipment back to the main town." Rob glanced more closely at her and flashed a smile. "I see you've got breakfast already. Do you need more time to finish? There's no rush as we've still to pack the car."

"I've just finished but can I get you something?" Thea noticed herself falling back into politeness to cover her awkwardness. "I'll see if I can sort out some coffee and rolls for you both if you're hungry," she said, grateful for an activity to distract herself.

"No, we're fine," Rob replied. "I ate earlier. Do you want to get your things from the room and we'll start loading the car. I'll come up and get my stuff in a few minutes." Thea nodded and with that he was gone.

Alone, Thea stepped into the room they had shared, the orderliness now disrupted by the pile of crumpled bed sheets and blankets strewn on the floor. Instinctively, Thea straightened the bed, smoothing down the sheets and covers, as if obliterating traces of any incriminating evidence. She started to gather together her few possessions and put them in her rucksack. For a moment, she held her copy of the Odyssey, idly thumbing through the pages, before placing it carefully into her day sack.

There was a quiet knock at the door, before Rob entered. "I've just come to retrieve my bag," he said, picking it up from the floor. "Are you alright," he asked solicitously, studying her face as she refused to meet his eyes. "You look pale."

"Just a little too much wine," Thea replied, feeling a slight wave of nausea wash over her. "I'll be alright."

"You're sure, as I could do with getting these samples back to the lab as soon as possible," he said and kissed her lightly on the forehead.

On the journey back, an awkward silence fell. Squashed against the hotchpotch of sample cases and equipment, it was difficult to think of what to say with the presence of a third person. Rob had been attentive as he helped Thea into the back seat, but now they both settled into polite conversation. Dionysios, the driver, had sensed the strained atmosphere, offering small talk about the weather, Greek politics and the logistics of getting a pick-up truck out to them.

After a while, they all lapsed into a stilted silence again. Thea watched through the window the sweep of the lagoon, as the car drove away from the gentle swell of Paliki. Despite having showered, Thea felt as if she carried the smell of him, a male scent imprinted on her body. A blush came over her cheeks, sure that the two men must also have noticed. As the outskirts of the main town approached, the emotional distance grew.

"We're going to take the samples back to the lab," said Rob shifting into professional mode, any intimacy firmly dispelled. "But first we'll drop you off at the hotel." He twisted his head round towards her. "You'll probably want to freshen up."

With the winding journey back to the town and civilisation, Thea's feelings of nausea had intensified. "That will be fine" she replied simply, feeling as if she was being dismissed.

Rob directed them through the town. The streets were quiet that Sunday morning and only a handful of people had ventured out, mostly elderly *yeia yeias* dressed in black, on their way to church. Or middle-aged women, clutching plastic bags from their trip to the patisserie, anticipating the arrival of the family brood later in the day. At last the car pulled up in front of the hotel and Thea swung open the heavy car door, gratefully taking a gulp of fresh air, whilst Rob courteously held it open for her.

"I'm going to be working most of the day," he said, "to get these samples processed. Would you like to go out later for something to eat?" For the first time on the journey, he looked at her directly and she caught an affectionate glance.

"Yes, I would like that," Thea replied, allowing herself to meet his eyes, though her skin prickled with a cold sweat.

"I'll be back in the hotel by early evening. Come and find me around eight o'clock. I'm in room 211."

After thanking Dionysios for coming to their rescue, Thea mounted the hotel steps as the car swept out of the hotel gates.

****

Darkness had fallen outside, as Thea made her way down the dim-lit corridor, trying the read the tarnished bronze room numbers. During the daytime, natural light flooded the space, with its airy white washed passage-way and high-ceiling windows. Her mood had been re-invigorated by the afternoon nap, which had cleared her head, and the fresh change of clothes. She had chosen to dress comfortably and for warmth, her lime-coloured tunic complementing her copper coloured hair. In front of a solid wooden door, bearing the numbers *211*, she stopped. She heard Rob talking loudly to some-one.

Had he forgotten their dinner? Thea wondered to herself as she knocked on the door, suppressing her feelings of insecurity. There was a delay before the door swung open.

"Come in. I've been expecting you," Rob grinned, steering her into the room. To her surprise, the room was empty. A laptop was sat open on the desk, where a chair had been pulled back.

"I'm just skyping my son," Rob explained, sensing her confusion. "Come and say hello."

Thea cautiously walked towards the brightly lit screen, which threw a blue-phosphorescent light into the room. Peering closer to the display, Thea could make out the features of a young male, casually dressed in a heavy checked shirt and pullover. The likeness to Rob was unmistakeable, only the features were softer and the skin less weathered by the sun.

"I'd like you to meet my son, Ryan," said Rob. "And this is my friend and colleague, Dr Thea Sefton." He ceremoniously introduced Thea with a sweep of his arm.

"Hello Thea," the camera shot of a young male casually replied, beaming out from the computer screen. "Dad's not mentioned you before," the voice continued. "I didn't know he was dating. Have you two been together long?"

Was it so obvious they had been intimate? she wondered, feeling her cheeks blushing, just as Rob stepped in to rescue her.

"Thea is working with me on the Odysseus Palace project." His words came breezily. "We were just about to go out for something to eat."

"You must be very privileged!" remarked Ryan, laughingly. "I've never known Dad to set aside his work so early in the evening. He usually lives a hermit's existence."

"Thank you Ryan," Rob interrupted, cutting his son short. "We'd better get going, so speak to you later. Can you pass on my regards to your grandfather? I'll see you both in a couple of weeks' time at the airport."

The younger man grinned, nodding "Will do, Dad. Good meeting you Thea." There was a familiar ping on the computer screen as the call was ended.

"Sorry about that," said Rob apologetically. "I'd forgotten that Ryan and I usually skype at this time. I hope you're not offended by what he said. He can be very direct."

"Not at all. It's good you both keep in contact."

"Shall we go?" he said, gesturing towards the door. He had changed his clothing and had made an effort with his appearance. His white cotton shirt was heavily creased and looked as if it had just been unwrapped from the packaging. His beard had been closely trimmed and Thea caught the pleasant aroma of sandalwood.

"I hope I look presentable?" he grinned. "I don't get much chance to shop for new clothes."

They headed out onto the promenade, where

a regimented row of street lights lit up the sea-front and waves lapped against the breakwater. On the opposite side of the gulf, the mountains were shrouded in darkness and only the glimmering lights dotted across the opposite hillside signalled the presence of small villages. As they walked, Thea noticed Rob kept a respectful distance as if the previous night's intimacy had created an invisible wedge.

"Where are we going?" asked Rob.

"There used to be a café close by," Thea replied. "The food's quite simple but always popular amongst the locals."

"That sounds like it meets the mark," he said, a good-humoured look on his face. "You lead on and I'll follow."

The restaurant was located on the edge of the town. Tables had been optimistically set out on the terrace anticipating the balmy summer, when office workers and guests might chat over a slow lunch, savouring the dramatic views across the gulf. A waiter greeted them warmly and ushered them into the interior, where a glass partition shut out the night chill. They were seated at a small table close together, so that their knees almost touched. Having surveyed the menu, they settled on a traditional Greek fare of hot chicken stew, steeped in wine and tomato and several plates of *mezedes*: giant beans, spanakopita, fried potatoes and *horta*, mountain greens. There were few other fellow diners that night, as others had either been put off by the chill of the wind or the still relatively early hour, for Greeks tended to eat late.

"Your son," said Thea, after placing their order, breaking the silence between them. "You resemble one another quite closely. Tell me more about him."

"Well," Rob said, resting his chin on his hand, his voice filling with pride, "as you know he's an only child. Following in my footsteps, he decided to study geophysics and earth sciences at Bristol. He would have joined the expedition but it clashed with exams."

"It must have been difficult for you both, being apart so much."

"It hasn't always been easy," Rob agreed, nodding his head. "As a child, he used to struggle with my absence and often took it out on his mother. He's always been close to his granddad, my father. It was he who taught Ryan how to play football, hunt for fossils and camp outdoors. Despite that, we're a close family." A look of pain, clearly visible, passed across his face. His absence was obviously a source of deep regret. He raised his head forcing a smile. "While I'm back in the UK, I'm hoping that we'll be able to spend more time together."

He turned and gestured to the waiter to bring more wine. "And what about you? Do you have children?" he asked.

"Unfortunately I don't," Thea responded lightly. She felt the heat rise to her face, remembering the herbal tincture she had prepared earlier, as a precautionary measure. She had been determined to take no chances.

"So what about the palace?" Rob asked, as the waiter deposited a full carafe in front of them and cleared away the assortment of empty plates. "You were keen on the idea that it is close to Mousatoi. Do you think we are any closer to finding it?"

"I'm not sure," Thea replied. "It's a hunch but there isn't much on the ground to see or in the old archives. I'm thinking of looking at the old archaeological reports for the village, but that would mean a trip to Athens. With Easter coming up next weekend, it may be quite tricky finding space on a flight."

Rob looked at her again, pausing as if weighing up whether to share a confidence or not. He lowered his voice, almost conspiratorially, as if not wanting their conversation to be overheard. "The provisional results we're getting from the tests seems to bear out the theory," he confided. "The samples show signs of marine life and you have to go a long way down before you hit solid bedrock."

"So what does that mean?" Thea asked, trying to figure out the significance of this information.

"It means that the geological evidence points to a channel of sea-water separating Paliki from the main part of the island." Rob raised his head towards her so that the clear blue irises of his eyes caught the light. "There must have been a massive landslide in antiquity, which isn't surprising given all the seismic activity in this area."

"Are you sure?" Thea could feel her excitement rising, like a hound picking up the scent of quarry.

"I can't be completely certain quite, but the findings so far fit the theory."

"How long before you will know for definite?"

"Six weeks' time, by the end of the field survey," Rob replied, sitting back in his chair. "Your plan to see what you can discover in Athens sounds good. It's better than the needle in a haystack approach and might help Richard more accurately pinpoint the palace location."

Thea raised her head, alert, her mind already formulating a plan. She had been considering going to Athens, but this decided the issue.

"I'll speak to Richard," she said firmly, "and see what can be arranged."

"By the way, you seemed to be unhappy after your conversation with Richard yesterday. Did he say something that upset you?" His perception startled Thea, as little seemed to escape his notice.

"He's wanting to set up a meeting between myself and our benefactor Mr Dimitri Kampitsis." At the mention of his name on her lips, her body stiffened, braced for the familiar surge of emotions. But as she tightened her grip around the wine glass, only a mild wave of dread washed over her. *The overnight trip to the uplands must have done me good*, she thought.

"And he wouldn't take *No* for an answer?" Just then Rob's phone went off with a buzz. Rob glanced at it before stuffing it back into his pocket, a fleeting scowl passing over his face and then vanishing like a summer shower. "Of course, you missed being introduced to him at the reception. Quite the local celebrity. Do you want me to join you at the meeting?" he asked, as if sensing her internal dilemma. "I noticed Richard can act quite deferential around our honourable patron."

"I can take care of it," Thea declined firmly, relieved not to be entangled by the gnawing dread but realising she had yet to come up with any plan. "Shall we get the bill?" she asked, keen to escape the gloomy topic.

Afterwards, they walked through the open expanse of the main square of the town, joining the procession of families, loving couples and young people out for an evening stroll. As they turned down the wide tree lined boulevard, Rob reached for her hand, entwining her fingers in his own. Just then, his phone started buzzing with an urgency.

"Someone is trying hard to get hold of you," Thea said, feeling a slight jolt in her stomach at the pressure of his fingers. Rob pulled out the mobile and snapped the button to silence it.

"It'll wait," he said, forcing a smile, staring hard at the offending object.

They were coming within sight of the hotel and Thea felt her heart began to thump, her pulse beating in her ears. It was then she realised that she had too much pride to ask the question directly weighing on her mind. *Where was this relationship heading?* Uncertain, Thea glanced across at Rob, trying to decipher his expression, but his face was inscrutable.

As they entered the hotel lobby, the shrill peal of Electra's laughter rang out. A dark-suited figure was leaning over the desk, as Electra flicked back a strand of hair. Rob had already let go of her hand, as Thea recognised, to her horror, the familiar figure of Stelios Ioannou.

"Ah, good evening Dr Sefton and Dr Hughes," Stelios came forward to greet them with exaggerated politeness, slightly bowing his head. "I dropped by in the hope of perhaps discovering you this evening, Dr Sefton. You can be a very difficult woman to track down."

"We've just been out for something to eat," Thea replied, the linguist in her intrigued by his Epiriot annunciation. It struck her Stelios came from a poor family and had to work hard to make something of himself. "Have you been waiting long?"

"No, not long, "Stelios replied. "And I have had excellent company," he said turning to Electra, who beamed in reply, bestowing upon Rob a warm smile. "I won't keep you from your evening only I wanted to confirm your meeting with Mr Kampitsis. Would this coming Friday be convenient?"

"I have some messages to check," said Rob, glancing down at his phone and snatching his key. "I'll say goodnight Thea and leave you to make your arrangement." His glance briefly settled on her face, before he turned and made his way up the stairs.

Thea now turned her full attention towards Stelios, forcing herself to meet his eyes flanked by dark eyelashes. For some reason, she had the feeling of being ensnared, like a wild animal lured into a trap. *If only she had time to think and come up with a plan.* Trying not to betray these thoughts, Thea simply replied "Friday will be fine."

"Good! Then I will arrange for a car to pick you up." A smirk played on his lips. "I know that Mr Kampitsis is very much looking forward to meeting you. And so," he said, turning his head towards Electra, "I bid you two ladies good night."

Chapter 13

Departures

Gradually throwing off *Sleep*, Odysseus slowly opened his eyelids. It must be getting late in the day as there was a coolness from the breeze stirring round him and the full heat of the day had softened. He became aware of the sleeping form of the woman besides him. She slept still, breathing softly, the long curls of her hair falling over the finely woven coverlets. He held her closely, enjoying the soft touch of her skin and fragrance of her body.

At first, during those early days, it had been an uneasy coupling. *Desire* for her had raged through his body, but he could not disregard the humiliation meted out to his men. Enchanted by a spell, the veterans of the Trojan War had grovelled in the dirt like pigs. But then all that changed on the tenth day.

It was growing late in the day, when Eurylochos had burst into the chamber, his eyes blazing and his mouth frothing. "The witch!"

he screamed. "A god has taken her wits and she is attacking one of the men." Odysseus had rushed out into the precinct and in the dim light had found her in an isolated spot, where the grove gave way to the dense forest undergrowth. She was stood panting over the warrior, who lay sprawled on the ground, clenching a wooden stick in her hand. The low moan from the crumpled body signalled the man was still alive, but he had been beaten senseless.

He had felt his fury rise up outraged at the impertinence of the woman. "What is the meaning of this, witch!" he snapped, rounding on her. "That you would thrash my men."

But Kirke had turned, squaring up to him. "And your man would force himself on an untried maiden and rape her." She lifted her face up to him in defiance. It was then he noticed one of the young novices lying on the ground, curled into a ball, sobbing. She was one of the fairest, whose task it was to feed the caged beasts. She was clutching her ripped robe against her naked body to protect her modesty, an upturned pail beside her. Kirke cast aside her cudgel and took the young maiden into her arms, wrapping her cloak around her. As she cooed and rocked the trembling young woman in her arms, like a lioness guarding its young, she looked up eyes blazing, challenging him.

"What would you have me do? If the man had forced himself on her, she would be cast out by our peoples and die childless without a husband."

And in that moment, he had finally understood her and why she practised these enchantments. They shared a common duty of protecting their people but chose a different weaponry: he by the sword and she through enchantments.

He signalled to Eurylochos, who had been patiently standing nearby witnessing the scene, a smirk on his face. "Take the man back to the camp," ordered Odysseus, "and see that his injuries are tended. I will deal with him myself, when he is sufficiently recovered from his wounds. But from now on, the men stay in camp by the sea-shore and do not venture into the precinct after dusk."

Eurylochos, nodded mockingly, raising an eyebrow. "Of course, *Basileos*, as you wish" As he dragged the man away, Odysseus turned to Kirke, speaking in a measured voice. "I would have done the same," he said, touching her on the shoulder. "And as the gods are my witness, I give my oath it shall never happen again."

That night he had lain with her as he had never done before. Only when the first light of *Dawn* appeared and the crowing of the cockerel, did he untangle his limbs from her. But news of the witch beating a companion spread like wildfire through the camp, only deepening the men's suspicions and disturbing *Peace* in the ranks.

As the darker stormier months of winter set in, they had fallen into a comfortable domestic pattern. At dawn, he would return to his men in the camp to organise the repair and refurbishment of the ship. Aware of his orders and still wary of Kirke, the warriors had kept to the shoreline, cautious to venture inland. Eurylochos in particular and those men who had been seized by the enchantment, steadfastly kept their distance, refusing to let go of the memory of their ordeal. And they passed on their fear and distrust to the others like a contagion. Nevertheless Kirke had been a generous and faultless host, each morning sending the men bread and wine from her kitchen. As the men worked, cutting timber to reshape into solid planking, they exchanged reminiscences of their time in Troy or their future plans for their return home. Sometimes they went hunting in the wooded hill above and afterwards sat around the campfire, cooking spits of meat over the crackling flames.

As the Sun's chariot fell once more below the sea, that was the time Odysseus spent with Kirke, observing her performing her duties, mixing her healing potions or lovemaking in her bed. And he had desired her with a passion he could hardly control, like a young pup he had found it hard to tear himself away from her side. But he had felt unnerved by her too, especially by the strange wild beasts, who lived in the clearing, penned in like domesticated cattle or pigs. When she and the young women had approached without fear the caged mountain lions and fierce wolves, as a herdsman might hand rear a sickly lamb, he and his men had gawped dumbstruck. When he had questioned her, Kirke had simply shrugged her shoulders. "Why do we have any reason to fear these creatures," she had replied, "when we treat them with due care and respect."

But it was more than that. The way she addressed him like an equal, as Nestor or Diomedes might have done, voicing her inner most thoughts and offering him counsel. The way she held sway over the sacred precinct, though a woman, drawing respect and deference from all who entered this strange world. But although he found her boldness and authority deeply unsettling, it was also irresistible, like a moth fluttering over a flickering flame.

When the goddess Demeter breathed new life into the earth and the time had come to plant the wheat, visitors arrived at the shrine travelling from the hinterland or sea. These strangers presented with a myriad of afflictions: toothaches that nagged day and night; limbs that had been torn from their sockets and women expectant with child. Each one Kirke warmly greeted, each one she guided into the inner part of the sanctuary, each one she would listen to with sympathy as she examined their infirmity. At her direction, the younger women would dart back and forth, bearing jugs of heated water, swaddling cloth, dried herbs or carefully prepared tinctures. Sometimes she had touched the unfortunate on the arm, shaking her head with a look of sorrow. She had later explained that this was because the gods had seen fit to number their days of life and nothing could be done.

At the same time the offerings placed on the shrine had multiplied, as people beseeched the goddess Feronia for assistance or expressed their gratitude for her divine intervention. There were metal plates of shiny silver and beaten copper, leather skins of wine, sacks of wheat flour for bread, olive oil in stone jars, vegetables for cooking and dried out fruits for when the earth slept. Sometimes visitors left on the stone altar small figurines carved out of clay representing the goddess herself or their personal afflictions. And Kirke was as skilled and knowledgeable in this craft as any physician Odysseus had encountered at Troy, even Machaon himself. The prosperity of the shrine testified to her fame and skills as a healer.

But then over time, something had started to mellow and change inside him too, like thawing snow. After all the years of conflict and hardship, a softness and warmth of sentiment had begun to take root. Perhaps the healing he had witnessed had touched him too, creeping into his darkened spirit. Bit by bit this new feeling had grown and with it had come a rekindling of *Strength* and *Hope*. He dare not name it but at its heart was Kirke.

He often accompanied Kirke into the forest. He had closely watched her face, as she attentively surveyed the leaves and plants underfoot for signs of some healing herb. It was as if some god had taken her to a different world, so immersed was she. One day his curiosity had got the better of him.

"Tell me, Kirke," he had asked. "There is something I don't understand. How can it be that you take such interest in the untamed animals you keep or these wild growing plants? Your goddess Feronia is not known to us Greeks. What is the purpose of her shrine that you worship and serve so dutifully?"

Kirke had looked up at him smiling, as if addressing a young child, not he a seasoned Greek warrior. "Have you not realised by now, Odysseus, for all your resourcefulness and after the moons you have spent here. Have you not seen for yourself the work of Feronia and her power? Our goddess is that of nature herself. We pay her homage for the bountiful resources she supplies. The game in our woods, which you and your men hunt and satisfies your hunger. The wild berries and fruits growing untended. The wood for our fires and pliable twigs for making baskets. The healing plants growing wild that soothe and give comfort to the sick. These are all the gifts of Feronia. Here we live in balance and harmony with the nature earth goddess and those creatures that share our world. This is what observing the rites of the goddess and keeping our faith with her ways has taught us."

She spoke earnestly, upturning her face to speak a truth. "You and I, Odysseus, come from different places and our life's course follows different paths. You are a warrior and I am a healer. What has being a warrior taught you? Does that help you to live in better harmony with the world around you?"

He didn't know what to say and for a moment had stood before her dumb-founded, as if a god had taken away his speech. Finally he had replied. "Kirke, I cannot answer you. It is so long now since I lived peacefully in my homeland of Ithaka, before the accursed war with Troy and all the trials hereafter. I can hardly recall this time. But my father taught me the importance of *kleos*. Of proving myself worthy through my deeds as a warrior that I may bring honour and prosperity to my family. That through good *kleos*, a man may be known and his name gain immortality like the gods themselves."

Kirke paused for a moment, a smile playing on her lips. "No doubt, Odysseus, you will have your *kleos*. But does this *kleos* help you live well and bring harmony, so that things are in their natural order?"

"Of course, how could it not!" His answer had come more abruptly than he had expected.

"But Odysseus, your pursuit for this *kleos* has taken you far away from all the things you hold most precious." The words had pierced him like an arrow. For he realised that a truth lay in what she had spoken.

He had looked at her, his words weighted with meaning. "Not all, Kirke."

It had been several moons ago since the long days had returned and the sea had calmed once more. Yet still he had lingered in this place, unable to tear himself away from her side. Now as they lay there in their bed, he reached over and pulled her closer. He noticed how her breasts had filled out like ripened fruit. And the swollen curve of her body. There was no mistaking there was a child in her belly. In the heat of their love making, the gods had seen fit for them, the warrior and this strange priestess, to create a new life. As if the unborn child sensed his father's presence, he felt a sudden movement under her skin like the ripple of a wave responding to his touch. He reached over and kissed her lovingly on the forehead and then the child inside the swollen belly.

There was a light knock on the wooden door. He quickly pulled his tunic over his body, covering his nakedness and crossed over to answer, not wishing to disturb Kirke as she slept. It was one of the attendants, a young woman, her face ashen with fear.

"Please forgive me for waking you, sir," she stammered, casting her head downwards. The maiden novices still feared him, ever since seeing Odysseus hold his sword to Kirke's throat.

"Your mistress is still sleeping. What is it?" he asked in hushed tones, sensing a disturbance approaching the peaceful slumber of the bedchamber.

"Your captain, Eurylochos, is here to see you at the request of your men. He begs to speak with you," she said, swallowing hard.

"That is fine." He replied lightly. "Tell him I will come soon." He quickly finished dressing and then followed in the woman's footsteps. Outside on the porch, Eurylochos was anxiously pacing, but turned at the sound of Odysseus' approach. He recognised the look of discomfort in his old comrade's face.

"Greetings, Odysseus."

"And you too, my dear comrade." He clapped the other man warmly on the back, aware that he seldom visited the precinct. "What brings you here so early? I hear that you wish to speak with me."

"Indeed I do." And yet Eurylochos remained silent, the muscles straining in his ox-like neck.

"Come tell me the nature of your business and do not hold back." At these words of encouragement, he could see the colour rising in his friend's face. At last, mustering his courage, Eurylochos spoke.

"There is no easy way to say this Odysseus. The men are restless. They complain that we linger here when long ago we could have left and be on our way to Ithaka. Already the days are past their longest and the air begins to cool. For a whole year, we have rested here, taking our fill of food and drink. But if we are ever to return to our native land and this is our fate, then the time has come for us to take our leave."

For a moment Odysseus stood speechless, as if his body had been hit by the force of a full fist. "But surely, that time has not yet come?" he protested. Eurylochos' words were truly spoken, but he could not bring himself to admit it.

"Odysseus, this woman has put a spell of entrapment on you. Have you become so soft with all her hospitality, even wearing the clothes she provides, that you have forgotten who you are?" Odysseus suddenly felt self-conscious, standing there in his earth-red tunic, which Kirke had presented to him. But now Eurylochos continued unabashed.

"Do you have to be reminded of your duty to your peoples," he said, his eyes aflame, "And what of your own father or your son, who you left as a young infant, and wife. We miss our homes, our families and loved ones. We worry what will become of them, while we dawdle here."

"Your words are spoken truely, Eurylochos," he replied thoughtfully. "I will dwell on them and consider whether the time is ripe to continue our journey home."

Kirke found him on the sanctuary steps as the day was turning and the sun god Helios was tethering his horses to give way to *Night*. Ever since he had parted company with Eurylochos, he had been turning over in his mind what he should do. She sat down close besides him, naturally leaning into him as he stared down at the hardened ground.

"What ails you, Odysseus, for I can see something has happened to grieve you?" Kirke had asked softly, nuzzling her head against his shoulder. His eyes were downcast as he had been staring at the same crack in the earth, where some ants scurried.

"I will tell you outright, Kirke, as you will find out soon enough." He heaved deeply, his voice blank of feeling. "Eurylochos came to see me today, while you were sleeping. He reminded me of my duty and said that the time has come to take my leave."

Kirke was silent for a moment, as if catching her breath, before she finally replied. "But of course you must go. You never planned to stay."

"I know I must go and it is my duty," Odysseus replied wearily, turning towards her. "I have seen what happens when a city and its people are left defenceless without their men and a strong leader." Briefly the accursed memory of Troy's destruction coursed through his mind, the blood running down the city streets, its slaughtered citizens and the pitiful wails of the women waiting to be taken into slavery. He shuddered. The images were too raw to dwell on.

Kirke reached over and lightly caressed him with her fingers. "Hush, you do not need to explain more." He felt her touch, trying to soothe him.

"But I must, Kirke," he burst out. "I would happily live out the rest of my days with you if that was our allotted fate. But I have also seen the madness and destruction of *Love*, when people give into feeling and *Desire*, forgetting their duties and position." He stopped and pressed his lips together in a slight grimace. "I witnessed with my own eyes the madness of passion between a man and a woman, Helen and the Trojan, which started the accursed war with Troy. Their desire was the cause of so much death and destruction to all who were touched by their love." He broke off for a moment, shaking his head, his eyes moist with tears. "I cannot give into my feelings, Kirke. Yet I don't know how to leave you, especially now you are with child." He reached over and took her hand in his own, clasping it with his fingers.

Kirke smiled, replying with soft soothing words. "You are right to have fears for your people, Odysseus. For you have seen much. We knew your departure would come as you were never destined to live out your days here. And yet it is now hard to leave, and you question your own path." She pressed her head against his solid shoulder. "There is a blind seer, Teiresias. He lives two days sail under canvas to the south, where the fruit ripens more quickly and the wide river meets the sea. You will recognise the land as it is low lying and wooded with tall poplars and willows. Go there and consult with him. He will tell you what you need to know to make this journey."

At her words, he felt his spirit lift. It would put

an end to his dilemma. "I will do as you say Kirke," he said, looking up towards her. "We will prepare the ship to sail at the first light of day after tomorrow, though the men will not be happy that we do not set a course for Ithaka."

"Nevertheless, Odysseus, they will follow you." Kirke pressed his hand. "They may grumble and complain, but they look to you as their leader. They will do as you say." She smoothed down the forest-green folds of her tunic over her swollen belly. "Now shake off this melancholy mood. Let us not waste this precious time the gods have granted us." And she pulled him up by the hand and led him back towards the house.

****

As the silver light of *Dawn* had filtered across the sweeping bay, he had broken the news to the assembled men. At first they had protested, but had nonetheless gone about the preparations for the voyage, relieved to be putting to sea at last. On the morn of their departure, there was no sign of Kirke, but a black ram had been tethered close to their camp for sacrifice on their journey.

The voyage was as Kirke had described. During the day, they sailed under canvass and oars, hugging the sea-shore, making good progress in the southerly direction. At night, they sheltered on a sandy cove or shingle beach, hauling up the boat onto the beach and making camp for the night.

Close to the wide mouth of the river *Acheron*, they found the blind seer living in the sacred wood. They tracked his simple dwelling through the sight of a smoking fire not far inland. The old man, came out to meet them, walking slowly with a stick to guide his steps; the gods had clouded over the orbs in his creased face. He greeted them warmly in Kirke's language.

"Greetings strangers, I have been expecting you." He looked towards them with his unseeing eyes. "Please come and sit with me," he beckoned them with his arm. "Tell me the nature of your business."

Odysseus frowned, as he tried to make sense of the jumbled words. "We seek the seer-priest Teiresias." The words came slowly as he tried to express himself in this foreign language, the sounds jumbling on his tongue like sand grains in a storm. "We come from the priestess Kirke, who said we must speak with you."

"*Basileos*," whispered Elpenor, the youngest of the warriors. When they had set sail for Troy, he had scarcely been out of boyhood, his face covered in a soft down. But the young warrior had a sharp ear for language and had quickly picked up the local dialect from the novice maidens. "I can speak for you," he said eagerly, "and tell you what the old man says."

Odysseus nodded his head. "Go on then."

Elpenor quickly repeated Odysseus' words, transformed into an unfamiliar string of sounds to which the old man responded with a deep utterance. "Tiresias says that Kirke, the priestess, is well known for her wisdom and healing. If she honours you as a friend then he must do likewise. He offers you refreshments. Afterwards you will make a sacrifice to the gods of the Underworld to summon the spirits of the dead."

"Very well," Odysseus replied. He gestured the others to sit on the ground and called over one of the men to bring the black ram from the ship. The old man called inside to the hut and a young woman appeared, bearing a pitcher and beakers.

"This is my granddaughter," Elpenor explained on behalf of their host. His eyes lingered on her slim body, as the young woman filled the vessels with wine. A blush rose across her cheeks, as she handed a beaker to each of the men, lowering her head modestly. When they had all slaked their thirst and were well rested, Odysseus ordered the men to dig a pit as Kirke had instructed him. Then the men poured offerings of mixed milk and honey, wine and finally water sprinkled with barley grains before sacrificing the black ram, its dark blood mingling with the earth. Suddenly the gods brought to Odysseus' mind that terrible sacrifice at Aulis and the look of horror on the innocent Iphigeneia's face. He felt himself flinched betraying his thoughts, when Teiresias turned to him speaking in his rasping breathless voice.

"These offerings of drink nourish the dead imprisoned underground," translated Elpenor, "allowing them to draw near. Once the ram has been roasted, he Teiresias will tell you what you need to know."

For a long time, as the fire crackled, they sat watching the ram's burning carcass roasting in the pit, the smouldering wood and the plumes of grey smoke. As the shadows began to lengthen, the seer bolted upright like a spear, crying out aloud.

"He says that the spirits of the dead are drawing near," whispered Elpenor.

"Then tell the other men to withdraw to the ship as I would hear this alone," said Odysseus. "But you stay!" The younger man did as he was bid and a short time later only the three men remained: the blind seer, Elpenor and himself.

"Odysseus!" The old man had begun to speak once more. He seemed to be in a trance, as if taken over by a god. "I see that you are destined to return to the land of your birth." Elpenor's eyebrows drew together and a look of dread passed over his face. "But this will not be the joyful return you seek. A god puts up barriers to block your way. For the sea god and earth shaker is angered at you for taking Troy and then harming his beloved son."

The memory of the Cyclops shot through his mind as suddenly the pieces fitted together. The wild man had called down a curse on him as his sight was robbed from him. *Were their troubles due to the god Poseidon, the protector of the Trojans, who had taken against them* he wondered?

"Will I reach Ithaka with my companions?" Odysseus pressed, his anxiety mounting.

The old man drew breath, the air escaping through his cracked lips. "It is hard to say. I see a pastureland with grazing cows that you will come across when you are in sore need. These belong to Helios the sun god and it is a test of your steadfastness. You and your men must resist your appetites and leave the cattle unharmed." He lifted his sightless eyes towards Odysseus. "Otherwise your ship will be lost and you will return home alone, late and luckless."

From the corner of his eye, Odysseus noticed his younger translator flinch, but he needed answers to his questions. He mastered his own spirit. He must find out now all he could, whatever might help him.

"And what is the state of affairs in my homeland of Ithaka?" he urged.

The old man lifted his head upwards. "Your father is alive, but your mother has passed over to the world of the spirits." At this news, Odysseus' eyes pricked with tears as sadness swept over him. His beloved mother, who had pressed him to her body so tightly, as he had set off on this ill-fated venture. Now he would never have the chance to behold her dear face once more or perform her death rites.

"And who governs the kingdom?" he demanded, sweeping aside his sentiment. He glanced as Elpenor, white-faced like ash, as he repeated the old man's words.

"Your wife holds steadfast and refuses to take another man as her husband. She remains true and your son administers your estates. But there are troubles ahead and suitors who will come to your house, eating your wealth, flocks and livelihood. They seek to seize from your son that which is yours."

At these words, Odysseus recoiled in horror as a bitter taste of saliva filled his mouth. His fears for the fate of his son and his kingdom were coming true. He had to return with full haste. He turned to Elpenor, whose colour had drained from his body and beads of sweat appeared on his lips. "We set sail at first light for Feronia and then onto Ithaka."

He started to rise to his feet, but the old seer raised his arm to delay him. "Odysseus, there is a man here who died in battle before his time. He towers like a god in shining armour. He claims acquaintance with you. He claims you tried to advise him in a quarrel, but he could not let go of his anger."

"Achilles?" he asked. His face came to his mind. Their godlike warrior, the very best of the Achaian Greeks. Brilliant but also temperamental, so moved by anger and pride. That terrible quarrel with Agamemnon had delivered so much death to the troops.

The seer nodded his wrinkled head. "Yes, that may be the man's name. He now laments his death, preferring to live as a lowly labourer or slave, than amongst the shades of Hades with glory. He brings a message to you. He urges you to live well according to the purpose of your life, so that one day you may have *kleos* and be known to all men."

The old man now put out his arm to restrain him. "I have one final prophecy for you, Odysseus," he said, his breaths now coming in deep gasps so the words scarcely escaped from his mouth. His sightless eyes stared at him milky like cooked eggs. "Your death will come from the sea. It will take you in the weakness of old age with your people prospering around you." He stopped and bent his head. "I have nothing more to say as the spirits draw away."

"I thank you for your words old man. For now I know I must return to Ithaka as soon as the gods permit." He stood up and started to fasten his sword belt around his waist, which he had cast aside. An urgency had come over him, now his son and his kingdom were in danger. "We will take our leave and go." He glanced at the seer, his body hunched over the pit, his head shrunken into his body. "I thank you for your prophecies and will make due sacrifice in your name once we reach Ithaka." The old man scarcely raised his head, as he bowed and turned towards the ship. The path he must follow was clear. If he delayed any longer, though it tore his heart, all might be lost and his family ruined.

A voice stopped him in his tracks. "*Basileos*!" It was Elpenor running up behind, panting and breathless. "Please stop! I would speak with you." His face was still pale and wide-eyed, with beads of sweat standing on his forehead. "I have heard and understood all that passed between you and the seer. I cannot come with you," he said, trembling with fear. "Please, I beg you my lord, leave me here. If it is my fate to die at sea, then I cannot go on. To be food for fishes is not the fate I wish."

"How can I let you, Elpenor, stay here alone?"

"And how can I hold my tongue and not speak to the others of our shared fate?"

Odysseus scanned the younger man's face and grasped at once his fear. "What you say is true, Elpenor," he said patiently. "This knowledge is a burden we must carry. But how would I explain your absence to the men, if you don't come?"

Elpenor replied without hesitation. "Say I fell drunk from the roof of the hut and broke my neck. Let them raise a burial mound for me at Feronia. For I would rather live my days here, then endure the fate of an early death swallowed by the sea." The younger man raised his head, an appeal in his face.

"Very well then, Elpenor. I will give you until tomorrow to consider your decision. But we will set sail at *Dawn*." He briefly clasped the young man to his chest, holding him close to his chest, momentarily thinking of his own son Telemachos on Ithaka. "Take care."

"Thank you *Basileos*," said Elpenor, the tears spilling over his face. With that the young warrior turned and retraced his steps to the seer's dwelling. Momentarily Odysseus cast his glance back to watch Elpenor's figure recede into the shadows of the woodland.

"He is always one for the pretty woman!" remarked one of the men bawdily back at camp, to the raucous laughter of the men. "And that granddaughter was a fine maiden, ready for the poke of a man!" Without question, they had readily accepted his explanation for Elpenor's absence. Even Eurylochos allowed a smirk to touch his lips.

At nightfall, he gathered the men around him, a plan now fully formed in his mind. "Men, my dear companions," he began, observing the bank of sullen faces. Even a full year of hospitality and being well fed could not undo the suffering and hardship inflicted under foreign skies.

"I have heard news of our destiny," Odysseus announced, "and I cannot pretend our journey ahead will be easy, but-" he paused, watching carefully to measure their responses: the curl of a mouth, the square of a shoulder, the raising of a brow. He continued, his words ringing out clearly for all ears. "But if you listen and obey me in all things, we will survive and return to our native Ithaka. This is what the ancient seer told me. We leave for Feronia at tomorrow's *Dawn*, where we will stay briefly to take on provisions for the journey. Then we set sail for Ithaka." A huge cheer went up, almost snatching away his words. The men were laughing and clapping each other on the back. Soon they expected to see their loved ones and home at last. "Take your fill of rest and food now, while you can" he shouted above the din, "for men cannot toil on an empty stomach."

Buoyed by the news of their imminent departure, there were high spirits in the camp that night. Some of the men broke into song, huddled round the flickering fire, thinking of home. But an anxiety hung over him. How could he break the news to Kirke? The thought of saying goodbye to Kirke disturbed his mind and felt worse than any misfortune inflicted by the gods. As he hunkered down for the night, wrapping a coverlet round him, Eurylochos whispered across to him.

"So at last Odysseus, you have finally come to your senses!" He chose not respond, but simply wrapped the blanket closer to him.

They were out at sea, when Odysseus broke the news of Elpenor's apparent demise. The young man had not reappeared, throwing his lot into stay in this strange land. Some of the men had let out gasps of anguish at the news of another loss. But they had all doubled their efforts and toiled on the oars, rowing with a renewed sense of purpose.

They raised a mound for Elpenor on a point overlooking the winter camp, fixing his oar aloft. When they were done, Odysseus went in search of Kirke. He found her in the inner part of the sanctuary, busying herself with preparing healing potions and salves. At his approach, she did not even look up from her work.

"So when do you leave?" she asked, without any hint of acrimony or recrimination.

"Tomorrow as soon as we take on provisions," he said, his heart beating fast, for he had feared this moment. "You are willing for us to take what we need?"

"Of course, Odysseus," came her easy reply. "Give instructions for your requirements to the maidens and they will see to it. For you will need supplies of bread, wine, water, dried fruits and meat too." She turned away from him, refusing to meet his glance. "Tonight you and your men will take your fill of my hospitality one last time, eating and drinking to your hearts' content, before your departure."

He touched her arm, lightly drawing her face around with his other hand to meet his eye. "Please Kirke, let us not be like strangers. Let me tell you what I have learned from the blind seer, Teiresias, so you will understand......"

She cut across him, interrupting his words. "You don't need to explain."

"But I do Kirke," he entreated her. "For I cannot bear to part other than we are." Kirke poured a pitcher of water to wipe her hands, pulling back a stray lock of hair from her face. She wore a robe of woodland green, her customary colour, beneath which the solid curve of her belly was conspicuous. Part of him wanted to cling to her, refusing to give her up even now.

"According to the seer, my kingdom of Ithaka is under threat." The words came tumbling out. "I have a son who is my heir and just entering manhood. My wife holds steadfast to our marriage but if she remarries, the kingdom will be lost. For this reason, I must go back. If the gods had not written my fate as such then... -"

"Hush, Odysseus. You cannot alter what the gods have willed. It is not our fate to be together in this life."

"But Kirke, how can you know that? Surely we have a choice over what fate we choose."

Kirke held a finger up against his lips. Then she turned and led him by the hand onto the lower steps of the sacred shrine. They sat together so that their thighs pressed against each other and he could feel the heat of her body. "Of course, this is not your life's course," Kirke said, raising her face to his. "The gods have been playing with us to imagine we might live out our days together, raising our children and then their children. Let us not dwell on this for it will only bring us both sadness. Rather listen to me carefully and I will tell you everything I know to find the route back to your island and all the dangers that may lay ahead." And she told him in detail, missing nothing out.

"And what of our child?" he asked, when she had finished, drawing her close to him and feeling her thickened waist.

"Don't worry." She reassured him. "I will cherish the child. When the time comes for the child to be born, there are many here within the sanctuary who will assist me." She stroked the round of her belly with her fingers. "If the child is a boy, I will call him Telegonos, the last born. He will be raised to know who his father is and that he is a great warrior. And if the gods will it, when he comes of manhood, I will send him to find you."

He drew her to him, suddenly overcome by sentiment, he the Achaian warrior conquered by a woman. "I love you Kirke," he whispered in her ear, as he held her to him breathing her fragrance.

"I know," she replied, and he had embraced her, feeling the child move inside her body. He felt he could have laid with her as the *Sky Ouranos* had laid with *Earth* at the dawn of time, coupling and impregnating *Gaia* with his seed for eternity.

****

"Father, wake up!" The pitch came more forcefully. "Wake up!" He felt himself being shaken awake. "Father, does something ail you?" Slowly he opened his eyes, acclimatising to the light, which was starting to fade. Telemachos was knelt in front of him, his eyebrows drawn together. "You seemed very deeply taken by *Sleep* as if in a different place. You have slept all afternoon."

For a moment he was still there with her. Then it came to him, he was back on Ithaka, sleeping and dreaming on his own lands. "I am fine, son." He said, blinking back *Sleep*. He peered into the light, as if expecting to see Kirke, but her image was gone. It took a moment for him to recognise the familiar grove and orchard. He shrugged reassuringly at his son. "Only old age and weariness catching up with me."

"Father, it is time to return to the palace. Tonight the feast is planned with food and entertainment ahead of tomorrow's festival. My mother, Penelope, will be expecting us."

Of course, Penelope! How could he have forgotten? "Come son, let us go." He drew himself up, stretching out the stiffness in his joints and followed his son up the track to the palace.

Chapter 14

Reunion

The daily journey across the island gulf to Paliki had become a familiar routine. She'd come to know by heart those recognisable markers of the landscape: the old olive press, the rising swell of the wooded promontory and the rotunda of the lighthouse before the open water. Yet, despite the arduous days spent sifting through old manuscripts and ledgers, Thea felt only mounting frustration. The palace was out there, somewhere on Paliki, but its very proximity only heightened her vexation. The trip to the peninsula had simply strengthened her resolve to find it.

The crumpled note lay on top of the desk, where it had sat for the past three days, discarded but not entirely thrown away. It felt like a metaphor for her situation. Three cursory lines, scribbled in Rob's distinctive handwriting to inform her of his sudden departure. It offered no explanation or date of his expected return. Outraged by his treatment, she felt the anger rising in her body once more. *How could she let herself be so naive?* She slammed shut the possibility of them as a couple in her mind. Until the pressing matter of Dimitri was resolved, she was determined not to pursue any relationship with Rob.

And there had felt an inevitability about the meeting today. Richard had been on the phone several times already, anxiously checking that everything was in place. He must have sensed her reluctance for he had lectured her at length about her responsibilities to the project and that meeting Mr Kampitsis had become her duty. Alone at night or during her isolated dining on the harbour quay, she had played over in her mind how today's encounter could be avoided. Gradually she had forced herself into the realisation that facing Dimitri again, sooner or later, was inevitable. Today was as good a day as any.

"And preparatory talks in Helsinki appear to have made a break through." The voice of the news reader on the television screen fired out a rapid succession of words like a machine gun disgorging bullets, breaking Thea's thoughts. The screen was bathed in a blue light displaying a carefully groomed woman with heavy black rimmed glasses. "Contrary to expectations, it is believed that all major countries have now agreed to attend the world climate summit talks later this year. And now more on the Greek economic crisis..."

Thea picked up the television remote and flicked the off button, before checking her watch for the countless time. As if arming herself for battle, she applied a coat of deep crimson lipstick, puckering her lips in the mirror. For the meeting she had chosen a dark business suit with an open necked sky-blue blouse, one she reserved for solemn occasions and University departmental meetings. To tame her unruly copper curls, her hair had been twisted into a tight coil, pinning down firmly any loose strands that escaped. Stealing one final look at herself, Thea smoothed her clothes down, steeling herself for what was to come. *Whatever happened, she would face it.*

The limousine was already waiting for her outside the hotel. A uniformed chauffeur ushered her politely into one of the dark upholstered seats. Even with the cool rush of air from the air-conditioning, the car interior felt oppressive, smelling of leather and formaldehyde. After a frenetic drive through a jumble of traffic, road lights and the town one way system, the car came to a stop in front of a modern glass faced building overlooking the harbour front. As Thea stepped out of the car, she breathed in the light fresh air from the sea breeze, allowing it to steady her nerves. There was no going back.

Richard was anxiously waiting for her, as Thea entered the waiting area. Quickly she scrutinised the new surroundings absorbing every detail: the pristine light coloured sofas; the large polished glass table and the bright modernist paintings. The receptionist sat behind a desk, elegantly groomed in her tailored suit, flashed a set of perfect teeth as a welcome.

Richard rushed over to greet her. "Hello Thea. I'm glad you were able to make it." He beamed broadly at her but his handshake was hot and clammy. The usual self-assured composure had been replaced by a nervousness, Thea had not glimpsed before. To arrive on time, Richard had obviously driven over from Kalodia early in the morning. He took out a handkerchief to wipe away a bead of sweat from his temple.

"Any progress with the trip to Athens?" he asked. They had both agreed on Thea's visit to Athens, but with Easter approaching, all the daily flights had been long booked up as families across Greece reunited for the holidays.

"Unfortunately not as yet," Thea replied. In the diversion of the meeting, she had overlooked her intention to check for flight cancellations. "I'm having difficulty finding a seat. I'll check again later today."

At that moment, a door adjoining the room opened. Stelios stepped out and with warm handshakes they were both ushered into a bright spacious office. Thea found herself in the very position she had longed for all those years ago. Now that moment had finally arrived, she felt overcome with dread.

"Allow me to introduce you to Mr Dimitri Kampitsis," said Stelios courteously. "Professor Mortimer you are already well acquainted with…"

"Of course, Richard!" Dimitri replied, shaking his hand. "I heard our press conference went down very well!"

"….and this is Dr Sefton."

Thea had already locked her eyes on him, before he had registered her presence. Close-up, he was as she remembered him: the square face and forehead, the fine equine nose perfectly balancing the almond brown eyes. Only the fine features were now no longer soft and boyish but those of a man full-grown. His hair had been closely trimmed, taming and masking the deep black curls. He was dressed in a well cut dark suit and open necked sky-blue shirt, expensive to the eye, which complemented the shape of his lean body. He wore his good looks easily and casually: there was no doubt he was a handsome man.

As his gaze fell upon Thea, his body give a start

and he hesitated, his hand poised mid-air.

"Thea?" he asked uncertainly, as if his eyes were playing a trick on him. "Is it really you?" He stood close, scrutinising her face.

"So you know one another already?" Richard enquired, breaking the awkward moment. It was hard to judge Dimitri's thoughts for both his smile and touch were welcoming as he shook Thea's hand.

"Yes, Dr Sefton and I are already acquainted," Dimitri replied smoothly, any momentary discomfort now evaporated. "It was many years ago when we last met, much younger than you see me now." He grinned, his glance falling on her face. "I didn't realise, Thea, you were back on the island. How is it possible? Stelios has kept me well informed about the project but I didn't recognise your name," he said turning to Stelios, who simply shrugged.

"Hello Dimitri," Thea replied evenly, determined not to be unnerved by this man. "I'm sure my presence on the island must come as a surprise. I go by my married name of Sefton these days," she said, feeling a need to explain. "So you wouldn't have recognised my name on the project list. I didn't realise that you were part of the Archontakis Foundation." And it was the truth. Had she known of Dimitri's involvement, she would never have signed up for the project.

"Of course, you would not know," Dimitri readily agreed. "The name comes from my wife who is from the famous Archontakis shipping family. It is her family who set up the Foundation. But I am delighted to welcome you back to the island, Thea" he beamed, her name lightly rolling off his tongue. "But, forgive my discourtesy to you both," he gestured them into the room, "please take a seat. Allow me to offer you some refreshments." He directed them to a plush cream sofa, taking one of the padded chairs for himself.

Refreshments were quickly summoned and when a cafetiere of fresh coffee appeared with some local pastries, Dimitri at once played the perfect host, pouring out the drinks. "Is this alright for you, Richard," he asked attentively, handing the older man a cup of coffee. "In my surprise at making the re-acquaintance of Dr Sefton, I hope I am not neglecting you."

"Not at all," replied Richard affably, settling himself comfortably on the well-padded sofa. "I am delighted that you two people know one another!"

Thea took a sip of her coffee and noted with pleasure it had a rich deep aroma, just as she liked it. As she savoured the hot liquid, her apprehension started to lift for the first time in days and she began to relax.

Dimitri sat forward on his chair, his eyes glued

onto Thea's face. "So your husband doesn't mind sparing you to help us out with our undertaking?" It was a simple question but it was loaded.

"Unfortunately we split up last year," Thea replied steadily. "So what I do is no longer his concern."

"I see. I'm very sorry to hear that," Dimitri said commiserating, his face full of sympathy and genuine concern. "So," he said, sitting now upright, "let us talk about the project instead. Professor Mortimer and Stelios have both kept me informed." He leaned back again in his chair. "I understand you've been working on the archives for the Paliki peninsula. How is that going?" The dark eyes, so familiar, darted again to her face. She noticed that Stelios had merged into the background, but was listening and watching attentively.

Thea drew a breath, bringing her mind back to the business at hand. "I'd planned to work slowly through the Venetian records to see if any of the original place names could be identified," she replied, the professional in her taking over. "Unfortunately, very little if anything has survived, certainly on the island. There may be something in the Vatican archives in Rome. Even if the records still exist, it could take a huge amount of time and effort to track them down." A flicker of disappointment passed across Dimitri's face and she realised that the outcome of the Project mattered to him.

Thea continued. "So instead I have been using the archive information to chart the villages known historically in the Upper Paliki area, which sit close to the project survey site. That would confirm, at least, we are looking in the right area. It is early days, but the research so far shows that in historical times this area was very fertile, with a higher population and agricultural yields." She smiled, remembering her own excitement as this pattern started to emerge from the jumbled and tangled letters of the old ledgers.

Thea continued, speaking rapidly. "I'm also cross referencing descriptions in the original Homeric source with local land features on Paliki. This is proving to be very promising and backs up the theory that Odysseus' palace is most likely situated on that part of the island. We have found one place already which matches Homer's description."

Dimitri threw up his arms, the smile lighting up his fine features. "So we are looking in the right place for the palace. Excellent! As I understand from Professor Mortimer the results from the field survey at Kalodia have been so far, how shall I put this...?" he paused. "Disappointing." He looked meaningfully at Richard as he emphasised the word.

Richard shifted uncomfortably in his chair, like a chastised young boy. The affable expression had dropped from his face and his colour could be seen rising. The reprimand of this highly respected scholar was excruciating to witness. The memory of that conversation with Rob darted through her mind. *Deferential* had been the word he had used about Richard. It was puzzling. Her suspicion was that Dimitri was behind Richard's decision to locate the field survey in the family village of Kalodia. Thea stepped in.

"I understand from Dr Hughes that the preliminary results of the geological analysis are very promising. It's early days but supports the theory of Paliki being an island and Ancient Ithaka." As soon as the words had left her mouth, Thea realised her error. From Richard's wide-eyed look of surprise, the information was clearly news to him. Rob must have told her in confidence. But this fresh knowledge had a transforming effect on Dimitri, who was now beaming widely at them both. Whatever shadow might have been there, had lifted.

"That is very good news," Dimitri said with pleasure. "I have high hopes that we will find our palace of Odysseus. And I have the fullest confidence in your team Professor Mortimer," he said, turning towards Richard, who weakly returned the smile. "May I thank you Dr Sefton for your dedicated work so far and assure you of my fullest and upmost support. I have a very personal interest in the Project's success." His gaze pointedly fell on Thea once more, his lips curled in a deep smile. "So please, if there is anything I can do or put at your disposal, then let me know."

"There is one thing, you may be able to help us with, "Richard began hesitatingly, clearing his throat. "Dr Sefton needs to travel to Athens to follow a line of enquiry regarding the old archaeological records. Unfortunately due to Easter, she hasn't been able to secure a seat on a flight. Is there anything you can suggest?"

Dimitri glanced at Stelios briefly and then back at Richard. "We have a meeting in Athens tomorrow and will return the following day. A place could be provided on our private jet and overnight accommodation arranged." Stelios nodded his agreement. "Would that be suitable for you Dr Sefton?" he asked smiling generously.

"I have a few phone calls to the archaeological schools, but I could be ready for then," Thea replied uneasily. The proposition wasn't what she wanted but with Richard beside her, it felt like a pincer movement.

"Then, it is settled," Dimitri spoke, leaving no opportunity for objections. "You can travel with us but bring an overnight bag. Stelios will make the arrangements and we will see you at the airport in the morning. I look forward to enjoying more of your company." An expression of easy charm sat on his face and for just a moment Thea felt a fluttering in her stomach and the beating of her heart.

"Until tomorrow then," she replied.

They drew the meeting to a close. "Well Thea, I don't know how you did it, but you seemed to make a big impression with Mr Kampitsis," Richard said buoyantly, as they stepped out into the lobby. All traces of his discomfort had now vanished and Richard was once more his jovial and outgoing self. "He seemed very charmed by you. But Rob hasn't said anything to me about the geophysical results," he said perplexed, rubbing his chin. "When did he mention it to you?"

"The other day, when we had dinner together," Thea replied lightly. "I assumed he had told you."

"Of course, he had to return to London at short-notice. I think I'll drop by the lab later for a chat," he said. "His flight is due in this morning." Thea watched Richard set off briskly, his figure retreating down the avenue towards the square. But the nagging feeling remained that unwittingly she had betrayed Rob's trust.

****

The plane was situated on the edge of the tarmac, perched like some rare exotic bird. Its distinctive coned shaped nose and white polished coat glistened in the morning sunlight. It was still early and a freshness hung in the air and over the verdant hillside, dotted with tall Cypresses and red-roofed buildings. At the airport, Thea had been greeted like a celebrity or film star and now she was being safely delivered to the waiting flight, like precious cargo.

Thea turned and thanked her escort, before ascending the short flight of steep steps leading into the plane cabin.

"Welcome Dr Sefton!" Dimitri's warmest smile greeted her, his head turned towards her. "Please take a seat and make yourself comfortable." Stelios nodded an acknowledgement, as Thea settled into one of the cream leather seats. "You catch us already at our early breakfast meeting." Dimitri continued apologetically. "Stelios and I have a few things to discuss before we arrive in Athens. I hope you will excuse our inattention to you."

"No, not at all. Please go ahead." Thea said, noticing the cabin was immaculate and smelt of polish or air-freshener.

"We have champagne on board, if you wish?" Dimitri's eyes fell upon her again.

"No thank you," Thea said declining graciously, strapping herself in with her seat-belt. "I want to keep my head clear as I have a long day ahead."

"Of course," he replied, bowing his head.

The two men fell into discussion, speaking in a flurry of Greek and talking hands. Thea took out her leather-bound notebook and began organising her day, prioritising the journals she planned to search. Most of the journals were non-digitised so would require physical searching by hand. From time to time Dimitri glanced towards her, trying to catch her eye. But the past with so many unanswered questions loomed over them. *In the presence of someone else, it was not the time or the place to talk.*

They were now approaching Athens, when the two men finally sat back from their papers. "I've arranged transport for you from the airport," Stelios began. "The driver will take you wherever you wish to go. Your bag will be transported directly to the St. Gerasimos hotel, Lykavettos, where you will stay as our guest." He turned his head towards her. "I hope that meets with your satisfaction." His words were spoken faultlessly but somehow had a ring of insincerity.

"That is most thoughtful, Stelios. Thank you," Thea replied.

"And I hope that you will do me the honour of dining with me tonight," said Dimitri, turning on his winning smile. It lit up his handsome features. "I think as old friends we have things to catch up on." His eyes beneath the long dark eyelashes lingered on her face. "Will it suit you if I meet you at the hotel this evening?"

Thea knew she was playing with fire, but her curiosity was now getting the better of her. She couldn't help herself: wanting to discover what had happened, since he had suddenly disappeared from her life without a word.

"Alright," she agreed.

"Until later then."

The rest of the day passed smoothly. In the archaeological school, between the tall stacks jammed with books and journals, Thea had sifted through innumerable old Greek archaeological reports. The tranquillity of the old library provided a refuge from her turbulent emotions. Quickly her mind became seized by the intellectual challenge of deciphering the formal *Katharevousa* Greek, favoured by scholars of the previous century. The words and sentence flow were more akin to the Ancient Greek tongue, more formal than the demotic Greek Thea spoke. Over the course of the day, the drama of the island's archaeological post-war years unfolded from the type-written records: the devastating earthquake of 1953; the destruction of the ceramic finds from the earlier excavations at Metaxata; the restoration and rebuilding of the archaeological museum and its proud civic re-opening in the 1960's. Then there were descriptions of excavations by the young Simon Karellis, the famous archaeologist born on the island, digging for traces of an earlier Mycenean past.

Had he suspected a connection between Odysseus and the island? Thea wondered.

The shadows were lengthening in the soft glow of the remaining sunlight as Thea walked purposefully through the streets of Athens towards the hotel. There was a restlessness about the city, with wave upon wave of sounds: car horns, traffic and the shouts of schoolchildren. Her attention was drawn to the brightly lit shop windows, tempting shoppers with a kaleidoscope of elegant goods for their bodies, their health and their homes. Some of the grey-washed walls of the apartment blocks had been plastered with posters, advertising a night of culture or scrawled with eye-catching graffiti. Billboards proclaimed the approaching local elections, where photogenic candidates promised a brighter future. In the tree-lined small triangular square, there was a swell of noise from people, young and old sitting in the cafes drinking and chatting, excitedly anticipating the weekend. Amongst the crowd, her attention was captured by a toddler, sitting on his mother's knee, reaching up with his chubby arms to clutch her neck. Thea blinked away the image.

In a quiet corner of the Kolonaki district, backing onto the steep wooded slopes of the Lykavettos hill, Thea found the hotel.

"The Archontakis Foundation has already settled all the expenses," explained the receptionist politely with a thin smile, as she checked Thea into her room. "Mr Kampitsis' assistant personally took charge of the matter and requested you be put in one of our best executive suites."

"And has Mr Kampitsis arrived?" Thea asked, noticing the receptionist's perfect manicured and painted nails as she handed her the room key.

"Not yet, but I believe he and his assistant are due later," she replied. "In the meantime, our hotel is at your service so please make yourself comfortable." She weighed up Thea with a sideways glance, measuring her appearance. "Would you like me to send up one of our beauticians for you?"

Feeling a touch judged, Thea shook her head. "No thanks. That won't be necessary."

The concierge showed her into an airy modern

suite, painted in varying shades of cream and white. The only colour dotting the room was the modernistic pictures and a vibrant bouquet of roses and tiger lilies carefully placed on the polished glass table. Her overnight canvas bag, scuffed and well worn, felt shabby confronted by the elegance of the suite. Thea glanced through the balcony windows and caught the well-known view of the acropolis, the luminous white marbled temple of the *Parthenon*, floating above the modern apartment blocks of the city.

Later refreshed from the city grime and with her hair still damp, Thea helped herself to a small bottle of wine from the minibar and stood out on the balcony savouring the view. The city spread out before her like a grid, its symmetry emerging into focus and the long wide avenue sweeping down to the sea, where Themistocles' wooden walls had stood in ancient times, built to repel the Persian invasion. Thea eased herself into one of the clear plastic designer chairs and took a sip of the sharp chilled white wine, breathing in the view. Her mind felt restless like the city below. All her unanswered questions came tumbling through her mind. *Why had Dimitri suddenly disappeared from her life? Why had he never written to her or contacted her? Had he ever realised the torment and agony he had caused?* She had wrestled with these countless times, but now finally she might discover the truth.

The telephone rang, startling Thea. Darkness had fallen and bright lights now illuminated the city. "Mr Kampitsis is here downstairs for you," the clipped voice on the line informed her.

When Thea got out of the lift, Dimitri was waiting. He was immaculately dressed, the formal suit now replaced by a spotless shirt and well-pressed chinos, similar to what he wore when he had walked back into her life several weeks ago. He greeted her warmly, leaning in to kiss her on both cheeks. As they touched, she could feel his smooth shaven cheek and the fragrance of expensive male cologne: her acute sense of smell picked out lemon, bergamot and oak.

"Shall we?" He steered Thea towards the hotel entrance, gallantly opening the glass door for her. "I have taken the liberty of booking a table for us. It is somewhere I wanted to show you and thought you would enjoy."

At the back of the hotel, the apartment blocks gave way to the wooded lower slopes of the mountain and the sound of cicadas. They boarded the old funicular carriage, which took them inside the steep Lykavettos hill to the summit. When they alighted into the darkness, all the city was now spread out before them. The *Parthenon* itself, glowing and shining in the dark, and beyond it the city lights stretching down to the deep blackness of the Saronic Gulf. There was a beauty and symmetry to the city at night time.

"I hope that you will enjoy my choice," Dimitri said guiding Thea towards the small restaurant, nestled into a rocky hollow beneath the summit. Thea could now see where they were dining. Dimitri had obviously chosen it for its intimacy, a place favoured by courting couples, with one of the most dramatic views of Athens.

The waiters attentively seated them at a table. Dimitri must have noticed her flinch as she read through the menu. "Please, order whatever you wish," he reassured her, "do not be concerned about the cost. Tonight you are my guest and it is my honour. The mixed fish platter here is excellent or there is lobster if you prefer." After they had ordered, a bottle of champagne was quickly produced elegantly wrapped in a gold-foil bottle.

"I propose a toast," said Dimitri, raising his filled glass and leaning forwards. "To the reunion of old friends." Thea clinked her glass but did not return the toast. She took a sip of the wine and allowed the bubbles, delicate and light, to fizzle on her tongue before swallowing. A warm smile played on Dimitri's lips which confused her, as if the champagne was clouding her judgement. With the alcohol and warm easy charm, her anger was dissipating.

"So, I can't believe that we are together again, here in Athens," Dimitri said brightly, clasping his hands together. He leaned forward to refill her glass. "I always wondered where you were. If we would ever meet again. And now you are here before me."

For a fleeting moment, the memory of that summer long ago came back to Thea. They had met almost on that first day, when Thea had arrived on the island, heady with examination results and fresh from leaving college. Thereafter they became virtually inseparable. Each day after work, Dimitri had rolled up on his motorbike to transport her to the beach to meet with friends, or excitedly introduced her to an eating place he had discovered, or a late-night drink in town. In those untroubled days, always he had been attentive and as the summer shortened, they had declared their love to each another.

That last afternoon he had turned up early, a frown etched across his handsome face. He had paced restlessly as he broke the news: he was leaving on family business and had come to say goodbye. In the quiet of the empty cottage, they had made love for the first time on the rusting iron bed as the old springs squeaked to the rhythm of their bodies. In his parting words, he had promised he would return to her. But he had stepped out of her life as easily and lightly as a player exiting the stage. A cruel act. She had been only nineteen.

Thea brought herself out of the memory. She looked across at Dimitri, trying to connect the man in front of her to the younger man she had loved. The face was fuller and more mature, the hair more tightly cropped, but the features and bearing were the same.

"So what happened," she asked bluntly, her anger now finally bursting out. "Why did you disappear? You led me to believe that you expected to be away from the island for two weeks." She could hear the reproach in her own questions and tears prickled her eyes. "The whole summer I waited for you without a word. I even wrote to you after I left the island, but you never replied."

"I'm so sorry," Dimitri said, reaching forward to try to take her hand, but she withdrew it. "I never wanted to leave you. I was told by my father that it was only for two weeks. They told me the truth, only when we arrived in South America. That it was a ploy by my parents. They disapproved of our relationship and feared I would marry you against their wishes. So they tricked me into going to South America and once there I was forced to stay and work in the family shipping office for a whole year." He spoke now earnestly, looking at her directly. "You have to believe me it wasn't what I wanted. I loved you and wanted us to be together!"

"Well they had their way!" Thea snapped, hearing the sound of righteousness in her anger. But his explanation had sowed doubt in her mind and she could feel her conviction already wavering. "And what about your wife? For I believe you are now married."

"Clemmie?" The question seemed to catch him by surprise, a slight frown pressing his forehead. "It was a dynastic arrangement, Thea, planned from when we were small children," he said, reaching out his hand towards her and then pulling back. "She's the daughter of the Archontakis family, the wealthy ship owners, an associate of my father. Our parents had always hoped that she and I would marry when we were older. We are fond of one another but our relationship is different from you and I. We had something very special, which doesn't happen often in a lifetime."

Dimitri reached out and squeezed Thea's hand. The sensation of his touch on her skin startled her. "You have to believe me, there was only ever you," he said, his hand still cupping her own and his eyes intent on her face. "Leaving you, knowing your upset, was the hardest thing I've ever done. But my parents adamantly refused our engagement and I couldn't go against them. But you have to believe I never stopped loving you."

It wasn't the explanation Thea had expected or rehearsed in her mind so many countless times, but still she did not completely trust his words.

"You planned to ask me to marry you?"

"I did," he admitted.

Pulling his hand away, Dimitri waved over one of the itinerant flower sellers. Placing a wad of notes in the surprised man's hand, he presented Thea with a single red rose.

"A peace offering," he said. The delicate crimson rose petals were still folded and the thorns had been removed from the stem to prevent injury. Thea held the flower close to her, breathing in the delicate perfume.

"Thank you," she replied, allowing a small smile to break over her face.

Dimitri leaned back, filling his chair with his limbs. "So tell me about your day, Thea. Did you have a successful visit to the archaeological school?"

She had planned to tread cautiously but after his disclosure, Thea felt lulled into the old feeling of familiarity. She described to him her day's search, sifting through the old archaeological journals, thumbing the index pages for any mention of grave discoveries in the Paliki area. She had pored over every journal published in Greek over the last century.

"So did you find anything?" asked Dimitri curiously.

"Unfortunately the main discoveries were made after the war and the records were destroyed by the large earthquake in 1953 that took place on Kefalonia?"

"Yes, all we Kefalonians know about this terrible time. Most of the main town was reduced to rubble and people were sleeping out in tents. So that is not surprising," he replied, raising his chin. "But you still think the palace is out there?"

"Yes, I believe so." Thea nodded. "I'm convinced it is somewhere on the northern side of the Paliki peninsula. My own hunch is that it is close to Mousatoi. The village is just on the edge of a very fertile valley, certainly no more than an hour's walk, which is perfect for cultivating olives, grapes and crops. It seems to intersect with the other geographical pointers from Homer, where Odysseus initially comes ashore when he finally returns to Ithaka. But at the moment I can't get any closer."

"So what's next?"

"I'm planning to go back through the local archives on Paliki next week and just keep searching. I'm also going to see if we can re-create Odysseus' journey on foot from where he first lands. It would allow us to pin down the radius of the search area, where the terrain matches Homer's landmarks. There is the island out in the bay," Thea paused. "But there is no way of getting there without a boat."

"Perhaps I can do something there to help you." Dimitri lifted his eyes and took a sip of the champagne. "So, you are keen to keep looking for this palace?"

"Absolutely!" Thea replied emphatically. "I came here to find it and I'm not done yet."

"So are you ready to get back?" Dimitri asked, now checking his watch. They had finished their meal and Dimitri waved over the waiter to settle the bill. They paused once more at the extraordinary view of the city stretched out in front of them, before retracing their steps to the funicular rail. As they stepped out into the quiet residential quarter of the city, they walked together companionably side by side, their footsteps echoing on the smoothed paving stones. At the edge of a small park, Dimitri took her hand and drew her into the shadows to a small wooden bench. The skeleton of a brightly coloured swing hung forlorn. They sat beside each other, Dimitri's features obscured by the darkness except for the pressure of his fingers and the fragrance of lemon bergamot.

"Is it too late for us Thea?" he whispered.

"Can we not give ourselves another chance?" Dimitri reached over, drawing her face close, his soft lips closing on hers.

Thea pulled away. "Please don't, Dimitri." He sat up still for a moment deep in thought, casually stroking her hand.

"Couldn't we spend some time together and just see what happens," he said turning towards her, the contours of his face catching the glow of the street lamps. "I've arranged to go away with Clemmie and the family over the Easter. Afterwards promise me that we can spend time together, just me and you."

"And your wife?"

"We go our separate ways and keep up appearances for the children's sake. A relationship with me would change nothing."

The explanation was plausible but Thea still shook her head. "And what about my work on the project."

"Don't worry," Dimitri reassured her, squeezing her gently, "I can take care of that. I'm considering renewing next year's funding anyway. Richard has been very anxious to secure our support for another season and that would put his mind at rest. Please Thea, just promise me. We owe it to ourselves to give us this chance." Perhaps it was the champagne or the agreeableness of the evening, but his words and familiar touch were starting to make an impression, stirring up old feelings.

"Alright then," Thea finally replied hesitatingly. "Let us meet again and see what happens." Dimitri placed his arm around her waist, pulling her closer, kissing her full on the lips. This time Thea didn't resist but responded to the embrace. He enfolded her in his strong muscular arms, so she felt the solidness of his chest, the feel of his skin and his masculine smell. He broke away first.

"Come on, we should go," he said drawing her up to her feet. "It's been a long day and you must be tired." As they parted in the empty hotel corridor, he leaned in and kissed her lovingly on her lips. "We have time," he said.

Chapter 15

Feasting

Helios' light was fading, when Odysseus and Telemachos reached the entrance leading into the yard. Crowning the swell of the hillock, the well-founded palace stood proud and upright. It was not as magnificent as the famed Mykenai, but nevertheless Odysseus still marvelled at the linear stone walls and square cut windows, red painted and deep set. Already a gathering of people, idly chatting, had assembled beneath the wide plane tree, having set aside their labours for the day. Glancing round, Odysseus recognised the faces: men who served him, working his fields and estates. Some he knew as the sons and grandsons of those companions, with whom he had endured so much. In those faces, traces of those companions lived on: a square forehead here, a pressed nose or rounded cheeks there.

"Welcome," he called out enthusiastically greeting each in turn. "We will all eat well this evening and take our fill of meat and wine, before tomorrow's feast of Apollo. There will be entertainment that would give a man joy." Broad grins broke out at his words.

As he spoke, he glanced up and glimpsed the white owl perched over the high gable of the roof. Turning aside, he caught one of the servants, hastening by with a flame to light the tallow candles hung inside the porch.

"The bird is still here?" he hissed, anxious not to be overheard.

"Yes, all day, master. The women have driven it off only for it to return a short while later. It will not budge from the rooftop."

A shadow passed over his body for he knew Penelope was superstitious of such occurrences, believing them to be portents from the gods. "Is your mistress, Penelope, aware for this would distress her?"

"I think not, master," ventured the loyal servant. "She has been occupied with her loom all day and has not wandered outdoors."

"Then that is good." He nodded at the man, before dismissing him. He would not dwell on these things. Dinner awaited them. "Come, Telemachos," he said clasping his son by the shoulder. "Let us wash off this grime from our bodies, before we dine." And father and son together entered the well-built stronghold.

Darkness had crept into the hall, as Odysseus took his place at the long wooden table. The tallows had been lit and bitter-tasting smoke hung in the air, which pricked the eyes. The raucous noise of human chatter filled the great hall, as the dinner guests had already been seated. At his right hand as always sat Telemachos, his skin well-oiled and his hair carefully groomed. A fresh robe covered his son's limbs, the fine handiwork of his wife Epicaste. Close beside, were seated Odysseus' two grandsons, the sons of Telemachos, now entering warrior-hood. The elder, Persepolis, in time being destined to succeed to the throne of the island kingdom.

It was at that moment, a hushed silence fell on the gathering as the lady of the house, Penelope, Odysseus' queen, stepped into the great hall. Flanked by her attendants and their daughter-in-law Epicaste, Penelope was modestly veiled as was her custom. Odysseus watched her move gracefully like a wild deer, as Penelope took her place at his side. Despite the passage of time, the gods had been kind to her. Within the privacy of their chamber, her uncovered face still bore her youthful appearance although flecks of grey streaked her dark hair. Tonight she wore a flame-coloured gown, woven by her own skilled hands and richly decorated with unending circles reminiscent of the cycle of life. He noticed her slim waist and how, despite her years, Penelope still bore herself nobly as a queen. Her entry signalled for the feast to begin. Hastily a troop of servants carried in plates piled high with roasted meats and the wine krater filled to the brim with dark wine, diluted with honey and water, before it was handed round for all to partake.

"Where have you been all day, my lord?" Penelope turned her gracious head towards him. She spoke modestly without grievance, her features obscured by her veil. "I noticed you rose early before *Dawn* and have been gone all day."

"I could not sleep, my love," he replied above the din of the feasting. "The gods disturbed my sleep again with dreams of Troy. So Telemachos and I departed early to inspect the preparations for the festival and to ensure all was in order. But in truth, I took rest in the shaded orchard, as I could not shake off the weariness of age and the visions that torment me."

"But would you not take more rest in the comfort of your own bed where none would disturb you? For your body no longer relishes sleeping on the hard earth, wherever you can lay your head." He knew her words were moved by feeling and held a truth. For though still a strong man, his limbs had weakened and now caused him pain.

"My dear wife, I am touched by your concern,"

he replied. "But do not trouble yourself, for Telemachos did not allow me to lack comfort but spread a coverlet over me." He turned his head to her face, but beneath the veil, her expression was inscrutable. "But," he continued, "now Helios beats down on the land again, would you not wish to accompany me outside, that we might enjoy our lands together and what the gods grant us." As the words left his mouth, he already knew her reply. They had had this exchange so many times before and always Penelope's cautiousness had prevailed.

She lifted her chin towards him. "You know I would prefer to stay inside the palace, attending to the domestic duties of the household," she replied graciously. "There is much to occupy my days, supervising the looms and helping Epicaste look after the children. Clambering about in the mud and undergrowth does not befit a noble woman. Rather it is the lot of a lesser-born woman who does not begrudge her face withering under Helios' rays."

Suddenly Kirke's image came upon him again and her haunting serene smile. It was if the gods dangled the memory in his mind to toy with him. It had been during *Spring*, when the woodland had come into flower and once more the heat had begun to rise. She had woken him early before the rest of the household had stirred.

"There is a place I want to show you," Kirke whispered in his ear. "It is a special place, known only to myself, where I go to set aside my formal duties and responsibilities." As the mist pooled over the sea plain, she had led him out along a narrow trail deep into the dense forest. In the hollow of the woodland, there was a lake, fed with waters from a mountain stream. Under the dappled light, where none could behold them, she had stripped naked and strode into the water, urging him to join her. He had gawped at her like a beached fish, stunned at seeing her flesh, the curved breasts and rounded buttocks exposed to the sight of the gods. Never had he seen his own wife's body uncovered outside of the bed chamber. He had pulled off his own mantle, feeling the weight of kingship and leadership lifting from his shoulders, until he stood there naked as a man. Then he had plunged headlong into the cool waters, gasping for air as he surfaced. Like village children, they had played, laughing, splashing and frolicking until Helios was high up in the sky. Even with her long tresses twisting down her shoulders and the water droplets dripping from her face, Kirke captivated him. Afterwards, under the woodland canopy, they had made love on the forest floor. Under the rustling of the leaves, protected by the circle of ash with its creamy blossom, perhaps then they had begotten the child.

"Husband, did you not hear me." He glanced up. Penelope had turned towards him poised for his reply.

He pushed the memory away and looked across at her. "Forgive me, beloved wife, something took my mind."

"I asked my lord, whether it is safe to roam by yourself? To sleep unprotected outside without your sword or a watchman to defend you." Penelope whispered to him, so he strained to hear. "Each day brings reports of people arriving from the mainland, seeking a safe place for themselves and their kin to raise a new roof." He heard behind her words her fears of the kingdom being ruined and the wealth of their house being diminished by too many mouths feeding off their herds and flocks.

Odysseus regarded her, the corners of his eyes crinkling. "What you have said is true, Penelope. There is unrest on the mainland and the skies have become blackened so that the harvests have failed for three seasons. These people come seeking refuge within our island kingdom on the island of Same. I have granted them land so they can set up new homes and through their toil feed themselves." He spoke soothingly as if comforting a child. "Telemachos is newly returned from Pronnoi, where he has been ensuring that all is carried out in accordance with my wishes. The kingdom of Ithaka is not affected and our own grain stores are full. All the estates prosper so there is enough for all. The newcomers' plight cannot be ignored for I was destitute once and only through the hospitality of strangers did I survive and return safely to Ithaka."

"Come, we are here to feast!" he said, turning his head away from her. "Let us have song to shake off this gloomy mood that some god has put in your mind." Calling out to one of the servants, he cried "Summon the bard to entertain us with music and song."

"Certainly, my Lord," came the reply.

The bard set up close to the hearth, next to the crackling fire, setting his well-strung lyre on his lap. He was a stranger, no more than thirty seasons of age, who had travelled with Telemachos from Pronnoi. The folds of his cloak were still soiled from the dusty paths. All at once, a sweet haunting singing descended over the hall and those hearing the sound quickly fell silent. The harmony was unknown to him, but quickly he recognised the unfolding story as his own, only embroidered under the callings of the *Muse*.

With a full sail and prevailing *Wind*, they had left the land of Aiaia but Odysseus had carried Kirke's instructions deep within his heart. The dangers had been as she had warned. Off a clutch of islands, the winds had swept in carrying the enigmatic echoes of sweet maiden singing. On his orders, the men had tied him to the mast with cords and sealed their ears with wax, refusing to draw near. He had railed at them, straining against the knotted ropes, as he begged them to release him so he might know these mysterious creatures, the Sirens.

It was on the ninth full day at sea that they had come across a beacon arising out of the foaming sea, whose flame and red glowing rock burned day and night. The men had been alarmed by the sight of the huge rocks and pumice hurled into the air, where no bird could fly safely, fearing the displeasure of the gods. But he had stayed faithful to Kirke's instructions. Keeping the Wandering Rocks to the right, he had steered the ship's course down towards the straits of Messenia. There, compressed by the land on both sides, the sea narrowed into a channel. Kirke had warned of *Charybdis*, the whirlpool who could suck a ship and its crew whole, carrying them down to the murky depths. He chose the course closer to the steep sided cliff. But no matter how hard they rowed, the sea-god Poseidon held them back with the currents. Only after they strained oarlocks, their foreheads hot and pounding, did the god grant them passage. It was then they saw strange creatures from the sea depths. Not the many headed monster *Scylla* of which the bard now sang, but tentacled and snake-fanged creatures, dead or half dying, that terrified the men out of their wits.

They then had passed into the calmer waters, the wide open swell of the grey sea ahead of them. He had been eager to continue on with their journey, but Eurylochos spoke up, laying down his oar.

"Can we not pull into this shore of Thinakia to take rest?" he demanded, his shoulders square and holding his head high. The sea journey had done nothing to temper his humour. "The men are weary from battling *Charybdis'* currents and need to take rest."

Odysseus looked at the men, who had lowered their oars, watching the exchange sullenly. Since their stay at Aiaia, they had become less responsive to his authority. No one had questioned his command outright but insubordination rippled below the surface.

"Very well then," he agreed reluctantly. "We will beach the ship and set-up camp for the night."

They found a sheltered bay beneath a sacred fire breathing mountain. Initially the verdant land offered promised respite to the weary travellers to regain their strength for the long sea crossing ahead. Only when Odysseus spotted the herds of cows grazing on the rich pastureland on the mountain slopes, was he seized with panic. Then the warning of the blind seer, Tiresias, came to his mind and he was filled with dread and foreboding.

That first night, he had taken the men by surprise. As they huddled round the campfire, the orange glow of the firelight flickering on their faces, he had made each and every one of them swear an oath. Not to kill or maim any cow they encountered under any circumstance, but to leave them unharmed. And the men had promised faithfully they would not touch a hair of the sacred cattle, an oath witnessed by the gods on Mount Olympos.

But then the fair weather had turned. Each day the gods sent storms and *Notos*, the south wind, keeping them trapped in that sheltered harbour. At first all had been well and the men had been content with their lot, happily idling away their time until the wind changed. Then they had fed on the rations of bread and wine supplied by Kirke. As the food grew scarce, they had tried to live on fish and birds caught in traps. But as their bellies began to empty and their muscles wasted, the complaints had started to swell. Eurylochos grew resentful, sowing the seeds of *Mischief* here and there amongst the men. As the heat and humidity of the place rose during that lunar month, so too did the men's tempers threatening to break out into full mutiny.

That morn Odysseus had been close to despair,

when he had decided to climb the sacred fire-breathing mountain. Only a murmur of breeze and light bee hum stirred the air as he purified his hands with water. He made libation with the last of the wine skins and prayed to the gods that they might at last provide safe passage. He looked around for some portent to answer his prayer, but there was only silence and the fertile grass valley stretching down to the shore.

It was when as he returned to the camp that he got the first warning of trouble. A plume of ashen smoke was rising up and there was a smell of meat roasting over a fire. The evidence was there to see. He strode into the camp, the full force of his rage upon him.

"Do you not realise what you have done?!" he cried out. One of the men, who had been about to bite into a chunk of meat, stopped and stared at him wide-eyed. A coat of meat scraps and animal fat encrusted his mouth. There were remnants of spitted meat and butchered cattle, but the men had already gorged themselves. He quickly counted the dead animals. Twelve slain beasts in all. "By killing these cattle sacred to the god, you have cut short your own days." He looked around, seeing a mix of despair and anguish taking over for these lost men. He left them to finish their impious feast, unable to bear watching. Whatever fate awaited them could not now be undone.

They put to sea the next day, hastily leaving that place as if they could outrun the *Fates* themselves. It would have been wiser to stay the winter now that windstorms had appeared, but Odysseus was convinced that they had offended the gods.

It was not long before his deepest fears were realised. A raging tempest sent by Zeus himself descended upon them, with no land in sight to take refuge. They had tried to battle the sea, straining on the oars with all their strength as the waves poured into the ship. But then disaster had struck. Odysseus shuddered to recall it. With a sickening groan, the mast had crashed down smashing apart the boat and hurling them into the water. As he fought his way up to take gulps of air, Odysseus recalled his last glimpse of his men, their heads bobbing in the waves crying out as one by one they disappeared. Even then, he had not been ready to descend to the dark of Hades. As he thrashed in the water, the *Fates* had put into his way the keel of the boat. Hastily he had scrambled to it and clung to the broken planking as a child to his mother. All through the darkness, he had held on tight, alone, refusing to give up his life.

Time passed in a haze. When the light of daybreak had come and the storm had finally quelled, he found himself drifting alone. There was no sign of those dear companions. He could not be sure how many days he was at sea. He remembered passing close to the straits of Messenia, where they had sailed but one lunar month ago, and being in danger of being sucked down into the whirlpool *Charybdis*. The sun god must have favoured him for he had cooled the heat of his rays, which would otherwise have beaten down remorselessly by day. But there was no comfort from the relentless thirst that racked his body or from the brine which permeated every crevice of his skin.

When the raft finally touched land, the local people discovered him near death, still clinging to those splintered timbers. That had been the land of Ogygia, where they had tended his broken body and nursed him back to health. In exchange for the gift of life, he had accepted the daughter of their chief as his bride, Kalypso. For seven long years, he had shared her troglodyte cave-dwelling existence, sleeping on the rock-hard floor and shivering with cold when the northerly *Boreas* wind blew. They had had some semblance of a marriage, but it had not been a love match. And though Kalypso had borne him three children, he had felt no joy in her company or ample figure.

As time passed by, Odysseus had grown ever restless. Walking on the shingled beach looking out towards Ithaka, he felt like a trapped bird wanting to escape its cage. His mind harboured a thousand fold fears for his kingdom, for his family and young son, while he dawdled here. Always there was the question that preyed on his mind. Would Penelope stay steadfast or would the kingdom be lost? As to what else he had left behind, that part of his mind was sealed like a tomb that he refused to open.

On that seventh year, a god must have put it in Kalypso's mind to help him. For she had noticed his low spirit, the way he took no pleasure in eating, love-making or evening story-telling around the cave fire. She had been a kind-hearted spirit and had petitioned her father to help him leave that wretched island. The chief had resisted at first until a kinsman had come forward to offer wedlock to Kalypso. He had not been a god, as the bard now described in painted words, but a mortal man ambitious for power. Then at last Odysseus had been equipped with a sturdy wooden boat. This time he had not lingered or prolonged his farewell to Kalypso. As soon as the fair weather arrived, he had put to sea steering by the Bear and the Pleiades stars.

For seventeen days, Odysseus sailed across that boundless sea, with only the endless swell of the waves for company. Even then the god Poseidon, the earth-shaker, had not quite done with him. On the eighteenth day, the god had whipped up a tempest, driving the ship off course and engulfing it with heavy waves. For two whole days, his body had clung tight to the mast, gripping the sail trusses. They had cut into his reddened chafed hands, burning the flesh like fire, but he had refused to let go. Even then, his mind was turning to how best he might survive refusing to give into death. When land finally appeared and the waves were threatening to engulf the small boat, he reasoned it best to swim for the shore. Quickly he had emptied out the goat skins and filled these with his breath to make a float. Then casting aside the heavy robe presented by Kalypso, he had thrown himself into the sea.

Now the bard was telling of his meeting at the shore's edge with a young Phaiakian princess, after the sea had finally deposited him onto land. Nausikaa had been her name, fresh faced and milky skinned. The other women had run screaming as he approached them, naked and destitute, only a leaf to cover his modesty. With soft and honourable words of supplication, he had gained her trust and her assistance. It had been she who had ordered her maids to wash and clothe him and instructed him in how to petition the help of her father, King Alkinoos, and her mother, Queen Arete.

The bard now was extolling Odysseus' qualities: his god-like appearance, his physical prowess, his noble countenance and how he could better any man in the athletic games so that even the young princess had fallen in love with him. Clearly the bard was expecting a good supper and generous reward for his efforts. Bawdy laughter rang out from the table.

"You are one for the women, Odysseus," one of his guests exclaimed.

"Perhaps that hospitality was too comfortable for you seemed in no hurry to return," shouted out another to raucous laughter.

Suddenly he felt ill at ease and awkward, sitting beside his honourable and steadfast wife. It was true that discovering his true identity, Alkinoos had offered him the hand of his daughter. He had graciously declined thinking only of his return. Nevertheless he had been accorded the full honours of guest friendship and provided with passage on a boat to take him at last to his journey's end, Ithaka.

The bard had now finished his song and the fellow guests roared out their approval, thumping the tables and calling out his name "Odysseus". The raucous sound filled the high beamed hall. But he still felt troubled in the knowledge he had not been faithful to his lawful wife and by all those years he had deserted her. He quickly glanced at Penelope besides him, trying to make out her reaction. Nothing could be discerned in her expression. There Penelope sat dignified and composed, no outward display of sentiment betraying her thoughts.

Chapter 16

Pascha

It was still quite early in the morning when Thea descended the staircase into the hotel lobby. Sunlight was flooding through the large bay windows, holding the promise of a warm spring day with a clear azure sky.

"Someone's got an admirer, I see," said Electra conspiratorially, as Thea handed over her room key. "Such beautiful roses that arrived for you yesterday! I think someone likes you very much." Thea blushed thinking of the extravagant pink bouquet in the modest surroundings of her room.

"And what's that I see?" Electra had noticed the flash of gold on Thea's finger, her eye drawn to the metal like a magpie. "Let me see!" Thea reluctantly volunteered her hand for Electra to inspect. "Very expensive!" Electra gasped excitedly as she examined the embossed gold ring on Thea's slender finger. "I think this admirer is very rich too!" With a slight nod, Thea accepted Electra's approval, trying to cover up her awkwardness. These outward extravagant displays by Dimitri were obviously being noticed and not just by her.

Across at the hotel entrance, Thea found Matthew looking pensive and pre-occupied. His face lit up at her approach and he greeted her with an open smile. Almost regretfully Thea noted he was alone.

"How are things?" she asked, noting the dark shadows underscoring Matthew's eyes. "You look tired."

"It's been a tough week," he admitted. "Rob and I have had a few late nights working to catch up on the analysis. Hopefully today will be more relaxed," he said buoyantly forcing a grin. "Certainly it will be good to escape the lab for the day."

"Is Rob not joining us?" Thea asked, her eyes circling the foyer, puzzled by his absence.

"He's on his way down." Matthew looked around furtively and lowered his voice. "I have to warn you," he began, "Rob's not in a good mood." Thea had wanted to press him more, but at that precise moment Rob's familiar figure appeared. He was dressed in cargo shorts and a bright close-fitting shirt, presumably local purchases, which emphasised the strong muscles of his shoulders and arms. But the relaxed casual clothes did not mirror Rob's expression and the scowl planted on his face. He gave Thea the briefest of acknowledgements, before striding out of the hotel. It wasn't a good sign for the day and already Thea's initial enthusiasm had evaporated.

"Enjoy your day," Electra called out after them, as Thea and Matthew followed Rob's receding figure through the wide glass doors.

It had been Mark who had proposed a team barbecue on one of the southern beaches on Paliki to celebrate Greek Easter, *Pascha*. It had seemed a good idea at the time, especially as the Greeks took the occasion very seriously and everything closed down to celebrate the holy day. Thea had come prepared for a rough hike, picking out a jade shirt and shorts to go with her sturdy walking boots. Into her rucksack, she had stuffed some beach items as a concession to the public holiday: a towel, a book, sunscreen and sunglasses. In her hand, she clutched the cardboard box, containing baklava pastries, which the assistant from her favourite bakery had decorated with a purple ribbon.

In the taxi, Matthew was first to break the awkward silence.

"So I understand we are making a detour before we arrive at the beach."

"Yes. I hope that's ok," replied Thea lightly. "Mr Kampitsis very kindly offered transport to take us over to the small island in the middle of the bay. It's called *Vardianoi*, meaning "Protector", as it guards the entrance to the gulf. I'm keen to visit it but it's only accessible by boat." She noticed again Rob's deafening silence as he sat in the front seat, his broad shoulders stiff and upright. The cold atmosphere was starting to dampen her mood.

"Does it have any significance?" Matthew enquired happy to continue the conversation.

"Of course. Homer mentions an island situated between Ithaka and Same, the old name for Kefalonia. It's here the suitors of Penelope dispatch a ship to ambush Odysseus' son Telemachos, after he journeys to the mainland for news of his father. By then, the kingdom is in a terrible state and the suitors are threatening to depose Telemachos as his father's heir," Thea explained. They all lurched forward as the car hit a pothole in the road. "I'm hoping that Vardianoi will provide more geographical evidence that Paliki is our Ithaka."

"And what happens to the son?" asked Matthew, interested. "Does he survive the ambush?"

"He has a premonition and instead decides to sail a different way up to one of the northern harbours. So he escapes and returns secretly to Ithaka, where he is reunited with his father." At these words, Thea noticed Rob throw a glance in her direction. The good humour had vanished, but she had not discerned him as a man of contradictory moods, blowing hot and cold like the wind.

They were now approaching one of the modern hotels in the resort area of the town. It was still early in the season and the area was only just starting to open up after the winter hibernation. There still were not many foreign visitors about. A speedboat was waiting for them at the jetty.

"Wow! Is that for us? I've never travelled this way before?" exclaimed Matthew enthusiastically, clearly impressed.

"Yes, I think so," Thea said noticing Rob remained stubbornly silent. She sensed the speedboat was Dimitri's doing, another display to impress her or at the very least, Stelios had been tasked with the job.

They were warmly welcomed on board by the skipper and his younger companion. But the atmosphere from the taxi followed them and hung over the speedboat like a dark cloud. It was dispelled by the hum of the motor starting as the boat pulled away from the jetty. Once out of the shelter of the harbour, the boat gained momentum, skimming and bouncing off the waves. They were now heading across the straits to a small island in the bay. As the breeze whipped up around them, Thea held tight to the side of the boat. It was hard to talk above the noise of the engine, the sea spray and gusts of wind.

The island quickly came into view and the stump of the old lighthouse, standing castrated on its plinth of concrete. Thea could feel her excitement rising, as she scanned the shoreline, tempered by growing nausea from the boat ride. There was no immediate sign of what she was seeking, only large boulders and rugged rocks.

The sound of the motor engine quietened as the boat now approached its destination, a small half moon bay, and with relief, Thea took in the white sand against the clay edge. *So there was at least one beach, where a ship could be brought aground.*

"So what exactly are we looking for?" asked Matthew, surveying the flat barren land.

"A second harbour," Thea replied, shielding her face from the dazzling sunlight with her hand. "The Odyssey describes the island as having two harbours. This one here is ideal for the Myceneans. They would beach the ships on shore, pulling them up above the water, rather than anchoring them in the bay. We just need to see if there's a second beach."

"This is as far as we can go into shore," said the skipper, raising his voice over the spluttering engine. An anchor was being dropped with a rumbling noise of metal scrapping against metal. It was hard to discern the Greek words above the din and the gusts of wind. "You will need to wade in from here. We'll stay on the boat, so let us know when you are ready to leave."

"Thank you," said Thea, starting to remove her boots. "Bring your footwear with you," she said, casting her glance at Matthew, "unless you are staying on the beach."

"Thea, why don't you use your Greek to ask the skipper if he knows anything?" The sound of Rob's voice surprised her. It was the first time he had addressed her directly all morning.

"Thanks for the suggestion." She glanced up at Rob for a moment, searching for a sign of friendship but only a stony expression greeted her. Their relationship had distinctly soured.

Thea turned to the skipper, noticing his surprising slight build and slender arms in comparison to other sea-faring Greeks she had encountered. "Do you know if there is another beach here on Vardianoi?" Thea asked, switching again into Greek.

The skipper hesitated for a moment and then shrugged. "Not that I know of," he said, throwing his arms back. "The island is surrounded by rocks everywhere except for this bay. But..." he paused, thinking out aloud. "My father worked the boats before. He told me that once the island was larger as they used to come here to hunt rabbits. It's possible there could have been another beach but it has been taken by the sea."

Feeling deflated by his words, Thea tried to enthuse her voice with optimism as she thanked him. Holding her boots aloft, she descended the short rope ladder, gasping as she entered the cold sea. The sand was soft-rippled beneath her feet making it easy to wade to the shore.

Perfect, she thought, scanning the shoreline, as she stepped onto the dry sand.

"So you are saying this might be the very spot where the suitors hid for their ambush?" Matthew had come to join her and was standing beside her. Clearly the idea captured his imagination.

"Precisely." Thea sat down on a smooth rock and started to dust the gritty sand from her feet, looking round. "On this north side, any boats would be hidden from view from anyone sailing into the gulf from the south. We are looking for somewhere a small ship can be beached. It only needs to be a short visit." She finished tying the final shoelace of her boot. "I don't know if this island has any snakes," she said pausing." It may be wise to make lots of noise so they scuttle out of the way." Without a second glance, Thea set off leading the way.

They clambered over the rocks and detritus to a small jetty, made of decaying planks of wood, nailed together. They climbed up the steep steps using an old rope banister. At the top, a disused chapel from the old monastery came into view. It was here, just above the sandy beach they found a single track, the red earth path picking its way through the scrubland of yellow gorse. From this vantage point, it was obvious the island was flat, treeless and featureless, except for the broken stump of the lighthouse and an old shipwrecked boat in the distance.

Rob had now caught them up and was quickly outpacing them. After a couple of minutes of trying to keep up his pace, Thea and Matthew both fell into a comfortable walking rhythm. As Rob's figure receded, it at least gave them a chance to talk.

"So how have things been going over the last couple of weeks?" Thea asked, trying to fathom Rob's ill-temper.

There was a discernible pause before Matthew responded. "Not great. You know that Rob unexpectedly had to leave the island for a couple of days, which threw our schedule." He adjusted his hat to shield his face from the strong sunlight. "Then we've had a series of visitors to the lab which has further disrupted things. First Richard, then Mr Kampitsis himself, both asking to see the ins and outs of our work. Ever since we've been hosting regular visits from the Foundation or local dignitaries at Mr Kampitsis' request. Rob was furious. I don't think it's just about being behind schedule. He and our great benefactor just don't seem to hit it off."

"Oh," Thea replied, taken by surprise. She could imagine Dimitri being excited by any new discovery like a child unwrapping a toy on Christmas morning. It brought to the surface her own recent experiences of Dimitri. Certainly it was clear he had other concerns in addition to herself. But she had an uneasy feeling that Rob's ill humour was connected to her in some way and perhaps what she had disclosed.

"Dimitri, I mean Mr Kampitsis," Thea said correcting herself, "can be very single-minded. But," she added, steering the conversation into safer territory, "the Foundation must be very pleased with the progress in the lab."

"Yes, the results so far are very promising," Matthew readily agreed. "Rob thinks that it's way too premature to draw conclusions. He tends to be very territorial about his work and isn't used to entertaining visitors. But evidence does seem to support Paliki being a separate island."

This was good news but still a part of Thea

felt uneasy. "I may have said something out of turn," she confided, biting her inner lip. "I mentioned to Richard and Mr Kampitsis that you were getting encouraging results. Rob told me in confidence and I'm afraid I may have inadvertently disrupted your work."

"Don't worry Thea," Matthew said reassuringly. "You're privileged for Rob to have entrusted you with that information. He must value you highly." For a moment, a wave of confusion swept over her, as Thea tried to reconcile this new information with Rob's aloofness. The curious mix of indifference but also attentiveness, verging on what exactly she could not say.

"Has the island always been called *Vardianoi*?" Matthew asked distracting Thea away from following this line of thinking.

"In Homer, it was known as *Asteris*, meaning like a star." They now had a clear view of the southern shoreline. "This isn't looking promising, Matthew," Thea said, noticing with disappointment the jagged rocky crevices at the water's edge. It would be impossible to beach a wooden ship here. She felt again doubt creeping over her. *Are we looking in the right place*, she wondered.

"Don't worry Thea," Matthew reassured her, picking up her tense mood. "If there's a second harbour on this island, Rob will find it. The man has got a sixth sense when it comes to geology."

"You think so?" Thea asked with incredulity. They had now reached the end of the track and the stump of the emasculated lighthouse. From the pile of stone and rubble, it was clear the beacon had once stood taller and prouder, guarding the straits before some earth tremor had toppled it. They were looking southwards over the rocky perimeter of the island towards the hazy mound of Zakynthos that rose up above the sea-line. Some way off Rob was gesticulating towards them. They made their way towards him, scrambling over the ruined debris of the lighthouse.

"I think I've found your second harbour," declared Rob, when they finally caught up, pointing towards a narrow strip of white sand enclosed by an outcrop of rocks.

"But how?" asked Thea, not fully taking in his words. "The shoreline here is far too rocky to beach a boat."

"That's true." A thoughtful expression played on Rob's face and a lively intelligence behind the slate-blue eyes. "What you're seeing here isn't necessarily the original shoreline. Rather with the seismic activity, I think this was originally a beach which became landlocked as the land rose over the last two millennia." He brushed away an insect, humming around in search of food. "The whole of the ground round here has been lifted up about five metres, equivalent to 20 H-bombs."

"So you think this could be the second beach?" Thea asked, surveying the shore-line. It was difficult to grasp the amount of physical force required to bring about that level of displacement of rock and earth, when everything looked so peaceful and solid.

"I suspect so. It would need a fuller geographical survey to confirm it and may be one for the future."

Thea turned her head upwards to look at him, squinting against the sunlight. "Thanks Rob." For the first time that morning, Rob returned her glance and smiled back. They walked along the stretch of silver sand, now landlocked, picking their way through the detritus that had been blown in from the sea: traces of old sailing boats, their wooden fixtures broken and splintered across the shore; bits of fishing nets; an old flip-flop; and a cluster of squashed plastic bottles, which had been lost or discarded into the sea. At the end of the beach, they came to the wreck of an old boat marooned on the rocks. The waves had tossed it unceremoniously onto the rocky shoreline, like a matchstick toy. Instead of being submerged in salt water, the stern pointed skywards suspended in clean air.

"Look!" called out Matthew, pointing at the calico sailcloth. "The sail is still attached to the mast." He hunkered down beside the wooden skeleton of the boat, where the fallen wooden mast now lay ripped from its fixture. The grey-coloured calico canvas had been shredded like rags, but the carefully tied sail remained trussed in place.

It was then that Rob appeared to falter. "Are you alright?" asked Thea, noticing his face had taken on a deathly pallor.

"For a moment, I felt unsteady on my feet," Rob replied sharply, throwing off her concern. "Just give me a moment to recover and I'll be okay. I suspect it's something I've eaten or the boat journey over. I'm not good on water."

"There's no rush," said Thea. "Take a seat on this rock for a few minutes until you feel better." She turned to Matthew. "Have you got some water?"

"No I don't need water," Rob responded, roughly pushing away the plastic bottle being offered. Nevertheless he sat down on one of the boulders, his head buried in his hands. Beads of sweat glistened on his forehead, which had turned ashen in colour. As Thea lightly pressed the back of her hand against his brow, he did not shake off her touch. The pulse was racing and although the skin felt cold and clammy, there was no fever. The cause appeared not physical.

"I can run back to the boat to let them know we've been delayed," said Matthew.

"That's a good idea," Thea agreed. "I'll stay here and we'll follow at our own pace in a short while." After Matthew had left, Thea sat close to Rob, the silence broken only by the light breeze and the sound of waves lapping against the shore. In the peacefulness of the day, it was hard to imagine the force of the tempest that must have smashed the sailing boat against the rocks, wrecking and splintering it into pieces.

After what seemed an age, Rob abruptly stood up and said "shall we go?" Without waiting for a reply, he set off striding ahead with Thea following as best she could. The path back across to the monastery was not so easy, narrowing in places where small brambles clawed at their ankles. It seemed that even the vegetation on the island was spiky and inhospitable.

Matthew was already watching out for them when they arrived at the small bay.

"Is he alright?" asked Matthew, as Rob sullenly walked past him, without a word removing his footwear and wading back to the boat.

"Who knows," replied Thea, shrugging her shoulders.

****

The sun was high in the sky, as the rugged shoreline of Paliki came into view, the grey clay mud cliffs crenellated like the edge of a serrated knife. In front of the cliffs was a distinctive narrow strip of red sand, where regimented lines of thatched sunshades had been planted. At the beach edge, a gazebo had been erected where small shapes gathered round. Gradually the blurred shapes filled out into recognisable figures, with hair, clothing and limbs. As the hum of the boat announced their arrival, faces looked up curiously to check the new arrivals.

The routine had become familiar, as they removed their footwear to wade to the shore. This time, as Thea started to climb onto the ladder, a hand grasped her own. She did not need to look up to recognise the touch of the fingers.

As they reached the water's edge, Belinda and Jamie ran up to greet them.

"Now that's called arriving in style!" Belinda exclaimed approvingly. "You look like celebrities!"

"Yes, I know. Isn't it cool," said Matthew, joining in with her enthusiasm.

"Do you think they will take us for a ride?" Jamie asked hopefully.

"Sorry mate," Matthew commiserated, as the

boat started to pull away, its motor gathering speed. "Maybe another time."

Grey plumes of smoke were already rising from the burning charcoal on the barbecue. Most of the group were clustered around the fire, chatting and watching the spits of roasting meat. Not everyone looked comfortable in this setting. Elizabeth sat detached from the group, stiff and awkward, concentrating on drawing in a sketchbook. The muted colours of her skirt and plain sweater seemed more fitting for a library and contrasted sharply with the red-sandy beach.

For once, Alistair had peeled himself away from his wife's side and now stood chatting with Richard, who appeared to be in his element. Dressed in loose fitting cream shirt and trousers topped by a Panama hat, Richard took on the appearance of the quintessential Englishman abroad. He had taken charge in almost military precision of the barbecue itself and the young men had been set the task of threading the assortment of meat onto wooden sticks.

"Happy Easter, Thea," Richard greeted her enthusiastically, looking up over the grey smoke, cooking tongs in hand. He nodded in the direction of the speedboat. "I see there's been no expense spared there. You really have made a big impression on our Mr Kampitsis!"

"It was very kind of him to go to such lengths," Thea agreed, inwardly grimacing. It was as if signs of their relationship were on show for all to see. She wondered what reaction Richard's words might have on Rob and looked around anxiously, but fortunately he appeared to be engaged in deep conversation.

"This all looks very organised. I brought this for later," Thea said, holding out the box of baklava. "Can I help with anything?"

"Just relax as we have it all in hand," Richard replied, gesturing sweepingly at the browning meat.

"Can I offer anyone some wine?" asked Mark embracing Thea on both cheeks. He held a large plastic water-bottle full of retsina in his hand and had a broad grin on his face. After conscientiously filling up everyone's cups of wine and handing these out, they sat down together on one of the rugs spread out on the sand beside Sophie and Belinda. Matthew had joined them and had now attached himself to Sophie's side. Thea could not help noticing the affectionate glance exchanged between the two young people. She looked around at the rest of the group: Alistair had returned to his wife and the couple were speaking together in low undertones.

"This is a pretty idyllic place, Mark," said Thea, taking a sip of the wine, savouring the chilled resinous flavour on her tongue before swallowing. "How did you hear about it?"

"I have my sources."

"Our housekeeper, Mrs Florakis, has taken a liking to Mark," commented Sophie with a gleam in her eye. "She keeps asking why such a handsome looking man is not married. She's always piling his plate up with the best food. I suspect that is his information source." Perhaps it was the effects of the wine, but a flush spread across Mark's face.

"You look positively glowing," Mark said, refocusing his attention upon Thea, studying her face. He lowered his voice, so only Thea could catch his words. "Like a woman in love. Is there something you're not telling your old friend?"

Thea pulled her knees close and wrapped her hands around her legs. "I confess I'm feeling good." She paused, catching her words, as she felt the sunlight warming her face. It had been a long time since she had felt happy and like herself. Mark had been right after all. It had been a good decision to return to the island. Her eyes inadvertently fell on Rob's resting figure, still recovering from his earlier fainting spell, where the air seemed to bristle like gathering dark clouds. "So how is the survey going Mark?" asked Thea, steering the conversation away from the thought.

"A bit mixed," Mark replied, restraining his

curiosity. "Richard perhaps wouldn't admit it, but the field survey so far has been a big disappointment. We've turned up only one or two small finds, pieces of pottery, but otherwise absolutely nothing from that period."

"You've still got time," Thea said reassuringly. "There are still a few weeks to go."

"I know", Mark replied, trying to instil some enthusiasm into his voice. "But I would have expected that we would have found some traces of occupation by now. I don't think it bodes well." He twisted his neck round to look at Thea, a grimace on his lips. "And it's been some of the most difficult survey terrain I've ever encountered," he said, speaking more openly. "Small pockets of land where either we can't trace the owner, or it's under heavy cultivation or it's so badly overgrown it is impossible. Everyone's legs and arms are covered with cuts and scratches. It's not been easy to keep up the motivation, walking up and down stretches of fields every day. Isn't that right Sophie?"

"It's still been a really interesting experience." Sophie replied tactfully. "We're learning a lot just by being here on the field survey. And the weather has been improving," she added. "I think we're just all keen to get as much done as we possibly can."

Thea thought for a moment. "Have you tried

moving the survey northwards, towards the village of Mousatoi? It's only six or seven kilometres away from your current site."

"We would have to get permits from the Greeks. Why do you suggest there?

Thea turned her face towards him, meeting his eye. "I discovered from the old Greek archaeological records Mycenean tombs were found just outside the village. I think it may be more promising."

Mark nodded, thoughtfully. "Alright," he agreed, "I'll speak with Richard and see if he is open to extending the survey in that direction."

At that point, Richard's voice boomed out, "FOOD'S READY!"

Gathering round the barbecue, they piled their plates with sticks of lamb souvlaki, Greek salad and bread. Belinda set out a plate heaped with generous chunks of green and blood-red melon.

"Are you alright Rob?" asked Richard, noticing Rob sitting listlessly picking at his food. He had hardly eaten anything. His face had still an unhealthy pallor and his colour had not fully returned.

"I'm just not feeling well from the boat journey," Rob said slowly raising his head. "I'll feel better once I've slept this off."

"Do you need anything?" Thea offered. "I may have something to help with nausea?" He shook his head and settled himself on one of the rugs once more, wrapping a blanket tightly around himself.

****

Once they were satiated with the heady mix of food and wine, a lull fell over the party. Thea found herself stretched out on a blanket, soaking up the balmy heat of the sun. In a semi-doze, her mind drifted back over the last few weeks and in particular to Dimitri.

Since returning from Athens, Dimitri had acted the part of an ardent and attentive lover. There had been daily phone calls, snatched texts, and extravagant gifts. One night, they had driven down a narrow twisting lane, through the orange and olive groves, leaving the small villages and tourist pensions behind. The restaurant, brightly lit, overlooked a secluded bay and offered a quiet refuge from the darkness. It was the kind of place where holidaying couples might come to share a romantic dinner. It had only occurred to her afterwards, that Dimitri might not just have chosen it for the intimacy but also the isolation: there was less chance of encountering someone he knew.

That evening they had been the only guests for dinner. Dimitri had dressed immaculately in casual jeans and an expensive looking fine-knit sweater. His cheeks were freshly shaved and smelt of spruce eau de toilette. A draught swept through the open-fronted building and Thea had hugged her cashmere sweater around her against the chill. They dined on sword-fish, green *horta* leaves picked from the mountain and salad accompanied with white *rombola* wine, with the hypnotic sound of the sea as a backdrop. The waiter had left them to their own company once their order had been placed and the food served. They had talked more about the project.

"I hadn't realised that you were so interested in the story of Odysseus," Thea had commented.

"Of course," Dimitri replied, pouring a generous portion of wine into her glass. He raised his own to his lips and took a sip. "He is the hero of our Ionian islands and of Greece itself." Settling back into his chair, he looked at her directly, his eyes gleaming. "He was a man who lived his life to the full and explored to the limits the world, with his cunning and intelligence. A man for all time." He paused, a smile poised on his lips. "I like to think of myself as being like him, only a modern Odysseus. And you will be my Penelope," he added, in an affectionate voice, reaching over and squeezing her hand. At his touch, a tingle ran down Thea's spine but she shifted her position and regarded him uncertainly.

"I am flattered by the comparison," Thea began steadily, "but I don't think Penelope was his true love." Her words caught him by surprise and a frown crossed Dimitri's handsome forehead.

"But everyone knows this is so." He spoke more high-pitched and his aspirated accent had become pronounced. "What makes you say such things?"

"My reading of Homer."

"But if Penelope was not his love, then who?"

"I suspect a woman he stayed with on his way back to Ithaka." Thea studied Dimitri again: the deep olive eyes, square cheeks and flawless features. He exuded a charisma and presence that seemed to fill the empty restaurant. She could see why she had loved him so much and how he reminded her of Odysseus. The old feelings of attraction were beginning to stir again, radiating from deep within her body.

"Wait," Dimitri announced, suddenly breaking the spell. "I have something for you." He reached into his pocket and produced a small box, elegantly wrapped. "This is for you, Thea. I hope it gives you pleasure. I just wanted to show how much you mean to me," he said with genuine feeling, his face upturned to reveal the prominent square cheek-bones.

Carefully unwrapping the gift, Thea discovered inside a golden ring in an unusual design. It was made of shiny-pure gold, beaten and edged with small rivets. It reminded her of the embossed jewellery from the tomb of Atreus at Mycenae, which she had once seen displayed in the National Museum in Athens.

"It's beautiful," she had exclaimed, examining it in her fingers.

"This is the ring I was never able to give you," Dimitri said, his voice brimming with emotion." I hope that when you wear it, you wear a small part of me." He placed it on her third finger of her right hand, like an engagement ring. It fitted perfectly.

Afterwards they had walked down onto the beach, past a closed up bar, the tables and chairs neatly stacked away. Where the restaurant light's gave way to pitch darkness, they had sat watching the endless stream of the white frothing waves rolling in and lapping against the sandy beach. In the clear dark sky, away from light pollution, the stars had been out and they had gazed at the constellations: Orion with his belt and the recognisable zigzag plough of the Great Bear. Only the distant lights of a sea port punctuated the darkness. Dimitri had put his arm around her and held her close to him, pressing his lips against her. It felt as if they had never separated. Slowly he moved his hands over her, feeling the contours of her body, her thighs, her stomach and then her rounded breasts. He kissed her now more forcibly, his weight pressing her body into the soft sand. His exploration now took on a renewed intensity as he fumbled with her clothing and Thea knew he would have made love to her there, if she did not restrain him.

"We can't do this," she said, forcibly pushing him away. She jumped up and started to dust the gritty sand from her hair and clothes.

"Can't you see the effect you have on me?" Dimitri's face was obscured by the darkness, but there an entreaty in his voice. "I love you."

"Not here," Thea firmly replied. "It's too indiscreet. If someone comes across us, they will recognise you instantly. It will be all around the island like wildfire and everyone will know. We must wait." She had started to walk back towards the bright lights of the restaurant, almost panicking that she could not trust her body and her feelings might get the better of her. Reluctantly Dimitri had followed, entwining her fingers in his hand.

Just before the hotel, he had stopped the car and leaned in to kiss her once more. "I have to go away with Clemmie and the family over the Easter," he said. "Promise me when I get back, we will go away together for a few days. I know a wonderful place in Switzerland, an exclusive hotel, overlooking a lake and mountains. We can spend some time there alone, just you and me. No one would know, not even Stelios. Can we do that, give ourselves that opportunity?" He seized her hand and pressed it to his lips.

She had nodded her head in agreement, knowing he intended to consummate their relationship. He had lifted up her chin with his fingers, kissing her on the lips and lightly running his fingers across her belly.

Thea fingered the ring once more. In the light of day, the thought of the hurt they could cause to his children and family unsettled her.

And yet, she reminded herself, *we loved each other deeply. Dimitri hadn't abandoned her intentionally. It had been against his will.* Always he had been the phantom in her marriage, always there to question, always there to compare against her love for David. She knew herself too well – that she was on the brink of giving Dimitri a second chance. Perhaps this time, they would finally be together. And with that thought, Thea felt the anxiety and doubt lift.

The clear sound of Sophie's voice roused her from her thoughts.

"Are you coming in for a swim, Thea?" she asked. Already a group of the students were in the sea, tossing a ball and splashing each other with water to piercing shrieks.

"Has your leg healed okay?" Instinctively, Thea picked out the pale pink scar running across Sophie's leg. Already the swelling had gone down and the skin was knitting together cleanly. In a couple of months, there would be no sign of the injury.

"The doctor said that it's healing nicely. Whatever you put on was a miracle treatment."

"Then, I'll brave it with you." Thea expected that the water would be cold but after the initial shock of the cold sea water, she quickly acclimatised.

"You and Matthew seem to be getting on well."

"He's been coming over every weekend to stay with us. We started to get closer over the last week or so," Sophie said, wrapping her arms around her body for warmth, as her body shivered. "I really like him."

"I've been impressed by him," Thea agreed, "especially his maturity and self-composure. You seem to fit well together." The younger woman smiled bashfully.

"We'll see," she replied.

When they emerged from the sea, Thea noticed Rob's head tracking her movements. Hastily she turned her back on him and grabbed her towel, covering herself with her shirt. Mark appeared at her side with more drinks.

"So you think Vardianoi Island may be the one mentioned in Homer, Thea?" asked Richard. He had come to join them, wine bottle in hand, playing the part of a bon viveur.

"It's looking that way."

"It would make a lot of sense," Richard continued. "As you know, anyone sailing from Pylos on the mainland would have come across to Poros on the south side of the island and then followed the coastline up to the straits. It would be the natural way to go. And I hear that you found your second beach." Thea nodded, assuming Rob had imparted this information. "That's a further sign we're on the right track," Richard confidently asserted, tipping his hat back. He was obviously still conscious of providing Dimitri with some good news.

"So where are you planning to look next, Thea?" Mark asked.

"I'm thinking of retracing the path taken from the landing site near Porto Katsiki towards one of the villages over a weekend." The plan had formed in her mind a few days before. "It would be at least a half day's trek."

"I could join you," said Mark good-naturedly. "We haven't seen much of one another lately and I'd enjoy a day out."

"It would be good to have your company."

Alistair had been standing nearby, his eyebrows raised. "Elizabeth isn't a keen walker, but the trail would be interesting and we could offer an archaeological perspective."

"Certainly your expertise would be useful," Thea readily agreed.

"And I could join you too." Thea looked up to discover Rob standing over her. It was the first time he had stirred all afternoon, since the excursion to *Vardianoi*. At last, a normal colour had returned to his cheeks and whatever ailed him had vanished.

"Alright," Thea replied hesitatingly, puzzled by Rob's sudden change in demeanour. "It sounds like the trip is settled."

The shadows had lengthened, as they prepared to leave. Most of the traces of the afternoon had been removed, the food packed away, the barbecue extinguished and the rugs refolded. The speedboat had not yet reappeared and Matthew had accompanied Sophie to the parked cars to say his goodbyes. To her surprise Thea discovered herself alone with Rob. He was looking out over the water towards *Vardianoi*, his face scrunched up against the dying beams of sunlight.

Thea drew her arms around herself, mustering her courage to break the awkward silence that lay between them. "I think I owe you an apology, Rob," she began cautiously.

"Why?" he asked, his voice toneless, as he stared out into the distance towards the sunset.

"For all the interest in your lab these past few weeks." Thea looked up at Rob, not quite sure what to say. He was obviously angry with her. "I didn't mean to betray your confidence," she said, swallowing hard. "Richard was in a tight spot and I mentioned what you had said to help him out. I'm really sorry if I put you in a difficult position," she ended apologetically.

Rob swung round to face her, glowering. "That's not the issue, Thea." His Adam's apple stood out in his throat and his face had flushed pink. "I know you're seeing Dimitri Kampitsis." He almost spat out Dimitri's name, through clenched teeth. "And it didn't look platonic the other night when I saw you two together!"

The force of his words caught her off balance and for a moment Thea stumbled to answer. She stared at him, feeling a rush of anger rising in her body. "I don't understand what interest it is of yours," she snapped, losing all patience. "You wrote me a cursory note and then left the island without explanation! How dare you complain about who I see!"

He flinched and hung his head, as if preoccupied by his thoughts. "You're right Thea," he finally said at last, his voice mellowing, turning to face her. "It's none of my business. But there was a reason for my sudden departure that I can't explain right now."

A gust of wind caught her hair and whipped it over her face. Evening was drawing in and she hoped their boat journey back across the straits would not be too bumpy. She suddenly felt a need to account herself to Rob, though perplexed why she had to explain. She pushed a loose strand of hair out of her eyes and turned to Rob.

"You're right, I did have dinner with Dimitri a couple of nights ago." Thea paused and fingered the ring on her hand, unsure how much to say. "Years ago, we were in a relationship together when we were both young. It's a complicated story. I hadn't wanted to see Dimitri again only Richard forced me into a meeting. It all happened after you abruptly left the island." She looked down, biting her lip, hoping not to sound reproachful. "I'm sorry if my relationship with Dimitri causes you offence, as this wasn't my intention."

"Then I hope you know what you are doing, Thea," Rob replied his voice tinged with regret. She felt between them a deep unspoken understanding, the source for which she could not fathom. But there was a connection. "If that is what you want. Only I'm afraid of you getting hurt," Rob continued more mildly. "The man just seems so full of himself. It's not Odysseus he's really looking for but the kudos of finding him, so he can become the next hero of the Greeks."

His words resonated and she suddenly recalled her dinner conversation with Dimitri earlier that week. "I know," Thea assured him.

Chapter 17

Home Coming

In the privacy of their bedchamber, Penelope had undressed, as always covering herself modestly with her arms. Then she had climbed beside him into the intimacy of their marital bed, carved by him from the trunk of a single olive tree. He made love to her, wanting to reassure her as she lay passively in his embrace. Afterwards he had held her to him, caressing her smooth milk-white skin and slender waist. Despite their years of love-making, she had not conceived again and now she had reached the end of her child-bearing years.

He cradled her in his arm and spoke to her with soft words. "I hope you will not distress yourself by what the bard sang tonight. For you are a blameless and faultless wife, outstanding in your virtue. Despite being hard pressed to take another as your husband, you held fast to preserve this kingdom. For that I am forever obliged to you and in your debt. We have spent these many good years happy together, living out our days in peace and may the gods grant us many more."

"Have no fear husband," she murmured. "I am content in our life together," and then she had given him her most loving and dutiful smile.

He didn't quite know what he expected from her, but some god unsettled his mood. Afterwards, when Penelope slumbered in his arms, he could not give himself over to sweet *Sleep*. From time to time the darkened room was illuminated by the distant flashes of lightning, soundless, sent by Zeus who thunders on Mount Olympus. Remembering Kirke disturbed him still and whatever thought a god was trying to plant in his mind, he shook it off.

Carefully he untwined himself from Penelope, trying not to break her slumber. Wrapped in heavy *Sleep*, she still slept soundly as a soft murmur escaped her lips. He crossed the familiar darkened room not knowing what to do with himself; this restlessness during the time of *Sleep* was becoming commonplace. Tomorrow would be the feast day of Apollo and he could not be absent in his bed. It marked the twenty years since his return to reclaim his island kingdom and for some time a plan had been forming in his mind. He seated himself on a chair, solidly carved, where he could ponder things in his mind until *Sleep* overpowered him. From time to time the room was brilliantly illuminated by the distant lightning flashes, revealing just for an instance the features of the room.

Odysseus now turned over the proposition in his mind this way and that to determine the best course to steer. When he had left Kirke, his purpose had been so very clear. It had been a long hard battle that he had fought to bring himself back from that accursed war to reclaim his natural and rightful place here on Ithaka. But now a new strategy for his kingdom kept occupying his mind, taking over his thoughts. He had tried to discuss it with Penelope, but she simply deferred to his judgement.

"Do as you think fit," she had said, lowering those compliant eyes. "For you are the *Basileos*."

Now as he pondered this matter, his thoughts led him back to that earlier time, when it had been so different, when he had set in motion that strategy to reclaim his kingship and authority.

When he had first set foot back on Ithaka,

there had been no big reception or thanksgiving feast for his long awaited home-coming. Indeed he had not even recognised that he had at last returned to his beloved island. For the Phaiakian boat that had conveyed him from the palace of Alkinoos had set him down in a remote long shallow bay, sheltered by two headlands that projected out into the sea.

He had cut a solitary figure on that isolated beach. Except for the gifts of guest friendship he, the great hero of Troy, was alone. No longer was he accompanied by those brave Kephallenian warriors, the companions alongside whom he had fought so long and hard to capture that cursed city. Those conquering heroes were long gone, scattered to the winds and his countrymen dead or lost at sea. He had done his duty and returned with his *kleos*, but it was a bitter sweet moment.

It was then he had recalled the words of the seer, whom Kirke had advised him to see and that had lodged in his mind all these years. "You will return home alone, late and luckless," the old man's words rang out. Standing there on that beach, it was just as the blind seer had described. But there were other words too that unsettled his mind and sent shivers down his backbone, "There will be those who come to your kingdom, eating your wealth and livelihood, trying to take what is yours away from your son." It had been a warning to Odysseus and he had come so far that he was not about to take any chances.

He sat on the sand, looking out across the calm water as the waves lapped against the shore-line. A plan had started to form in his mind perhaps sown by his patron goddess, Athena herself. It was too perilous to present himself to his household unexpectedly as he could not be sure of what reception he might receive. He had no way of knowing which retainers had stayed true to him and which had become loyal to another. He could be set upon and murdered. Until he knew for certain who was now ruling the palace, he would enter as a stranger disguised as a beggar.

A small cave at the water's edge caught his eye. Covered by an olive tree, it had not been immediately visible from the beach. *A good place for hiding the precious gifts*, he reasoned, thinking of the pile of tripods, precious metals and finely made clothes. It took some time to stow them in a corner of the cave, which he then covered with rocks. He uttered a prayer to the water nymphs to protect the precious stash, promising gifts in return. He then stripped off his well-made clothes, provided by his host, down to a simple tunic which he tore in places and smeared with earth. Likewise he splashed himself with saltwater to shrivel his skin and rubbed dirt into his hair and beard. Once done, he was ready.

At the far end of the strand, he discovered a small path leading up the steep slope between the hollow of two hills. He followed it. The land was lush and verdant on this side and he noted the well-tended olive and lemon trees loaded with ripe fruit.

Signs of human labour suggested a dwelling place could not be far away, he thought to himself. He would spin a story to cover his sudden appearance on the island. He considered this in his mind: to avoid suspicion, he must stay true to the lie even if it meant bearing insults and dishonourable treatment from others.

The light of Helios was fading when he finally reached the top of the hill. Sitting at the entrance to his hut, he had come across a swineherd. The man was watching his drove of pigs foraging for acorns and woodland fruit. There was the sound of excited grunting, as the animals greedily snuffled the ground. It was the barking of the dogs which had alerted the man to his presence and he would have suffered injury had the stranger not called them off, scattering a handful of pebbles.

"Welcome stranger," the man greeted him. "You look as if you have travelled some distance." His eyes flashed bright but kindly. "You must be weary." Beneath the full black beard of curly whiskers, it was hard to discern the man's features except for the skin tanned like leather hide.

"I have indeed," Odysseus had replied, noting with satisfaction the well-constructed yard. Care had been taken to divide it into sties to house the swine. "I would welcome a place to sit and take some rest for my tired bones."

"Then please allow me to give you hospitality according to the rules of Zeus himself. My name is Eumaios," the man continued, "I work in the service of Odysseus, king of Ithaka, who has been absent these twenty long years."

The sound of his own name jolted his ears, like the twang of the bowstring when discharged. He could almost have wept in relief at the kindly greeting. He studied the swineherd more closely, but it was hard to discern his features. He judged him as a servant, perhaps taken as a slave during a raid. The fellow had an open and honest demeanour, but prudence held him back from revealing his true identity.

He allowed himself to be led by the man inside the small wooden dwelling, furnished with a thick goatskin pelt for a bed.

"Please sit and take some rest," said Eumaios, clearing a place on the floor and scattering brushwood. He then left Odysseus to go and prepare food for them both. It wasn't long before the swineherd returned with a plate piled with cooked pork and a wooden bowl of wine, which he set down on the floor, urging his guest to eat. Suddenly hunger overcame his body at the sight of the roasted meat, the crackling fat golden and glistening.

When their bellies were bloated with food and wine, only then did Odysseus question the servant, his curiosity getting the better of him.

"So tell me, good Eumaios, what land is this that I have come to and who rules here? For you said that your master is absent."

"It is hard to say," the other man replied wearily, casting his eyes downwards. "For my master has been gone such a time. He was called to fight on the battlefield of Troy by King Agamemnon himself, the *Anax* of the Greeks. But since the war ended over ten years ago, he has not returned and no word has been heard of him. He is thought now lost, perhaps wandering hungry and destitute in some foreign land."

The words cut Odysseus like a knife. "And what became of his kingdom," he asked feigning indifference. "Did he leave behind a family and children?" He could feel himself stiffen and alert to the man's reply.

"That is a woeful business! Even though we live remotely here, a whole half day's walk from the homestead, bad news still reaches us. Suitors lay siege to his house daily, pressing their suit on his wife, Penelope. They say that she is beside herself. His father, Laertes, could not bear the situation as it sorely vexed him, so he retired to another part of the estate. Through the gods' blessings, his mother did not live to see this day as she suffered terribly at the loss of her son."

He flinched at the mention of his mother's passing. It pained him that he had not been there at her funeral rites to mourn her death as her dutiful son. He pushed down the tears welling in his eyes. He had come too long and too far to betray himself at this point.

"What else have you heard?" he pressed, concerned that the seer's words appeared to have become true.

"They say each day these suitors, though high born, abuse the hospitality," the kind-hearted Eumaios replied. "They deplete the wine stores and demand more flocks to eat and feast upon, making a poor man of my master. Each day we receive a summons for more animals to be sent to the homestead for the suitors to feed upon." The man shook his head at the dismal situation he described, his shoulders hunched. "But I believe the gods will one day dispense their justice."

"So the wife Penelope has not taken a new husband?" Odysseus asked casually, quickly calculating the situation in his mind. "And what of the son?" He quickly corrected himself. "The eldest son, I mean, if there is one. How does he manage this state of affairs in his father's absence?"

A broad grin broke out on the other man's face. "There is only one son, Telemachos, a fine boy now in young manhood. He is desperate for his father's return and has gone away to Sparta on the mainland, seeking news of his father. For the situation is intolerable to the young man as each day he witnesses his inheritance being diminished and consumed by those wretched suitors. May the gods bring down a curse upon their heads! But that apart, my master was a good and true man as ever lived. I greatly grieve his absence."

The words of this good and faithful servant filled his heart with shame at his deception. For the man had remained loyal to his memory through all these long years. He tried to offer reassurance. "I have heard of your master Odysseus on my travels, Eumaios, and tell you truly that he is on his way. When I last saw him, he was mustering a ship and will be here by the month's end."

Eumaios eyed him courteously and without malice. "I know stranger you are only trying to offer comfort for our situation, but that time will never come." He let out a deep sigh, staring blankly into the distance. "Had he returned in time, I might have looked forward to my freedom from service and been provided with small lands so I could take a wife and raise a family." He shook his head as if throwing off his mood. "Let us speak of things less grievous to the spirit. Tell me old man, from where do you come?"

Odysseus had been waiting for the questions to come and had prepared his story. He spun a false tale of being a Kretan wanderer weaving in details of his own plight: the fighting at Troy, a sea voyage going badly wrong; being ship wrecked and finally trying to make his way to the island of Doulichion. He had not been sure as to how much of the story Eumaios had believed.

"And so I plan to seek out the palace on this island and throw myself at the mercy of their hospitality."

Eumaios had stopped him, his eyes wide with horror. "Don't go," he had urged. "For I fear those haughty young suitors will disrespect you. Stay here for a while until you regain your strength. You will be quite safe for we are remote. When you are ready, I myself will show you the way."

Even then he had not been content to trust the words of the swineherd but had devised other ploys to test out the servant's loyalty. He shuddered to remember his attempts to deceive and catch out this good and loyal man, spinning more falsehoods of fighting alongside Odysseus at Troy. If Eumaios had suspected his ruse, he did not betray his doubts. Instead he made up a bed of sheep and goatskins by the fire for his guest, offering up a thick woollen cloak and vacating his comfortable bed to sleep in the sties.

It was now the third day that Odysseus had stayed with his amiable and excellent host. The two men had been gathering firewood and preparing breakfast over the open lit fire for the herdsmen, who had gathered before departing for their day's work in the fields. Already bowls of food had been dished out and jugs of ewe's milk set down, when the excited barking of the dogs announced the arrival of a newcomer. Eumaios got to his feet to see who this visitor was to his humble dwelling. It was then Odysseus first set eyes upon a young man standing at the gateway, dressed in a *chiton* tunic covered by a cloak, his garments clearly sullied by the dirt of a long journey. Although lightly built, he could see the young man's limbs were none the less those of a warrior, strong and powerful. He was fresh-faced and of mild countenance with a beard of soft down whiskers. At once he recognised the stranger. It was his son, Telemachos. The son whom he had left all those years ago when he had set sail. His body gave a start at the recognition.

"Telemachos, my beloved master!" Eumaios quickly confirmed Odysseus' assumption, clasping the young man in a warm-hearted embrace. "Do my eyes deceive me? Can it be that you have returned from your journey to Pylos and the gods saw fit to grant you a safe return?" He stood back from the young man, assuring himself he was in good health. Then a look of puzzlement appeared on his brow. "But why do you come this way and not go straight to the palace?"

"For some reason, the gods put it in my mind

that the suitors might lie in ambush for me," said Telemachos, stepping back from the older man's embrace. His face was lit by a wide smile. "You know the small island in the straits, where there is a sandy bay for beaching a ship. It made me decide to sail around the island and land at the bay near here, the one rounded with the ox horns."

Eumaios nodded in agreement. "You were perhaps wise. And does your mother, Queen Penelope know of your return yet?" he asked anxiously, a shadow flitting across his brow. "Or your grandfather Laertes? They will be mightily comforted that you are safe and well."

"Not yet, my dear Eumaios. I came here first to gain news of the palace," the smile now fading on his lips, his fingers tightening on his sword belt. "Has anything yet changed? Is my mother still without a husband?"

"She is, master," said Eumaios nodding, "and the marriage bed of Odysseus remains untouched. Though they say your mother cries in despair each night."

"Then all is not yet lost," responded the younger man, momentarily lost in thought, biting his lip.

"Come Telemachos! Eat with us," said Eumaios, seeing his concerned look. He beckoned the younger man into the small hut and they sat together on the fleeces set on the brushwood floor. And so Odysseus found himself brought face to face with his beloved son, his own identity masked by his disguise. This was not the reunion he had envisaged during those long years at Troy. As the tears welled up inside, he fought to hold himself back from rushing over and embracing the young man. Instead silently he watched the two men, relieved by Eumaios' attentions to his son who was ravenously filling his mouth with food.

When they had eaten their fill, only then did Telemachos turn his attention to the new stranger.

"And who is your guest, Eumaios?" he asked, casting his glance over him in his ragged clothing. "Will you not introduce us?"

"He is from Krete, a man for whom the *Fates* have spun hard times," answered Eumaios evenly. "I have offered fresh clothing but he refuses. He comes as a supplicant requesting *xenia* and I hoped to entrust him to your hospitality and care."

Telemachos quickly glanced from Eumaios to the stranger, weighing up his appearance. "Forgive me, old man," he said courteously but his brow was furrowed. "I cannot offer you the full rights of hospitality and this pains me dearly. My house is not safe and is troubled by men who covet my mother's hand. They would steal away the kingdom from my absent father, the famed warrior Odysseus. If you came as my guest, I cannot guarantee your protection and the suitors may use their mistreatment of you to humiliate me. I can accord you gifts of guest-friendship and provide you with passage to wherever you need to go, but it is better that you remain here and receive hospitality."

Odysseus could feel his anger rising at this outrage to his son but he needed to know more. "I am saddened to hear of the discord in your house," he responded calmly hiding his true feelings. Already his mind was calculating the best approach forward. "But tell me, do the people tolerate this state of affairs or are they resentful of your birthright to rule?"

"No," replied Telemachos perceptively, "it is simply that I am the only son, as was my father Odysseus before me and my father's father before him. So when the young suitors arrived from Same, Doulichion, Zakynthos and Ithaka itself, seeking to seize the kingdom through marriage, there was no kinsfolk to rally to our defence through blood ties."

He turned his attention now away from his

father, speaking quickly to the swineherd. "You must go now Eumaios to the *polis* to tell my mother that I am safely returned." He lowered his voice and his eyes shifted over the yard, as if expecting to see a murderous suitor lurking nearby. "None must know of this news and you must give this message to her and her alone."

"I will at once," replied the faithful servant, rising to his feet. "And shall I take the news also to your grandfather Laertes too, for your absence grieves him sorely?"

The younger man motioned his head indicating no. "I'm afraid not. We must leave him in his sadness a while longer. You must take this message with all haste and then come straight back. I will wait here for your return."

"I will set off at once," replied the older man, "for it will take the best part of the day." Quickly Eumaios made himself ready for the journey, gathering a wineskin and food for the journey. When the faithful servant had departed, Odysseus stepped out into the yard to breathe in the clear air to steady himself. The urge to clasp his son to his bosom and hold him there was overpowering. He could not keep up the pretence of his identity. This was his beloved son he had fought so long and hard to come back to, through all those trials at Troy, the calamitous sea journey and tearing himself from a woman's comfort. Always he had held in mind this object to return to his kingdom to evade the fate of the fatherless child falling on his own son.

Quickly he cleaned himself from a pail of water, washing off the dirt and soil from his face and body so that once more his bronzed skin could be seen. He had been away on foreign shores so long, as a warrior and then a wanderer, he had almost forgotten who he was. That here, on Ithaka, was his natural place.

When Odysseus walked back into the hut, the other man starred at the transformation in his countenance. "Forgive me, stranger, but I mistook your appearance and did not take you for a warrior. Are you some god sent to test me?"

"No, dear Telemachos." Odysseus shook his head slowly, measuring his next words with great care. Now the time had come, he hardly dared to lift his face. "I am your father. It is on my account you have suffered much over these years."

For a moment, the son stared at his father dumb-founded, struggling to take in what he had heard. "Surely you are playing a trick on me, an imposter come to take advantage of our plight."

"No, my dear Telemachos," he said, speaking patiently. "I am indeed your father. Is it such a surprise that after twenty years, finally my long expected arrival has come and I stand before you?"

A look of bewilderment flitted across the younger man's face and then he broke into joy as father and son fell into each other's arms, each embracing the other and neither holding back the tears. Long into the day they spoke, narrating their story to each other until they lapsed into silence. Odysseus finally spoke, looking his son in the eye.

"I'm sorry my son, I left and abandoned you for all those years. A son needs his father close to protect him and support him in becoming a man and a warrior. I regret I was so long in coming." Momentarily a flicker of a feeling came across him, remembering another child he had left behind. This was not the time to dwell on that.

"But tell me now, Telemachos, all you know regarding our situation. Who is loyal to us and who has turned?"

"I fear, our plight is dire and that you have come too late," he replied sorrowfully. "There are too many suitors entrenched in the palace for us alone to defeat."

Odysseus raised his head. "Have no fear my

dear son," he said calmly, his mind already turning over different plans. "Now we are reunited and with the gods on our side, this too we will overcome. But we must keep my return a secret known only to ourselves. No one else must know. Not your grandfather nor good Eumaios but especially not your mother, Penelope. Not until we can ascertain who within the household has remained loyal and true to us and who has turned." Telemachos consented with a nod.

The moon was already in the sky, when Eumaios returned from his mission. He found the two men in the fading light huddled round the fire, roasting a slaughtered hog, still deep in conversation. He glanced over at the beggar, still sat in his ragged clothes covered in filth. The pair made a strange coupling. He shrugged his shoulders and hunkered down to join them.

****

Odysseus suddenly woke with a start, looking around the darkened room. He rubbed *Sleep* from his eyes, slowly remembering where he was. Those memories, so vivid, happened a long time ago. Many years ago. Zeus' thundering had now passed and he sensed Penelope's sleeping presence in the marital bed. How had he forgotten? When it had all been so clear. That his young son Telemachos was the reason for his homecoming. He had made his choice years ago when he had left Kirke pregnant. His mind was set. Tomorrow it would be twenty years since he regained the kingdom of Ithaka. Apollo's feast would be a fitting time to announce his judgement to his people. And yet still the unsettling and disquieting feeling lingered.

Chapter 18

Revelations

"Thea! Is that you?" A shrill female voice rang out cutting the air.

Thea had been walking down the main thoroughfare of the town, flanked by inviting boutiques and brightly lit shops. On the white polished stone flags, metal stands had been set outside, enticing prospective customers like an eastern bazaar: beachwear, wind charms, jars of honey, sugar coated almonds and olives in an array of guises. The afternoon was drawing on and the air had lost the heat of the day. For once, Thea had finished her work early and had taken the opportunity to stroll along with the evening shoppers. The sudden call of her name, brought her out of her thoughts. Looking up, she saw a woman about the same age but who appeared familiar and the memory clicked into place.

"Despoina!" She paused a moment to take in the other woman's face. The thick curly dark hair was tied loosely back and there was still the wide open smile, revealing perfect white teeth. Her skin was a smooth olive complexion but there was a weariness behind the hazel eyes. The two women stared in disbelief at one another, before embracing each other.

"I can't believe it's you," Despoina said, her face full of joy, breaking away from their embrace. "When did you get back? How long have you been on the island?" A hundred questions hung in the air and it was hard to know where to start.

"Just a few weeks ago," Thea replied, glowing with pleasure. "I'm here working on an archaeology project. I would have called you but I didn't know whether you still lived on the island."

If there was any neglect of the relationship, it was quickly forgotten. "I'm on my way to take my mother-in-law to hospital," Despoina replied. "But come I have a little time. Let's have coffee." Despoina steered Thea towards one of the cafes in a small square, overlooked by a white marble building, temple-like, now the local post office. They sat at an empty table, beside a small garden of leafy shrubs, away from the noisy hordes of shoppers.

"I can recommend the ice cream," said Despoina skimming through the menu card, displaying pictures of calorie-loaded sundaes topped with whipped cream. "And they do a good Cappuccino."

"That will suit me fine," Thea replied, setting her menu back down on the table. "I'll go for the pistachio." The young waitress was attentive, keeping an eye out for new customers, and quickly came to take their order. The other tables were now filling up with groups of people, relaxing from their weekly work, excitedly chatting together. The place was abuzz with voices, deep laughter and children's playful squeals. For a moment, the two women sat surveying each other in silence, as if breathing in each other's essence.

"So tell me about yourself?" Thea started, sitting back in her chair. "All that has happened to you?"

Despoina shrugged and looked around. "Well as you can see, I still live here on Kefalonia. I married my childhood sweetheart, Yiorgos. You remember we used to hang out together when you were here." She rummaged into her handbag and produced a creased photograph of a happy smiling family. "We have two boys now, quite a handful and full of energy," she announced proudly, thrusting the picture into Thea's hand.

A look of weariness and worry fleetingly passed across Despoina's face. "You know about the Greek financial crisis," she said, her voice more restrained. "I do a little work in one of the offices here and Yiorgos works in his father's business, so we get by." Quickly the easy smile returned, lighting up her face. "I'm so happy to see you," Despoina said, reaching over to squeeze Thea's arm. "And that you're back on the island. So tell me about yourself. What have you been doing?"

"There's not much to say really," said Thea, feeling her own story was a let-down. "I still work at one of the London Universities. I married some years ago, but David and I are in the process of getting a divorce."

"I'm sorry to hear that," said her friend sympathetically. "And do you have any children?" she asked.

Thea shook her head. "I'm afraid not." She spoke casually, but her feelings gripped her like a vice.

"I don't think you ever really got over Dimitri, did you?" Despoina glanced at Thea knowingly. "He was your first love."

"Perhaps," Thea conceded. The waitress now appeared with their order so they settled on eating the ice-creams and coffees, idly chatting about their lives.

Despoina checked her watch and called over to the waitress to settle the bill, handing over a wad of notes. "I'm sorry Thea, I have to go. But we must meet up again. Here are my contact details," and she hastily wrote down a number on a torn piece of paper and handed it to Thea. "I can't believe it, that you're here. So call me, won't you," said Despoina emphatically. "And don't take twenty years this time!"

"I will. Of course I will," Thea promised, thrilled to see her friend again.

Despoina had started to turn away but then stopped. "By the way, does Eleni know you're back on the island?"

Thea's stomach knotted as a pang of guilt swept over her. How had she forgotten Eleni her dear mentor and friend from all those years ago? Eleni, the person who had taught her to recognise the herbs that grew wild and what relieved digestion, inflammation or menstrual pains. It had been to gain from her vast store of knowledge, Thea had first arrived on the island as a young woman but then somehow other things had crowded in.

"No, she doesn't," Thea admitted puzzled, not knowing how to explain her omission.

"You must see her," said Despoina reassuringly, looking down at her. "She would be so delighted to see you. You know that she still lives in the old cottage on the edge of the town. But she hasn't been so well lately."

"I will," Thea agreed nodding her head, inwardly marking in her mind that she must do so. And yet it had taken several days since the two women had parted company before Thea found herself standing on the pavement outside the house. The old cottage stood where it had always done, but now dwarfed by high rise buildings instead of alone on the edge of town. It looked strangely out of place, with its modest and drab exterior, against the pastel-coloured apartment blocks and high-end boutiques.

The metal hinges complained loudly as Thea pushed open the old gate and mounted the red-marled steps up to the entrance. The front door was still the same, with the wrought-iron grille twisted into ornate swirls. The dusk-pink paint was faded or streaked with brown-rust. An air of neglect overhung the garden, where a tangle of foliage was slowly enveloping the building and threatening to erupt out into the public street. On the front porch, more care had been taken. Thea cast her eye over the jumble of brightly decorated plant pots and white-washed oil cans, recognising a whole medicinal larder: camomile and marjoram for inflammation; rosemary for circulation; fennel, juniper and lemon to refresh the body; cloves for troublesome toothache; sage and red clover for feminine ailments; and lavender and rose to soothe the agitated body. Thea smiled to herself, perceiving Eleni's touch at work.

The cottage's interior was shrouded in darkness giving the impression that no one was home. But on closer inspection, the smell of sweet cinnamon filled her nostrils and there was the noise of activity deep inside the house.

Thea knocked loudly and then tested the door. It was unlocked. Entering, she called out the Greek greeting "*Yeia-sas*." From within the interior came a muffled answering response. After a few moments a woman emerged, small and rounded in shape, the freshness and glow of her face at odds with her slow shuffling movements.

"*Koritsi mou!*" The older women came towards her, embracing and holding Thea closely to her as if she would hold on for ever. For several minutes, they held on tight to each other, trying to cross the years that had separated them. And then Eleni stood back from her at arm's length, reading in Thea's features, as if deciphering all that had happened since they had last occupied the same space.

"*Ela*," Eleni motioned Thea into the kitchen, where there were several pans boiling on the old ceramic stove. "*Kathiste, etoimazo cafe*". As instructed, Thea seated herself at the small table covered in a floral primrose-yellow oilcloth. As Eleni busied herself making coffee, it gave opportunity to glance round the kitchen. The shelves were cluttered with a collection of bottles and glass jars. Each was carefully labelled in Eleni's neat handwriting, declaring the herbal contents or medicinal remedy. There was the scorch mark from the old water element, circular and coffee-coloured, branded on the formica worktop. Suddenly all the memories came flooding back as if a curtain had been lifted and they had stepped back in time.

Thea watched Eleni, taking in her awkward and laboured movements as she went back and forth across the kitchen. She was dressed in an unassuming loose-fitting dress, the colour of blanched aubergine. Her hair had turned whiter and the lines more deeply etched, but the spark in her eyes was unchanged. A plate was produced of sugar coated *kourabiedes* shortbread and lemon polenta cake oozing with honey. After setting down a large steaming tea-pot, Eleni sat down, her eyes locked on Thea, beaming with joy.

"*Fate, fate!*" she instructed Thea, gesturing to her to tuck in. Complying Thea began to eat, realising the origin of her taste for Greek pastries as a burst of sweetness filled her mouth. Not only had this woman fed her but had stirred love and kindness into the sweet dough mix.

"So when did you arrive back?" asked the older woman, speaking in Greek, enunciating each word in the distinctive Ionian accent.

Thea swallowed a mouthful of pastry, her fingers now coated in powdered icing sugar. "A couple of weeks ago. I'm working on an archaeological project." Eleni passed her some sheets of kitchen roll, before allowing her to speak on. "I'm here until next month," Thea continued, anticipating the next question already forming on Eleni's lips. *How could she have so easily set aside and forgotten this friendship*, she wondered? A wave of guilt passed over Thea as she looked up at the older woman who was nodding encouragingly.

"I'm so sorry, I didn't visit earlier. I hadn't meant to stay away-," she began.

"Shh, shh, don't worry *koukla mou*." Eleni's clucked, as if comforting an anxious child. "I always knew when the time was right, you would come back." Eleni patted her arm, squeezing it affectionately, a look of joy on her face. Thea lifted her head and returned the smile.

"So tell me more about this project that brings you here."

"It's a survey to find the palace of Odysseus. Most of the team are based in Kalodia on the field survey. I've been working on the old archives and trying to match the topography with the Homeric descriptions. There are a couple of geo-physicists doing a soil and rock analysis." She hesitated, trying not to let her thoughts dwell on Rob. "So far, everything is pointing towards Paliki but we haven't located the site yet."

Eleni had been listening, her head cocked to one side. "I think I've heard about this. It's a big thing on the island, did you know. It has been in the local papers. Everyone is talking about it. Isn't it sponsored by the Archontakis Foundation?"

Thea nodded her head, her mouth full of pastry. "It would be a big prize for them," Eleni continued "if they do find Odysseus' palace. You know how important the hero Odysseus is to us Greeks. Whoever finds that would become a national hero and right now we could do with heroes." Eleni leaned back, looking down at her wrinkled hands. "Here in Greece, it hasn't been an easy time with austerity," she observed. "But this would bring a little light to our world, if you and your colleagues are successful and I hope you are. It would mean a lot to us Greeks."

Thea looked across at her friend. "I will do everything I can to find it," she promised. They talked on for several hours, eating and drinking, until the evening was well advanced. The light had faded some time ago, when Thea started to think about leaving.

"I need to go very soon," Thea said checking

the time on her watch, knowing she must tear herself away from the side of her dear friend. "I start again quite early tomorrow."

Eleni nodded and clutching Thea's arm lowered her voice, as if afraid someone was eaves-dropping. "Did you know Dimitri Kampitsis is back on the island?"

"I did."

"He's a very important man now. Very rich and big in the Archontakis Foundation. Does he know you're here?"

"Yes, I've seen him," Thea replied calmly. "He's asked me to go away with him this weekend." She paused, waiting for Eleni to digest this information. "I know he's now married but he swears he loves me."

Wordlessly, they both shared the story. It was Eleni who had witnessed her distress, after Dimitri had been summoned away on family business. At first Thea had immersed herself in the work, busying herself in preparing healing potions, studying late into the night, learning all she could under Eleni's experienced guidance. But as the last days of summer passed, the deafening silence grew.

"You should write to him," Eleni had said as she brought one of the countless brews of herbal teas into Thea's room. She had sensed from the beginning that something was amiss. Thea had tried to hide her tears, but her swollen eyes betrayed her grief. "Tell him what has happened."

She had shook her head. "He'll return when he can. I know he loves me." If Eleni had had her doubts, she kept them well hidden.

Early one morning the bleeding had started. Lying in the bed, Thea had felt a wetness between her legs and the sickly sweet smell of blood staining the white cotton bedsheets. Distraught, she had cried out in agony and despair and Eleni had come rushing to hold her. Afterwards, it had been Eleni who had nursed her injured body back to health through those endless days and stifling heat. And still there had been silence. Not a word. Dimitri had walked out of her life, like an actor exiting a drama after a turn on the stage. As the chill of autumn arrived, the truth had finally sunk in. He was not coming back.

At this very table, Thea had told Eleni of her decision. She could no longer bear this waiting game. Turning her back on healing, Thea had set her mind on returning home to follow a different path.

"You're a gifted healer," Eleni had protested. "How can you reject these natural skills?"

"And how can I help others, when I am wounded myself," Thea had replied. For Dimitri had inflicted a wound to her spirit as surely as if he had twisted a knife into her chest. She had reached over and squeezed Eleni's arm to reassure her. "There is a language course I can enrol on, where I can use my love for your language instead."

Tears welled up in Eleni's sympathetic eyes. "Then go with my blessing," she had said.

And now across this same table, Eleni faced Thea squarely in the eye. "Don't do it, *h koukla mou*. You will only plough a field of stones. From that man you will harvest only pain and heartbreak." The words came as no surprise to Thea. Even though now an adult in her prime, she recognised Eleni's fierce maternal instinct to protect her. "But you need to tell him. He needs to know the truth."

"I will give it some thought," Thea assured her.

"And do you have children of your own?" the older woman enquired.

She could feel the denial sticking in her throat. "David and I broke up but parenthood never seemed to be our priority. Work always demanded more the attention, so it never happened."

"You're a natural mother, Thea. And I think it won't be so long before you have a baby in your belly," the older woman said, reaching over to touch the rise on Thea's stomach.

Thea looked again at her, this time slightly perplexed. There was always the rumour that

Eleni was gifted with the second sight. Believing in her intuitive powers, sometimes people would come seeking her guidance. Was this a statement or a prophecy, Thea didn't know. She rose to leave, embracing Eleni on each papery cheek but Thea hovered by the door, unwilling to turn the handle.

"I'll come again Eleni. I promise. I won't leave it so long next time."

"I know you will. Goodbye *h koukla mou*."

Stepping into the dark, the town felt as if it had already put itself to bed. There was little traffic around and even fewer people, as Thea picked her way through the dimly lit streets. Her phone began to ring, as she crossed the wide open expanse of the main square. As she answered it, she recognised the distinctive sound of Dimitri's voice.

"Did I wake you?" he enquired solicitously.

"No, not at all," Thea replied, trying to keep her answer light and breezy. "I'm just on my way back from the town after visiting an old friend."

"And how did you find them?"

"A little bit more worn from the years, but otherwise in good spirits." Still remembering the conversation with Eleni, she was aware she was holding back. "And how has it been going with you?"

There was a pause over the muffled line. "Clemmie has been in a bad mood all day. The children have been boisterous which has bothered her. She has gone to bed early with one of her headaches." Suddenly Thea could imagine Dimitri alone, clandestinely stealing away to ring her from some quiet corner of a building. "I can't wait to see you again in two days' time. Then we can go away together." He spoke more animated now, eager to share the details. "Everything's arranged. I'll pick you up on Friday. Make sure you bring warm clothing and your passport. We're going to have the most wonderful time!"

"I will. Dimitri?" Thea asked hesitatingly, a question hung in the air.

"What is it?"

"There is something I need to tell you."

"Will it wait until Friday? We'll have all the time in the world to talk."

"Of course," Thea agreed reluctantly.

"Alright baby. I can't wait to be with you. Love you. Goodnight."

"Goodnight." She was about to say back those three words, when the call ended. There was only the dead monotone sound of the ringtone and once more he had vanished into the ether.

Chapter 19

Restitution

It was in the great *megaron* where Telemachos found him the next morning. He was taking his first meal of the day. The bread and fruit, which a servant had set before him, remained untouched. Hunched over the table, he held himself awkwardly, his muscles aching from sleeping on the stiff upright chair. At least his mind was still as lively and alert as before, even though he could feel his strength slowly ebbing away day by day deserting him. The dreams the gods sent to him, whether as punishment or a reminder, disturbed his nights, leaving him weary and exhausted whenever *Dawn* finely rose.

His son must have sensed his discomfort.

"What ails you father?" the younger man enquired worriedly. "Are you sick? Do I need to send for my mother or some healer?"

"No, calm yourself Telemachos." He noticed the worried look on his son's face. No doubt he saw the weakening muscles within his aging body, the wilted lined skin and the silver-metal streaks that ran through his coppery hair. "I am not sick, but the gods have put a stiffness and weariness in my limbs today. *Sleep* eluded me in our soft bed and now I pay the price resting on a wooden chair. I would have slept on much worse, when I was a younger man, but today the gods let me know all too well my years and how my age overcomes me."

He studied his son more closely. His warrior body was still lean and powerful, built like an ox and well-toned by the strenuous discipline of training. Like his father he excelled in fighting skills and in the wrestling circle, throwing the finest of Ithaka's men onto the mud-baked dust to claim victory. But age was beginning to tell also on Telemachos, lining his face and weathering his body, like leather stretched out and tanned in the burning sunlight. Touches of silver now flecked his thick mane of hair. The realisation jolted him, as if he had just woken up. Telemachos, his devoted son, was the age as he had been when he reclaimed the kingdom of Ithaka. Pride stirred his chest for the man his son had become. Why had he not seen it before, as if the gods had veiled his eyes? And yet still he lived beneath his father's roof.

He turned his stiff neck towards him, his eyes gleaming. "When you have taken your fill of sustenance, son, I would speak with you about something that has been occupying my thoughts lately. I would have spoken with you yesterday but my mind was befuddled by *Sleep*. Let us sit under the old plane tree together out in the yard, where none can ease-drop or over-hear our words. There is something I would say to you."

"There are matters also of which I too would speak, father. Concerning my journey around the kingdom. I also heard news of changes that are afoot."

"Then let us speak further." And with a slight nod of the head, Telemachos withdrew.

****

The old plane tree was still there, as it had been always, only wider grown and fuller in leaf. The coolness of its foliage still provided protective shadow against the burning rays of Helios. A slight breeze stirred the air, which felt pleasant in the increasing heat of the day. This view, with the tall mountains in the far off haze and open sea gulf across to Same and then purple-misted Zakynthos, never failed to please him. From here, he could cast his eye over most of the island kingdom, except for small Doulichion hidden behind the towering mountains of Same.

Odysseus turned his neck to glance at the palace behind him. The well-apportioned walls with the high gabled roof were imposing and impressive, unchanged from his father's day. Over the years, the tiles and mud brick had been repaired, replaced or repainted, but still the sight of the palace never failed to please him. It came to him how he had sat here with his own father Laertes as a boy, many moons ago. His father was long dead, buried alongside his mother in the family tomb on the main thoroughfare towards the harbour, so any visitor to the palace might stop and pay due honour. The old stools had been replaced with a sturdy wooden bench, which he had crafted himself. The dusty earth was pitted with red stains like over ripened figs falling and rotting from the tree. Now he sat in this same spot, beside his own son in the fullness and maturity of manhood. Despite the passage of time, no stranger could have mistaken them for other than father and son.

Odysseus looked around surveying the tended fields below them, noting with satisfaction the abundant crops coming forth from the ground. The granaries across the kingdom were still well stocked with last year's grain and there were signs of a good harvest to come. The golden-haired barley was ripening under Helios' soft glow. If the crops failed, they need have no fear: there was enough grain stored away to feed them through several poor harvests. If, as it was claimed, the fertility of the land echoed wise kingship and stewardship, then he could feel proud-spirited.

Telemachos was waiting attentively for him to speak, his gaze fixed on his father's face. Odysseus began.

"So are our plans in place, my son, as we agreed?"

"They are indeed father. The local leaders accept your proposal and await your directive."

He turned to face Telemachos, his ears alert. "And did they all acquiesce or was there some dissent?" If there was any resistance, he needed to know about it.

"They consented readily to our proposal. They are afraid," he admitted, a shadow sweeping his face. "For each day brings more people from the mainland, seeking shelter in our island kingdom. They say that *Strife* has broken out in some of the great cities and the people fight amongst themselves." Telemachos paused and glanced across at his father, who was listening closely.

"Go on."

"Even the great cities of Mykenai and Tiryns have not escaped," Telemachos continued, an uneasiness creeping into his words. "A strange darkness has come over the land of Pelops, so that the day is in perpetual gloom and without Helios, the crops fail to grow and thrive. The grapes rot on the vine and people starve for want of food. They offer sacrifice each day but the gods show no pity for their plight."

"And are we any clearer as to the cause?"

"It is rumoured that the peoples of Atlantis, a sea-bound island, offended the gods. So they destroyed their city with smoking fire and ash, but the darkness stays in the air."

Odysseus raised his eyebrows. It was not his place to question the actions of the gods, but it whetted his curiosity. "You have done well, son," Odysseus replied steadily and he affectionately clasped Telemachos by the shoulder. "We must make sure that we are protected here in our island kingdom and do what we can to ward off this danger." At least the barrier of the sea offered some security to the kingdom from the madness stalking the mainland. "Let us hope, my son, that it does not come to war." He lapsed into silence, slowly nodding to himself.

"Is there something else on your mind, father?"

Odysseus allowed himself to venture a smile, his mind still wrapped in thought. "You know me too well Telemachos!" he said glancing up. "Do you remember that day when I returned to the palace? It was not long after we were first reunited in the humble dwelling of Eumaios, our dearest and most loyal friend. He who took me in, though dressed as a beggar, and gave me food and shelter."

"How could I forget that day, father. For the gods have kept the memory of that time clear in my mind. We had waited so long for your return that *Hope* had all but abandoned us."

"Do you recall, how I travelled alone to the palace, still disguised as a beggar to hide my identity?" The other man bowed his head slightly to indicate his agreement, so Odysseus continued. "Before I entered the town, I stopped at the water fountain, the one below the hill of Hermes to take a drink of its sweet waters. As you know, the water is very cool as it comes from high up on the hillslope." He paused, taking a deep breath. "I drank from the spring and it shames me to say it now, for a moment I doubted my course. Whether to go on with our plan or to take flight. It came to me that the way that led here to the palace was my destined path and this was the journey I needed to take. It was that which determined my decision to carry on."

"Why are you telling me this, father?" asked Telemachos, perplexed, gazing up at his father. "I don't understand."

"That too was a terrible time, son. Our house was in disarray when the natural order of things had been overturned and broken down.

Guests in this very palace acted as masters, causing disorder, sleeping with the female servants and insulting you and your mother. Here in my own palace, I was dishonoured as a beggar and assaulted by those with no regard for the normal rules of hospitality." At the memory, he clenched his jaw and irritation flashed through his mind. "Their arrogant and overbearing behaviour spread like a pox passed from man to man, corrupting and despoiling the normal bonds that hold men together and the natural order of the *Cosmos*. Thus those who previously knew their place, either as nobles or humble workers grew emboldened, overstepping their rank, believing they were all kings together."

Telemachos momentarily shuddered in front of him, recalling that terrible spectacle of the bloodletting. When the slaughter had begun in the great *megaron*, there had been assembled the highest born young men drawn from across the kingdom seeking to seize his father's authority. One hundred and eight men in all, wedding suitors, greedy for power and the wealth it bestowed: the lands, the herds of goats and sheep, the hard-won precious metals piled in the treasure room and control of the well-founded palace itself. With the arrogance of young nobodies, they had sought to replace their king even in the marriage chamber without *kleos* or merit.

"We stood together then, Telemachos," he lifted his chin, as he looked his son full in the face. "Shoulder to shoulder. The two of us together with the loyal and trusted Eumaios, then only a lowly herdsman. With our swords and our weapons, we cut them down each and every last man."

"And the faithless servants too," added Telemachos, remembering his part also in the killing. The palace hall had been covered in blood. Even the intense cleaning and scrubbing of the servants and the purifying pots of sulphur could not eliminate the stain for years. The bodies had been piled high here in the yard, awaiting to be claimed by their kinsmen to be given ceremonial and proper funerary rites.

Remembering the horror of the scene, Odysseus' eyes inadvertently fell on that part of the yard, as if seeing once more where the earth had been pitted with dried blood. "The suffering was terrible, son, and many families within the kingdom grieved for their young men, departed sons or lost brothers taken early to Hades."

"Do you now doubt father whether it was right?" asked Telemachos perplexed.

In his darkest moments Odysseus had indeed questioned the slaughter. He grasped the pain and suffering it had caused. When he had fought at Troy, it had all been so simple and straight forward. To follow the warrior code at any cost to seek *kleos* and individual heroic glory of the hero. Now he was less convinced. He wondered whether his warrior's heart had softened under Kirke's influence like wax in the flame's heat.

He drew himself upright, his back rigid like forged metal. "No it had to be done. Not from hate or rage of the *Furies* who exact vengeance and punish wrong-doers. But it was accepted that this violation and pollution of the natural order had to be stopped. For else we would all suffer retribution from the gods and Zeus himself, the arbitrator of justice." For had the price not been paid and what was necessary done, Zeus' vengeance would be visited on the next blameless generation or the next, until full recompense had been made. For that would be the price for disrupting the balance of the *Cosmos* created by the gods. "There was a high blood-price paid," he said slowly, the words almost sticking in his throat, "to restore the kingdom and to return things as they should be but that was the necessary path."

"I still do not understand why you speak of these things now father," said Telemachos unable to read his expression. "That grievous time is in the past and now *Peace* encircles the kingdom."

"That is indeed true and there is a reason why I speak of such matters," he said gathering his thoughts closer together. "It is now twenty years since those dreadful events. I have lived for sixty years and am now reaching a ripe old age. I have watched you these many years and taught you everything I know about kingship." Odysseus paused, his eyes now moist with tears. The guilt still pained him like a knife that he had not been there during his son's childhood. He took some comfort that they had been inseparable since. "Now you have reached the same age as when I returned to these shores, twenty seasons ago, I believe the time has come to pass onto you the kingship of Ithaka. The gods give me no doubt that you are ready to shoulder that responsibility and will rule wisely and justly." He could see the effect of his words. Telemachos was vigorously shaking his head.

"But father, you are still …" But Odysseus put out a hand to stop him speaking, not allowing the younger man to finish his speech. His mind had already anticipated all the arguments and objections.

"Telemachos, I know what you will say. That I am not yet descended into Hades, the land of the dead souls. That I have more years to live. All this may be true. But Ithaka needs new vigour and strength to govern and protect it, especially in these troubling times. Not that of a weakening man." He looked up at his son, feeling sentiment well in his throat and spoke more soothingly. "This was always on my mind when I battled my way back here from Troy and endured all the misfortunes along that cursed home journey. That one day you would succeed and be king of this island kingdom. My task is done." He felt calm and clear of purpose. "The gods have blessed me that I live to see that day. That day I believe has now come and is my most heartfelt desire." He reached for his son's hand and held it against his chest, above his beating heart. "Do you agree, Telemachos, and consent to my wishes?"

The man glanced up, as if reading his thoughts and then he motioned his head in agreement. "If this is what you desire."

"Good, then at the feast today, when the people are assembled, I will present you to the gathered people as their new king and leader. We will speak no further of this until then. And how are those two boys of yours, my grandsons?" Already the elder was showing promising signs that he would make a fine warrior. The younger one had a different disposition, more given to handling a lyre than a mighty sword. But he had astute observation and a quick turn of words, like his grandfather.

"They are excited by the prospect of the feast."

"It won't be long before we will need to find them brides," Odysseus said knowingly, feeling pride stirring in his chest. "But come then, let us go and make our preparations to join the celebration. There is still much to do." He started to rise to his feet. While sitting, his back had stiffened and the sinews tightened on his limbs. No longer was he so quick in movement. He could see that Telemachos still delayed. He knew the bonds of father and son kinship ran deep between them overcoming every obstacle.

Telemachos turned his face upwards to him, the emotion clear on his rugged bronze face. "Father, though you suffer the weakness of old age, may the gods keep you here yet with your people prospering around you."

"Of course, my dear son," he responded, inwardly perplexed. Strange those were the very words spoken by the old seer all those years ago. Again the gods brought Kirke into his mind and that disquieting feeling. Now Odysseus had remembered, he could not seem to shake off the past as if some god was tormenting him. At that very moment, the outline of a winged creature swooped down low, a tail feather slowly weaving its way to the ground. It perched high on the roof-tiled gable of the palace, where no stone could reach it. There was no mistaking the white owl.

Chapter 20

Rejection

The overnight case lay on the bed, inside a pile of clothes neatly folded. Thea gave the contents a final check before decisively zipping the cover. The metal teeth complained as they snapped shut.

"So you're going away, *kyria*?" Electra enquired, her attention falling on the piece of luggage, as Thea handed over her room key.

"That's right. For the weekend."

"Anywhere nice?" The inquisitive smile invited a confidence.

"Just seeing an old friend," Thea answered casually, feeling her ears beginning to burn and a tightness in her throat. She liked Electra and her straightforward nature, but any suspicion or knowledge of her plans was dangerous and explosive if it became common knowledge.

"Do you want me to call you a cab," Electra called out after her.

"Thanks but that really isn't necessary," Thea replied lamely, feeling the heat spreading out across her face, as she hastily dragged her bag out of the hotel lobby.

The small square was just around the corner from the hotel. It was quiet and deserted when Thea arrived. It had been Dimitri who had suggested this meeting spot, seeking discretion. She took a seat on the wooden bench, in the shadow of a flowering oleander, overlooking a modest patch of coarse grass and cultivated lavender. Thea checked her watch and waited, watching the empty street. Just opposite was a marble column, the whiteness almost luminescent and elaborately carved. Thea recognised the winged figure of the god Hermes, the messenger of the gods, standing in repose.

Just then a figure came into view, walking with the familiar distinctive stride. After seeing so little of him since the Easter barbecue, it was an unfortunate coincidence Rob should turn up right at this same moment.

"Hello Thea." Rob greeted her affably with a wide grin. "What are you doing here? Are you going somewhere?" he asked with lively interest, immediately taking in the packed suitcase. His clothing was lighter in style, which blended in with the local Greek dress code and the colour accentuated the blueness of his eyes. Before she could reply, the deep guttural sound of a sports car engine interrupted, as Dimitri pulled up in his racing-green car.

He quickly got out of the car and came over to them, almost sprinting. "Hello, Dr Hughes", Dimitri said acknowledging Rob's presence. "Are you ready to go Thea," he asked, checking his watch, clearly keen to leave.

"I didn't realise that you two were going away together?" Rob commented, looking at Thea questioningly.

"Yes, Dr Sefton has kindly agreed to accompany me to an event over the weekend," Dimitri smoothly replied on Thea's behalf before she had a chance to speak. "So we're travelling together." He continued without pausing, "Thank you for kindly letting us visit your lab the other week. You know that the Foundation, including myself, are very impressed with your work and the results you are producing. We may have to look into some extra financial reward for your efforts." The words were meant to be flattering but had the opposite intended effect. There was a distinct reddening of Rob's face and a look of pure hatred. Clearly Rob had no time for Dimitri, even as a financial benefactor.

"I'm not around this weekend Rob but I'll be back first thing on Monday morning," Thea said stepping in to punctuate the tension. "Are you still on for the walking trip next week? I'll finalise the details with Mark once I return."

"No, you go on with your weekend, Thea. I can make the arrangements." The colour of Rob's face was still flushed but the tone was conciliatory.

"Can I drop you off anywhere?" Dimitri asked, unperturbed by his effect on the other man.

"No, no," Rob replied abruptly, putting out his hand as if warding off an evil spirit. "I can make my own way," he said still glowering at Dimitri, rejecting the offer out of hand.

"That man is a brilliant at his work, but quite strange at times," said Dimitri good-naturedly as they pulled away from the kerb. Rob was still watching them but with a peculiar wistful expression on his face, his eyes tracking the moving vehicle. As they drove through the town suburbs, the look stayed with Thea unsettling her thoughts and she could feel the old doubts resurfacing. They had now left the town behind them and were quickly speeding along the airport road, eating up the distance. They were approaching the turning for the airport itself, when Thea suddenly called out.

"Pull over! We need to talk."

"What now? When we are so close to the airport?" Nonetheless Dimitri complied with the request, pulling the car up to a sudden stop, the tyres screeching on the tarmac.

"This will only take a few minutes," Thea said soothingly. "There's a small *taverna* over there, let's go in and get some coffee."

There was a flush of irritation on his dark handsome face, but Dimitri courteously helped Thea out of the car. An awkward silence followed, after their order for coffee was taken. Thea noticed Dimitri glancing round impatiently, tapping the floor with his foot and shifting in his chair. She waited until the coffees were brought by a young boy, no more than twelve years, who slowly set the cups down his hands trembling, trying not to spill a single drop, until they were finally left alone.

"So what's so urgent that couldn't wait?" Dimitri began. "Surely we've the whole weekend to talk."

"Yes, we do," Thea replied, her voice steady. "But I need to ask you something."

"So ask away?" Dimitri said, a look of good-humour playing on his face, as he took a mouthful of coffee. "What do you need to know so urgently?"

Bracing herself, Thea took a deep inward breath and asked the question. "How was it decided that the survey should be based in Kalodia, your family's village?"

Dimitri laughed out loud, throwing back his head to reveal a row of perfect formed teeth. "Is that all? For a moment I thought it was something more serious. That you'd changed your mind." She noticed the long eyelashes and the smooth shaved skin, as Dimitri turned towards her his deep pooled eyes. "Of course Kalodia is my family village and I can't deny that. Everyone on the island knows that. I suggested it to Richard and he readily agreed. I didn't think it was a problem." He beamed reassuringly at her and reached out to stroke her hand, but Thea drew back.

"But Richard is under your spell. I don't understand how but you seem to have this influence over him," Thea said struggling to find the right words. "Do you not see that? He will do whatever you ask him."

"Yes, Richard has been very accommodating," Dimitri readily agreed, looking up over his coffee cup, as he took another sip. "But if you think that Kalodia is not the right location, then we can move the project next year to the site of your choosing. Where ever you want, you decide." He lifted his eyes to her now smiling, seducing her with his words and easy charm.

But the nagging doubt and unease would not abate. Looking at Dimitri across from her, this time Thea summoned up all her strength and determination.

"I can't do this Dimitri," Thea finally said, shaking her head. "It doesn't feel right."

Dimitri gasped banging his coffee cup down onto its saucer, so the contents spilt over. "What do you mean Thea, you can't do this," he demanded, his voice loaded with exasperation. "What's the problem? You're an adult, I'm an adult. We no longer have to care about everyone else, we can do what we please. Next year choose where you want to do the survey. Lead the project yourself if that's what you want. Just as long as we're together."

Thea hesitated and took a deep breath, realising her next words might only infuriate him. "But there isn't just us. You have a family, a wife and two children. We have to think of the hurt and pain we might cause others."

"Thea, why are you doing this?" Dimitri was regarding her steadily through deep olive-coloured eyes, the irises clear and glassy. "We love each other. We've done so for years. That's all that matters. You know this is the truth. I can give you whatever you want. Take you wherever you want to go. Set you up in your own place, so we can be close. I'm one of the wealthiest men in Greece. We'll have a wonderful life together. How can that be a problem?"

Briefly an image came to her of the two of them growing old together, snuggled beneath a thick blanket, watching the sunset over a snow-capped mountain. For a moment, Thea's resolve almost wavered before she banished the notion.

"I'm sorry Dimitri, but no," Thea said firmly, shaking her head.

"You can't mean that. Are you stupid?" A flash of anger now lit up Dimitri's fine-featured face. "Why would you throw away this chance, of us being together?"

And then it came out, from nowhere, catching even Thea by surprise. "Because you abandoned me! You left me pregnant!"

For a moment, Dimitri sat visibly shocked, his mouth dropped like a fish gulping for oxygen. "What are you saying?" he demanded, as the questions came urgent and pressing. "There was a child? Where is it now?" A nervous look passed over his face as if he was trying to grasp the implications of this revelation: the thought of having a grown-up child, the financial repercussions or the possible disruption to a life so carefully crafted.

"I miscarried at three months," Thea added, her words barely audible. "I lost the baby here on the island, twenty years ago."

"Oh my god!" Dimitri exclaimed. "No one told me. Who else knows?" He now glanced anxiously around the *taverna*, suddenly taken by paranoia that their conversation might be overheard.

"No one," Thea reassured him, "only Eleni who nursed me through it. But that's the reason I can't do this. Our relationship is built on a destructive love. And if it is discovered, it will only cause hurt and suffering to others."

"But we could start over. I love you." Desperately Dimitri scanned her face, searching for any glimmer of feeling but Thea refused meet his eye.

"Dimitri, this isn't love," Thea replied finally, at last raising her face to him. "You're mistaken. Love is a force for good, not a destructive self-centred act. How can this situation you propose be love? I'm not going to be your dirty little secret, who Stelios or some other hanger-on knows about. A mistress who you shut away. Do you think I'm still that naive girl of nineteen?" She paused, meeting his eye directly. "We owe it to the child we lost to act honourably."

"But I can't let you go," Dimitri said, almost childlike, now pleading with her. "Not now!"

"You can and you must," Thea replied firmly, "if you really and truly care about me. This isn't the life I would choose for myself. It's a poor substitute. I may be no longer married, but this isn't what I want either."

"And what about the project?" The mood now had suddenly shifted to something darker and menacing.

"What about the project? What are you implying?"

"If you walk now, then the project does too." Dimitri was staring at her, the dark pupils of his eyes dilated. An ugly crimson mottling flushed his handsome features. "Do you want that on your conscience?" he continued. "How you let your colleagues down?"

"Oh no Dimitri!" Thea said, shaking her head, feeling her body begin to shake with rage. "You aren't putting the blame for your actions onto me. What you and the Archontakis Foundation decide is up to you. But that should not determine whether or not I have an affair with you!"

And then a veil that had been there for years finally lifted. Suddenly Thea saw him for what he was: the ego, the vanity, the conceit covered by an easy superficial charm. And with it the realisation that she had wasted most of her adult life yearning for Dimitri Kampitsis only to be confronted by a shallow shell of a man.

"I was mistaken," Thea calmly replied, meeting his glance head-on. "I thought you were someone else." Decisively she stood up, picking up her bag to go.

"Wait!" Dimitri cried out desperately. "Surely we can work this out? You can't leave like this. At least let me run you back to the hotel."

But her mind was set. "You go on with your weekend plans. I can make my own way." Almost as an afterthought, Thea turned back towards him and removed from her finger the expensive gold ring. "I'm sorry Dimitri but this doesn't belong to me." And she carefully placed it on the wooden table in front of him. He stared down at it, his nostrils flaring, speechless.

The loose grit scrunched under the suitcase, as Thea wheeled it along the side of the road towards the airport. A large billboard announced the services of a car hire office. The procedure was straight forward. After rummaging through her bag to produce some ID, her driver's licence and credit card, Thea was handed the keys of a small compact Korean car. The interior smelt of strong polish and synthetic plastic. She opened the electric window allowing the clear air to flood in. She wasn't quite sure where she was going, as she clasped the metal-grey steering wheel but found herself driving back along the coast towards the main town. To the only place that felt right.

When Eleni opened the door, Thea fell into her arms sobbing, her body contorted with anguish. For several minutes the two women stood, the older one comforting the younger. Finally without a word, Eleni quietly led her into the kitchen, seating her at the table. A pot of tea and cups were produced. The china had seen better days: the painted roses had faded and the porcelain was chipped and cracked.

"*Ela, koritsi mou*, tell me what happened." Eleni glanced up at Thea, her face brimming with sympathy.

"I told him Eleni. I told him everything," Thea gasped between the sobs, the tears now falling quickly. "It's over. Finished." She took deep breaths, trying to steady herself so she could get out the words, blowing her nose on the tissue that Eleni now passed to her. She shook her head. "I don't understand why I feel so upset. It feels like a huge gaping wound."

"You're not crying for him." Eleni stroked her forearm, looking intently into Thea's face. "You're crying for long ago and the child you lost. This man has affected your life far more than he deserves. What he did to you, abandoning you without a word, was cruel and callous. Come. Cry if you must! Far better this comes out then keeping this sorrow bottled inside," the older woman reassured her with an understanding look, rubbing Thea's back. "Stay here until you feel okay. Stay for the weekend. We'll make up your old bed together."

Thea smiled at her weakly through her tears. "Thank you," she murmured.

As darkness had fallen, the two women made up the bed together. The covers were worn but scrupulously clean, smelling of washing powder and mountain lavender. From an old-fashioned wardrobe, Eleni had pulled out a heavy woollen coverlet in the hues of autumn red, green and orange. Other signs of her loving touch sprinkled the room. A collection of coat hangers had been placed on the bed. And on the bedside table, a small bouquet of fresh-cut flowers and beaker of water to quench any night-time thirst. Under bedclothes, Thea had curled herself into a ball and for the remainder of the night, she didn't stir. She had sobbed her heart out until at last, the pillow wet with her tears, she fell asleep.

The light was already streaming through the half-closed shutters, when Thea awoke the next day. Her watch-face told her the morning was already well advanced. Eleni would have been up several hours already, completing her daily tasks and chores. Thea looked around, absorbing the familiar features of her old room, but something was different. Her head and spirit were clear. As if a burden she had been carrying for many years had been lifted, like a pack-animal relieved of its load. Opening up her suitcase, Thea pulled out a loose tunic to match this new mood. Something had shifted as if an internal knot had been undone.

When Thea entered the kitchen, she was met with the sight of Eleni bustling around and already several pots were bubbling on the stove. The metallic rims were streaked with ingrained marks, which neither scrubbing nor metal scouring pads could dislodge. Eleni was cooking up salves or herbal remedies.

"Would you like something to eat," asked Eleni, reaching out to kiss her on both cheeks. "My neighbour has just delivered some fresh eggs. We could have omelette with tomatoes and new bread." It was the typical maternal response of countless mothers across Greece to feed away all troubles. Thea accepted gratefully, submitting to Eleni's ministrations.

"*Pos eisai simera?*" Eleni asked, as she took some eggs from a brown paper bag and cracked them into a bowl. The familiar polite enquiry took on an extra meaning.

"*Eimai kala,*" Thea replied and meant it. Although she still felt drained from the release of the emotions so carefully stored away, she did feel fine. "Can I help?" she asked, keen to turn her attention to something other than her newly found insight and dwelling on Dimitri.

Eleni responded with the typical Greek tilting of the head back to form a nod for *ochi*, meaning *No*. Instead, Thea sat as she was urged, watching the stooped and laboured movements of the older woman as she prepared breakfast. The kitchen electrical equipment was rudimentary: an old four-ringed stove for boiling or frying and a small fridge for chilling especially during the summer heat. And yet they belied Eleni's formidable cookery skills and the mouth-watering feats that could be produced in that simple space.

They ate together in silence, which was only broken by Thea. "Eleni, thank you for taking me in yesterday. I was glad you were there."

"You were very upset, *e koukla mou.*" Eleni studied her sympathetically, pausing to take a mouthful of food. "But you did the right thing."

"I nearly went away with him," Thea shrugged, shaking her head. "But in the end I couldn't do it. It seems that this love between us is like poison. It hurts anyone who comes into contact with it." She looked down, as if analysing the piece of torn bread in her fingers, a blank stare on her face. "But I've realised something else. All these years I've been carrying this love only to discover I've been infatuated with an illusion." She gave a thin smile and looked up at Eleni. "And you know, the funny thing is that it has come between me and any relationship. Eleni, if I am being truly honest it was there in my marriage to David." She paused. "I was drawn to him precisely because he was safe and steady." Tears started to well up but she brushed them aside. She wasn't going to let go of this new-found clarity for self-pity. "And I wanted to protect myself from being hurt or abandoned again."

"Perhaps now this love has gone," Eleni said quietly, steadily regarding her, "there is space to cultivate something else."

"Yes," Thea agreed, nodding her head thoughtfully. "Perhaps this is where my obsession with Odysseus and his palace comes from. I've actually spent most of my adult life immersed in the meaning of words and texts so I can avoid interacting with a real living and breathing man." She laughed out aloud. "After all you can't be let down by a mythical hero from four thousand years ago!"

"*Vevaios* Thea! I always deeply believed you were born with the gift of love and healing. You deserve to be surrounded by the love of those who hold you dear." Eleni paused, emphasising her next words. "And I believe that you will be a mother yet."

Thea looked up at her bewildered, a frown crossing her face. That statement again. "Perhaps I have become too independent and self-reliant," she conceded. "But I doubt motherhood. My thirty-eight years are against me."

"*Mi forvasai*! There is still time, *e koukla mou*." Eleni's kindly eyes crinkled underneath her heavy eyelids and she pressed Thea's hand. "Would you like to help me?" she asked, turning away to look at the pots still boiling on the stove. "Your company would be *mia chara*."

"It would be a pleasure." Thea stood up, smoothing down her tunic and tied an apron around her waist. For several hours the women worked, heating pans of different concoctions. Some they made into herbal tonics to be drunk, others were reduced down and then squeezed through fine mesh and mixed with oil for a salve or tincture. Thea glanced across at her friend. Her indefatigable energy and vitality contradicted her advancing years.

"Do you not have anyone who can help you," Thea asked at last concerned, wiping a bead of sweat from her brow.

"Of course," Eleni replied gathering her breath, "but you are the only one who knows exactly what is required."

When they were hungry, they stopped to eat a simple fare of coarse bread, cheese and lettuce, just harvested from Eleni's garden. As the daylight faded to darkness, they sat outside in the garden, covering themselves with blankets to keep out the night chill, talking about different medicinal linctus and treatments. They ate more lemon polenta cake, drank local wine and talked into the early hours until it was time for sleep.

When Thea awoke the next day, it was another clear azure sky, the chill dissipated by April's silvery sunlight. Not only had the deep sleep refreshed her but a greater clarity was permeating her mind. It had been her idea to drive up the mountain and forage for wild medicinal plants that grew on the wooded slopes of Mount Oenos. Eleni had been initially cautious, reasoning that she could not walk far, but had eventually come round to the proposition. Now they were driving in the rental car up the track leading to the higher slopes of the mountain. The landscape was ablaze with a hotchpotch of wild spring blooms: yellows, reds, whites and golds all competing for the attention of the pollinating insects. Thea's trained eye instinctively categorised the wild mountainside shrubs into fennel, mint, sage, chamomile, valerian and rosemary. But her interest was surpassed by Eleni, who was growing more excited with each passing moment at the sight of the hillside in bloom.

Under the shaded cover of the woods, Thea parked the car, near a picnic area with wooden tables. There was an air of dereliction, as if the spot had enjoyed happier times, hosting long summer evenings of campers or young people strumming guitars. The two women got out of the car, taking a couple of plastic bags to stash their foraging.

"You look like a *yeia yeia*," grinned Eleni, as Thea emerged with her hair bound beneath a headscarf, a plastic carrier bag in her hand.

"I'm not a grandmother quite yet," Thea replied laughing. "Do you think we will find *horta* here?" The wild green leafed plant grew wild in the hills and was traditionally collected and served up as a delicacy.

"No, I think it's too shaded here. But there are other plants which only grow in this place." Without hesitation, Eleni set off leading them up one of the narrow dirt tracks into the woodland, where the trees thickened. Despite the slowness of her body, her head darted from side to side, scanning the woodland floor searching for the rare but familiar medicinal plants.

It was well past noon and they had lost track of time, when Eleni leaned against a tall tree trunk, panting heavily. "I'll be alright in a moment," she grasped as she caught her breath. "It's just old age catching up on me."

"Shall we go back to the car?" Thea asked anxiously, studying her friend and reaching out to take her carrier bag. It was bulging with green cuttings foraged from the forest floor and garlic, which gave off a pungent smell. "We could snack on the fruit and cinnamon pastries we brought with us." Without protest, the older woman accepted Thea's arm as support and allowed herself to be guided back down the path.

"*Oreo,*" Eleni commented, as they sat chewing. They were occupying one of the deserted tables and the earlier moment had been forgotten. There was a look of contentment on Eleni's face, being close to this beloved landscape and the natural woodland. "*Einai poly amorfa.*"

Thea inwardly concurred, the peacefulness of the place was indeed very striking. The leaves of the ancient forest showed not just one colour green but a whole spectrum of different shades: from khaki to lime; olive to sea-green; bottle-green to jade. Sunlight was now breaking through the forest canopy, providing a dappled light where clusters of insects danced in the sunlight.

"You know there is a special kind of tree, that we only have here on Kefalonia," Eleni commented pointing to the foreground, her eyebrows knitted together. "The Kefalonian fir." Thea nodded as she followed the direction of Eleni's gesture and noticed several deciduous trees. She knew this fact well from reading Homer. The boat oars of Odysseus' Kefalonian contingent had been constructed from this native tree.

"What is it? What's wrong?"

"The trees shouldn't be like this at this time of year! Look at the needles, they looked dry and parched. They ought to be greener after the spring rains." Thea glanced up at the towering upright giants. It was true, the shaggy pine branches were browning at their tips. The ground must be very dry. "It's not a good sign for when the summer heat comes," Eleni continued, her voice racked with concern. "You know our summers have become hotter. I'm afraid that the heat strains our Kefalonian fir. It would be a great crime to lose it. *Ena krima!*" Eleni tutted to herself. Thea looked up again at the tree with renewed respect. This magnificent species, standing lofty and proud, had witnessed Odysseus and the Kephallenians sailing off to Troy and over the millennia the countless comings and goings from the island. It was hard on this day, sat amongst the lush woodland, to envisage that this might become a casualty of a changing climate. That the natural order of the planet might be changing imperceptibly little by little, day by day, year by year. In silence, they finished their improvised picnic, breathing in the natural beauty that connected them to the generous and fertile earth.

On their way back to the main town, Thea suggested stopping at a *taverna* in one of the small villages that dotted the mountain hillside.

"Please, it will be my treat just to say thank you for your hospitality," Thea explained to a reluctant Eleni. She already anticipated the familiar tussle over the bill, where the honour went to the person paying. She made a mental note to settle it early, before her friend could pre-empt her.

When they pulled up outside the *taverna*, the place was deserted. It was still too early to expect the Greek families, who usually ate much later in the evening. They ordered a plate of grilled chicken, *choriatiki* salad, *tzatziki* and baked salty *kefalonitis* cheese. Thea poured out a glass of wine for Eleni from a carafe, before taking a sip of her own soft drink. It was still too cool to dine *al fresco*, so they had taken a seat near the balcony window. There was still a breathtaking view across the bay to the main town, fanning out over the facing hillside. Beyond, Thea could see the low lying swell on the Paliki peninsula, which inadvertently drew her attention. Eleni noticed and followed Thea's gaze.

"So is the work going well?" the older woman enquired, squinting out over the lagoon to the land beyond.

"I think so-so." The Greek that rolled off Thea's tongue, *etsi ketsi,* expressed the meaning perfectly. "I've located a number of places that seem to match the Homeric descriptions for Ithaka. An island that has two beaches and a landing place with a sheltered harbour and cave. The geological work so far confirms Paliki was once a separate island." Thea noticed her throat constrict as she thought of the lab. She did not allow her thoughts to dwell on it. "But the field survey has been disappointing and they haven't picked up any archaeological signs of habitation. And we're running out of time," she added resignedly. She looked up at Eleni, who had been listening attentively in silence. "But I feel it in my bones we're on the right track. So close, I can almost touch it."

Eleni gave her a long look, which the younger women found hard to decipher. "Perhaps our island palace is not quite ready to be discovered," she said slowly and deliberately. "But I think Thea, maybe you are close to discovering something else but not as you expect."

Eleni wiped her hands on the serviette. They had done justice to the freshly prepared food and only a few chicken bones and remnants of the meal remained. "So are you ready to go back?" asked Eleni, looking pointedly at Thea, "and face the world again?"

"Yes," Thea firmly replied. "I'm ready."

Chapter 21

Apollo's Feast

When Odysseus entered the bedchamber, newly fashioned robes had already been laid out ready. He took a moment to admire the finely woven garment. The hemline was decorated with a perfect row of symmetrical squares representing the unending path of life. The cloth was light in colour to offset the gold foil sewn into the collar to signify his kingly status. It came to him that this was the reason Penelope had been so occupied during the last cycle of the moon. To ensure the robe was ready for this important feast day.

He fingered the robe and was moved by the great delicacy and fineness, a reflection of his wife's mastery of the loom. He realised this was her precious gift to him. A god brought back to him the memory of when Penelope had first crossed the threshold of the palace as a blushing maiden. His own dear mother, now long dead, had delighted in his choice of young bride. She had cultivated the young woman, taking great pleasure in instructing her new daughter-in-law in the skills of the loom and cloth making. And Penelope had been a gifted and willing learner; there was no doubt that the two women had both been endowed with the skills and crafts of the goddess Athena herself.

Penelope had already dressed in her new robes for the occasion, her raven hair carefully coiled into a knot at the nape, pinned with elaborate gold spirals. Her single calm presence masked the frantic comings and goings of the servants. Her own garments mirrored those before him, only instead of precious gold, her collar had been embroidered with elaborate stitching. The shoulder was pinned with a bronze fibula decorated with blue faience, a guest friendship gift, and she wore a necklace of amber beads. It was obvious she had been waiting, wanting to observe his reaction and to see if her gift pleased him. He nodded towards her as a sign of approval.

"This is a fine garment, Penelope," he said, looking up at her. "And more than fit for today's Feast of Apollo. You have indeed excelled yourself and the gods have blessed you, good wife. Do you want to help me dress?" He started to strip off his old clothes, hastily thrown on in the darkness of the night. As he exposed his body, he noticed Penelope casting her eyes downwards to avert her gaze. Even now, after years of marriage and lovemaking, she was awkward at the sight of his naked body. This was not the day to upset her. He chose to ignore it and finished dressing by himself. The robe fitted perfectly and he drew across his waist a belt, embossed with gold foil sewn into the leather. Although he could not see his own reflection, he felt outwardly clothed in the full symbols of his kingship and authority.

"How do I look to you, wife. Is my appearance to your satisfaction?" He turned round so that she could admire the full effects of her creation.

"It is indeed, husband. It is a garment well befitting the king of Ithaka."

"And his queen," he added, touching her cheek affectionately, "also looks beautiful and regal." He kissed her lovingly on her forehead. "Are we ready to go?" He noticed Penelope adjusting her veil over her face, a custom she had always observed as a dutiful and noble queen. A feeling rose up inside him: a frustration or irritation given by the gods he dare not name. He pushed the feeling away from him aware that this was not the time. It could wait. There were more important matters at hand that needed to be attended.

As Penelope and Odysseus descended the stairway, Telemachos and his family were already gathered in the great *megaron*. His wife, Epicaste, stood at her husband's side, her face modestly downcast. She had come from Pylos, the daughter of his dear friend Nestor, and was renowned for both her intelligence and her beauty. It gave Odysseus great pleasure that marriage had joined the two families together, further strengthening the ties of kinship and guest-friendship. Epicaste had borne Telemachos two healthy sons: the elder who was now entering manhood and a daughter, Arete. She had recently married a noble from Zakynthos and had returned with her young husband for the feast. Now she stood in her finest attire beaming, proudly clutching her young babe. At the sight of his family, Odysseus' heart swelled and he thought with satisfaction how the fortunes of the House of Arkeisios, his father's father, had flourished since his return.

Now that the full extended family and the retinue of attendants had assembled, Odysseus with his queen Penelope led out the procession from the palace. They walked at a steady pace slowly winding their way down towards the open fields leading to the shrine of Apollo, close to where Odysseus had slept so long and so deeply only the previous day. A canopy had been raised across the trees to provide shelter from the fierce rays of Helios and the long banqueting table and benches set beneath. Straining and sweating under the solid weight, the servants had carried it down from the great *megaron*. For those unable to be seated at the table, brushwood and chaff had been scattered over the ground. A throng of people had already assembled, having travelled from all the different corners of the kingdom: from Same, Doulichion, Zakynthos and from Ithaka itself to celebrate Apollo's feast. Many of the faces were familiar but there were also some strangers, their dress slightly different and their faces haunted as if chased by the *Furies*. He assumed these people must be from the mainland. From the corner of his eye, he noticed Telemachos embracing a man of similar age and stature, his brother-in-law Peisistratos. The two had become close from Telemachos' journey to Pylos and his marriage. He had newly arrived to join them in their celebrations to the god. Peisistratos would make a worthy ally for the kingdom in time of need.

In the crowd, Odysseus picked out a familiar face and singled him out at once.

"Welcome dear friend. Your face and that of your family are a welcome sight to me." He greeted Eumaios, embracing him. He stepped back, taking in Eumaios' appearance. His beard had been neatly trimmed and the thick black curls now edged with silver. He was clad in a fine robe, crafted by his younger wife, who waited patiently at his side. For Eumaios had had his wish for freedom and a hearth of his own. Three manly sons stood behind and he could see that soon brides would need to be sought.

"Thanks that the gods have let us live long enough to see this day," Odysseus said, clasping Eumaios on his broad back. "For it is twenty years, since we fought shoulder to shoulder to reclaim the kingdom from those insolent suitors so this good could come of it."

"Indeed, my lord. It is a fine sight," the other man said, his eyes watering with tears. "To do honour to Apollo this day. "

"And I would invite you to sit beside us and your family as our most honoured guests." Eumaios bowed his head and nodded his agreement. "But first we must give our attention to observing the ceremony to honour the god Apollo and give him his due rights", Odysseus said seeing the priest approaching him. He felt in good spirits. Already there was a rich aroma of meat and dark smoke filling the air from the roasting spits. In preparation for the feast, fifty lambs and fifty goats had been delivered from the upland pastures, all now cooking over the open fire-pits.

"*Basileos*, we are ready to make the offering to

the god," announced the priest, a mild-looking fellow. He gestured to a cooked meat carcass that had just been removed from the fire. Odysseus took the knife proffered by the priest, taking care to cut away the juiciest and most tender meat cuts for the god. He did not wish to invoke the divine punishment as Prometheus had done when he had deceived Zeus, wrapping bone and gristle in succulent fat. When the metal platter was brimful, the priest carried it the short distance to the shrine, holding it aloft and intoning a supplication to Apollo.

The priest then set the platter down on the altar, together with a *kylix* full of sweet honeyed red wine, sprinkled with herbs. All bowed their heads and observed silence while the ritual was performed giving full honour to Apollo, he who shoots from afar, the god of prophecy and healing. When the ceremony had been performed to the priest's satisfaction, a signal was given for the herald to announce the start of the festivities.

They now took their seats at the table, Odysseus leading his queen to her place beside him followed by Eumaios. Already attention had turned to the shooting contest, which was creating a great stir amongst the young men. It was the feat Odysseus had accomplished when he finally had shrugged off his beggar's clothes to reveal the truth of his identity to those ill-starred suitors twenty years ago. Now each of the contestants took their turn to string the great bow, bending it to their will, and then to shoot the arrow through the twelve grey axes of iron. Howls of merry laughter arose as the bow got the better of the young men. Odysseus took pleasure in seeing his two grandsons trying their hand. It would not be so very long before the eldest, Persepolis, mastered it. Only when Telemachos stepped forward for the challenge, turning the bow over in his powerful hands before effortlessly stringing it and sending an arrow through the handle hold of all the axes, was the competition done. Then loud cheers and shouts of praise rang out from the people at what the son of Odysseus had accomplished: the re-enactment of his father's feat.

He was the first to applaud his son, embracing and holding him in front of all assembled. "I have no more dearer prize I can give you," Odysseus whispered under his breath out of earshot, "for the kingdom of Ithaka is now yours, my son." Turning towards the herald, feeling tears welling up from his eyes, he spoke loudly for all to hear. "Come, announce the feast and let us eat!"

Bowls piled with roasted meats, bread and ripened fruit were swiftly set before the guests and the heralds distributed the drinking bowls filled with diluted honeyed wine. Odysseus surveyed the scene with great satisfaction, relaxing under the glow of the wine. This outward display of his wealth, now shared, could not be begrudged by the people or the gods.

When all had taken their fill, the bard was summoned and started up in song, his clear voice ringing out to the accompaniment of the well-strung lyre. For a moment Odysseus drew an inward breath, waiting to discover which heroic story the bard would treat them to. It was with relief that he realised it was the *nostoi,* the songs of the return from Troy of the Greek conquering heroes. The stories were familiar. And yet, in this strange nostalgic mood that had descended upon him, it struck him what had become of them all. The ending had not been as they imagined, as they set out bright-eyed and clean-shaven for the shores of Troy. It had not been the glittering and glorious *kleos* they had been promised.

The brilliant but hot-headed Achilles had met his untimely death, shot in the heel by a coward's poisoned arrow. Perhaps the gods had been outraged by his defiling of the Trojan dead and his excessive mourning for his beloved companion, Patroklos. And then there had been Ajax "The Big-one", that giant wall of a man. If only he Odysseus had realised in time and loosened his grip in the wrestling match, perhaps that tragedy could have been averted. For a madness had descended upon Ajax and he had taken his own life, unable to bear the humiliation and shame of not being crowned victor. Death piled upon death.

And now the gods brought to his mind Ajax Oileus. He shuddered to recall that wretched brute of a man. Shipwrecked and drowned on his journey home, the beast had paid dearly for his sacrilege of Athena's temple. Even Diomedes, Odysseus' dearly loved friend, had not escaped unscathed. He had survived shipwreck only to discover another warmed his wife's bed. And so Diomedes had departed Argos, the city of his birth, to become an exile from his own lands.

And what of Agamemnon himself, their leader, the *Anax* of the Greeks, with his haughty and foolish arrogance, the man who had been so eager to grab the spoils of war for himself. But all that wealth and power, all the precious metals, all the plundered weapons, all the fine woven garments and all the beautiful captive women, had not saved him in the end. Rather they had sowed the seeds of his destruction. For stripped naked like a babe, he had been murdered in his own bathtub by his wife Klytaimnestra and her lover, Aigisthos. It was said that she had never forgiven Agamemnon for the murder of her innocent daughter,

Iphigeneia. But when the captive Kassandra was installed in the palace as the new mistress, Klytaimnestra's anger had turned to murderous rage.

Only Nestor had escaped the painful fate that had awaited them, the conquering heroes of Troy, living out his days wisely and justly. They had been the pride of the Greek warriors, fighting bravely and heroically side by side at Troy to win individual *kleos*. But this *kleos*, which all his life he Odysseus had followed, in the end had done none of them any good and had come at a terrible price.

And as for his own *kleos*, Odysseus wondered, when life had left his body, what memory would be left behind and what account given of him by the bards down the generations. He did not dwell further on these thoughts as the song was drawing to a close and the bard was playing the final chords. This was his signal to put his plan into action.

"Grandfather!" A sweet voice caught him by surprise. He turned to see his youngest grandson, standing at his side. The boy was bright-eyed and soft-featured compared to his elder brother, but already he had a way with words. "When I am older, I want to be a bard and sing of your heroic deeds," he proclaimed in his clear child voice, his eyes flashing with excitement.

"You will do me proud if you remember half of all the stories I have told you." Odysseus laughed and fondly patted him on the head.

"Homer, come here," whispered his mother Epicaste. And she dotingly led her son away by the hand. Odysseus nodded at the herald, who called for silence now the cheers and appreciation for the bard had calmed.

He rose to his feet, hoping that the winged words would not desert him in what he was about to say. He began, his clear voice ringing out steady and strong to the expectant throng. "People of Ithaka, Same, Zakynthos, Doulichion and our guest-friends, I welcome you all to this great feast and celebration of the god Apollo. Since I was a boy at my father's side, I have always done my duty to win *kleos* for myself and this island kingdom to show myself worthy of being your king. As a young man, I was called to serve the great king of Mykenai, Agamemnon himself, and for ten long years did my duty as a warrior fighting on the plain of Troy. I have seen the loosening of men's limbs in battle and the destructive force of the war god Ares. During that grievous time we all lost many dear ones: your fathers, your sons and your brothers, both in battle and on the journey home. Living here in peace and harmony amongst ourselves and with bountiful nature is perhaps our greatest achievement." As the words left his mouth, it tore him like a blade: Kirke had spoken the same words all those years ago, but he had not understood then. For a moment, a god took his breath away.

He grasped the solid table to steady himself. "Are you well, father," enquired Telemachos, noticing the sudden change in his father.

"I am quite well," he replied in a hushed whisper. He paused for a moment to compose himself and then continued. "My greatest desire is that no longer do we witness the death, the destruction and the slaughter of young men for personal greed or vainglory. Rather a new way is found that honours our dead. But these are troubling times. On the mainland, disturbing news reaches us that the old order is breaking down." His glance fell on the strange faces, their appearance strained and haunted. "New peoples arrive each day fleeing violence, unrest and hunger that hold sway over the great Mykenaian cities. If *Strife* brings troubles to this kingdom, then we must be ready and prepared."

He glanced around at the sea of heads awaiting his words: old and young, men and women, parents and children drawn from across the kingdom. "I have deliberated this much in my mind and at my request Telemachos has been visiting the islands. Discussing this with my son and advisors, we propose to found fortified towns across the kingdom, each having strong walls where its people can take refuge and seek safety in case of war. Each shall have the right to raise an army from all who are freemen and farm the land. Thus if danger comes, we can act quickly to avoid calamity or invasion and its people can rally to its defence." A murmur had risen from those listening, as they turned to one another and he put up a hand to silence them. "Further, to help ensure good governance, each town shall hold an assembly each season of the year where the *politai*, its free citizens shall have a say and vote on decrees. Thus we may maintain this state of harmony and no more witness the death and destruction of bygone times. On the island of Same, these cities will be known as Same, Krani and Pronnoi. And here on Ithaka, Pali."

"Finally," he said now turning towards his son, "a new order requires a new king. One who has the vitality and strength to accomplish this task. I believe the time has come to hand over the kingship to my beloved son, Telemachos. It was always on my mind when I battled my way back from Troy that he would succeed me and be king one day. Now he is a man full grown, that day has now arrived and my duty is done. The gods give me no doubt that he will be a good king and will rule you wisely and justly. I give to you your new king and leader, Telemachos." For a moment, there was stunned silence and no one spoke but slowly came chants of approval and the banging of tables until the clamour rose to a great upsurge.

****

In the still of the evening, he sat once again under the old plane tree to gather his thoughts before bed. Penelope had already taken her leave and retired to their bedchamber with her circle of handmaidens to make her preparations. It had been a most auspicious day to see Telemachos take possession of the kingdom and become king at last. For so long and through all the many trials he had endured, this had been his heart's desire. In the distance he could hear the sounds of raucous laughter and clapping. The revelry was continuing into the night. He had decided to withdraw, leaving Telemachos as the new king to lead the festivities and entertain his guests. This was the time for his son's star to rise and shine full and bright.

"So it is done," he said to himself, in the quiet of the darkness. The moon was full above him, casting a silvery light over the mountain tops and dancing on the waters of the lagoon. He had at last dispatched his duty and was now free to live as he wished. If the gods favoured it, he and Penelope might retire to one of the country estates as his father, Laertes, had done before him, living out his days. Yet he noticed this thought gave him no pleasure. Then it came again this unsettling feeling as if the gods were stirring his mind to tell him something.

What was it that so disturbed him? Penelope was still a fine-looking woman, with her quiet dignity and noble bearing. She had put up no resistance to his plans but had readily acquiesced to his wishes. She had dutifully and faithfully acted as his queen beyond reproach, tending the household well; he could never abandon her as he was forever in her debt. He thought again of when they had first married and how she had entered the palace as a young bride. This union had been the dearest wish of his own mother, Antikleia, whom he had deeply loved. Antikleia had favoured as his bride the young Penelope, who already had a reputation for her beauty and her noble nature. Like her daughter-in-law, his mother had been skilled in the crafts of women and had been content to rule the household and keep it in good order for his father. It was then a thought struck him, like a spear shooting through his mind. It was hard to swallow its truth: that he had married his mother's likeness. His wife was steadfast and loyal, but the marriage wearied him and sparked no flames of passion.

And then at last, he allowed himself to admit it. Penelope was not Kirke, who spoke and acted like a male equal. For all these years, he had done the right thing as a husband, but it had not brought him the strong affection and companionship he craved. That was Kirke, the woman with whom he had met his match in the ways of Aphrodite. The woman who unnerved him with her strong independent ways, so different and yet the same. Though she might no longer walk above the earth, even now the arrows of Eros were bombarding him with *Desire* for her. Somewhere out far away, there might be their son or daughter, a love-child, full-grown. But he had made his choice of duty over love and that journey was now done.

A resolution came to him suddenly, perhaps sent from the goddess Athena herself, his wise protector. At the break of *Dawn* tomorrow, he would set off early and make purification down by the sea, facing towards the land of Aiaia where Kirke lived. He would wash off the pollution and contamination of the warrior, but also cleanse himself of this *Desire* for her once and for all. For otherwise it would drive him mad, pursuing him like the *Furies* and unable to take pleasure in his wife's company. It was said when forgetfulness took over, a man lost part of his *psyche*. But if that was a requisite, then he was willing to pay that price.

His decision was made. He would leave at first light.

Chapter 22

Discovery

A hushed stillness hung over the small square, except for the tread of car wheels on the concrete surface. It was still early on a Sunday morning, but the rusting church gates were padlocked and the bells of the small belfry stood motionless. Somewhere in the distance, a cockerel crowed as if forsaken in the empty village. The sky was grey and overcast. *Hopefully not a portent for the day* Thea thought to herself.

"You obviously know your way round," said Mark peering over at her from the front seat, opening the car door. Since they had left Mousatoi, Thea had driven through a labyrinth of twisty small lanes, without a second thought. "You've become quite the local over these past few weeks."

"I suppose I have." Thea replied breaking into a laugh. With a car at her disposal had come a new found sense of freedom, independence and self-assurance. It had been a relief, when Thea pulled into the driveway of the base house at Kalodia, that there was no sign of Richard. Over the last few days, he had left a series of terse voice messages on her mobile. Otherwise it had gone silent since that last fateful encounter with Dimitri.

The other passengers started to emerge out of the rear of the car, unfurling their arms and legs. Alistair awkwardly got out of the car, his body tall and gangly. He was dressed conservatively in the stereotypical check-sleeved shirt and beige slacks favoured by classical archaeologists. And then there was Elizabeth, her body camouflaged by a wide tweed skirt and a high-buttoned blouse. Her hair had been scraped back severely, giving the impression of a stern spinster schoolmistress. And finally there was Rob. He had been distant since their departure from Kalodia, choosing to squeeze his broad frame into the corner of the back seat. She had caught a glimpse of his stony-faced head, bobbing in the rear seat, each time she glanced in the rear-view mirror. Not for the first time that morning, regret came to her for Sophie and Matthew's absence. The presence of the young couple might have added a lighter social touch to the day, but at least she had Mark's easy companionship. With only a week left of the project, a consolation was that Elizabeth and Alistair's expert presence gave the best possible chance of discovering the palace site. For now there was an urgency to their search.

They started to retrieve their possessions from the car. Walking boots were more suitable for the rugged terrain and they had brought plenty of water and a packed lunch for the hike. Thea noticed Mark and Rob had their heads bowed, studying their mobile phones.

"The satellite reception isn't great," observed Rob. "However we can use the phone to record the time and distance. Perhaps we can synchronise the devices and then compare numbers at the end."

"Good idea," said Mark. "How long do you think the walk will be, Thea?"

"It's hard to judge," she replied, observing Elizabeth and Alistair had already detached themselves. From the vantage point of the square, they were deep in conversation observing the landscape. It occurred to her that light conversation might be a challenge. "The large scale map indicates about twelve kilometres. Depending on the roughness of the track, we ought to arrive in Mousatoi in just under four hours."

Mark glanced up at her. "Is that significant, Thea?"

"It would fit the time-frame in Homer of the goatherd Eumaios being able to journey to the palace back and forth within a single day. It would be a substantial day's walk, especially as the tracks would be poor in those days."

Thea shut the boot with a dull thud. "Shall we go?" They started to make their way through the small village, which hugged the ridge of the hillock. All was quiet as they walked past the jumble of small red-tiled cottages punctuated by modern flat-roofed concrete homes, their footsteps echoing on the asphalt. There might be little sign of the occupants but the gardens were well tended: multi- blooming roses and brightly coloured bougainvillaea, amber-orange or cherry-red, covered some of the white washed walls. Thea noted the planted vines and flourishing fruit trees, orange, apricot and fig, providing an extra larder to the occupants in the summer months.

At the edge of the village, they joined a small track which led them out of the village towards the coastline and the distant upland hills. The carefully tended plots and grassy meadows now gave way to scrubland. In the distance, the asphalt road on which they had travelled could be seen cutting an undulating swathe through the rough terrain like a grey serpent.

Thea watched the two men striding out ahead: Rob's strong broader frame against Mark's tall slender figure. Thea recognised Mark's favourite trilby hat, the long blue scarf and cross-swung satchel, which always gave him the air of an artist. The two were engrossed in conversation and seemed to be enjoying each other's company, which for some reason gratified her. Thea slowed her pace and fell back into step with Alistair and Elizabeth.

"So how is the field survey going?" Thea asked, breaking the stiff silence but also out of genuine curiosity. The couple had the responsibility for recording and cataloguing any finds, Elizabeth particularly being an expert draughtswoman. Despite the painstaking and time-consuming nature of the work, no doubt Elizabeth excelled at it through her meticulous attention to detail.

"There's been some bits and pieces, mostly from the late Classical or Hellenistic period," Elizabeth replied coolly, barely raising her head. "It's not surprising really as the land is close to the old classical city of Pali."

"Anything earlier?"

"It's hard to tell," Elizabeth replied, her expression inscrutable. "There are some cruder pieces of pottery, handmade domestic ware impossible to date."

"So nothing from the right period?" Thea persisted, trying to make sense of the information. Despite her grasp of languages and natural fauna, her knowledge of archaeological pottery was limited.

Alistair interposed, coming to Thea's rescue. "Nothing that can be convincingly attributed to that period. And we have catalogued most of the finds. A bit of a disappointment really, I suppose," he said pinching his lips together. They lapsed once more into an uncomfortable silence except for the scrunch of footsteps.

It did not take long for Elizabeth to fall back and Thea found herself walking by herself. The rocky stone path was now closely following the contours of the cliff-line, but every footfall required attention so as not to skid on the loose stones. Thea paused to absorb the landscape, looking across to the distinctive cone-shaped hill in the distance and down to the gulf, the island's watery navel. In the absence of human cultivation, there was a panoply of wild shrubs and flowers: broom dotted with small yellow star florets, silver-green sage, red hot pokers standing erect with their spiky tips and delicate purple crocus that clung to the gravel path. Then a sound caught her ears, the unmistakable jangle of bells from a grazing herd of goats or sheep. A smile broke across Thea's lips for slowly the land was giving up its secrets. It would be perfect pasture land for the flocks of Eumaios, described so long ago by Homer. In that moment, she knew intuitively they were on the right path and closing in on the palace. Her hero could not be far away.

It had started to drizzle, a slow gentle mizzle, but the clouds remained high in the sky. They had been covering the ground well and the scrubland now gave way to cultivated patches of fields and olive groves. At a small farm, a smooth asphalt lane replaced the stony path. Thea quickened her pace, more confident of the firm surface beneath her boots. Eventually she caught up with Mark who had paused to wait for her.

"Rob is outpacing us all," said Mark panting, slightly out of breath. Beads of sweat lined his brow. "He's such a fit man, it's hard to keep up."

"You're not the first to remark on that."

"But at least, I've got the chance to speak to you alone." Thea looked up at Mark, alerted by his tone. There was a serious expression on his face. "You remember your suggestion of relocating the survey closer to the village of Mousatoi." Thea slowly nodded her head, encouraging him to speak on. "Well I brought up the idea with Richard and he didn't take it at all well. In fact he downright refused."

Thea paused for a moment, trying to make sense of Richard's intransigence. She was so sure they were close to the palace. They were just not looking in the right spot. With time running out, the opportunity was slipping through their fingers, like grains of sand in an hour glass. At last she responded. "That's not like Richard. Do you know the reason for his refusal?"

"He's not been in a good place all week. He's under tremendous pressure to deliver the palace site within the next seven days. Otherwise there are plans to terminate the project."

The word "terminate" resonated in her ears. It sounded such a brutal final word, as if all the hopes and energy invested in the project had become surplus to requirements. "What makes you say that?" enquired Thea, a feeling of dread gripping her chest.

Mark looked across at her, a puzzled look on his face. "Have you not heard?" Thea shook her head, now recalling the terse pressing messages left on her mobile phone. "Richard was summoned urgently to a meeting with the Foundation board at the start of the week." Thea stared at him in disbelief, mentally calculating the days from that aborted weekend. "He was assuming that they going to renew the funding for at least another season," Mark continued steadily. "Things didn't go well. Apparently Mr Kampitsis expressed his dissatisfaction with the progress of the project in front of everyone. The board then voted and declined any future funding. Richard was devastated."

So Dimitri had acted quickly to set in motion his threats. It was easy to visualise the meeting in that manicured room behind the glass panelled fronting. It must have been a bombshell to Richard's considerable sensibilities as a well-respected and renowned expert in his field. No doubt Dimitri had instigated this move against the project and the other board members had followed his lead. *Had her rejection so bruised his ego that he had retaliated in this way and damaged the palace project which mattered so much to him?* It didn't make sense when they all stood to lose. "So is it definite?" Thea asked, suspecting she already knew the answer.

"Pretty much." Mark glanced across at her, catching her eye. "Richard was pinning his hopes on you interceding on the project's behalf. He seems to think you carry influence with our Greek patron." Thea frowned, a shudder running down her spine. This action was personal but she didn't want to have any part in it. The cost was too high and she was not willing to pay the price.

She shook her head. "I'm sorry Mark, I don't think there is anything I can do. The last time I saw Dimitri Kampitsis, it didn't end well. I'm probably the last person to whom he will listen."

Mark grimaced and turned his head towards her. "Looks like our job may be nearly done then. It's unlikely we will make a big breakthrough in the last week. Pity, as I've rather enjoyed it here."

"I suppose you're right," Thea reluctantly agreed, not completely willing to accept the possibility of defeat.

"Thea!" Mark spoke hesitantly and a slight flush now coloured his pale cheeks. "Since you broke up with David, Laurence and I have missed your company. You must come over again soon for dinner, even if it is now only the three of us."

"Of course, I would love that," Thea replied with a deep smile, nodding her head. "I didn't stay away deliberately, I just didn't want to burden you with my misery. But your suggestion of joining the project has helped me enormously."

"I think we will see a new stronger woman emerge from the ashes when we get back to London. And the haunted look is no longer there. But we'll have to have a final get together before we leave," Mark continued more positively, trying to dispel the gloomy atmosphere. "As you know the island pretty well, is there anywhere you could suggest?"

"Actually," Thea nodded, remembering the bay below the pension from the previous month. Angeliki, their hostess, had mentioned a pebbled beach with stunning views and a seafood *taverna*. "There is a place. Now the weather is heating up, it would be ideal for spending the afternoon eating and swimming."

"Sounds good. I'll look into it. You will come of course?"

"Absolutely!" exclaimed Thea. Whatever the outcome, it was important to mark the ending.

Close to midday, they stopped for lunch, where the track crossed a tarmac road. They spread out across the rocky outcrop to sit together, eating the packed food they had brought. They were now overlooking a wide cultivated valley with old derelict farm buildings and stone barns dotted across the landscape. At last the sky was brightening up and the sun was breaking through the clouds.

When it was time to move on, Thea was surprised to discover Rob at her side. It struck Thea, how comfortable it was to be in his company. She glanced across at him. With his rugged features and skin furrowed by the extremes of weather, he wasn't the handsomest of men. And yet there was a charisma, not like Dimitri's born out of a superficial charm, but a deep solidity and dependable mental strength. The kind that men would follow even to their deaths. It was then questions crept into her mind. *Could that night have grown into something else?* But Dimitri sat like a wedge between them. He knew she had planned to go away with Dimitri and that knowledge could never be undone. Even with Rob's admirable qualities, it was too much to expect his ego could accept and forgive her.

As if sensing Thea's inner quandary, it was Rob who initiated the conversation.

"So how was your weekend and Mr Kampitsis?" he asked without any recrimination in his voice.

"It didn't quite go to plan, but it was fine," Thea answered steadily, hastily glancing across at him. "You seem to have a particularly strong aversion to the man!"

"Yes," Rob readily agreed, "there is something superficial and shallow about him. He revels in over-consumption and high status. Perhaps he is just one man, but he sets a dangerous precedent for others on the planet. I didn't think you were like that," he added half-questioning. He suddenly turned round abruptly to face her, catching her off balance. "Look Thea! It's up to you who you see. Things had been left very open between us and I had no right to any expectations." A look of regret crossed his face as he averted his gaze, as if speaking into the distance. "I realise that now but I would still like us to be friends."

The old Thea would have shrunk away from an emotional connection. But with her newly found insight, instead she looked up at him and spoke openly. "I would like that too. And-" He was standing close to her, his blue-slate eyes keenly studying her. "What we shared that evening was very special and will always be so. But I thought you were indifferent and taken up with your work, especially after you left so abruptly. But I would be glad to be considered your friend."

Suddenly Rob stopped and threw back his head, laughing. "Of course! I didn't realise how it looked," he said, the half-smile still hanging on his lips. "I was urgently summoned to an international panel on climate change but had to keep it hush hush. One of the allies was threatening to pull out of the Helsinki talks so it couldn't go public." Rob shook his head as he read the expression on her face. "So you mistook my departure for disinterest. I thought my feelings were obvious and that I respect you deeply, even though I don't necessarily approve of your choice of companion." Clearly Rob still believed she was with Dimitri but Thea couldn't bring herself to enlighten him and disturb the reconciliatory moment.

"So what will you do after the project?" Rob asked, changing the subject, so that the instant had passed. They were approaching a small farm, where a dog was barking excitedly at the approach of potential visitors.

"I have my lectureship at one of the London

Colleges. But over the last few days, I've been thinking of a new venture. I've spent such a lot of my adult life trying to locate the ancient palace of Odysseus." Thea shrugged her shoulders. "I think it's time for something new. Something linked with my knowledge of plants and perhaps climate change." Rob was now looking at her attentively and she felt almost her whole face blushing under his scrutiny.

"So you'll be coming back to the island again, Thea?"

"Of course. Now I have a reason, I am thinking of basing myself here each summer." She had decided to cast aside the years of omission and had promised Eleni to visit more regularly. "And what about you?" Thea asked. "What are your plans?" They were crossing a river bed and the path was now steadily climbing upwards.

"First I'm going to spend some time with my father and son. My father is quite elderly now so we won't travel too far."

"And he's been appointed director of the Coverdale Centre," said Mark clapping Rob on the back. He had just joined them and caught the end of the conversation. "It's the prestigious group that works on climate research and informs government on policies. Our Rob is going to join the great and the good."

"Congratulations!" exclaimed Thea, noticing the modest smile on Rob's lips. The appointment obviously pleased him. "But don't you need to be based in the Antarctic with your work?"

"As long as I can access the data, it doesn't really matter where I'm based. And I have left good colleagues down at the Halley station, who are more than capable of taking care of the fieldwork. I can do more good in the UK working with a team of analysts. We need to get the message across to governments and legislators to take the issue of climate change seriously." As he looked across at her, there was a fire and passion burning in his eyes. "It's probably the biggest challenge of our generation."

"Put like that, my ideas seem almost trivial."

He hastily shook his head. "Not at all, Thea. You seem to have a vast knowledge of the natural world. We need people like you to demonstrate the local effects on nature and the things that we take for granted."

They were approaching the outskirts of the village of Mousatoi, their destination. The fields had given way to more intensive farming and they passed several enclosures where young piglets were being raised. The unusual cone shaped hillock now loomed above them. Below it, they came across a spring coming down from the hillside, where the water had been channelled into metal pipes leading to a public tap. Above had been written in Greek lettering, "*frontizete tin kathariotita*".

Thea gasped as she saw it. "Would the spring have been here four thousand years ago?" she asked, turning to Rob, her excitement mounting.

"Probably," Rob replied. "It would take thousands of years to shape the hillside through soil erosion, but the limestone will probably be riddled with springs." Elizabeth and Alistair had finally caught up with them and were crowding round curiously.

Alistair leaned in to take a closer look. "This looks like an old public water system," he said in his light Scottish accent. "Perhaps the whole village may have accessed it at one time to get fresh drinking water."

"What does the Greek writing say, Thea?" asked Mark. The sound of his voice brought her out of her stupor. She had been stood scrutinising the water system, staring in disbelief.

"It says *take care of the cleanliness*," Thea repeated slowly. She reached inside her rucksack and pulled out her copy of the Odyssey. At one of the marked pages, she opened it and read out a translation of the Ancient Greek.

"*There is a fountain for the town along a rocky path. Water comes from a rock high at the top*".

Thea glanced up at the others, her hands trembling as she clutched the book. "A spring is mentioned close to Odysseus' home. The spring of the Hill of Hermes, the winged messenger of the gods. Could this be the actual place?"

"How far have we travelled?" demanded Alistair, looking back at the way they had come.

"My mobile indicates thirteen kilometres," said Rob, flicking open his device. Mark nodded in agreement. "It would be a viable day's walk from where we have just come, if Katsiki is the site of your Eumaios' hut." Rob looked across at Thea, a quizzical expression on his face. The modern village was just above them, further along the track, nestled in the hollow of the hill.

"And the village is well hidden from the sea," commented Alistair.

"Is that significant?" asked Rob.

"Yes of course." Elizabeth had suddenly joined the conversation. The tone was slightly cold and patronising. "It is well known that due to piracy in the Mediterranean, Greek villages even in recent historical times were located where they were hidden from view from the sea for protection."

Alistair turned towards Thea. "I think you may be right," he conceded. "The palace is somewhere in this vicinity. Can we get the survey team up here, Mark?"

Mark shook his head. "I'm afraid Richard has given a categorical refusal."

Thea scanned the horizon. Somewhere close by was the palace. There was a flattened ridge occupied by some modern dwellings that looked promising. She glanced across at Rob, who was stood transfixed, the sunlight catching his copper streaked hair: his attention drawn to the very same spot.

"Let's continue along this path," he said.

****

When they arrived at the base camp at Kalodia, Richard was waiting for them at the top of the steps. Immediately Thea sensed that something was wrong. The affable smile was gone, replaced by a fierce-lipped expression and feverish eyes. He wiped a bead of sweat away from his forehead with a white handkerchief.

"Are you staying Thea?" Richard asked, dispensing with all preliminary greetings.

"I was planning to run Thea back to Katsiki, so she can pick up her car," Mark said casually.

The words did not seem to register. "Did you know the Foundation has refused our funding for next year?" Richard demanded aggressively, his face angry and flushed. "Do you know anything about it, Thea? Your name came up when I was informed of the board's decision. Mr Kampitsis said to speak to you."

Instantly Thea grasped the situation. Dimitri was using Richard to exert pressure on her. It was blackmail. She felt her stomach lurch but then calming down her feelings, she turned to face him. "I'm sorry Richard, this is not my doing. Mr Kampitsis makes his own decisions. I would never influence him to do something like this."

Richard looked down at her, glaring. "Then why did he mention your name. Have you said or done anything at all that might have compromised the project? Think!" The director's voice had become more strident and insistent.

"Absolutely not," Thea said, vehemently denying the accusation and refusing to flinch from Richard's heated stare. "I've had nothing to do with this decision."

"Then can you not speak with Kampitsis and get him to reverse the decision? Surely you can do something, after all he is an "old" acquaintance." Sarcasm rolled off Richard's tongue as he pronounced the words.

The exchange had become very heated and public. Thea noticed they were not alone and that their audience must have at least partially overheard the conversation.

She looked up at him, sadly shaking her head.

"I'm really sorry Richard but I can't. You are asking me to do something I'm not prepared to do."

"Shall we go now, Thea?" Mark had stepped forward to rescue her, a concerned expression on his face.

Thea turned her head towards him, grateful Mark was a good friend and ally. "Yes, I'm ready."

Mark glanced over his shoulder at Richard. "Did you know that through Thea's efforts today, we may have pinpointed the area of the palace?" Mark said, trying to diffuse the situation.

"Then it's a pity," Richard snapped, "that she has just compromised our funding."

****

When Thea entered her hotel room, she lay on the bed feeling weary to her bones. It was not just the long walk that had drained her, but the deeply troubling exchange with Richard. Mark had been reluctant to desert her, as he dropped her off by the car abandoned in the quiet square.

"Are you sure you will be okay," he had asked, anxiety written over his face.

"I'm fine," she reassured him smiling, partly

convincing herself. Mark naturally shied away from conflict, a childhood remnant from witnessing bitter recriminations between warring parents. "I'm an adult and can take care of myself."

"You know," Mark continued thoughtfully, "Richard was hoping to go out in a blaze of glory with the discovery of a lifetime, Odysseus' palace. He had his sights set on a trip to Buckingham Palace and a knighthood as his crowning glory, so he can recount at length the tale to his fellow gentlemen academics at college reunions. Don't worry," he said, his face showing genuine warm-heartedness, "this rift will blow over and soon pass. Richard may be pompous and full of his own self-importance but he isn't one to hold grudges."

He turned the ignition key and started the car engine. "It's going to be pretty hectic over the next few days, but call me if you need anything."

"I will," Thea replied as she closed the car door with a heavy thud, before waving him goodbye in the empty square. But it was disturbing to see the lengths to which Dimitri was prepared to go to have his way. Like a spoilt petulant child demanding a new toy. It wasn't an attractive proposition. Involuntarily she shuddered at the thought of making the same mistake twice. *At least she had the good sense to end it.*

At that moment, her mobile phone rang and reluctantly Thea reached over from her bed to answer it. Immediately she recognised the mild spoken voice on the crackling line.

"Sophie!" Thea held the handset to her ear. "I'm sorry I didn't get chance to speak with you. Things got a bit heated earlier. How can I help?"

There was a slight pause at the end of the phone. "Well, I have been thinking about when I finish my degree. I really admire your work and before the project ends, I'd really like to talk to you about doing a postgraduate under you."

Thea ears pricked up, as she contemplated the possibilities. "Of course. I would enjoy that conversation too. We'll find time to sit down together and talk through some ideas," she said, already making a mental note in her diary.

"That would be great," Sophie replied enthusiastically. A pregnant pause hung between them on the crackling phone line.

"Was there anything else?"

"Listen there is something I think you should know."

"Go on," Thea said encouragingly. She could hear a sharp intake of breath down the line.

"Well, after you left, there was a massive quarrel. Richard was discussing next year's project funding and how your involvement was an absolute condition of the Foundation, but apparently you declined." Thea felt a stab of pain but bit her lip. She knew it wasn't true and that Richard blamed her, but it felt uncomfortable that this business was being aired so publicly.

"He was complaining how you refused to meet Mr Kampitsis, when Rob came to your defence. He said you were absolutely right and shouldn't be forced into anything against your will. He got so furious that Rob refused to discuss it further and then stormed out. Even Matthew was surprised as he's never seen Rob so enraged."

"Thanks Sophie for letting me know," Thea said, unsure what to do with this information. She sensed that it had taken some courage for the younger woman to dial her number after all the disturbance and raised voices. "Things aren't quite as they appear but I'm sorry you had to witness that. I'll see you before you go and we'll have that chat."

Just as Thea replaced the handset, the phone rang out again. Registering it was Stelios' number, Thea sighed resignedly. *Could the day get any worse?*

****

It was later the next day, Thea stood in front of a large gated mansion, overlooking the sea, set back from the main coastal road. The drive down had not been unpleasant, with the sweeping views of the sea glinting in the sunlight, beneath the shadow of Mount Oenos. Somehow her modest Korean car seemed incongruous within so grandiose a property. She peered through the grille of the security gate. Within the high white-washed walls and security fence, the garden was immaculately kept, with its closely cropped jade-green lawn and manicured borders. As Thea pressed the intercom buzzer, she almost expected to be turned away, even though Stelios had set up this meeting. Her response must have satisfied the maid or housekeeper as the electric gates swung open. As she steered the car up the endless driveway, she could see the manicured gardens stretching back and the outline of a swimming pool, with the sound of children's laughter. *Dimitri really had entered the realms of the super-rich.*

In the hallway, Thea encountered Stelios. He was dressed casually in an open neck shirt and seemed to have been awaiting her arrival. For some reason, he seemed slightly anxious as he loosened his collar with his fingers. He was as deferential as always. "Allow me to show you the way, Dr Sefton. I don't think you have had the pleasure of meeting *Kuria* Kampitsis."

They entered a spacious open plan living room, which could have come straight from the cover of a high-end home magazine. It was exquisitely decorated with white sofas and fleece-piled rugs. There were several pieces of modernist artwork dotted around. The door on the opposite side suddenly opened and a woman walked in. Dimitri's wife. Her body was elegantly clad in a pale silk blouse and matching wide chiffon pants. As she held out her hand to greet Thea, the gold bracelets that adorned her wrists jangled. Her hair had been bleached and her face was perfectly formed, except for the hard sculptured features.

"Please, Dr Sefton, sit down," she said, speaking in English with a trace of an American accent. "I'm Clemmie Kampitsis, Dimitri's wife. Stelios has told me a lot about you. Please, you can leave us now," she said, gesturing to Stelios. Beneath the cordial reception, there was a chill in the air and this woman exuded anything but pleasantness.

She gestured to Thea to sit. "I understand that you and my husband have been spending a lot of time together," Clemmie began, heavily emphasising the words. There was a cold smile on her face. "I wanted to inform you, that you are not the first woman to catch my husband's eye."

It suddenly clicked with Thea the purpose of the meeting. *It was to warn her off.*

"If you have any concerns in that respect, then I can reassure you," Thea said facing her squarely, raising up her chin. "I'm not in a relationship with your husband. I simply know Dimitri from twenty years back, when we were both young. We were engaged briefly but he chose to break it off."

Clemmie turned towards her, her eyes blazing. "Do you think I'm a fool?" She threw her head back indignantly, her voice ice-cold. "I know you've spent time together. I know about your trip abroad. So," she collected herself, "please tell the truth. I know my husband and that he can be very persuasive and determined when he wants something."

"I'm afraid you've got it wrong! We travelled to Athens together, but it was purely as part of the Odysseus project. Your husband kindly paid for my accommodation in Athens and then took me out to dinner on a couple of occasions. I did initially agree to accompany him to Switzerland but I changed my mind. I assure you," Thea said with emotion now creeping into her voice, "it has not gone further than that."

Clemmie's eyes had narrowed like a serpent, poised to strike. "Forgive me, Dr Sefton, but I find that hard to believe. That you would refuse one of the world's richest men and simply walk away. Usually women are all too willing to oblige him. So what is it, I wonder," she said thinking out aloud "that made you run away from him." Clemmie got up and stood looking out on the garden, where the joyful squeals of the children playing drifted through the open window. *Dimitri's children*. At the sound, fleetingly tears pricked Thea's eyes before she dismissed them. But in that moment the other woman had glimpsed her pain.

"Of course, he hurt you very badly. Didn't he?" Clemmie thought for a moment, as if studying a blemish on the polished marble floor, before turning her attention to Thea once more. "You were pregnant, weren't you? But I am informed you don't have any children. So what happened?" There was a sudden intake of breath as Thea flinched, taken by surprise. "I think I understand. He abandoned you pregnant, didn't he? That is the truth!"

Without waiting for a response, Clemmie continued. "And he hurt you so badly, that through the pain and shock, you miscarried. Is that what happened? He sacrificed you and the child for his own ambition."

Thea had been listening to Clemmie's words horrified. *How could she discern that information?* "You're mistaken. He didn't abandon me," Thea replied firmly, trying to rally to

Dimitri's defence. "His family forced him to leave for South America."

"You said this happened twenty years ago?" Clemmie asked casually. "Is that correct?" Thea nodded hesitantly, hearing a note of triumph in Clemmie's voice. "I'm afraid to inform you Dr Sefton, he lied. At the behest of his family, he was in South America for a very short-time. But the rest of the time, he was in Athens wooing me with large cow eyes as the heiress of the Archontakis fortune." She paused choosing her words carefully. "There were rumours that the family had packed him off to South America because he had become, how shall we say ..., entangled with a foreigner. I'm sorry to say Dr Sefton, you didn't stand a chance against the wealth and prestige that his marriage to me brought him."

Thea stared at the woman in disbelief. As if the woman had uttered a stream of poisoned barbs aimed at her chest. *Was it true? That Dimitri had deliberately turned his back on her, leaving their unborn child to bear the consequences.* That this man whom she had naively trusted, had treated her so badly and callously. The truth sickened her to the core. Her face must have betrayed her emotions for the heiress of the great Greek shipping dynasty now continued with a hint of sympathy.

"Don't worry, Dr Sefton, you're not the first

my husband has deceived. He has broken the hearts of many others before. This fact I know well as his wife. But always the allure of wealth and power has brought him back. Truly I am sorry for your loss." She lifted her head, an enigmatic expression on her face. "I know how hard it is to lose a child."

Clemmie picked up a small bell and rang it. The shrill tinkle rang out across the room. "So, I understand the Odysseus project ends this week." She now adopted a more formal tone. "I do not know if our paths shall cross again but I wish you a pleasant stay on the island." Thea realised she was being dismissed.

As Stelios entered the room, Clemmie Archontakis turned to address her once more, a forced smile on her face. "Goodbye, Dr Sefton. Please don't be too disheartened. One day he will pay for his actions but I believe revenge is always best served cold."

It was a relief to escape the mansion. As Thea drove back up along the coast, she turned over the conversation in her mind, trying to make sense of what had just happened. It was puzzling how Dimitri's wife knew so much about her, knew her movements and the planned trip abroad. *It could not just be coincidence*, she reasoned. And then it dawned on her. It was there staring her in the face, as she entered the hallway. *Stelios!* Dimitri's *Mr Fix-it*. His faithful and trusted right-hand man. Always there to arrange things and do Dimitri's bidding. But Stelios' attentiveness and the way his glance lingered on her didn't feel the whole story. Perhaps Clemmie Kampitsis had secrets of her own. Certainly the gilded wife lived up to her ancient namesake of Klytaimnestra.

Chapter 23

Endings and Beginnings

He rose before *Dawn's* first light and quietly left the bedchamber. Without disturbing any within the household who slept deeply, carefully he picked his steps down the broad smooth-stoned staircase. A dusty smell of charcoal hung in the air as the palace ovens were lit for the day. In the kitchens, he came across an elderly servant already risen and kneading the bread dough to bake in the hot ovens. His presence had startled her as she had not expected anyone one roaming the palace before first light.

The woman looked up from her work, her knobbly hands encrusted with the milky barley flour. "Good morning, *Basileos*." She bowed her head towards him. "You startled me, master. I did not expect anyone would be astir yet. For I heard the sound of revelling going well into the darkness of the night."

He nodded at her, recognising her as one of

the older retainers within the household. "And greetings to you also, Hypomone. I planned to travel early by foot to *Keratios*, the ox-horned bay, to make libations to the goddess Athene. Is there any food and drink that I might take with me?"

"Yes, master," the woman replied. Although her skin was furrowed and the face hooded, there was an alertness in her eyes. "There are meats left over from the festival and several goatskins of wine." She dusted off the yellow flour from her hands and wiped them against her simple brown tunic. "I will fetch them for you. But first sit and take some barley broth, master. So that you will not tire on your journey."

He did as the woman instructed, sitting close to the fire and allowing the heat to creep into his limbs. He ate the bowl of porridge placed in front of him, slowly sipping the runny gruel. By the time he had done, the servant had returned with the provisions. He slung the heavy goatskins around his shoulder ready to leave.

"Is there anything else you require, master," Hypomone asked attentively, anxious to ensure he had everything for the long day.

"No, this will do fine" Odysseus reassured her with a nod of the head. "But let your mistress, Penelope, know of my intention and that I will be gone the whole day. Tell her not to have fear if I am late returning."

"Of course, but take heed master." She raised her head upwards at the rafters. "For that cursed white bird is still hanging around and I fear it can only herald bad news." He turned and kissed the faithful servant lightly on the forehead, noticing her eyes misting up with tears. With that he left, without a further glance back.

The well-trodden dirt track out of the *polis* was easy to follow, under the silver light of the full moon. He glanced over in the direction of the olive grove, where the feast had been held. The shadows of the pitched tents could be seen in the darkness, but otherwise all was quiet and still. By the time he passed the spring of Hermes, already the rose-coloured fingers of *Dawn* had started to creep across the lands and the cultivated fields. The air was soundless except for waking birdsong and the light touch of a *Zephyr*.

He walked on, keeping the steep mountain on his best side, where the skin was less scarred from wielding a sword. The path wound round the edge of the mountain, before cutting through a low pass towards the sea. He felt high in spirit, his body and limbs loosened by the early morning walk. At the cliff edge, he slowed, following the rocky track leading to the bay, where the dazzling clear sea-green waters sparkled below. From this height, the distinct shape of the ox-horned bay could be discerned. This was the place where Telemachos had landed, when he had sought to evade the ambush of the suitors. Beads of sweat now stood up on Odysseus' forehead, as he took care to place each footfall so not to plunge headlong to the depths below.

By the time he reached the sea shore, already Helios had reached his peak in the sky. Not far from the path, he found a clear stream and refilled a goatskin, taking a long draught of the cool waters. When his body felt refreshed and his thirst slaked, he made his way along the white shingle to a point where it faced out westward towards the land of Aiaia. There at the waters' edge, he poured a measure of red wine into the finely decorated two-handled *kylix*. The cup had been brought especially for the purpose of libation. Holding the vessel high above him, he now spoke these words.

"Oh goddess Athena, you brought me home safely and always have protected me, despite the many hardships and sufferings I endured. You provided me with intelligence and quickness of mind to survive the trials that the *Fates* spun." As he held the *kylix* upwards, there was the gentle sound of the sea swell rippling over the pebbles. "Accept now these offerings of wine and meat and take the portion due to you." He poured the wine out onto the rocky ground and carefully positioned the roasted meat on a make-shift slab of stones, as if a small altar. "And grant your favour to this kingdom and to my son, Telemachos, so that he may rule as a just king over the kingdom of Ithaka."

He paused, squinting into the sunlight. "For myself, goddess, I have only one request. Help me find peace from these torments that afflict me, the sufferings I endure and trouble my sleep from the slaughter of that accursed Trojan war and the ill-starred journey home." The next words almost stuck in his throat. "And cure me of this love I feel for the woman, Kirke. For I can find no rest now in my old age."

When the libation was finished, he smashed the *kylix* on the stony ground, where it broke into large jagged pieces. Approaching the water's edge, he removed his footwear and entered the sea, bathing his body in the salt waters. He cupped the water in his hands, vigorously splashing it over his hair, face, and arms, as if the water could wash away the warrior's stain and the mental pain he carried.

There was a rock, not far from shore, square in shape and smoothed on top like polished metal. It looked as if it had been hurled from the mountain cliff by the earth-shaker Poseidon or a Titan, when the primitive gods had battled each other. He hoisted himself onto it, stretching out his body, allowing Helios' rays to dry out his wet tunic which clung to him like a second skin. Slowly, lulled by sound of the waves and the sweet gentle *Zephyr,* he closed his eyelids until *Sleep* slowly overtook him.

****

It seemed unclear what drew her back. The decision to book a room for the night had been on impulse, catching even Thea by surprise. As she mounted the pension steps, the exterior of the pension looked reassuringly the same: the high glass-fronted windows, the paved tiles and swimming pool, now inviting in the late spring sunlight. The sunbeds were unoccupied as it was still early in the day. It had only been one calendar month ago since their stay, and yet so much had changed. Her hostess had instantly recognised her and greeted her enthusiastically. "And is your friend not with you?" Angeliki had enquired as she handed over the room key.

"I'm here alone," Thea had answered with a shrug, trying to dismiss the memory.

"Never mind. You look so well together and the *kyrios* was so attentive!" Thea just smiled politely. It was too complicated to explain.

Situated at the darkened end of the corridor, the room was smaller this time. Apparently new guests now occupied their former room, but the simple whitewashed walls, pine furnishings and the smell of freshly laundered sheets remained the same. Thea pulled open the shutters and stepped out onto the balcony, taking in a breath of the clear air. The view was unchanged. The dazzling turquoise sea below, framed by steep-sided cliffs and the half-moon chalk-white bay. She surveyed the scene, her lips pressed together, unsure what she expected but mildly disappointed.

Thea stepped back into the room and stuffed a silk-green tunic and some beachwear into her rucksack. *If this was to be the last day of the Odysseus Project*, she thought, *she was determined to make the most of it*. She checked her watch. There was still plenty of time to walk down to the beach. Someone was sure to offer her a lift back for the upward journey.

It was a good hour's walk down the cliff-side. The sun was now high up in the sky, beating down on Thea's back and making the descent dry thirsty work. The beach road coiled downwards to the sea, closely hugging the contours of the rock face. Occasionally a small dusty path would cut across the rugged ground, avoiding the wide meandering loops of road to lessen the distance. Even then it required hard concentration not to slip on the loose stones underfoot. Hardly any vehicles passed by. It was a welcome sight when finally, nestled against the edge of the white pebble beach, the *taverna* came into view. It was a peaceful spot, with the gentle heaving of the waves against the white pebbled strand soothing like a lullaby. As Thea approached, the sound of metal striking metal announced the waiters setting the tables for lunch.

Richard was instantly recognisable, dressed in his light linen suit with his Panama hat and red bow tie. He was sat alone slumped over a large table, a carafe of wine in front of him already half drunk.

"Do you mind if I join you?" Thea asked, unsure of her reception.

He looked up distracted and for a moment didn't appear to recognise her. "Of course, my dear, please sit down!" He rallied himself and pulled out a chair. "May I offer you some wine?" he asked, pouring out a large generous helping into a tumbler without waiting for an answer. Close-up his face had visibly aged and the greying hair had whitened overnight. He sat stooped and deflated as if the life had been sucked from his body. Clearly the last few weeks had taken their toll.

The wine tasted lightly resonated but perfectly chilled. "Where is everyone?" A high pitched female squeal rang out and Thea turned her head to see Belinda in the distance surrounded by a bevy of young male students splashing each other in the sea. Richard followed her glance and nodded in their direction.

"They wanted to take a morning dip," he said, "so we arrived early. Helen and Alistair are still packing the final find boxes, ready for dispatch to the local museum." He took a large sip of his wine, studying the drained glass in his hand. "Mark will be coming over shortly, bringing Mathew and Sophie, but he had a couple of things to take care of. Everything has to be cleared out before tomorrow morning."

Without thinking, she looked around searching for Rob's presence, when Richard interrupted her thoughts. He coughed to clear his throat.

"I think I owe you an apology," he said, his eyes resting steadily on her face. A subdued hesitant tone had replaced the self-assured voice. "Unfairly I pressurised you to intervene with Mr Kampitsis. I don't know the circumstances of your relationship, but it was wrong of me." He clutched the empty glass in his hand, as if carefully studying its content. "I hope you can forgive me. I'm just disappointed we failed." The sunken and hollowed cheeks suggested a broken man. In the twilight years of a glittering career, clearly Richard had been hoping for this one last glorious discovery.

Thea reached out towards him, gently touching his shoulder. "Thanks Richard. Your apology means a lot. I'm disappointed too as I was convinced we're very close." She smiled reassuringly, remembering Eleni's words. "Perhaps the palace is just not ready to be discovered."

He put the glass down on the table and was studying her closely. "You know Rob warned me about him some time ago." He obviously was referring to Dimitri but the mention of Rob's name on his lips startled her. Richard shook his head slowly. "About this all being a vanity project. But I wouldn't listen and dismissed it." Had Rob really seen through Dimitri, she wondered, and taken her side. "I did you an injustice, Thea," Richard continued, "when I refused your advice about Mousatoi. It just seemed easier just to scapegoat you for things not working out."

"Perhaps there will be a next time, Richard," she replied brightly, refilling their glass tumblers with wine. There were no hard feelings. "And if so, we will find the palace!"

"Let's drink to that." As they chinked their glasses to a toast of *yeia-mas*, her mind suddenly darted back to the end of that day, when they had walked the coastal path from Katsiki.

They had stood at the edge of the village, looking out over a promontory, where a cluster of modern dwellings barred their way. They had stopped besides a boundary wall of one of the properties.

"This looks a natural place for a Mycenean palace complex," Alistair had declared in an authoritative voice, exchanging a knowing glance with his wife. "It would sit high up commanding the lands around, but be strategically defended by the natural slope of the hillside. What a damn shame we can't get any closer as it's all privately owned."

She noticed Rob had detached himself and was standing alone, the strange faraway look settled on his face. "I know this view," he remarked, looking round puzzled at the sound of her footsteps. "The tall mountains across the gulf and Zante way in the distance. I've seen it somewhere before either in a book or photograph." He cupped his hands over his brow as he squinted at the landscape westwards towards the deepening glow of the setting sun. "And I can't shake the image of a plane tree from my mind." He looked up at her, as if trying to read an answer on her face. "It makes no sense!"

She had glanced down at the earth and for a moment, she thought she glimpsed the ground pitted with the red flesh of crushed figs. But then the image was gone and there was only the hardened dried out earth.

"And is Rob joining us?" Thea asked, trying to keep her voice light, noticing some of the dullness had lifted from Richard.

"Oh, I think he's left for the airport already," said Belinda. She had appeared suddenly at the top of the steps leading from the beach, her blonde hair dripping with sea-water and a bright coloured sarong tied around her body. From the weeks of field-walking, her skin had changed to a deep brown colour like a ripened nut. "I overheard Matthew saying he had to leave early."

They both looked at Belinda astonished. Clearly this was news to Richard too. Their argument earlier in the week must have caused a rift. "I suspect he's had to return to take up his new position," Richard answered thoughtfully, smoothing over any awkwardness. "Did you know he's just been offered the directorship at the prestigious Coverdale Institute for climate studies? That one will go far!"

"I'm sorry I missed him," replied Thea steadily, disappointment gripping the pit of her stomach. Even though she had hardly glimpsed Rob these past few weeks, his proximity somehow mattered. She drained her glass, tilting her head back to swallow the last dregs of the wine. "I think I'll take a short walk to get some air," she said briskly, setting the glass down on the table.

"There's no hurry," said Richard affably, some of the colour restored to his face. "Lunch isn't for some time."

In the changing room, Thea swapped her walking clothes for a bathing suit and the loose fitting fern-green tunic. She unwound her hair, allowing her copper hair to cascade down her back in thick ringlets. She emerged to a commotion. A small crowd had gathered at the back of the restaurant, watching intently the noisy television screen. The news commenter spoke in a torrent of fast flowing Greek, the words firing in quick succession. The words "Newsflash" and "Archontakis Company" caught her attention. Curious, Thea stopped and peered over the shoulders, as pictures of the Piraeus headquarters flashed up on the screen. The television picture now changed to a press conference where Clemmie Kampitsis stood centre stage, regally dressed in an elegant silk-cut suit. Her words, sophisticated and elegantly crafted, carried over the airwaves as she announced the appointment of the new chief executive of the Archontakis shipping company. To rapturous applause, Stelios Ioannou stepped out of the shadows and took his place at her side.

Thea raised her eyebrows in surprise. There

was no sign of Dimitri, but the puzzle was quickly answered. An image flashed on screen of a man, being hastily bundled into a car, hunted by a baying pack of journalists. Unshaven and startled, the target blinked and gaped in the scrum of the crowd and the flashing camera lights. His fine features were the same but bewilderment and shock had now replaced the charming smile and self-assured confidence. The large Greek caption on the screen caption announced "Dimitri Kampitsis – Embezzlement of Archontakis Funds."

So this was what Clemmie's parting words had meant, Thea thought to herself. Her revenge had been swift and brutal. To hurt Dimitri where it hurt the most. To depose him in favour of Stelios, her lover. Had something been stirred at their meeting? Just for a moment, there had been a glimpse of something. Then it suddenly struck her. Could it be that Clemmie too had suffered a loss, perhaps like her losing a child? Whatever had happened was no longer her concern. Thea turned her back on the blaring screen, the speaker now speculating wildly on the turn of events and Dimitri's downfall, and started to walk down the white pebbled beach.

There was a large square rock at the end of the beach, a short distance from the shore. It caught her eye, the smooth flat surface.

Discarding her shoes, Thea waded through the current of the water, the waves pressing against her shins and calf muscles. Finding her hand-hold on the sharp jagged edges, she climbed up onto it, taking care not to graze her skin and lowered the weight of her body onto the rock's smooth flat surface. The balmy breeze on her skin lulled her senses and she thought again about the project. Richard was right in his assertion they had failed. It was as if her whole adult life had been built around finding this place. Like a bolt from the blue, the realisation came to her. Had she simply wanted to get close to this man, this mythical hero Odysseus? And yet inexplicably she felt so near.

****

He did not know how it happened. The light shimmered like a thousand splintered shields of highly polished silver. It dazzled and befuddled him. The face was paler then he remembered, a translucent white and sprinkled with freckles. And the eyes had become clear blue. But his senses recognised at once her fragrance of lavender and mountain herbs. And then the hair, the colour of spun copper, falling around her shoulders in the swirling mist. She wore a garment he had never seen before, dyed fern-green, the colour she most favoured.

He was unsure if he dreamed again. He reached over and grasped a handful of the thick bronze tresses, lifting them to his lips and breathing in her essence. He reached over to enfold her, embracing the moment to hold her in his arms once more.

****

There was a kaleidoscope of colours, like a thousand splintered mirrors. He looked more worn and aged than she had imagined, but she recognised his face and the copper flecks running through his silver hair. Through the shimmering light, he reached out, holding her hair to his lips. She felt the touch of his hands, the skin rough and calloused, touching and caressing her. Her senses defied reason. That she could see and feel him across the span of four millennia. Together. As if in this brief moment, time itself had dissolved and melted away. But for now, she surrendered to his embrace content to be in his arms.

****

He held her closer to him. Even if this was a *phantasma*, he was grateful that the goddess had allowed one more glimpse. He stroked her hair, the lush copper-spun curls, holding her body tight to him. "My love, Kirke," he whispered over and over in her ear.

****

"Kirke!" The voice was coming from somewhere in the distance, as if in a dream, calling her. Thea sat up befuddled and disorientated. Re-accustoming her eyes to the blinding daylight, she blinked and looked around. The rock was deserted. The vision, whatever it was, had vanished. But the name came again, this time more distinct and louder. "Kirke!" Twisting her head round, she saw Rob wading out towards her from the nearby shore, the waves splashing against him.

"What did you say?" Thea asked, her mind confused, refusing to grasp what she had just witnessed as Rob reached her.

"I called you Kirke." The look on his face was sincere and an easy smile played on his lips. He was stood almost level with her, refusing to be thrown off balance by the breaking waves. "It must be wearing your hair down," Rob said looking up at her. "You look as I always imagined Kirke did when Odysseus first met her."

She stared at him wide-eyed. "I thought you had left the island. Belinda told us you had gone to the airport."

"To meet my father and son." Rob grinned, barring a row of white teeth. "They've just flown in to holiday on Kefalonia. I've been telling them about the island attractions and they couldn't resist." There was a teasing look on his face, as he caught her eye. "But surely you knew," he said, his voice thick with emotion, "I wouldn't have left without saying goodbye?"

She shook her head, the recent image still lingering in her mind, confounded by what to make of it all. "I didn't. You always seem so distant or angry."

He threw back his head, imitating the Greek gesture for *No*. "Then that's my fault. For some irrational reason, I deeply resented your relationship with Dimitri Kampitsis. The man's such as fool! If you were being kind, I guess you would call it jealousy." His eyes lingered on her face, as if seeking her forgiveness.

"He's just been deposed from the company and arrested for tax evasion. It looks like he's upset one person too many along the way."

He brought up a finger to his lips to silence her, shaking his head. "Thea, let's not talk about that man. Not in this place. Not right now. But there's something I do want to ask you." She nodded her head, raising her ears, as he released his finger.

"Go on," she said encouragingly.

Dressed in his cotton shirt, the sleeves rolled up and the light dancing on his face, Rob shifted awkwardly and nervously. "When we return home, would you like to meet up? I mean, spend time together, like watch a movie or go for a meal," he asked, almost stumbling over the words, the muscles in his throat taut. "What I'm trying to say is I care about you and want to know you better. Would you like that too?"

Thea looked down at him and felt a burning attraction that only intimate lovers can feel. *Could this passion or whatever it was transcend into something more steady and stable? Could it be the stuff of slow burning love and lifelong companionship?* For a moment she paused, trying to grasp this unexpected twist. "Yes," she finally answered, leaning her face towards him, "I would like that too."

He reached out and pulled Thea down to him, meeting her lips with his own. As they embraced, he wrapped her in his strong arms and held her, as if he would not let her go for a long time to come. For several minutes, they stayed that way, locked in a kiss, until Rob broke the spell.

"Come," he said, offering her both his hands, the skin rough and calloused, helping her down from the rock. "I want you to meet two very important people in my life: my son and father."

****

When the light had started to cast long shadows, Odysseus finally stirred himself from his reverie. He decided to make camp that night on the beach. His mind reasoned that soon the orange glow of *Dusk* would appear, making it too late to make the steep ascent uphill. But in his spirit, he knew he was not ready to tear himself away from this place or disturb the memory the gods had bestowed on him. Not when he had felt finally so close to her. He scoured the beach edge and discovered a small sandy hollow protected by boulders, where he could bed down for the night. He built a small fire and ate the remaining rations. When night came, he lay down under the starry constellations, looking into the fathomless blackness known only to the gods. Order was breaking down on the mainland, the crops were failing and the northern Doric tribes were on the move, pushing hard down into the lands of the Achaian Greeks. *Would there ever be peace to this land,* he wondered. Could they ever live without grim *War* and *Strife*? When the moon had risen high in the sky, casting its silver light over the dark expanse of water, he finally fell asleep her name on his lips. Kirke.

Telegony

Across the water, under the same silver moonlight and the bright constellations of the gods, a boat had been hauled up. The planking had been hammered firm and the timbers well-pitched for that long sea crossing to foreign shores. Close by, under its shadow, the crew slept soundly. All fresh-faced young men, keen for adventure but untried in battle. They carried a deadly cargo. A son in search of a father, the warrior father he had never met. The father who had left even before the young man had departed his mother's womb and taken his first gulps of air as a new-born babe. The son, whose hair was flecked with copper and whose mother had given him the name Telegonos. *The Last Born*.

Now as a man full grown he came seeking the same path his father had taken many years earlier, hoping to claim a warrior hero's destiny. High expectations of prowess on the battle-field and glorious victory filled his dreams as the son slept. And close beside him, his spear stood upright, planted in the sand like a sentry. The long tapered arm had been crafted from an ash tree, a gift from his mother not to destroy but to protect him from harm. But the metal head, bronze-tipped and dipped in the venom of the stingray, was fated to unloosen the limbs of the Achaian hero who had sired him.

But for now Telegonos slept, untroubled in *Sleep*. For this one final night, he dreamed sweet dreams. Gently he exhaled, the breath escaping from his soft lips, unaware of the intersecting destinies that awaited father and son. At the first light of *Dawn*, he would be ready to put to sea and complete the journey that the *Fates* had decreed.

Ithaki by Konstantine Kavafy

Σὰ βγεῖς στὸν πηγαιμὸ γιὰ τὴν Ἰθάκη,
νὰ εὔχεσαι νά 'ναι μακρὺς ὁ δρόμος,
γεμάτος περιπέτειες, γεμάτος γνώσεις.

Τοὺς Λαιστρυγόνας καὶ τοὺς Κύκλωπας,
τὸν θυμωμένο Ποσειδῶνα μὴ φοβᾶσαι,
τέτοια στὸν δρόμο σου ποτέ σου δὲν θὰ βρεῖς,
ἂν μέν' ἡ σκέψις σου ὑψηλή, ἂν ἐκλεκτὴ
συγκίνησις τὸ πνεῦμα καὶ τὸ σῶμα σου ἀγγίζει.

Τοὺς Λαιστρυγόνας καὶ τοὺς Κύκλωπας,
τὸν ἄγριο Ποσειδῶνα δὲν θὰ συναντήσεις,
ἂν δὲν τοὺς κουβανεῖς μὲς στὴν ψυχή σου,
ἂν ἡ ψυχή σου δὲν τοὺς στήνει ἐμπρός σου.

Νὰ εὔχεσαι νά 'ναι μακρὺς ὁ δρόμος.
Πολλὰ τὰ καλοκαιρινὰ πρωινὰ νὰ εἶναι
ποὺ μὲ τί εὐχαρίστηση, μὲ τί χαρὰ
θὰ μπαίνεις σὲ λιμένας πρωτοειδωμένους.

Νὰ σταματήσεις σ' ἐμπορεῖα Φοινικικά,
καὶ τὲς καλὲς πραγμάτειες ν' ἀποκτήσεις,
σεντέφια καὶ κοράλλια, κεχριμπάρια κ' ἔβενους,
καὶ ἡδονικὰ μυρωδικὰ κάθε λογῆς,
ὅσο μπορεῖς πιὸ ἄφθονα ἡδονικὰ μυρωδικά.

Σὲ πόλεις Αἰγυπτιακὲς πολλὲς νὰ πᾶς,
νὰ μάθεις καὶ νὰ μάθεις ἀπ' τοὺς σπουδασμένους.
Πάντα στὸ νοῦ σου νά 'χεις τὴν Ἰθάκη.

Τὸ φθάσιμον ἐκεῖ εἶν' ὁ προορισμός σου.
Ἀλλὰ μὴ βιάζεις τὸ ταξίδι διόλου.
Καλλίτερα χρόνια πολλὰ νὰ διαρκέσει.
Καὶ γέρος πιὰ ν' ἀράξεις στὸ νησί,
πλούσιος μὲ ὅσα κέρδισες στὸν δρόμο,
μὴ προσδοκώντας πλούτη νὰ σὲ δώσει ἡ Ἰθάκη.

Η Ἰθάκη σ' ἔδωσε τ' ὡραῖο ταξίδι.
Χωρὶς αὐτὴν δὲν θά 'βγαινες στὸν δρόμο.
Ἄλλα δὲν ἔχει νὰ σὲ δώσει πιά.

Κι ἂν πτωχικὴ τὴν βρεῖς, ἡ Ἰθάκη δὲν σὲ γέλασε.
Ἔτσι σοφὸς ποὺ ἔγινες, μὲ τόση πεῖρα,
ἤδη θὰ τὸ κατάλαβες οἱ Ἰθάκες τὶ σημαίνουν.

Ithaka (English Translation)

Once you set out for Ithaka
hope your road to be long,
full of adventures, full of knowledge.

Don't be afraid of the Laistrygonians and the Cyclops,
the angry Poseidon
you'll never find them on your way
if you keep your thoughts high,
if rare excitement touches your spirit and your body.

You won't meet the Laistrygonians and the Cyclops,
the wild Poseidon
unless you bring them along inside your soul,
unless your soul puts them in front of you.

Hope your road to be long
may there be many summer mornings
when you'll enter with pleasure, with joy,
the harbours you've seen for the first time.

Stop in Phoenician trading stations
And buy fine things
pearls and corals, ambers and ebony,
and sensual herbs of every kind
as many sensual herbs as you can.

Go to many Egyptian cities
to study and learn from the educated ones.
Keep Ithaka always in your mind.
Your arrival there is your destiny.

But don't rush the journey at all.
Better it lasts for many years,
so you're old when you reach the island,
wealthy with all you've gained on the way
without expecting Ithaka to make you rich.

For Ithaka gave you the beautiful journey.
without her you wouldn't have set out.
She has nothing more to give you.

And if you find her poor, Ithaka hasn't fooled you.
Now that you have become wise with so much experience,
you'll have finally understood what Ithakas mean.

Translation adapted from Miley lovato for Lyricstranslate.com
https://lyricstranslate.com/en/ithaki-ithaki-ithaka.html-0

Glossary

A list of Ancient Greek words and place names.

Achaia: A term used to describe an area on the Greek central mainland.

Achaian: The peoples from Achaia, an area of central and southern Greece in the Peloponnese. Often used interchangeably with "Greeks".

Aiaia: Thought to be Cape Kirke, a distinctive promontory located on the Italian southwest coast.

Aphrodite: The Greek goddess of Love, including the sensual qualities of beauty and love-making.

Argos: A city located in the Peloponnese, southern Greece on the fertile Argive plain.

Atlantis: Believed to be the ancient name for the island of Santorini, destroyed by a cataclysmic volcanic eruption approximately 1200 BC.

Anax: The overlord or chief leader.

Basileos: A king or lord.

Boreas: The North Wind.

Chiton: A woollen tunic worn next to the body.

Doulichion: A separate island within the kingdom of Ithaka and most probably the modern island of Ithaka.

Hermes: The god of travel and communication, Hermes often acts as the messenger of the Greek gods.

Himation: An outer garment worn like a cloak or shawl.

Hubris: An excess of arrogance, pride or ambition that will ultimately cause the transgressor's downfall.

Kephallenia: The ancient spelling of Kefalonia.

Kephallenians: The tribe of people from ancient Kefalonia and the surrounding areas.

Kleos: Lasting fame or glory from heroic deeds performed on the battlefield.

Krani: An ancient city on Kefalonia, located 3km from Argostoli to the southwest of the Gulf of Koutavos.

Kylix: A two-handled drinking vessel with a conical foot.

Lokris: An ancient town thought to be located in Phrygia, northern Greece.

Megara: A city close to Athens, situated on the Corinthian Isthmus.

Megaron: The large central hall within a palace. The plural is Megara meaning rooms.

Moly: Thought to be garlic.

Mykenai: The ancient name of Mycenae, a citadel located in the fertile Argive plain on the northeast Peloponnese. One of the first Mycenean sites to be excavated, the archaeologist Heinrich Schliemann used its name to define the Bronze Age civilisation found in central and southern Greece.

Myrmidons: The inhabitants of Phthie and Hellas now modern Thessaly, central northern Greece.

Notos: The south wind.

Oikos: The household, including the family, home and property.

Ogygia: An island thought to be Malta.

Pali: An ancient city located on the western side of Kefalonia.

Phaiakians: The inhabitants of Scheria, thought to be the modern island of Corfu.

Phantasma: A phantom.

Philoxenia: Hospitality or the rights accorded to a guest.

Phrygian: From Phrygia, a region in western Thrace, northern Greece.

Phthie: A town in modern Thessaly, one of the most northerly Mycenean kingdoms.

Polis: A town consisting of a citadel and lower town.

Politai: The male citizens of the town.

Pronnoi: An ancient city located on the adjacent island of Same to the south, facing towards the Greek mainland.

Same: In Homeric language used to refer to the main part of the island of Kefalonia after the town of Same. This area in modern times forms a single landmass with the Pale peninsula and the irregular shaped island of Kefalonia.

Thinakia: The ancient Mycenean name for Sicily.

Tiryns: A Mycenean citadel located in the fertile Argive plain in the northeast Peloponnese, renowned in Homeric times for its mighty walls. The modern archaeological site has distinctive cyclopean tunnels.

Xenia: The honour and hospitality accorded to a guest.

Xeno: A stranger and therefore due the rights of hospitality.

Yeia Yeia: Grandmother in Modern Greek.

Zakynthos: The ancient name for the island of Zante, the most southerly of the Ionian Islands.

Zephyr: The west wind, known for its light gentle breeze.

Zeus: The patriarch of the gods and ruler of the sky, thunder and lightning.

Selected Bibliography

Although a fictional novel, this work is hugely indebted and built upon the previous scholarship of others. Where possible, great care has been taken to reflect accurately existing information known from historical and literary sources. In terms of the epic poems The Iliad and The Odyssey, the following translations and commentaries have been invaluable primary sources:-

Green, Peter (2015) Homer's Iliad Translation (University of California Press)

Hammond, Martin (2000) Translation of Homer's The Odyssey (Bloomsbury)

Jones, Peter (2004) Homer's Odyssey: A commentary based on the English translation of Richard Lattimore. (Duckworth)

Jones, Peter (2010) Homer's Iliad: A commentary on three translations. (Duckworth)

Lattimore, Richmond (1961) The Iliad of Homer Translation (University of California Press)

Lattimore, Richmond (1967) The Odyssey of Homer: A Modern Translation (Harper and Row)

Other Sources on Mythology, Topography and Location

Bittlestone, Robert, Diggle, James and Underhill, John (2005) Odysseus Unbound: The Search for Homer's Ithaca (Cambridge University Press)

Bradford, Ernle (1964) Ulysses Found (Century Publishing)

Ferry, Luc (2014) The Wisdom of Myths (HarperCollins)

Graves, Robert (2011) The Greek Myths (Penguin Books)

Roller, D.W. (2014) The Geography of Strabo (Cambridge University Press)

Le Noan, Gilles (2001) The Ithaca of the Sunset (Tremen)

Main, Tom (1975) "Some Psychodynamics of Large Groups," in Kreeger, L. (ed) The Large Group: pages 57-86. London: Constable. Republished (1989) Main, T.F. The Ailment and other Psychoanalytic Essays. London: Free Association Books.

Morkot, Robert (1996) The Penguin Historical Atlas of Ancient Greece (Penguin Books)

Acknowledgements

They say that it takes a whole village to raise a child, in the same way I am grateful for the help and support of a whole host of people in bringing this work to fruition. First among those is Gill, with whom through numerous conversations the characters and storyline of the novel slowly evolved and took shape. Alongside Gill, also Janet McCarthy, Artemis Hionides, Ant Devonport and my lifelong husband and partner Derek, for their reading of an early draft and offering suggestions. My particular gratitude to Artemis Hionides, not only for her dry wit and encouragement when the going got tough, but also for her considerable knowledge and insights into Greek language and culture, both ancient and modern. Also Alex and Freya, my adult children, who helped keep me grounded and humble.

In terms of editing, I owe a huge debt of thanks to Barbara Windle for her formidable critical eye and astute copy editing, along with Terry Kay for his generous and expert proof reading.

Regarding the researching the historical background to the novel, my thanks for the help and support of the staff at the Iakovitis Library, the Corgialenos public library and local archive on Kefalonia, as well as the Hellenic and Roman Library in the Institute of Classical Studies, London. In addition by correspondence Mina Theofilatou on Kefalonian colloquialisms, Andrew Shapland of the British Museum for sources on Mycenean domestic architecture and UCL London regarding Bronze Age archaeological sites on the Ionian Islands.

Finally I am indebted to the people of Kefalonia, past and present, who provided the essential inspiration. Any shortcomings or faults contained within this work of fiction are my own.

About the Author

Anna Harvey has always been fascinated with Ancient Greece and read Ancient Greek, Ancient History and Archaeology (BA) at Bristol University. While later pursuing her doctoral degree, she lived and worked in Greece for several years where she first encountered Kefalonia and the Kefalonian people. After returning to the UK, Anna retrained as a clinical psychologist and has worked in mental health for almost three decades, gaining a unique insight and perspective into human psychology. In addition to her clinical work, Anna is a passionate advocate of sustainability and wellbeing. She is involved in a number of initiatives, including writing a psychological health blog, mentoring and political campaigning. Anna now lives in Leeds, West Yorkshire, with her husband, the family cat and an array of hedgehogs. This is her debut novel. To find out more about Anna, future publications, news and events please visit her website at anna-harvey.co.uk.

Printed in Great Britain
by Amazon